Praise for Lau[...]
and The Magick Trilogy

"Navarre has concocted this stew of historical, paranormal, medieval and renaissance romance that is sure to please all.... Readers will find it enchanting with a slew of characters good enough for a fantasy film."
—*RT Book Reviews* on *Magick by Moonrise*

"A promising start to what looks to be an intriguing series.... Navarre effortlessly crafted a story brimming with elements of Arthurian legend, Faerie lore, Tudor history and fallen angels."
—*Urban Girl Reader* on *Magick by Moonrise*

"Navarre exquisitely interlaces the adventure of Arthurian legend, the timelessness of angelic lore, the intrigue of the English Tudor court, the magic of the Faerie realm, and deliciously passionate love scenes in this spellbinding novel."
—*Chanticleer Editorial Book Reviews* on *Midsummer Magick*

LAURA NAVARRE

Magick by Moonrise

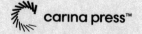
carina press™

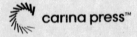
carina press™

ISBN-13: 978-0-373-00424-9

Magick by Moonrise

Recycling programs
for this product may
not exist in your area.

www.CarinaPress.com

Printed in U.S.A.

Dear Reader,

If *Magick by Moonrise* were a blockbuster screenplay, I'd place the cast of characters from sword-and-sorcery film *Excalibur* in the setting from *The Tudors*, add a few fairies from Ridley Scott's dark fantasy adventure *Legend*, then garnish with a dash of chivalry, a heaping dose of romance and lots of steamy heat.

Tudor England hovers on the brink of war. Bloody Queen Mary is burning heretics. And the Veil between the Faerie realm and the mortal world is thinning. Beltran is one of my favorite heroes— trained by an order of fighting monks, sworn to chastity and the Inquisition, a holy terror in battle. Innocent Faerie healer Rhiannon teaches him the hard lessons of mercy and forgiveness. When Tudor England and the Faerie kingdom collide, the players risk all for power. But only love can save them.

In these pages you'll also meet shy scholar Lady Linnet Norwood and Zamiel, the irrepressible Angel of Death, whose full story appears in *Midsummer Magick*. Please keep in touch at www.lauranavarre.com and friend me at Facebook.com/lauranavarreauthor.

Here's wishing you your own happily-ever-after!

Laura Navarre

Every writer is blessed with her own guardian angels—those generous souls who provide critical encouragement and belief even when all hope seems lost. For this book, my guardian angels were talented author and mentor Leigh Michaels and my agent JD DeWitt at The View Literary Agency.

As for the literal angel in this book, burning with determination and integrity, my inspiration is always Steven—my own real-life hero.

Magick
by
Moonrise

ONE

Tudor England, April 1556

TORRENTIAL RAINS LASHED the countryside with cataclysmic force, a mighty river pouring from angry clouds to punish the drowning lands. The deluge pounded the frost-nipped forest, stripped away pearl-gray daylight and churned the English soil into a sucking sea of mud. Through this treacherous mire, their valiant steeds galloped full out.

Rhiannon twisted to slant a desperate glance behind her, where the last of her defenders hammered at her heels. Faithful unto death, just as they'd sworn before the Goddess, no matter their hidden misgivings about this dangerous mission.

From the rear, a horse's whinny pierced her like an arrow—the familiar timbre of Nineve, the white mare she'd raised from a foal.

An angry growl of thunder muffled the rider's shout of despair as he tumbled from Nineve's saddle. Rhiannon felt the lightning crack of pain through her own tender flesh as his shoulder struck the ground with crushing force. Her heart nearly stopping, she cried out as though stricken herself.

"Halt!" Healer's instincts taking over, she struggled to slow her panicked mare.

"Nay, princess!" her foster-father shouted, pound-

ing alongside. "Those brigands are but a breath behind.
The devils ride as if hell-spawned."

"But Nineve and Cynyr—I will not abandon our
friends." Violently she shook her head, damp tendrils
of silver hair flying around her shoulders. "Halt, I command it!"

"Nay, child." Lord Ansgar Emrys gripped her bridle in his gauntlet and urged the mare on. "Your safety
must be our paramount concern. Cynyr himself would
be the first to say so."

As their flight opened distance between her and the
fallen, the searing bolt of pain eased, until her own
healer's bones no longer throbbed with Cynyr's agony.
But she would hear Nineve trumpeting for help until
the day she died.

Cynyr could save them both if he kept the presence
of mind to summon the Veil, thicken the mist swirling among the ancient oaks and wish himself back to
Faerie. But nothing could mend bones snapped like
kindling, save time and her own healing touch.

Tears of sorrow stung her rain-washed eyes, because Rhiannon knew her foster-father was right. If
they were overtaken by that howling band of brigands—the horde who'd come ravening down on them
from nowhere the moment they cleared the Veil, and
hunted them for three days as though bewitched—
if they were captured, all her friends' precious lives
would be lost in vain.

Only four of us left. A pang of grief and terror
stabbed through her. *Goddess, will they all fall—all
those faithful souls who believed in me enough to follow me from Faerie?* Every one of the stalwart seven
she'd lost tore her heart anew.

But she would honor their sacrifice. Later she would grieve for them, those shining souls who should have lived forever, their immortal lives cut cruelly short by the sword. If she survived, she would never cease grieving them.

But they'd made their choices just as she made hers, sworn to preserve the fragile peace between the mortal realm and the Summer Lands behind the Veil where the Fae dwelled. She'd sworn to reach Catholic Queen Mary at the Tudor court, to deliver the precious treaty the Faerie Queene had crafted, to trigger the spell that would bind mortals and Fae to an enchanted peace. The desperate scheme had been Rhiannon's, the Faerie magick her royal mother's—and nearly every high noble at her court violently opposed the plan.

If Rhiannon failed to reach the Tudor Queen and persuade her to sign, the enchanted peace could not be triggered, and both realms would bleed. And as the Faerie realm faded, so too did the Faerie Queene. The bloody tide of war would rage between the realms and sweep Rhiannon's mother from the throne. Then the Convergence would be upon them: the apocalyptic clash between mortals and Fae that erupted every thousand years when their twin realms, like ships on the sea of time, drifted too close in the mist between the worlds and collided in the night.

Beneath her, mist-gray Astolat stumbled and nearly went down. Rhiannon clung like a burr to her saddle, grimly ignoring the dull ache in her back and thighs.

It was the gray mare's keen senses—that sudden veer of alarm, the startled prick of ears—that alerted her to the trap: a ragged line of horsemen, carnival-bright in a muddy patchwork of stolen finery, spread across the track before them. With a shout, Lord Ansgar wheeled their brave little band in a tight jostling arc, away from this new peril.

His stolid strength supported her, as he'd always done. Beneath a thatch of gray-streaked black curls, cropped short in the Roman style, her foster-father's eyes flashed steel. Swiftly he scanned the gnarled oaks looming over them, too tangled for passage, storm-tossed branches lashing in the tempest.

"Too late," Rhiannon whispered. "They've found us."

Now the twisting road behind them filled with a black tide of men. Seeing their prey brought to bay, the pack slowed, horses jostling between the high sloping banks of the Queen's Highway.

Chilled through from their desperate flight through this bewildering, half-drowned land, her hands turned to ice. Trepidation fluttered in her chest and knotted her stomach as she searched the harsh faces that ringed them.

"Trapped!" Ansgar cursed. His wicked saber flashed into view. He held the blade slantwise before them, cold fire burning in his lined features. In that instant, her foster-father was the knight of legend once more— the divine spear, the Queen's champion. Except that the Queen he'd loved in his mortal life was a thousand years dead, and now his sword was Rhiannon's.

Still, he was mortal. Blessed by the Faerie Queene with long life, he could yet die by violence—just as they all could. *Lord and Lady, this will be a massacre. Our quest shall fail, and my people drown in blood and darkness.*

The steel of resolve stiffened her spine. Tilting her

chin, she spurred Astolat forward from the thin protection of their huddled quartet. Rashly she tossed aside her hood to bare her head. Sleet stung her face, drenching the pale ringlets that slipped from her coronet.

"Why do you hunt us through this realm like animals?" Her brave question echoed through the trees, words strong, voice shaking as she summoned the foreign mortal phrases. "We have done naught to thee. Indeed, we are strangers to this land, traveling the Queen's Highway on a diplomatic mission to the Queen's own Grace. For the sake of both our realms, I command thee, let us pass!"

Through sinking heart, she glimpsed no flicker of compassion in the ring of filthy faces, no trace of comprehension though she spoke clear English, even if her dialect was ages old. Truly, these mortals must be little better than beasts, just as her full-blooded Fae sister Morrigan always taunted her.

For Rhiannon bore their blood, her half-mortal strain mixed with the blood royal of Faerie. Surely, she could make them understand her—

Among a tall stand of firs on the high bank, a flash of movement drew her eye, where a ragged brigand knelt. She barely recognized the weapon stretched between his arms before the resonant thrum of a bowstring propelled the arrow toward her. Wildly she flung herself flat against Astolat's neck. The clothyard shaft buried itself in her saddle, a handspan from her thigh.

Despite her fierce determination to betray no fear, Rhiannon flinched from the terrible weapon.

"Unchivalrous cur, to attack a lady!" Lord Ansgar spurred before her, a blur of motion wrapped in swirling wool, mailed hauberk glittering as his arm snapped forward. Silver streaked through the air. With a gurgling cry, her attacker toppled from the bank into the road, the knight's dagger sprouting from his chest.

As though the stroke had unleashed them, the pack of human wolves howled and leaped toward them. High on the bank, more ragged figures slunk into view. Nearby, her companion Lady Linnet Norwood uttered a cry of dismay.

Merciful Goddess, this blind pursuit is unnatural. Even beasts would seek shelter in this unrelenting gale. Do mortals so thirst for blood, or is this Morrigan's doing?

Suddenly her skin tingled, hair rising along her forearms with an electric charge. The air glowed blue around her. Then a blinding flash turned the forest white as a sizzling bolt of lightning slammed into a stately poplar. Horses screamed as the percussive crack of wood tore the air.

Astolat shied and reared, forelegs churning the air. Desperately Rhiannon flung her arms around the mare's neck and let her scramble where she would, away from the smoking leviathan that swayed dangerously above.

The deep groan of wood sent men scattering in all directions, away from the massive shadow blotting out the heavens. The lightning-blasted tree slammed through a thicket of branches, smashing them to splinters and crashing across the road. Somewhere, lost in rain and darkness, a man's shrill scream cut short.

Rhiannon huddled in her saddle and shuddered, sodden mantle doing nothing to warm her frozen flesh. For one dreadful moment, her head swirled.

Lord Ansgar gripped her arm, hauling her upright. "There, into the trees, child!"

Peering through the rain-lashed twilight, she spied the dark gap the fallen tree had made, beating down the high bank between road and forest. Astolat needed no second urging, but pounded into the darkness as though devil-driven.

So THIS WAS how it ended. She'd led them all to their deaths.

Rhiannon battled the rising tide of despair and stared at the turbulent river, tumbling in angry white eddies over jagged rocks too treacherous to cross. To her left rose a jumble of mossy rocks. To her right, a thorny thicket barred any passage. Behind, their pursuers were closing in.

Ansgar, at least, would go down fighting. Bravely his silver blade rang against steel, over the rush of rapids and the patter of rain. She, too, must arm herself.

Heart beating in her throat, Rhiannon reached for a sturdy oaken limb. The branch rooted deep in its mother tree, but she closed her eyes and whispered to the wood her desperate need. At last the branch yielded, coming away in her hand—the sort of minor magick she could sometimes summon, but rarely control. Beneath her touch, the barren bough flowered into unseasonable green.

As she wheeled her mare to face their attackers, her companions spread protectively before her—the guardsman Caedmon putting his back to the rocks, Lady Linnet slipping toward the thicket, her fosterfather braced for battle ahead.

"Goddess protect us." Rhiannon gripped the leafy

branch until her fingers ached. At her belt, the unsigned treaty in its pouch pulsed warm with enchantment. She doubted the bandits would deliver it for her, nor even be able to read it after she'd perished.

The clash of steel on silver rang out; both Ansgar and Caedmon had engaged the foe. Rhiannon searched the darkness, every sense straining. She smelled the metallic tang of blood, the musky scent of wet horse, the faint stench of rotting earth. The looming Convergence sickened the very soil itself, as the twin realms of mortal and Faerie drew toward their fateful collision.

Yet beneath the smell of death, like a flicker of dying hope, she nosed the fresh green aroma of shoots and buds sleeping beneath the cold spring rains, waiting patiently for rebirth.

Caedmon toppled with an axe buried in his skull—two thousand years of wisdom and beauty crushed into fragments like an eggshell. Lady Linnet's small cry sounded like a stricken rabbit. No help to be had from that quarter. Now Ansgar fought alone, saber whirling through the darkness, punctuated by the grunts and curses of the two-legged predators—a pack of snarling jackals around the lone knight.

You are a daughter of kings! Help him, she ordered her shaking limbs. *Or he will perish defending you. You know what they'll do to Linnet—what they'll do to you. Even if we all die here, anything is better than waiting meekly for the slaughter.*

But what could Rhiannon do? She, a healer who believed all life was sacred, had never wielded a weapon.

She heard the low evil thrum of a bowstring as someone loosed another wicked shaft. The sound curled her into herself, flesh shrinking. But it was Ansgar whose pain-filled cry pierced the night.

Silent lightning flashed through the clearing. Illuminated for an instant, a dozen brigands fanned across the muddy ground. Two crouched before Caedmon's crumpled form, already pillaging though the man was not yet cold. More struggled to subdue Ansgar's coal-black stallion, his saddle empty. The stallion reared, forelegs slashing the air, with a trumpeting scream of rage.

Lady Linnet was a slender struggling figure, tangled in saffron skirts, slipping and scrambling across the river's moss-slick stones. Rhiannon caught a glimpse of her white face, those gentle eyes wild with terror. Water foamed around the girl as she fled—and who could blame her? The Fae had kept her against her will, a half-Scottish noblewoman who'd blundered through the Veil by mischance, with her precious knowledge of the Tudor court. The Fae had beguiled her to spill Tudor secrets while her family grieved and months stretched into years in the mortal world. What loyalty did Linnet owe them?

On the earth, Ansgar the divine spear lay thrashing, a clothyard shaft jutting from his shoulder. A dark tide of blood spilled over his silver hauberk. Two human wolves circled him, eyes gleaming through matted hair, wary of the saber still flashing bravely in the fallen knight's fist.

Rhiannon stared at the stricken form, the world spinning to a halt around her.

Directly before her, close enough to touch, reared an ogre of a brigand. Rotted black teeth showed through a thicket of dripping beard. Clutching her improvised

weapon, she bared her teeth and hissed at him like a
wildcat.

"Here be the girl," he growled. "Kill her—and catch
t'other one, ye half-wits."

"Damn you for a pack of spineless huddipicks!"
Ansgar's furious voice rang over the howling wind as
he struggled to rise. "Attack *me*, blast you!"

To Rhiannon's heightened senses, outlaws seemed
to rise like demons from fissures in the ground. At last,
her nerve failed her.

"Blessed Mother," she whispered to the Faerie
Queene and the Goddess herself. "Protect Ansgar, save
your champion. Hide Linnet from their gaze, for she is
innocent of all. As for myself, forgive me…"

As if indeed she'd summoned forth a spell, though
her half-mortal blood held no such power, the rain-
lashed night went still around her. The forest held its
breath. Falling rain shimmered in the dusky air.

From the forest a figure strode—a solitary man,
storm-winds lashing the black cloak around him, ad-
vancing sure-footed across the treacherous ground. He
gripped a cross-guarded broadsword in both hands,
blazing gold like a cross of fire. To human eyes, he
was a lone mortal. Still, Rhiannon knew at once he
was more than human.

Her Faerie Sight discerned a fiery halo around that
striding figure as he swept through the carnage. Su-
perimposed over that mortal frame blazed a warrior
clad in shining white-gold mail, a banner of silver hair
streaming around features stern and fearless. Rising
from his mighty shoulders, the shadow of iridescent
wings spread wide: a shimmer of opal and turquoise

and garnet feathers. Cold fire spilled from burning cobalt eyes to illuminate the clearing.

As this vision of divine wrath strode toward them, his mouth opened and he roared like a lion. On the ground, Ansgar dropped his sword and covered his ears—the stricken ears of a mortal who'd dwelled too long among the godless Fae.

The outlaws gaped at the fury bearing down on them as though their God himself had blown his trumpet. She could hardly guess what they saw—perhaps only the glimmer of an aura. Yet the man nearest that shining figure fell to his knees, crossing himself and babbling. The form of fire roared again, blazing sword sweeping around to cleave the air. When it struck the outlaw's head from his shoulders, a blinding flash of white made Rhiannon cover her eyes. Sparks danced against the blackness of her closed lids.

When her vision cleared, the bandits were cowering on the earth. The bravest scrambled for fallen weapons. The bearded ogre who'd threatened her roared his own challenge and waded through the mud toward that dreadful apparition, hefting a blacksmith's hammer baptized with Faerie blood.

Rhiannon sat frozen to her saddle as the outlaw's brawny arm whirled his hammer overhead. Again that flaming sword carved the air and parted the fabric of night. When the sword smote, thunder shook the heavens. The smith's hammer tumbled in two pieces from a nerveless grip. The outlaw himself fell screaming, legs cloven from his body.

Now the beast who'd slaughtered Caedmon rushed forward, his murdering axe dripping with gore. "God damn ye!"

The Name of God doubled Rhiannon over in the saddle. Though she held nothing against the Christian God, her mixed blood gave her all the Fair Folk's vulnerabilities, and few of their strengths. Still on the ground, Ansgar moaned and covered his eyes.

As for the winged fury, he seemed to swell until that streaming hair brushed the wind-lashed branches overhead. The light that spilled from his eyes burned blue as the heart of flame, stabbing Rhiannon's vision until she was nearly blinded.

Roaring like an avalanche, the fiery warrior extended an arm to point at the blasphemer. Before that accusing finger, the bearded face went blank with terror. Dropping the axe, the bandit fell stricken to the earth and covered his head with his arms.

The remaining outlaws required no further urging. Babbling with fright, they scattered in all directions. Some splashed into the river, lost their footing in the tumbling waters and vanished. Some flung themselves headlong into the thorny brambles, plunging into the thicket on foot when their horses balked. Their abandoned steeds veered away.

Rhiannon found herself alone in the clearing with that vengeful vision—alone save for Ansgar who lay like a dead man, arrow jutting from his shoulder.

Scarcely daring to breathe, she groped for the moonstone pendant that hung at her throat: the charm that disguised her Fae fairness from mortal eyes. But she feared no makeshift magick could deceive the godlike creature before her.

Indeed, her movement drew its gaze. Slowly, those burning cobalt eyes turned toward her. When their eyes met, a tingle swept through her, prickling her skin into gooseflesh. A breeze stirred her rose-red mantle, lifted her tumbled ringlets and tossed them around her shoulders.

For the first time since she'd ridden through the Veil into the mortal realm, she was warm, even burning. A scent like cherry blossoms drenched the air. Somewhere music was playing, and she was drowning in the cerulean fire of those unearthly eyes...

"Lord of Light," she whispered. "What are you?"

The fiery figure opened his mouth and spoke a word that sounded like the blast of trumpets. Sudden dizziness rushed through her; the earth seemed to shift beneath her feet. On the ground, Ansgar cried out and half rose as though lifted by an invisible hand. Then a silent flash of lightning washed the world white.

When the painful brightness faded, the wrathful angel had vanished. Around her, the storm had gentled, the wind gone still, rain soft as mist bathing the battle-churned soil.

In place of that fiery vision knelt the man himself, head lowered, weight braced on spread arms. Just a man in stark black garments, not even armored, with a cross-hilted broadsword strapped to his back.

Rhiannon fought to collect her scattered senses, make sense of what she'd seen. Ears ringing, the afterimage of that burning figure still seared into her eyes, she slipped from her saddle. When her legs buckled beneath her, she clung to the mare and braced her shaking limbs. As Astolat sidled, she stroked the damp silk coat and whispered reassurance—a comfort she herself badly needed.

Night had fallen, creeping through the clearing like fog. Overhead, pale clouds parted to reveal a lavender moon. By its unearthly glow, she fumbled for her basket of healing herbs and simples.

Ansgar's plight compelled her immediate attention, though he'd wadded his cloak against the wound to slow the bleeding. At least he was still conscious and capable of rational thought, which was nearly more than she could manage herself. She started toward him and encountered the newcomer, still kneeling on hands and knees in the mud.

At her very feet he panted, head bowed, each exhalation a low groan of pain.

He saved our lives—he or whatever appeared through him. Duty and decency obliged her to aid him if she could. Yet she hesitated, curiosity mingling with caution, and stared down at his bent head.

Rain had soaked close-cropped golden hair in tawny spikes around his head. Massive shoulders bunched beneath a doublet of stark black velvet, broadsword strapped across his back, a scene of the Christian Day of Judgment stitched in gold and silver on the scabbard. The stiff white lace of a nobleman's ruff framed his neck like a halo, stark against a sinewed column of sun-browned skin.

Though she understood poorly the sumptuary laws that governed how a man might attire himself in England, clearly this one possessed his share of wealth.

She stared at those capable hands spread in the mud, blunt-fingered, rough-knuckled—no lordling's pampered paws, whatever his clothing might suggest. A heavy gold ring weighed one finger to the knuckle: the Scales of Justice stamped there like an accusation, smeared with what appeared to be fresh blood. That decided her.

Laying a gentle hand on his shoulder, she summoned her antiquated English. "Sir, thou art wounded?"

Without raising his head, he flung out an arm to thrust her away. Through the wet velvet beneath her fingers, the tensile flex of muscle bespoke strength. But his powerful frame was shuddering—too subtle for eye to discern, but she felt it.

Impressions flooded her healer's senses, the floodgates opened by her tentative touch. Exhaustion burned in each trembling muscle. Every nerve in his body was raw, seared by the divine fire channeled through him.

He knelt in the soil because he lacked the strength to rise.

Still, miraculously, he seemed uninjured. Neither blade nor axe had so much as grazed his skin. The blood must belong to the men he'd slain, the tumbled corpses strewn around him like discarded dolls.

"Stand back." Barely audible, a weary voice scraped from his throat. "It could happen again."

Startled to hear a mortal voice rumbling from his throat, she dropped her hand and stepped back. Fresh alarm sparked through her. If that monstrous form of fire came roaring back, would this tortured figure be unable to control it?

Yet the man was in agony. And mortal dread, if she read him right.

"Let me help thee," she breathed. "I'm a healer."

He uttered a harsh noise, somewhere between derision and a groan of pain. "No power under Heaven can heal this. If you love life, stand back."

To this, she found nothing to say. She could not help the man if he refused to let her touch him, no matter his obvious torment. When her foster-father groaned, Rhiannon started and hurried to his side.

"Ansgar!" She dropped to her knees beside him, the fragile cage of her unfamiliar farthingale bunching beneath her skirts. She paused to wrestle with the accursed thing, the stiff point of the stomacher jabbing her belly like a dagger.

"Now why did you remove the arrow?" she said softly in the Roman tongue. "Do you want to bleed to death here in the mud?"

A bitter smile creased his pain-worn features. "If only I thought I might."

Lord and Lady grant me patience! 'Tis my day for difficult patients.

Clearly seeing her distress, the knight sighed and yielded to her careful fingers as she examined the wound. "Never mind, child. With Queene Maeve's own blessing on these old bones, I'll be striding the English isle until Christ's second Coming."

By that slip alone, he betrayed his own exhaustion. Half-mortal as she was, the Name of Christ caused her no lasting harm, but the word made her flinch like a shout in her ear.

"Forgive me," Ansgar murmured. "I am—not myself."

"Hush, dear heart." Swiftly she sorted through her healing basket for ground comfrey to knit the torn flesh. "No major vessel was severed, but this wound is wide. Lose enough blood, and the loss *will* kill you, whether you be blessed or nay. Once we stop the bleeding and I bind it up, you're going to need rest."

"No time for that. Those wretched curs could return at any moment. I can't understand what—" Sudden alarm flashed in his gray eyes, and he struggled to lever himself up. "Where's Linnet?"

"Be still now." Firmly Rhiannon eased him back to the ground, though fear for the hapless girl tightened her own chest. "She fled across the river. She is mortal, don't forget, and lost a year or two of mortal time in Faerie—or so we hope." Time seemed to flow ever faster in the mortal realm, though she'd thought just a few days passed while Linnet dwelled among the Fae. "Perhaps she'll return to us. If not, she'll seek shelter with her own kind, and manage well enough."

Either way, Linnet stands a better chance of surviving these benighted mortal lands than we do. One grieving knight who last strode these shores a thousand years past, and a misfit princess who'd rather die than lift a weapon in her own defense. How long are we likely to last?

Like most warriors, Ansgar made a poor patient. His chivalrous nature wouldn't allow him to rest while a lady might require his aid, and his stubborn struggles reopened the wound. His efforts ceased only when his eyes fluttered closed. Concerned, Rhiannon bent over him, pressing hard to stop the bleeding.

He was going to require true healing. Never mind that the enormous expenditure of healing energy would render her, too, helpless.

Uneasily she glanced toward the stranger, still hunched in the mud. Still breathing heavily, but no longer groaning with each breath. He'd managed to push to his feet, hands braced on knees as he fought for breath. Darkness obscured the rugged lines of his face. She glimpsed a strong jaw scraped free of whis-

kers, the wary flash of eyes, but could not read him.
Still, undoubtedly, he was watching her.

Well, there was nothing to be done. Ansgar had
nearly died, and could die still if she didn't stop the
bleeding, or fever set in.

Shaking her head, she bent over the unconscious
knight and laid both hands against the mangled shoulder, fingers light as butterfly wings. Through the contact, she sensed the sluggish seep of blood, the raw
pain of torn muscle and something else—the cruel cold
touch of an evil wish, the tingle of dark enchantment,
the taste of rust and iron in her throat.

It was as she'd suspected. Those brigands who'd
hunted them so doggedly had been bewitched. Impossible to say who'd done it, with the long-buried magic
of this ancient isle welling like blood from the war-torn
lands as the two realms drew toward their fatal cou-
pling. But Rhiannon had her suspicions.

Closing her eyes, she silenced the clamor of worry
and focused on the evil wound. She gathered her
strength like hanks of rough wool twisted into a spin-
dle, spun the raw energy into a spool of smooth thread,
woven of her own life force. Hands moving as though
she drew needle through fabric, she used that pulsing
thread of light to stitch the wound.

The dark spell evaded her, twisting and coiling like
smoke around her fingers. Ansgar mumbled and tossed
in his sleep as she clipped and knotted the thread. She
fretted lest she'd sewn some trace of that vile sorcery
into his flesh. Already the wound felt over-warm to
her touch, but that might be no more than her own
healing energy.

Weak as though she'd spilled her own blood, she

swayed, almost fainting. For that was the price of her healing magick. The energy she consumed must be borrowed from her own body. And if she borrowed too much…

"A healer, are you?" The man's gruff voice at her shoulder nearly made her leap from her skin. Startled as a flushed hare, she whirled toward him too quickly. The world blurred and revolved around her.

"More like a witch, if you ask me," he rumbled. A trained orator's voice, speaking the new English with an accent she could not place. Beneath the mortal words, she heard the clarion ring of distant trumpets.

"Nay, I'm a healer," she murmured, hand raising to her brow to clear her head. He stood before her, flesh and blood, yet she could almost see that shining warrior with his flaming sword looming over her—at rest, but watchful, translucent hands folded over the cross-shaped hilt.

"The witch is my sister," she said absently.

This made him pause. Eyes narrowing, the man stepped back and surveyed the carnage. For a man of his bulk, he moved lightly, lithe in high boots and traveling hose. A wicked-looking dagger swung at his belt, sinuous dragon twining around the hilt.

"She is far from here." Hardly knowing what she said, Rhiannon clung to consciousness with both hands. She needed food, fire and a bracing cup of wine—none of which she was likely to get. "Thou cannot see her, unless she wishes to be seen. For which blessing thou should be thankful."

"It's not your sister who concerns me." Intent, he studied her. "When you laid hands upon this fellow, your form and his were rimmed with unholy fire. What is that if not witchcraft?"

Uneasy with the threat of him looming over her, the sudden sense of danger, she deemed it wise to change the subject. "That fiery being who came to our aid— was it thou, or thy demon?"

"Demon?" He reared back as though she'd struck him, that proud tawny head coming up. Behind him, the angel's eyes glowed like banked coals.

Respectfully, she gestured to the Presence, though now she could barely discern its fading form. "I see thy wings like a shadow looming over thee."

The mortal frowned, jaw clenching with unease and impatience. "You speak nonsense, healer. You're in shock, asleep on your feet or mad."

"I know what I saw, sir." Stubborn, she struggled to rise. The effort brought another surge of dizziness. Suddenly she found herself sitting on the ground again, crushing a carpet of pale snowdrops that had pushed too early from the soil. Ivory skirts spilled around her as she stared up at him.

Whatever had ailed the man, he towered over her fully recovered, swirling black cape pinned carelessly back, greatsword jutting above one broad shoulder. Austere and unadorned, but for the ring with the Scales of Justice and the gold-and-steel medallion swinging over his heart: an inverted sword wide as her palm, cross-shaped, wreathed in flames.

"This must be what thou mortals call irony," she said faintly, eyeing the holy symbol and his somber attire. "I am saved by a Catholic priest."

Senses dulled by exhaustion, vision swimming with black fog, still Rhiannon found the wit to appreciate her dilemma. It was this very collision—between the Romish influence that guided devout Mary Tudor's every step, and the wild Faerie magic bursting its boundaries as the two lands approached their thousand-year conjunction—that caused the looming crisis Rhiannon must prevent.

"Thou should have let them kill me," she murmured. "Thou wilt not appreciate this quest of mine."

"Quest, is it?" The man frowned, tawny brows knitting above cold eyes whose color she couldn't discern by moonlight. "Why do you ride with only this man and his slain comrade for escort, if your need is so dire? Surely you know these English roads are plagued with cutthroats and thieves, displaced tenants and lesser rogues. These are no easy times for England."

He spoke as though this realm weren't his own, though he seemed easy as a native with the English tongue. With furrowed brow he studied her, as though puzzling her out.

For a moment she lost herself looking at him. He was the first mortal man she'd ever beheld, except for Ansgar—and of course her father, in the vault where he'd slept since his mortal life ended—and both had dwelled too long among the Fair Folk not to be marked by it. But this priest was mortal to the marrow of his bones: earthy and formidable, pensive brow furrowed beneath close-cropped hair sparkling with rain, a raptor's nose, firm lips pressed together. Droplets of mist clung to a stern jaw glittering with tawny stubble.

He was nothing beautiful or refined, despite his elegant cloth. The Fae would find him alarming and uncouth. Physical strength shouted from the muscled form beneath his stark attire.

To say nothing of the form of fire, though that un-settling image was thankfully fading.

She must think how to deal with him. Should she confide in him, beseech his assistance for her mission, when a Catholic priest must surely oppose it? Or should she lie, when she did it so poorly?

Uneasy with her vulnerable placement, spilled across the soil with only an unconscious knight for protection, Rhiannon scrambled to her feet—too quickly. The world darkened around her.

Suddenly the priest loomed over her, one muscled arm closing around her waist to hold her upright. The rich dark aroma of frankincense seeped from his cloak as the heavy fur-lined garment swirled around her, making her head spin. Worse was the sharp clean scent of steel from his blades—anathema to any Faerie.

If not for the ensorcelled rings that banded her little fingers, and the half-mortal blood that blunted the deadly aversion to steel, she could never have borne his touch.

"Stand back, I pray thee," she gasped, even while her weakened body leaned into his thrumming heat. She gripped the hard calloused hand at her waist, a tingle like magick seeping through her blood. "Thy steel…"

"Frightens you, does it?" His gaze narrowed, grew thoughtful. "I mean you no harm in this place."

"Only in this place?" She meant it for a jest, but she was weary and frightened, and her voice too plaintive. "I tell thee I cannot bear it. I command thee, release me!"

He stepped back as she demanded, but gripped her hand in his warm hard fingers, so she couldn't flee.

"Madam, no more of this evasion. What manner of creature are you?"

Oh, she could show him evasion with a right good will; no mortal creature could evade like a Faerie. Yet the notion repulsed her—she, the daughter of Arthur of Camelot and the Faerie Queene, was proud of her honor as any knight. She was not her half-sister Morrigan, a full-blooded Fae who lied by instinct as well as inclination—the very rival who'd sworn on her own blood to undo Rhiannon's plan for peace.

Nay, Morrigan might be heir to the Queene's throne, but Rhiannon had inherited their mother's gentle spirit and her father's fabled fairness.

Clearly, this priest was a man of wealth and probable influence. She and Ansgar, and Linnet if she lived, desperately needed help from some quarter. Perhaps this man could be prevailed upon to bring her to the Tudor Queen. She couldn't think it through, weigh risks and advantage, with him standing so near. The presence of his steel prickled her skin like an allergy. Any proper Fae would be screaming by now.

If she looked with her Sight, one of the few minor magicks aside from healing she could summon, a halo of fire still burned around him.

Through the desperate exhaustion swirling through her, she seized upon a strategy.

Chin tilting up, she summoned the pride of a king's daughter. "I am Rhiannon le Fay, daughter of Queene Maeve and the Dreaming King Arthur, dispatched to the English court as a royal ambassador by the Faerie Queene herself. If thou art loyal to the Tudors, I command thy aid."

When she spoke her name and titles, harsh breath

hissed from his lungs. His free hand sliced through
the air, signing himself with the Cross. A fresh wave
of weakness rolled through her. On the soil at her feet,
the half-conscious Ansgar cried out.

"Woman, you must be a witch, a madwoman or a
fool." The stranger's jaw hardened. "Don't you know
this symbol?"

Uncomprehending, she blinked at the flaming cross
on its chain over his heart. "'Tis the symbol of the
Christian God, inverted, so it does not pain me to look."

He released her suddenly, with a flicker of distaste,
as though he could no longer tolerate her nearness.
Fired by a lifetime of survival instinct, she stepped
quickly back—too late. His sword-calloused hand
closed like a manacle around the fragile bones of her
wrist: not cruel, but unavoidable as destiny.

"Peace, Father," she whispered, frightened pulse
fluttering like a trapped moth against the hollow of her
throat. "I mean thee no harm, and I've no true claim
upon thy service. Betimes the habit of command is too
strong in me, I fear."

"I'm no priest," he said abruptly. "I proved unworthy of that honor long ago, God pity me."

After her terrifying flight and the dreadful drain of
healing, the holy Name proved to be too much. With a
despairing cry, she felt her knees turn to water beneath
her, vision narrowed to a pinprick of feeble moonlight.
Then even that much was gone. He was lifting her into
his arms, handling her weight in her sodden skirts effortlessly as a feather. The dangerous aromas of steel
and incense were filling her nose. Dizziness swirled
through her. Floating, barely conscious, she sagged
against him.

"Merely let us pass, I beseech thee." Her faint voice sounded insubstantial as a spirit's in her ears.

"Let you pass?" His voice rumbled through his chest, mighty heart thumping like a hammer against her cheek. "A witch and alleged Faerie—a self-proclaimed princess, no less? It's God's doing that I've found you, and God's will that I keep you."

"Keep me? What does that mean?" A shaft of fear pierced her heart.

"I mean, you foolish, misguided girl, that I'm a witch-hunter and inquisitor," he said flatly. "In the name of His Holiness the Pope, by my authority as a Blade of God, I'm placing you under arrest."

TWO

DEEP IN THE WOOD, someone was watching him. Lord Beltran Nemesto felt the weight of hostile eyes like an itch between his shoulders. He'd pushed hard to clear the scene of slaughter, avoiding hidden roots and branches by instinct as the darkness thickened.

His strength was dangerously depleted. Bad news that. Coming two full years after the last such episode, he'd begun to think himself cured. Now he dragged his reluctant cavalcade through the thicket by raw determination—three horses, that strange girl and her wounded paramour bound witless to their saddles.

When his strength finally failed, taxed by weeks of fasting and hardship, he found a cave. Beltran made camp there—a makeshift citadel of tumbled rocks to guard his back from whatever stalked them. Patiently he coaxed a fire from damp wood to ward off the wolves and wild dogs who'd be drawn by the rich scent of blood.

Moving slowly as an old man, groaning with effort, he fought the dragging weight of exhaustion, the burn of overused muscles and sinews stretched beyond human bearing.

Clearly, despite his prayers and fasting, his grueling penance during this dolorous Lent, another fit of holy madness had seized him. He'd heard the unmistakable clamor of combat in the woods, an instant of warning as his blood ignited in his veins, then the burning darkness had fallen. He recalled none of what followed, nor why he was afflicted with these unsettling gaps in memory. Beltran knew only that when his vision cleared, he'd found himself panting on hands and knees, blood on his hands and slaughtered men tossed about him like kindling.

And that uncanny girl with her silver-gilt hair and archaic speech, this girl dressed richly as a princess whose flawless skin glowed like moonlight, had babbled about wings and a form of fire.

He clenched his fists against the frustration that chewed through him, perilously close to despair. Despair meant turning his back on God.

For the moment, he'd work to do. He stripped the blood-soaked tunic from the graying knight who tossed and mumbled in a stupor, buried the garment far from their camp, hauled water from the spring he hoped led to the Queen's Highway.

He tethered the horses close—the girl's mist-gray mare tame as a kitten, the knight's skittish black barely tolerating him, his own white Serafin stalwart as a rock. The strangers' bulging panniers he didn't touch, unenthusiastic about riffling through others' possessions, no matter what his duty required. He unrolled a damp bearskin and eased the wounded knight into it, though the man muttered fretfully and brushed his hands away.

Then, steeling himself against the sin of intimate contact, he lifted the girl's slight weight and carried her to safety in the moss-lined hollow.

She lay in his arms, fragile as a newborn foal beneath the spill of ivory skirts, slashed sleeves lined with a fortune in silver cloth. Well, she styled herself a princess, didn't she? And dressed to play the part. Her beauty was so ethereal, her weight so feather-light in his arms, he could almost believe her some enchanted creature, some wood-nymph or dryad, if the Church didn't forbid such heathen nonsense.

As he bore her to shelter, a torrent of gilded curls cascaded over his arm nearly to the forest floor. Her lids fluttered, a fringe of dark lashes kissing porcelain skin. Slim black brows arched like bird's wings against her brow, lending her an air of mischief, even unconscious. When he knelt to lower her, the faint sweetness of violets rose like smoke from her garments.

He gritted his teeth against it. The scent of a woman, enough to make flesh harden and blood quicken, even after a lifetime of hard-fought denial.

Breath rasping in his lungs, Beltran settled her and spread her rose-red mantle to dry. A filigreed belt clasped her slender hips, holding a jeweled knife and an elegant sealskin pouch. Those he removed for caution's sake, and for later examination.

Though he strove to keep distance between them as he worked, inevitably his fingers brushed the warm silk of the girl's white throat, where the crescent-shaped moonstone glimmered. The gentle swell of her breasts, perfectly formed and no larger than ripe apples, rose against the square neck of her bodice.

Cursing softly, Beltran turned away. Women were his besetting sin, the weakness that had kept him from the priesthood. Despite a lifetime of guilt and grim denial, his all-too-human flesh still betrayed him—most recently with that fetching and quite willing widow who'd shared his ship during the Channel crossing.

Another sin to confess before the Cardinal when he returned to Rome. Another lashing for a penance, until the blood ran down his back for it.

As he rummaged in his saddlebags for brown bread and a wheel of sharp English cheese, stomach growling from the day's Lenten fast, his neck prickled again. He doubted those brigands would follow him, if he'd left any alive, for he recalled nothing of the battle when the madness took him. By what he'd gathered from those who witnessed these strange and vexing episodes, though the tales verged upon the hysterical, he was a holy terror when the killing rage seized him.

He was God's Vengeance.

Gripping the loaf of barley bread in a sword-hardened hand, he loosened the broadsword in its sheath. From the dark heart of the forest, a throaty chuckle sounded.

Beltran pivoted toward that wicked mirth, bread tossed aside, his sword hissing free. Wrapping both fists around the hilt, back to those he defended, he slanted the blade across his body. Firelight blazed down the honed blade, gilding the etched figure of St. Michael driving the Devil into Hell.

Deep in the forest, at the very edge of hearing, a woman whispered, *"Your mortal blade cannot slay me, Vengeance."*

The evil voice raised his skin into gooseflesh, even as holy fire made his blood burn. *Christ's Blood, don't let the madness take me. I must know what evil hunts me.*

Jaw knotting, he gripped his blade before him and strode boldly into the forest, bellowing, "In the Name of Christ whose power compels you, be gone!"

A shriek of pain tore the darkness. The cloying sweetness of apple-blossoms suddenly filled his head. From the cave, the wounded knight cried out hoarsely. Beltran pivoted and charged back to the camp, the red heat of madness searing through him until his skin seemed to smoke.

Jesu—not now! Lose my wits and I could slay them both, the girl and her lover.

Barely holding the madness at bay, he burst into the clearing. Near the fire, the senseless knight tossed restlessly, cheeks flushed, sweat glistening on his brow. Clearly, fever had set into the wound, all healing efforts notwithstanding.

And there, a slim white figure etched against the darkness, stood the girl—flown from dreamless slumber to full alertness in a heartbeat. She posed like a wild doe on the edge of flight, pale skirts gripped in her fists, gilded curls tumbled wildly past her hips. In the frame of her delicate features, her enormous leaf-green eyes were riveted to his.

I should have shackled her, like any suspect witch. But she seemed so innocent. Careless of me…

"Easy, now," Beltran rumbled, as though calming a skittish horse. Better for her if she didn't try to flee. Perhaps she could yet prove innocent. "There's nothing to fear."

A faint scornful smile curved her lips. "Do not thou fear my sister Morrigan?"

"I fear no creature that walks God's earth." That much was certainly true. He'd slain his demons years ago, except the one who lived inside him.

"Then thank thy Creator thou hast never met my sister." A pulse fluttered in the girl's throat above her travel-crushed finery. Absently her hand stole to her waist. A cry spilled from her lips.

"My pouch!" Her eyes blazed with emerald fire. "Thou hast stolen it!"

"Merely laid away for safekeeping." Spirited then, as witches tended to be. Despite her archaic speech and all that sweet beauty, she would prove no different than the others. He swallowed an unexpected tinge of disappointment.

"Thou art a thief, to trifle with items that do not concern thee," the girl said stubbornly. When her skirts brushed the fallen knight, she glanced down at him. With swift concern, her brows drew together. "Lord Ansgar is feverish. I fear I did not fully draw the poison. He requires proper tending, in a proper bed."

"If he's one of the Fair Folk," Beltran said, to test her reaction, "he can't die."

Fingers knotted in her splendid skirts. Pain flickered across her elfin features; her glow dimmed, as though a shadow slid across the moon. "He is mortal. Believe me, he can die. Or if not die, he will fall into dreaming and waken nevermore."

"There's an abbot with some claim to healing where we're headed." Beltran divided his attention between the dark trees that clustered around them and the girl, still poised for flight. He harbored no doubt that, if not for her wounded comrade, she would already have bolted. If she managed to elude him, Beltran would hunt her down and drag her back to camp in chains.

Far better for her if she hadn't named the Fae and their demon Queene. His duty bound him now to track her to Hell itself, if it meant one less witch to plague Catholic Mary's troubled realm. Never mind that the

Archbishop awaited him in London, and Beltran was already late.

"You intend we venture forth together?" Apprehension and relief mingled in her face, she cast him a guarded glance.

"Briefly. I've pressing business in London."

She hesitated. "An abbey…is it a Christian church?"

"It is." He watched for her reaction.

Alarm widened her leaf-green gaze. "Then we cannot go there. In his condition, Lord Ansgar would not survive it."

Heaving a breath, Beltran thrust his sword over his shoulder into the scabbard, the certain movement honed by decades of repetition. Now for the usual interrogation, to circle back on the girl's own words and tangle her in her lies. Though he'd little time or taste for it tonight.

"If he isn't Fae—"

"He's bespelled." Impatience sharpened her words. She knelt gracefully in a pink carpet of early primrose, a cloud of sweetness rising around her. "Mortal, but subject to all a Faerie's weakness. For he has dwelled too long among the Fair Folk."

"Among your folk?" he pressed, attention divided between the shadowy perimeter of their camp and the gentle hand—light as a butterfly's foot—that touched the fallen knight. Somehow, he didn't like to see her touching him.

Carefully she adjusted the bandage, paying no heed to his likes and dislikes. "This fever will require my basket of healing simples. Praise the Lady I brought it. He must have hot water, fresh linen, and willow-bark tea to draw out pain and fever."

The girl glanced up expectantly, as though Beltran would spring to obey her like a kitchen-boy. Hoisting his brows, he planted his feet in the soil and folded his arms. She stifled a sigh.

Supple as a willow herself, she flowed to her feet and stepped lightly toward their piled possessions. When she discovered the rawhide tether around her ankle, she halted abruptly. A woman heavier on her feet would have fallen, but she scrambled deftly and managed to stay upright—a mark of the Devil's favor.

"Why…?" She traced the cord knotted around her slim ankle to the tree where he'd bound her. Her brows rushed together, eyes incandescent with anger. "By what right, sir, do thou bind me, as mortals bind their poor wretched beasts? Dost thou fear I shall stray?"

Lo, how the color rose into her fair skin now! Being thwarted had flown her into a fine temper, a spoiled child rather than the haughty princess she claimed to be. Any less poised and she would have stamped her booted foot in its fine-tooled cream leather. Unexpectedly, Beltran's lips twitched.

Briskly he strode to her bulging panniers, hoisted them into his arms and dropped them at her feet. "Find your healing tea. The restraint is a trifle. When we sleep, as I shortly must, I'll tie it to my belt."

"Thou…thou…" Clearly, she couldn't quite bring herself to say *knave*. "By what right am I held?"

"I'm detaining you for interrogation," he said coldly, hardening himself against her outrage as he would to her tears. He'd a lifetime of experience dealing with women's wiles. "My right derives from the Holy Catholic Church and the Lord himself."

She stared, her face softened by pity. "Poor fellow. Thou art deluded."

Despite his years of experience, this annoyed him. "I'm a Blade of God, madam, sworn to root out vile sorcery. By your own words, you name yourself one of the Fair Folk who steals innocent babes from cradles and dances in witches' circles by moonlight. Do you wish now to recant?"

For the first time, doubt flickered in her face. He could see her working it out, recalling what she'd told him, wary eyes moving from the flaming cross at his throat to the Seal of Justice on his hand. She didn't rush to justify or explain, nor deny the charges, which he found interesting. Instead she hesitated, nibbling at the pale pink flesh of her lower lip.

As the firelight played over her still figure, Beltran was distracted anew by her beauty—high slanting cheekbones, those slim brows winging upward from tilted eyes, a cat's pointed chin. She was slight and delicate as a sparrow beneath the soiled opulence of her gown, one sleeve coming away from frayed laces at her shoulder, any trace of a lady's hood long gone.

And, God's fury, that splendid curtain of silver curls tumbling free around her. He could well believe the Devil had crafted her beauty, despite the deceptive air of innocence that lingered about her.

"I'm not a witch, as thou would name it," the girl said at last, her sweet voice laced through with certainty, like the chime of a silver bell. "I am Rhiannon, as I told thee. Forsooth, I can prove it. Merely fetch the letter of safe-conduct from my belt-pouch—the pouch thou hast taken." Pointedly, she paused. "I bear Queene

Maeve's own writ to negotiate with Mary Tudor the terms of a lasting peace between thy folk and mine."

Ah, now we come to it. Again, inexplicably, a twinge of disappointment stabbed through him. She entangled herself deeper in guilt with every word, this girl. *Rhiannon.*

The Devil had led her well astray with these delusions. Perhaps she even possessed some such letter, either the Devil's mark or some charlatan's forgery, which he would examine in due course. From written evidence of witchery, if such existed, even recanting would not save her.

"A princess of the Fair Folk," he repeated, giving her this last chance.

"I am," she said proudly. So heedless of her peril.

"Shall I call you 'Your Highness'?"

A hint of discomfort flitted across her face, and her lashes lowered. "'My lady' will suffice. I'm hardly a proper princess with my blood, though my mother insists upon the title."

Casually, he found a small cauldron and rigged a spit over the flame. "And who is this fine fellow? Your prince?"

"I told thee. He is mortal." Which was no answer at all. The girl—Rhiannon—knelt to sort through her possessions. Carelessly she tossed aside a swath of opulent fabric in pale green sarcenet, a court gown. She paused to caress the silver curve of a lap-harp, tucked among the fabric. That, she laid aside gently.

As he sliced twigs from a branch with a few capable strokes, Beltran kept a watchful eye trained on her.

"He is Lord Ansgar Emrys." Again, that hint of

hidden things stirred behind her eyes. "In the ancient tongue, they call him the divine spear—or lance."

She crossed toward the water-bucket, steps gossamer-light on the uneven ground, only to be pulled short by her tether. Annoyance sharpened her tone. "I command thee, unbind me! I must have freedom to tend my comrade."

"In a moment." The lie rolled from his tongue without effort. The Cardinal had taught him God's holy work justified any tool—dishonesty, coercion, threats, even torture. That was another reason they called him God's Vengeance.

He followed her toward the bucket. "Tell me your purpose in this wood."

"I told thee, I'm bound for London, to negotiate a treaty of perpetual peace."

"So much faith in a treaty? Most aren't worth the parchment they're written on."

"Ah, but this is an enchanted treaty." Her elfin features lit with conviction. "The Faerie Queene has already signed. Once the Tudor Queen does likewise, the spell is triggered for both parties. My people are protected from mortal violence, and Morrigan's faction is bound to the Summer Lands for a thousand years, but only if the treaty is signed before the Convergence. If not, the spell is nullified."

In the midst of setting water to boil, the girl fell silent. Still as a woodland creature, she searched the black forest that crowded close. Skin prickling, he listened, stretched all his senses for another evil whisper. Above the soft crackle of flames and the knight's feverish mumbling rose the distant cry of a hunting owl.

"The Convergence? What's that, madam?" Truly,

the Devil had gilded her tongue. Rarely had he heard lies so elaborate. Perhaps she truly believed them. If so, Bishop Bonner would burn them out of her.

As if she sensed the fire's purifying heat, sensed the danger that threatened, she shook her head stubbornly, curls swinging around her winsome face. "These are matters for the Tudor Queen. Tell me, sir, who art *thou*?"

Again, Beltran found himself fighting an inappropriate urge to smile. Quick-witted and brave, this girl, that much he'd grant her.

"Lord Beltran Nemesto." He swept back his cloak from one shoulder and bowed shortly. Might as well use the title the Holy Roman Emperor had encumbered him with. "Sworn Blade of God. We're a sort of Templar, a monastic order of fighting men in Spain, trained from early youth to serve as Church enforcers."

"Thou art far from home," she said lightly. "I have studied the geography of the mortal realm. What is thy purpose in England?"

"I'm dispatched by His Holiness the Pope, at the invitation of Bishop Bonner and the Archbishop of Canterbury, to advance the Inquisition here." He paused. "Were you aware that, under the authority of Their Graces King Philip and Queen Mary, the good bishop has burned more than two hundred heretics?"

He said it deliberately, to provoke a response, and saw the girl whiten—as well she should. Had she encountered Bloody Bonner or any of his henchmen in these woods, she'd already be on her way to the dungeons beneath St. Paul's Cathedral, for an appointment with the rack or the witch-pricker.

She might well end up there, if she but knew it.

Now at last she feared him, though she took pains to hide it. Beltran wondered why the knowledge gave him no satisfaction. A frightened prisoner was a compliant one, in most cases. An effective strategy, notwithstanding his secret distaste for terrorizing these misguided souls.

"Now do you see, you foolish girl," he said softly, "why it's unwise to wander this land babbling wild tales about Faeries and enchantment? I can never release you now."

If possible, she grew paler, and stumbled back to the limit of her tether. "W-what does that mean?"

"My duty's clear. I intend to bring you before the Church for interrogation."

THREE

HER FORMIDABLE CAPTOR was asleep at last.

Swallowing a sigh before the tiny sound escaped, Rhiannon laid aside the lap-harp she'd been strumming. She was all but useless at enchantment, but she'd always been neat-handed. She could spin a restful melody easy as thread from a wheel; the man's exhaustion had done the rest.

A spear's length away, Lord Beltran Nemesto sat propped against a slanting beech, black hood fallen over his eyes. Dim firelight flickered over his square jaw, dusted with golden stubble, and the corded sinew of his sun-bronzed throat. A hard man, even in sleep, but the ruthless set of his mouth had relaxed. He slept with broadsword across his knees, one gauntleted hand resting on the hilt. His powerful chest rose and fell with the rhythm of slumber.

Heart thudding painfully, she slid one hand beneath the fur covering Ansgar's still form. Her foster-father slept easier since her tending, but Rhiannon knew she could never leave him behind to this Blade of God's uncertain mercy. They must escape this stern Catholic. She dared not chance being locked up—not now, with the Convergence looming.

Nor did she care to suffer torture in the name of Spanish King Philip and his Inquisition.

When her fingers brushed the cool silver hilt of Ansgar's dagger, still strapped to his belt, her eyes fluttered closed in relief. Stealthily, she eased the blade from its sheath.

Steel-hard fingers closed around her wrist. Rhiannon barely stifled a scream. Ansgar's gray eyes were open, the cold light of battle sparking in their depths.

As her gaze locked with his, recognition flashed through his face and he drew breath to speak.

Imploring, she raised a finger to her lips and inclined her head toward Beltran Nemesto's still form. He followed her gaze. A muscle ticked in the knight's temple as he grasped their situation.

Easing the dagger free, she sawed gently at the rawhide cord that bound her to her captor.

Barely daring to breathe, she whispered, "The horses..."

Her foster-father jerked a nod of comprehension and struggled upright. Though the pain made him whiten, he managed it. Her dainty Astolat was already straining toward them, testing the strength of her tether, ears swiveled forward as she sensed Rhiannon's wordless call. Beside her, Ansgar's coal-black stallion was alert yet quiet. But Lord Beltran's white charger stamped a restless hoof.

For a heartbeat, the Blade of God's deep breathing hitched. Rhiannon's heart nearly stopped.

When the slow rhythm of his breath resumed, she wasted no time. While Ansgar crept across the clearing to untie their horses—moving haltingly, but at least moving—she flung aside the severed cord and crept catlike to her captor's saddlebags. Distasteful though she found pilfering another's belongings, she could not leave without the enchanted treaty.

Bent over his possessions, she cast a careful glance around the glade. Half-hidden in shadows, her foster-father was working one-handed to tighten Astolat's girth, wounded arm bound to his chest. Against the tree, Lord Beltran was still slumped, hood pulled low over his eyes. By the faint flicker of the dying fire, she glimpsed that shadowy form imposed over his—a giant in silver mail, fair hair streaming around his face, great wings folded around his sleeping body.

Cold with dread and the deep chill of night, she sorted through a bundle of rich garments to find doublets, shirts, hose, all enveloped in the rich sweetness of frankincense. A wrapped crucifix and gilded Bible that made her eyes burn, a portable reliquary where a traveler might pray. The man seemed to carry an entire chapel in his saddlebags—

"Are you searching for your heretical documents?" His voice rolled across the clearing like a lion's growl. "You won't find them there."

Rhiannon froze, stomach knotting, heart sinking like a stone. Fearful of seeing that fiery Being fully roused and wrathful, she dared not even look toward her captor, still reclining beneath his tree.

"Thou cannot keep me here," she whispered, voice taut. "For the peace of both our realms, sir—"

"Rhiannon!" Ansgar's shout rang over the sudden thunder of hooves. Springing to her feet, she caught a pale blur of movement, her beloved Astolat flying toward her, perfectly attuned to her needs. Across the clearing, metal whined as her foster-father unsheathed his blade. Black wool swirled as Lord Beltran unrolled to his feet, firelight flashing red on his holy sword.

As the mare swept past, Rhiannon launched herself

toward the saddle. The tooled leather struck her belly hard, knocking the wind from her, but she scrambled deftly into place. Needing no reins to guide the mare, she had only to spy Ansgar's mounted form and they were sweeping toward him, her steed's mane floating like a silver cloud around them.

The mare sailed over the dying fire as though winged, the wind of her passage billowing Rhiannon's pale skirts around her.

"In God's name, *halt*!" Lord Beltran's bellow sounded like the blast of trumpets. The holy Name struck her like a blow to the belly. Beside her, Ansgar cried out.

Forewarned by that uncanny bellow, Rhiannon twisted to glance behind her. What she found filled her with panic—the Blade of God fallen to hands and knees, pure cobalt fire spilling from his eyes, strong features contorted with pain. Around him, above him, a halo of flame was burning.

Goddess save us.

The mare leaped into the trees without slowing. Rhiannon ducked wildly as a gnarled branch nearly swept her from the saddle. Catching a bare glimpse of her foster-father's grim features as he raised his sword, she screamed at him.

"You cannot fight him. Flee!"

As they raced through the darkness, twisting among trees they could barely discern, branches reached from the night like the Hand of God to pluck her from the saddle. Twigs snared her skirts and tore at her flying hair. Sightless, wind stinging her cheeks, ears filled with her own crashing flight, Rhiannon clung to the mare's neck and let the faithful creature find her own

way. Unless they stumbled across the Queen's Highway, they'd be lost in the forest.

Better even that, than the form of fire.

Above, through a web of trees, a violet moon hung
low in the heavens, surrounded by a glittering net of
stars. Using these celestial signposts, Rhiannon steered
a course southeast toward London. Here she was in
familiar terrain; the moon served as her compass for
navigating through time and space behind the Veil.
Even the stars shifted in their courses in that enchanted
realm.

Now, as she fled, the trees seemed to shift around
her—here a tangled thicket of malevolent oak, there a
moon-threaded glade of slender aspens, somewhere the
roar of a river cascade such as never poured through
this mortal wood. Was it Morrigan's vengeful hand
that spun the sinister thread of enchantment? Rhiannon must not allow herself to grow befuddled, or all
was lost.

Behind her, the cherry-red glow of fire edged the
black trees in silhouette.

Though he'd started out behind her, she could no
longer see Ansgar. She fretted for his safety but feared
to cry his name, lest she lead their pursuer straight to
them.

Her mare burst into a familiar clearing, hemmed
by a high jumble of rocks and a rain-swollen stream.
Twisted forms littered the ground, dead men and dead
horses, reeking of blood and loosened bowels. Her
stomach rose into her throat as she galloped through
the glade where they'd fought for their lives, and the
last of her Fae escort had lost his.

Before them, suddenly, a shadowy figure cried

hoarsely and struggled upright—some chance survivor of the slaughter. Astolat shied violently and reared,
hooves striking out at the apparition and thudding into
flesh. A scream tore Rhiannon's throat as her grip on
the saddle dislodged. The world spun around her, the
star-strewn heavens somehow below her, the ground
rushing to fill her vision.

The slam of impact knocked the breath from her
lungs. For a few moments she lay crumpled on the
damp ground as the mare thundered away, bones aching beneath the voluminous skirts that had cushioned
her fall, the farthingale crushed flat beneath her.

When she could drag breath into her lungs, she
pushed to hands and knees, head spinning too madly
to risk her feet. Frantically she kicked free of the ru-
ined cage of fashionable wire and scurried across the
soil, tangled curls falling forward to screen her vision.
Clinging to her wits, she sensed Astolat's panicked
presence, snorting and shying, crashing through the
trees and struggled after her.

Mortal, not monstrous, that creature who'd risen
before her. Just one of the brigands Ansgar smote before he'd fallen. If the grievous wound that had torn
open his chest didn't kill the man, she knew with her
healer's instinct that Astolat's hooves had cracked his
skull. Scrambling across the soil, she assured herself
the doomed man behind her was nothing to fear.

Yet, somehow, fear closed her throat and dried her
mouth.

Around her, smothering silence fell like a hammer
blow, obliterating all sound including her own gasping breath. Dread spilled through her like ice-water,
pressed her flat against the soil like the wrath of the

Christian God. Beneath her palms, the earth trembled. She knew what had entered the clearing behind her.

Lady of Light, Goddess, Mother, protect me. Her lips moved soundlessly as she struggled against the soil like a crushed insect. Easy prey for the Blade of God, or whatever vengeful angel he'd become.

Suddenly, the crushing pressure eased. Sound leaked back to the night—Astolat's distant snort of alarm, her own desperate breaths, the scrape of wind against leaves and branches. Behind her, the wounded mortal was sobbing.

Gathering her courage, Rhiannon risked a glance behind her. Surprise riveted her in place as surely as divine wrath had done a moment past.

Lord Beltran Nemesto had indeed arrived, but only in mortal form. Astride his white charger, he frowned down on the wounded bandit, ebony cape unfurled and snapping behind him in the wind. Even as she watched, the fire dimmed and dwindled to a shimmering halo around his form, burnishing his cropped hair to tawny gold. At his feet, the bandit groveled.

"Lord Jesus Christ—forgive me," the poor wretch groaned, clearly fighting for every breath. "I need a priest—before ye—take me."

Flinching from the holy Name, Rhiannon shook her head sadly. By his lights, the poor man was dying with mortal sin upon his soul. Without confession and whatever sacred rite the priests performed to absolve him, the wretched creature was destined to burn in hell. For her mother had taught her that as men believed of the life beyond, so it became. Each soul created its own reality.

Moving with a catlike grace that belied his powerful frame, Lord Beltran swung a leg forward over his saddle and leaped down. The cloak swirled around him as he strode forward and dropped to one knee beside the dying man.

"Jesu forgive me!" The bandit's voice splintered. She sensed the bleeding inside his skull, pressure building against his brain.

"Such a terrible waste of life," she whispered, a healer's pity welling in her heart. The least she could do was ease his passing. Driven by a lifetime of habit, the instinctive need to comfort, she gathered her trembling legs beneath her.

Heedless of her halting approach, the Blade of God leaned forward to cup the man's head gently in one large hand. Based on her limited knowledge of Beltran Nemesto, she would never have dreamed he could touch a living creature so tenderly, display such compassion as the terrible wrath eased its grip on his harsh features. That voice that could roar like a lion or the blast of trumpets rumbled soft, bringing sudden tears to her eyes.

"Your soul requires no priest, Rurick son of Angus." Those fiery cobalt eyes glowed like banked coals. "Repent sincerely. Ask God for forgiveness. I shall intercede on your behalf."

The amber glow of Beltran's aura spilled across the man before him, lighting the bandit's grizzled face with a child's wide-eyed wonder. Staring into those glowing eyes as though they were windows into the Christian heaven, the poor creature gasped. Rapture lit him from within until the last breath seeped from his lips. Slowly then, the divine fire faded, until Beltran Nemesto knelt over a dead man.

Rhiannon stood riveted, too awestruck by his strange magick to move.

"What manner of creature art thou?" she whispered. "I vow this poor soul thought thee his Maker. And how did thou learn his name?"

Without lifting his gaze, Beltran voiced a bitter sound. Propping one elbow on his bent knee, he heaved a breath.

"I'm only a man, no better than this poor wretch. Will you make me hunt you into the ground, Rhiannon le Fay, and bind you hand and foot like a criminal?" he asked the soil wearily. "I managed to control it—this time. Surely now you realize it's wiser if you don't provoke me."

AFTER THAT FOOLHARDY escape—an attempt that had nearly succeeded—Beltran decided to bind her. Last night's debacle had already cost him one prisoner. He'd lost her wounded paramour with his antique armor, who'd eluded his dead-of-night search.

Pity, because Beltran would have liked very much to interrogate the fellow. His relations with the strange girl alone made him suspect.

Now, as shafts of morning sunlight slanted through the trees, Rhiannon le Fay swayed gracefully in the saddle, as though heedless of the rope that bound her hands before her. Her dainty little mare, the color of smoke and moonlight, stepped gamely along without protest beside his Serafin.

Still, though his captive seemed to be behaving for the moment, a tinge of rose stained her slanted cheekbones. Imperious as any princess, she rode with her chin tilted at a mutinous angle. She'd been adamantly opposed to leaving her comrade behind and argued passionately that his wounds required tending.

"Your faithful protector abandoned you to your fate," Beltran said curtly, as he knotted the rope around her fine-boned wrists. "I suggest you resign yourself to doing the same for him."

She'd looked as though she wanted to run him through with his own sword.

The girl was still simmering as she rode beside him, one gilded ringlet swinging against a rigid shoulder. Still no sign of a proper hood. When they watered their horses, she'd knelt beside the tumbling brook like a river nymph and coiled that mass of silver hair into a coronet around her head. It gave her the illusion of respectability, despite the travel-stained cream velvet billowing around her. Her red mantle spilled over the mare's silken haunches like a royal banner.

By daylight, the girl's beauty was undeniable. Light as a bird, she perched in the saddle, waist small enough to span between his hands, her breasts round and sweet as apples beneath her tight-laced bodice...

Damn it! *Remember your oath, man.*

No good. Even a man sworn to celibacy—though he routinely tumbled into sin—couldn't be immune to her enchantment, her ethereal innocence, those flashes of wildness like a forest creature.

Fashioned by the Devil to beguile, no doubt. He'd have to be blind not to want her. Just to kiss her once, feel her startle and kindle beneath his touch, yield against him as her arms stole around his neck...

Beside him, the girl slanted him a guarded look, as though sensing his lustful thoughts. "Where dost thou take me, Lord Beltran Nemesto?"

He cleared his throat and banished his carnal cravings, forcing his thoughts resolutely away from the cock-stand beneath his codpiece. "To the abbey for questioning, to determine whether formal charges of witchcraft should be brought."

Her leaf-green eyes widened with trepidation. Firmly, Beltran quashed a pang of discomfort. The time for subtlety had passed, with the lady flown and barely recovered. He could only thank God he'd managed to hold another fit of holy madness at bay when he woke from a sound sleep to find her fleeing him.

Now he hardened his heart against her plight and adjusted Serafin's course, angling them away from the stream. If his reckoning was correct, they should be emerging on the Great North Road near Hatfield.

He'd leave her at the abbey there, explain the situation and be on his way within the hour. The abbot was noted as a rigid doctrinarian and a strict questioner. He would have time to bother with the girl as Beltran did not, to question and counter-question her, pick apart this outlandish tale she'd concocted and get at the truth of the business.

Possibly, he would find Rhiannon le Fay to be merely deluded. If not, the abbot would turn her over to Bishop Bonner—and then God help her.

"Why cannot thou question me, as we ride along?" she asked. "If question thou must."

He kept his voice curt. Now was no time for sympathy; better for her to grasp the gravity of her situation. "I've no time to oversee your interrogation. Questioning a suspect properly takes days. The business can't be rushed, though some enthusiasts barrel through it to judgment."

Hearing the censure in his own voice, he checked himself and made his face impassive. "The best interrogators build a relationship, of sorts, with the accused. One must establish credibility and authority as well as fear."

"Thy performance thus far seems more than adequate," she murmured, slim fingers twining in the mare's flaxen mane.

Heat kindled in his blood. On the lips of another woman, a comment like that would have been an invitation. Was she truly so innocent of seduction? Or did she play his passions like the lap-harp she'd used to sing him to sleep?

Grimly he halted these dangerous speculations. "I'm expected in London, and long overdue. But I place full faith in the abbot. He's questioned dozens—if not hundreds—of suspect heretics and witches. He'll know how to question you without botching it."

"I've nothing to confess," she whispered. "I've done nothing wrong. I'm a stranger to this land."

When her lip quivered, a twinge of remorse plucked at him. Forsooth, needful though it was, he never relished making these poor unfortunates fear him.

"If you're innocent of the charges, girl, you've nothing to fear," he said gruffly.

"I fear nothing." Her pointed chin lifted, battle-ready once more. "Have thou examined the documents in my belt-pouch, my letters of introduction and safe-passage, the treaty with Queene Maeve's own seal?"

"I've said I have no time, girl. Your interrogator will examine the evidence in due course." He paused. "Frankly, unless those letters come from Pope Paul himself, I don't care who's written them. It's unfortunate you've fallen into the hands of the one man in England least able to show you mercy, Rhiannon le Fay."

Indeed, he'd worked hard to become so ruthless, to become the terror on the battlefield and in the interrogation chamber known to God-fearing Christians as God's Vengeance. Compassion had no place in the holy work he did, or so he'd always believed. His place was to carry out judgment, not cozen the accused with mercy and sympathy.

Beneath their hooves, bracken crackled as the smoke-colored mare sidled, no doubt sensing her rider's distress. The girl murmured under her breath, and the mare settled.

"If thou wilt not question me," she said tightly, "then will thou listen? And open thine eyes to the evils that bedevil this land? Plagues, famine, flooding such as England has not witnessed in generations. Crops have rotted in the fields three years running because these villages have buried all who would harvest them."

Beltran nodded grimly at that. All of Europe knew of England's misery.

Looking encouraged by this small acknowledgement, the girl rushed ahead.

"England is drawn into the bottomless pit of Spain's unceasing wars. Queen Mary is hopelessly besotted with her Spanish husband, enslaved to the will of his brother the Holy Roman Emperor. They've been burning Protestants here for years, though once the English isle was known for tolerance and moderation. This entire isle teeters on the brink of civil war."

"Aye, they're burning more heretics than ever," he conceded, drawn against his will into this matter that concerned him so closely. "Though, with proper handling, many of those might be saved. Some of God's servants are too quick with the torch."

Sensing her apprehension, he allowed her a tight smile. "You needn't fear. The abbot will be just. Honest repentance and willingness to take instruction in the Catholic faith will avail you greatly—"

"Repentance?" she cried, brows rushing together above stormy eyes. "For what should I repent? For being who I am, and what I am—half Fae and half mortal, a misfit who belongs nowhere, neither in one world nor the other? An oddity dwelling always on the fringes, peering through the window at a fellowship I'm not permitted to share? What have I done my whole life but regret and grieve for that?"

Startled by her passion, he stared at her. For a breath, the English forest melted away around him. He was a boy again, weak with hunger, face still swollen from his father's fists, the shabby peasant rubbing elbows with his betters at San Miguel. How the noble brats and the merchants' sniveling sons at the monastery had hated him!

Yet he'd grown to manhood among them, learned to swim in that sea of scorn and venom, watched with hidden satisfaction as the weak and the unworthy broke beneath the lash of discipline. He'd overcome gnawing hunger from the everlasting bread-and-water fasts, ignored the ache of sleeping on stone floors with nothing but a threadbare blanket and his prayers to warm him.

And the peasant-lad had thrived. Though he'd proven unworthy of a priest's chasuble, the Blades of God had welcomed him. And this strange girl beside him, with her incandescent passions, she too had thrived, dressed richly as the princess she styled herself. Her wealth had come from somewhere. Men willingly laid down their lives to defend her.

But who would protect her from him? Against the Church's wrath, Rhiannon le Fay would be utterly defenseless.

Slowly the shadows of his past receded. The forest coalesced around him, cold sunlight slanting through spears of brittle poplar, cruel wind biting exposed skin.

Damn cold for April, and that's God's truth. Looks like England's destined for another famine year. Whatever the cause, this girl spoke truly about the ill fortune cursing this land.

Riding alongside, Rhiannon studied him curiously. "What is it, my lord? Thine aspect is most severe. More so than usual, I mean."

The corners of her lips curved wryly, but her concerned gaze invited him to trust her. The realization that he felt tempted to do just that brought cold sanity rushing back.

She was a suspect witch. What greater evidence of her enchantment did he require than this—the fact that she tempted *him*, of all men living.

"Look after the state of your own soul, lady." Abruptly, he spurred ahead. "For the abbey lies yonder, and your interrogation."

At that moment, a horse and rider exploded into the road before them.

FOUR

FOR ONE MAD MOMENT, as the fiery chestnut stallion erupted from the trees, Rhiannon feared some new assault. Her departure from Faerie on this mission of peace had not occurred without rancor. Her sister's faction, violently opposed to the scheme, had nearly overwhelmed those loyal to the ailing Faerie Queene.

Too well they recalled the last Convergence, when her father King Arthur had reigned. This time, they burned to avenge his bastard son—their traitorous prince Mordred whom Arthur had slain—and howled for mortal blood.

Don't be foolish. Sternly Rhiannon put steel in her spine. *My brother Mordred is long dead at our father's own hand, and the dead do not return. As for Morrigan... Mordred's mother, Arthur's lover, Arthur's bane...as a creature of darkness, she cannot walk the mortal realm until nightfall.*

Not that it ever thwarted her when Morrigan wished to work her mischief. Her sister was a mistress of illusion, one of the best in Faerie. She'd tricked her mother's own lover into lying with her by weaving a simple glamour. Morrigan had merely assumed the likeness of the Faerie Queene and summoned Arthur to Avalon.

Beneath her, Astolat shied violently, nearly flinging her from the saddle. Lord Beltran's firm hand on the bridle steadied her. As the chestnut stallion bore down on them, the Blade of God drew his sword in a single sure stroke to plant himself between Rhiannon and danger.

The stallion skidded to a halt before them, flaming mane tossing, red as the tumbled curls beneath his rider's stylish French hood.

"Dear God have mercy upon my soul!" the newcomer gasped in a clear, frightened voice. Rhiannon glimpsed her white face stark against the severe black of her riding habit. Her eyes blazed like wheels of silver fire.

Not Morrigan then, for certain, Rhiannon thought wryly, wincing from the holy Name.

The rapid tattoo of hooves and the violent snap of foliage heralded the lady's pursuers, whoever they might be, closing in. The redhead's sharp eyes fixed on the flaming cross that swung against Beltran's chest.

"I beg your protection as a gentleman and a Christian knight!" she cried, glancing frantically over her shoulder.

"You have it," Beltran said.

Whatever his shortcomings might be—and Rhiannon had determined they were many—cowardice and indecision didn't appear to be among them. Swiftly he kneed his charger forward, sword angled across his body *en garde*, and stationed his stalwart frame protectively before both women.

Rhiannon cast him an appreciative glance. For the first time, the width of his shoulders, the bulge of biceps beneath his doublet, the resolve knotting his jaw promised not threat, but reassurance—protection from any foe that threatened. As formidable a foe as he'd proven to be, he lacked nothing as a guardian.

The redhead wheeled her chestnut neatly into place beside Rhiannon and shot her a swift assessing look.

"Who are you?" the lady whispered, eyes sweeping over Rhiannon's disheveled finery, the silver gleaming on Astolat's fine-tooled bridle, and the coil of rope that bound her wrists before her.

"I'm Rhiannon." Fascinated, she stared at the fiery-haired newcomer—not beautiful, but blazing with drive and spirit. Her energy crackled in the air around her like an aura, as though the woman were Fae herself.

"Follow my lead," the redhead urged. "Otherwise, say nothing."

Rhiannon was unaccustomed to following anyone's lead, but she was given no time to protest. The next instant, a trio of riders burst from the undergrowth. Encumbered with swords and armor, the scowling men sweated freely in the crisp air as they plunged to a rearing halt.

The foremost figure, tall and dashing in plumed cap and shoulder cape, nudged his fine-blooded stallion toward them in a prancing walk. Armed to the teeth, two surly-looking guards followed his lead.

"If you love life, gentlemen, keep your distance," Beltran said calmly.

The leader's pale eyes, set in ascetic features, assessed the Blade of God standing like a castle in his path. That icy gaze flickered indifferently over Rhiannon to the redhead.

"My lady Elizabeth." Curtly, he bowed. "You've led me a merry chase."

"Why, Sir Henry Bedingfield!" The redhead pressed a white hand to her breast. "God-a-mercy, you should have identified yourself. I fancied a gang of cutthroats pursued me."

Her lordly pursuer brushed a miniscule speck of dust from his brocade hose. For a man who'd just been galloping madly through a forest, he appeared bored by the entire affair—a player who'd lost interest in a too-familiar role.

"You knew well enough who followed, Your Grace. Do you still think to slip my vigilance?"

"Indeed, sir, you do me great disservice!" the lady cried. "I spied a fox in the bracken, the very fiend who's been terrorizing our poultry all winter, I've no doubt. Why, Sir Peter Killigrew told me this very fox bit a sleeping babe in its cradle, can you imagine?"

Sir Henry plucked a dried leaf from his well-barbered beard. "The only fox in this forest is the one who sits before me, pleading innocence so prettily. Who are these new confederates, Your Grace? More conspirators in the Dudley plot?"

Beltran kneed his horse forward. "We're no conspirators in some Protestant plot against your good Queen Mary, man, merely travelers chance-come upon a lady in distress. Why do you hound and harry this lady?"

"By the Queen's own writ, this 'lady' is charged to my keeping. It's my duty to ensure she's not caught up—unwitting or otherwise—in another anti-Catholic plot," the newcomer said stiffly. "Although Sir Dudley has failed in his heretical scheme to overthrow our rightful Queen Mary and her Spanish lord, the innocence of certain persons in this household has yet to be proven."

Rhiannon's thoughts raced. Could this be true? The Tudor Queen's own people now sought her downfall?

Had the Faerie Queene chosen the wrong sister for their treaty?

"I'd advise you to step aside, stranger," Sir Henry finished gruffly. "This is no affair of yours."

When the man placed a casual hand on his belted sword, a current of tension crackled visibly through Beltran's frame. Around them, the forest held its breath, all the customary sounds of wind and woodland fallen silent.

"Sir, I implore thee!" Rhiannon leaned past him and appealed to Sir Henry. "Do not provoke him, or I swear thou shall rue the moment."

"Indeed?" Sir Henry arched an elegant brow. Discreetly, Rhiannon tucked her bound hands beneath her mantle. She'd hoped this man might prove an ally who could help her reach the Tudor Queen he proclaimed to serve.

Yet her disastrous encounters with mortals in this realm had taught her to approach them with caution. This one, she now sensed, would prove unsympathetic.

"And who might you be?" Sir Henry murmured. "His fancy leman?"

Rhiannon was uncertain of the word, but the disdain in his tone was biting.

Lady Elizabeth gasped. "For shame, sir! These are still *my* estates, no matter what my sister suspects of me. I'll see no woman so abused on Hatfield lands."

"Enough!" Clearly Sir Henry had lost patience with the charade. The two guards sidled forward, seeking to flank Beltran, who loomed like a fortress in their path. One eased a hand toward the knife in his boot.

Beltran flung back his cloak and leveled his sword at Sir Henry's throat. "Keep your distance. And tell your underling to keep his hand away from that boot-knife unless he wants my sword through his throat. I won't warn you again, man."

They all froze. The standoff stretched the air tight between them. Lady Elizabeth's hand stole to Rhiannon's arm and squeezed tightly. When Rhiannon glanced at her pale face, resolve burned there like a white flame. The lady wasn't frightened witless. Far from it. Her clever eyes measured the scene playing out, and Rhiannon could almost *hear* her thinking...

For a confused moment, she wasn't certain what to wish—for the conflict to escalate, allowing her and the beleaguered Elizabeth to flee? But then, surely, men would die. How could she call herself a healer and wish for that?

Indeed, Beltran Nemesto had saved her life when the bandits attacked. If he were injured, how could she leave him to bleed out his life on the forest floor while the cold-eyed Sir Henry dragged Lady Elizabeth off to imprisonment?

Swallowing a sigh, she straightened her shoulders and assumed a commanding tone—the tone Queene Maeve deployed to compel instant obedience. These foolish men, like strutting roosters, would be at each other's throats in a heartbeat unless a woman took charge.

"Thou heedless creature, dost not recognize the man before thee?" she declared grandly. "He is Lord Beltran Nemesto, Church enforcer. Thy lady has appealed to him as a Christian knight for protection."

When she declared Beltran's name, Sir Henry blinked. One of his guardsmen edged his horse back.

The other guard crossed himself and muttered, "God's Vengeance."

At her elbow, Lady Elizabeth's fingers tightened.

"Ah," Sir Henry said softly, eyeing Beltran with new respect.

"There, you see." Fiery head lifting, Elizabeth spurred fearlessly forward. "This man's reputation precedes him from Rome. Will you cross swords with a Blade of God over trifles? Certainly I ought not to have pursued the fox so heedlessly, but my intention was never to disobey the Queen, my sister. Let us all return to Hatfield, these good travelers included, and warm ourselves with hot mulled wine and a brisk fire."

The Queen, her sister...

A new awareness stiffened Beltran's shoulders; the wind ruffled his cloak around his boots like ebony flames. In passing, Rhiannon wondered how she'd grown so attuned to the man's reactions after so few hours in his presence. She sensed the coil of caution tightening around him, clear as the nervous skip of her own heart.

Sir Henry swirled his cape and bowed elegantly, this time to Beltran. "My lord, this situation is regrettable, but I have my orders from the Queen's own lips. I fear you must step aside."

"When did my sister ever say I could not converse with a servant of God's own Church?" Elizabeth smiled winningly all around. "Indeed, I am supposed to take instruction for the betterment of my soul, am I not?"

At this, the beleaguered Sir Henry raised his eyes toward heaven. After a moment, he signaled subtly to the men behind him, and his henchmen relaxed. For the first time, Beltran shifted his attention away from the threat.

"Your Grace." In a single forceful movement, he sheathed his blade and bowed from the saddle. "Forgive me for failing to recognize you. We haven't met."

"You're forgiven." Lady Elizabeth extended a regal hand, which Beltran raised to his lips with surprising style. Clearly, the Blade of God knew his way around a royal court.

As she acknowledged him with a dazzling smile, Elizabeth's eyes danced with mischief. She looked like a woman who could appreciate a man who'd ridden fearlessly to her defense and ably defused a dangerous situation.

Rhiannon, well schooled in mortal etiquette, rummaged through her store of knowledge on the Tudor court—the treasure-trove of gossip and custom Lady Linnet had shared while she lingered, beguiled, in the Summer Lands. She'd spoken of the difficult history between Catholic Mary, proud daughter of Katherine of Aragon, and the Protestant Elizabeth—daughter of the witch Anne Boleyn. Mary had always considered her half-sister a bastard, though the English Parliament had legitimized the girl years ago.

Suddenly, the pieces dropped into place.

"Thou art the Tudor princess," she whispered, so surprised she said it aloud.

"Nay, not princess," the lady said swiftly, with a glance toward Sir Henry. "I was barely two years old when I was first proclaimed a bastard, and my good Catholic sister has shouted my status to the heavens ever since. I can never inherit the English throne. Thus,

I am merely Lady Elizabeth. Indeed I aspire to nothing more. You'd do well to recall that."

Clearly relations between the sisters had not improved since Linnet's sojourn at the Tudor court. And how not? English King Henry had renounced the Pope's authority and divorced Mary's mother—his wife of twenty years and the mother of his only living child. Then he'd cast aside both mother and child like a pair of boots he'd outgrown, banished them from court to shivering misery in some remote estate. All to wed the upstart Anne Boleyn in a dubious dead-of-night undertaking. Their daughter Elizabeth was named a princess, Mary herself stripped of title and property and forced to wait on her half-sister like a servant. Was it any wonder Mary showed rancor to her now?

As for Elizabeth, she herself had known her mother beheaded, her royal title stripped and herself proclaimed a bastard by that selfsame father before she was three years old. She'd seen herself replaced in his changeable affections by his son with his next wife, Jane Seymour. Though the pair were sickly and short-lived both, Elizabeth had never regained her place.

Rhiannon felt an unexpected sense of kinship with this spirited mortal—a woman whom, unless she was much mistaken, had more than a drop of Faerie blood coursing with the Tudor through her veins. Lady Elizabeth sparkled with it—her hair flame-bright, eyes burning like twin stars, every word she spoke crackling with magick of which she likely had no notion.

Both of them bastards, both of them outcasts, both of them tainted by mixed blood.

Still, Elizabeth Tudor was Mary's sister. If Rhiannon could not reach Mary's distant ear, perhaps she could entreat this quick-witted royal sister to adopt the cause of peace.

To succeed, of course, she'd have to elude Beltran's vigilance. Elizabeth was the heretics' great hope for a Protestant Queen, and Rhiannon a suspect witch in his custody. A frown furrowed his tanned brow as his keen eyes searched her, as though he sensed the current of hope eddying through her tired body.

"Your Grace, we cannot linger," he told Elizabeth abruptly. "I'm overdue in London on papal business. The Archbishop of Canterbury is expecting me."

"Why, all the better, sir! I'd never dream of keeping the Archbishop waiting. We must ensure you're well refreshed and provisioned for hard riding."

A brittle note had invaded Elizabeth's voice when she named the Archbishop—Lord Reginald Pole, the supreme Catholic authority of England, Mary Tudor's most loyal ally. Rhiannon recalled that the Protestant princess and her sister's Catholic magnates were nothing close to friends.

The flickering candle of hope flared higher in her breast. Since Lady Elizabeth and the Church were rivals—the lady's own mother beheaded for witchcraft, among other crimes—surely the Tudor princess could not entrust an innocent woman to Rome's tender mercies.

Judging by the muscle jumping in Beltran's rigid jaw, he entertained the same suspicion. He ducked a perfunctory bow.

"Your Grace is generous, but we need nothing—"

Swiftly Rhiannon stepped into the breach, doing her best to mirror Lady Elizabeth's blithe assurance. "Marry, sir! Hast thou forgotten my encounter with those bandits? Look upon me well, Lord Beltran. I'm all over mud and brambles!"

He looked upon her indeed, slow fire kindling in his cobalt eyes as they lingered on the pale curve of her shoulder, half-exposed where her sleeve had torn away from her bodice. An unexpected heat slid over her bare skin, warmth rising in her face.

"My lady," he began, his voice dark with warning.

"And what of my lost comrades?" Still tingling from that smoking look whose meaning she couldn't comprehend, Rhiannon was beginning to enjoy herself for the first time since she'd entered this bewildering mortal realm. "Both Lord Ansgar and Lady Linnet are lost in the wood, as I've attempted to explain to thee. If we linger but a few hours, they may catch us up."

"Absolutely not," Beltran growled. Of course, being caught by Ansgar would complicate his plan to have her locked up and interrogated.

Smooth as though they'd rehearsed it, Lady Elizabeth took her cue. "Lost comrades, in this benighted weather? There'll be hard frost by nightfall, no doubt of it. Sir Henry must dispatch men to search."

"Sir Henry must do nothing of the sort," the owner of that name said crossly. "My orders are to guard your safety, Lady Elizabeth, not tear about the countryside searching for stray vagrants."

"We ask for nothing and need nothing." Looking irritated at being spoken around as though he weren't present, Beltran grasped Rhiannon's bridle. "This lady's bound for St. Edward's Abbey, and I must deliver her forthwith."

"But I don't *wish* to—"

"Oh, St. Edward's?" Speaking over Rhiannon's

cry of protest, Elizabeth pressed a dismayed hand to her bosom. *What a talented player she is*, Rhiannon thought admiringly. "My dear Lord Beltran, I regret to bring you unhappy tidings. That monastery has been disbanded for months. All the good monks fell victim to the plague that has ravished this land—the abbot included, may God assoil his soul."

"Disbanded?" Beltran stared. "The Pope told me nothing of this."

"Well, the Pope has been busy, has he not?" Elizabeth said archly. "He's thick as thieves with the French these days. My sister and her Spanish kin are most troubled by it."

Carefully tucking away these tidbits, Rhiannon saw the observation did not please Beltran. His face was shuttered—all hard jaw and hooded eyes. He bristled with ill-concealed impatience to be rid of this delay and on the road again.

By rights, he should terrify her to witlessness. She should be willing to plunge into any mad scheme to escape his vigilance. Yet somehow, she'd never doubted he would protect her when Sir Henry and his lackeys came thundering toward them.

Still, she could not fail to recognize the opportunity the spirited redhead represented. Mary Tudor was nearing her fortieth year, ancient by mortal standards, and had already miscarried one child. If the Queen died without issue, this bastard Tudor princess with her wild Fae blood would become the next Queen of England—with authority to sign the treaty.

While these thoughts raced quicksilver through her mind, Beltran was stating his intent to make for some other church and deflecting Lady Elizabeth's obvious interest as to why. Rhiannon shivered in the biting wind, which drew his immediate attention.

His eyes sharpened. He swept the folds of Rhiannon's rose-red mantle briskly around her. She could have imagined a flash of concern in his gaze, if she hadn't already known he despised her.

"Come," he said gruffly. "We can make the church at Yardley by Nones."

"Yardley!" Elizabeth was quick to seize her cue. "God-a-mercy, you cannot mean to take her half so far. She's frozen through, poor creature!"

That much was no lie. Rhiannon hadn't been warm or dry since she'd come through the Veil to these benighted lands. Though she'd fought to keep a brave face, her reserves were depleted by fear and exhaustion. Her eyes stung with sudden tears.

Swiftly she blinked them back. Yet her voice rang forlorn in her ears. "Forsooth, my lord, I'd welcome an hour within walls and warm water for washing. Surely thou cannot mean to lead me among thy people in this condition. I look like a beggar-girl!"

"Hardly that." As he surveyed the cream velvet glittering with silver stitching, his hard mouth twitched with a flicker that was almost amusement. "The priest will extend you every comfort."

Then at least I shall be comfortably fed when they drag me to the pyre, she thought tartly. "Only see the clouds piling in the north, my lord. I fear 'twill shortly rain."

Indeed, the words had barely left her lips when thunder muttered overhead. Beltran slanted a disbelieving glance toward the heavens, where the sun had shone all morn.

Briefly Rhiannon closed her eyes and sent a grateful thought toward her mother. High time Queene Maeve bestirred herself to intervene, after days of Morrigan's spells and interference.

Of course, time passed at a different pace in Faerie. Likely, from Maeve's perspective, only an hour had passed since Rhiannon rode through the Veil. Moreover, the Faerie Queene could influence little in the mortal realm—else she need never have sent Rhiannon at all.

"There, you see!" Lady Elizabeth declared. "We'll be roasting our toes before a fire at Hatfield before the first drop falls. Truly, I insist upon it."

Captive to her sister's will she might be, but Elizabeth Tudor had issued a royal command.

THEIR ROYAL HOSTESS led them thundering in a spirited gallop from the forest across the green. As they pounded through the rolling park, spotted deer scattered before them. Beyond, the great quadrangle of a manor house in russet brick rose among the stern geometry of clipped hedges, so unlike the untamed tangle of wild forest Rhiannon knew and loved. As she eyed the rows of mullioned windows, a rush of excitement stole her breath.

A mortal dwelling, peopled by my own kind—my father's folk. Perhaps I'll feel more at home here than ever I did among my Faerie kin, ever mocked for my weak magick and mixed blood—a circumstance Morrigan did all in her power to aggravate. My father asleep and dreaming in his vault, shielded from death by the Faerie Queene's blessing, until the day England's need calls him forth again. And my mother the Queene too

otherworldly, too absorbed with the lure of her own
magick to heed anything I might have needed.

More likely, I suppose, these mortals will sense my…
Otherness, just as the Fae always did. Then shall I be
outcast here as well.

Surreptitiously, she touched the moonstone charm
swinging against her breast. The movement drew her
guardian's hawklike gaze. No doubt wary she'd slip
away, Beltran hadn't left her side for an instant as they
followed Lady Elizabeth through the wood. Now his
gloved hand claimed her bridle, easing Astolat to a
walk. Gradually, they fell behind Sir Henry and his
guards.

Rhiannon slanted him a cautious glance, the cross-
hilted broadsword jutting over his shoulder—an un-
necessary reminder of his Church allegiance. So close
he towered over her, his black-cloaked form blocking
out half the sky, cropped head bare in the misting rain
that drifted across the green.

His keen eyes searched her upturned features. Eyes
as shattering blue as a midsummer sky, possibly the
bluest eyes she'd ever seen. Looking into them made
her strangely breathless—even when the great winged
Presence that shadowed him was seemingly absent.

"My lady," he said flatly, "it seems we're obliged
to break our journey here. Once Sir Henry and his
cronies learn your circumstance, you'll be made…un-
comfortable."

"Will they chain me in their dungeons like a criminal?" Determined to know the worst, Rhiannon lifted
her chin. Secretly, the prospect made her quail, but she
would never let him know it.

He hesitated, and her heart plummeted. "They've

no tolerance for strangers now. Whatever sympathy for
you our Protestant hostess may feel, she's under close
scrutiny, with more damning details of this Dudley plot
against the Queen coming to light every day. They say
Elizabeth's in it to her ears. One misstep, and they'll
toss her back in the Tower. This time, she'll meet her
mother's fate."

Rhiannon shivered at the thought of imprisonment
behind cold gray walls—the grimmest punishment
imaginable for her, whose greatest solace and sanctuary from her mother's narrow-minded court had always
been the wild wood.

"I would do nothing to harm Lady Elizabeth, sir.
Whatever they do to me here, I'll say not a word against
her."

Clearly, her assurance did nothing to placate him.
His proud golden head turned to search the rain-swept
hedges marching stiffly beside them. No doubt the
weather kept them all indoors, whoever dwelled here
in exile with the princess, the deer park and gardens
deserted and desolate around them.

"I'll have your vow," he said suddenly, drawing his
dagger.

"My lord?" She cast the steel blade a wary glance—
hard steel, thrashing serpent, haloed warrior spearing
it into hell. Any proper Fae would be shrinking from
the thing. Yet she couldn't believe he meant to harm
her. He could have killed her last night while she slept,
or a dozen times since, if he'd wanted that.

"I'll have your word of honor you'll not attempt
another trick like last night's." Voice hard and impatient, he scanned the rows of windows staring down on
them. Already Lady Elizabeth had flung herself from

the saddle, seemingly heedless of her hovering guards. "Give me your oath, by whatever you hold sacred, that you won't try to escape. Then I'll let you walk free beneath this roof."

Judging by the scowl that darkened his rugged features, Beltran made the offer against his own better judgment. Was it a kind impulse—like the surprising compassion he'd shown the dying bandit, at odds with his unyielding mien—or more of the cold, correct courtesy he'd shown her all along? Indeed, harsh and judgmental though she found him, she could have fared far worse, stumbling alone and unguarded upon an armed man in the forest, with all a mortal man's hungers.

Such mishaps befell women in the mortal realm. Her sister had taunted her with it.

Rhiannon shivered beneath her damp mantle, but met his gaze steadily. "You have my word as the daughter of the Dreaming King, whose honor is legend among my people and thine. I shall not seek to escape thy vigilance while I rest beneath this roof."

His eyes searched hers for any sign of treachery, but she'd spoken true. She knew no better oath than her father's famous honor. Though the Fae could be treacherous, they too were bound by certain laws. If a Faerie swore an oath, she stood by it, though they might weave their words with a loophole.

No doubt of it, his eyes were steadfast blue as a mountain lake. The fine lines of hardship etched in his tanned brow, the mortal years that lay upon him merely added strength and determination to his chiseled features. If ever he gave his word, she thought suddenly, he too would honor it.

"Very well." He jerked a nod. "Let's have your hands."

When she extended them, he reined close against her. His knee brushed her thigh, making her tingle. When he gripped her forearm to steady her, warmth pulsed between her thighs. She marveled at the novel sensations, wondered if they were part of the strange magick he wielded. His big hands were impersonal, strong and hard as the rest of him, not ungentle as he laid the dagger against her bonds. With one swift motion, he sliced through them.

As his cloak swirled around her, the rich aroma of frankincense filled her head; his garments and skin were rich with it, laced with the cold tang of steel. Again she shivered, thankful for the silver warding rings on her fingers. Thankful, for once, for her mortal blood.

As she trembled beneath his touch, he shot her a swift glance. Gold-tipped lashes dropped over his eyes as they swept the exposed swell of her breasts, laced tight against her bodice, where her skin was pebbled with goosebumps.

"You're cold," he said gruffly. "You'll soon have fire and a hot meal."

"Oh, yes," she agreed fervently.

Still he gripped her arm. Now, as though involuntarily, his gloved hand rose to trace the bare skin of her collarbone. One finger slid down the fragile ridge of bone to the vulnerable hollow of her throat, where her pulse jumped. Shivers raced across her skin, hardened her nipples to pebbles against her chemise.

Abruptly, he reined away, jaw hard as he stared straight ahead. "Step carefully here, my lady. This household will be thick with the Queen's spies—fervent Catholics all. Utter one of your heretical assertions in the wrong ear, and you'll find yourself locked in a cell for Bishop Bonner's personal attention."

His brusque warning dissolved the fog of strange and wondrous sensations like a knife slicing through cobwebs.

"And see that you honor your word," he said grimly. "If you flee, I'll hunt you down like a wolf with a rabbit. Never doubt that for a moment."

Abruptly he spurred his white stallion forward, toward the waiting guards—and left Rhiannon staring after him, cold with foreboding.

FIVE

When Beltran strode into the banqueting hall, he was simmering. After abandoning his prisoner reluctantly to a tiring-woman, he'd bathed quickly, just in time for prayers in the Hatfield chapel at Sext.

Yet Rhiannon le Fay hadn't appeared. When he returned after psalms to collect her for dinner, the lady wasn't in the chamber allotted to her.

Now he braced to find he'd been made a fool by a mere slip of a girl, that she'd cheerfully broken her oath and slipped away. If she had, he vowed darkly, he'd hunt her down and bring her to ground if it took him a year to do it. He had his orders from Rome and the Archbishop was waiting, but the English Inquisition was rolling briskly along beneath the combined enthusiasm of Mary Tudor and Spanish Philip, with little encouragement needed from Beltran.

Striding into the hall, therefore, he was fully prepared to turn Hatfield House inside out to find his wayward charge. If Elizabeth's grooms had taken his money but defied his orders and let Rhiannon and her mare vanish into the forest, he swore heads would bloody well roll for it.

As a king's daughter and a queen's sister, Elizabeth Tudor should keep a splendid estate. Indeed his mentor, the Cardinal, scorned her extravagance. But this princess was in deep disgrace, immured under guard in this remote country manor since her release from the Tower of London under a cloud of suspicion. They were still seeking evidence to behead her.

Beltran had a keen nose for sniffing out mischief, and the odor of treason tainted these halls like a miasma.

Perhaps that explained why the great hall stood abandoned, only a handful of whispering courtiers clustered anxiously beneath the coffered ceiling, huddled for warmth before the roaring hearth-fire. *Protestants all, no doubt—and likely to find themselves much closer to those flames than is healthy for them, if Philip and Mary have their way. Though it's my way too, isn't it? I'm sworn to support this bloody business.*

His nostrils flared. These fearful heretics knew who he was, no doubt of it. Under the acrid bite of wood-smoke and cloying perfume, he smelled the sour sweat of Lutheran fear.

Still, danger hadn't taught decorum to these ladies, breasts white and plump as pillows in their low-necked finery, waists pinched cruelly in their tight-laced stomachers. He steeled himself not to see the blatant invitation in those gleaming eyes and met their murmured offers with cold silence. For a man with his unsavory reputation, the softer sex seemed uncommonly fond of flaunting their charms before him.

He was only a man, after all, flesh and blood driven by a man's hunger. The holy fits of madness that seized him had done nothing to change that.

Today, though, he saw no one else, gaze drawn like a magnet to the leaded glass window where a lady stood, slim and graceful in leaf-green sarcenet, one hand lifted so her fingers touched the glass. An errant beam of sunlight gilded the curls swept decorously beneath her flat hood, and edged her delicate profile with light. Framed by the high elegant collar of her gown, her white throat was supple as a swan's. Cone-shaped skirts swept from her narrow waist to brush bottle-green slippers.

Rhiannon.

She hadn't flown the nest after all…hadn't fled him. Relief unclenched his belly and loosened his balled fists.

She stood alone, light-footed as a butterfly, while the green ivy pressed against the glass as though yearning for her touch. In that moment, she was the soul of purity and innocence, and something in him longed for her—both her haunting sweetness and her flashing fire. For the healing grace only her gentle soul could offer.

Heedless of his surroundings, Beltran brushed past the hopeful ladies who loitered casually in his path and strode across the floor straight toward her, boot-heels ringing on the wood.

As though she heard him or sensed him, Rhiannon dropped her hand and turned. Her dark brows winged up. Her eyes widened, the same vivid green as her gown. Her breasts rose against the demure sarcenet bodice as though her breath quickened to see him.

And the sight made him harden, damn it to Hell.

Her lips parted to speak.

Beltran pivoted away from her, scrubbing a hand against his face, and seized upon the first distraction he glimpsed—an elegant figure in a mulberry doublet and trunk hose.

"Ah, Lord Beltran, there you are." Sir Henry Bed-ingfield bowed. "A word with you, if I may."

Beltran suppressed the urge to glance over his shoulder—just to check on her, make sure she hadn't moved, admire her lissome silhouette before the window. But he refused to stare at the girl like a love-struck suitor. If for no other reason, he'd cause a scandal. The Blades of God were supposed to be celibate.

Belatedly, he made the popinjay a courteous leg. The man was worth his effort to cultivate—Mary's creature through and through, trusted watchdog over Mary's treasonous sister.

"Your servant, sir," Beltran muttered.

Sir Henry gestured for wine. "You'll understand, my lord, that Lady Elizabeth is not generally permitted visitors. This measure is for the lady's own good, if she wishes to prove her innocence in the Dudley affair. Matters may yet go badly for her if she doesn't."

"No doubt," Beltran said shortly. Her guardian didn't seem overly concerned by the prospect.

Beltran beckoned the hovering servant for a cup. The midday meal, no liturgy until Nones; he could allow himself a little bread and wine without breaking the Lenten fast. He suppressed his impatience as the servant crept fearfully forward, tray shaking in her hands—a mouse bearding the lion in its den.

"There, child, I'm not going to eat you up," he said gruffly, claiming his cup before the fool dropped the entire lot. "Fetch mulled wine for Lady Rhiannon there. Sir Henry, I've heard little on the road, but rumors are rife in Rome. The way the Pope heard it, the French are ready to invade this isle in Elizabeth's name, and the Protestants to rise. Evidently one of Dudley's con-

spirators panicked and confessed the entire mess to
Archbishop Pole. His Holiness charged me to learn
what I could."

Sir Henry's gaze flickered at this strategic mention
of the Pope. "As a good Catholic and dutiful subject of a
Catholic Queen, of course I can refuse nothing to God's
Vengeance. Your reputation precedes you, my lord."

Sir Henry made a courteous leg, which Beltran
waved away. "Never mind that, man. Save your bow-
ing for God and your sovereign. Are the French coming or nay?"

"The plain truth of the matter is, we've no idea."
Sir Henry downed his wine like a man who needed it.
"Harry Dudley is Elizabeth's man, like all the Dud-
leys. His son Robert shared her imprisonment in the
Tower in '54, and there's strong affection still between
those two. The Dudleys are kin as well to the Duke of
Northumberland—a connection not to be trifled with."

Beltran grunted his assent and swirled the tart vintage around his tongue. At San Miguel, he'd learned
to drink pig swill after a three-day fast and praise God
for it, but this Burgundy was exceptional. Disgraced
and under suspicion she might be, still Elizabeth Tudor
lived like a princess.

"Now Dudley's somewhere in France, raising an
army to march on London." Bedingfield shrugged. "Or
so it's said. A considerable sum was stolen from the
Exchequer to pay for the rising, caches of arms turning
up places they shouldn't. And that arrogant fool Courtenay's in it to his eyebrows. He has Plantagenet blood,
you know, and they still consider themselves rightful
kings of England, though the Lancasters trounced them
utterly in the Wars of the Roses."

"I'm familiar with English history," Beltran said impatiently. Next the man would begin reminiscing about how Owen Tudor had bedded the widowed Lancaster queen and thus fathered the royal Tudor line, all of it well over one hundred years past. "What about Courtenay?"

"You'll scarcely credit the man's conceit, but he proclaims to all and sundry that he'll marry Elizabeth and seize the throne."

"Good Christ." Beltran glanced darkly around the hall. White-rimmed eyes stared back at him. They saw him as the Pope's man, enforcer of the dread Inquisition. The stench of fear in the room was thick enough to choke on, and now he understood why. "Is she part of it, do you think?"

Sir Henry voiced an elegant snort. "Her? Who can say? I've been her guardian for more than a year now, and the woman has made my life a merry hell, I can tell you. Nothing suits her, nothing pleases her, she confesses nothing and commits to nothing. She'll obey no one and go nowhere she's bidden. If I insist, she takes to her bed and carries on like she's dying! I've never seen anything like it. Forsooth, this very day—"

Beltran intervened before the man could settle into what was clearly a familiar grievance. "I've no doubt she claims innocence, though a skilled questioner would have the truth from her. What of her people, her servants and intimates? Can no evidence be found, either to clear her or condemn her?"

Henry hesitated. "There are letters, written in code, found in the French ambassador's saddlebags. Supposedly from her, but that can't be proven. Predictably, the French king invoked diplomatic immunity for Monsieur de Noailles and recalled him to Paris. Therefore, he can't be questioned."

"But her folk here—"

"Put to the question." At this casual mention of torture, Beltran frowned. "They've already arrested her servant, one Francis Verney, and seized her neighbor, John Bray. As for Sir Peter Killigrew—another neighbor and one of Elizabeth's confidants—no one's seen him in days."

"No wonder this entire household's starting at shadows."

"The net's tightening, never doubt it. If that redheaded vixen had anything to do with this conspiracy, even if she merely suspected it and said nothing, with even a little more evidence they'll have her head off. Just like her mother, that adulterous witch Anne Boleyn."

Beltran gave him a quelling look. He'd been an idealistic young knight of twenty when Henry Tudor's second queen was beheaded in '36. He'd sleep-walked through that summer, devastated by his failure to earn a priest's chasuble solely because he hadn't been able to keep his cock inside his codpiece.

Despite his personal tragedy, Anne Boleyn's gruesome end had been the talk of Europe. The wronged husband, Old Harry himself, had served as judge and jury. So much for the showy trappings of English justice. And Beltran had always questioned the verdict.

Now, for some reason, his brain skipped from the travesty of Anne Boleyn's trial and sentencing to the elfin beauty he'd found in the forest—the lady he resolutely kept behind him now. The same fate awaited her in the Inquisition's hands if she couldn't prove her innocence...if he did nothing to protect her.

But protecting a suspect witch wasn't his job. Far from it. Forgiveness was a priest's work. God required utter ruthlessness from his Vengeance.

He looked coldly at the pompous prig before him, whom he neither liked nor trusted. "Has it occurred to you, sir, that if Mary Tudor dies without issue, this 'redheaded vixen' becomes your Queen and sovereign? She'll not remember you fondly."

"'Tis treason to predict the Queen's death." Sir Henry glanced warily around the banqueting hall, where subdued servants in green-and-white Tudor livery bustled to set the long table for dinner. "She's devoted to her husband, and King Philip's a proven breeder. A father of sons."

"Father to an imbecile." Beltran snorted. "That hunchbacked whelp from his last marriage, Don Carlos, is a bloody monster. Tortures his own horses to death for pleasure. Yet Philip thinks to wed the wretch to Elizabeth, since Philip can't have her himself."

"For the love of God, have a care!" Sir Henry murmured. "She's his own wife's sister, and he's never offered her an unchaste word, no matter what the rumors. We'll have our English prince from his union with Mary, never doubt it."

Beltran had never been comfortable tiptoeing among the quagmires and shifting terrain of court intrigue. Until the Cardinal found him in that stinking coal-pit of a Yorkshire hovel, he'd been a mongrel with dirt beneath his nails. His own father had come close to crushing his skull with blacksmith's fists the size of anvils. Thus, diplomacy had been a hard-won skill for Beltran. He placed far greater faith in violence.

Now he confined himself to a shrug. "The Holy Roman Emperor's dying, God assoil him. As his heir, Spanish Philip can't leave the Netherlands. He'll need to farewell his Danish mistress and return to England if he wants an heir, or your Queen must go to him. Either way, at her age, conception would take a miracle."

"I thought you believed in miracles." Sir Henry eyed the holy emblem that swung against Beltran's chest.

"That's someone else's job." Beltran's mouth hitched. "I'm the Church enforcer, not its saint."

I'm the hired sword, nothing more, a glorified constable who hastens the guilty to Hell. And content with my calling, damn it.

"My duty toward the Queen requires constant vigilance," Sir Henry said primly. "Forgive me, my lord, but I must inquire about the purpose that brings you to Hatfield. Who the Devil is that woman who rides with you? And, by the way, where has she gone?"

RHIANNON WAS STARING longingly through the mullioned window at the verdant green beyond—freedom, if only she could reach it. If only she hadn't sworn an oath to remain. Despite the sprinkle of plump crystal droplets on the ivy over the sill, the last clouds had scudded away. A torrent of sunlight, like honey from a pitcher, poured through the glass to warm her.

Though she'd placed her back to the whispering courtiers, none of whom had extended any overtures, she sensed the sudden presence that silenced the muted court like a hammer blow. Slowly, as if drawn by enchantment, she glanced over her shoulder. When she recognized Lord Beltran, the breath spilled from her lips, as though all the air had been sucked from the hall.

For once, he'd abandoned his austere black. Now he commanded the doorway without effort, broad shoulders encased in sapphire-blue brocade so dark it was nearly midnight. With his slashed doublet and dashing cape, heavy links of hammered gold spanning his chest and the sword in flames swinging over his heart, his shoulders nearly brushed the lintel on either side. A velvet cap, tilted at a stylish angle, set off his dark golden hair and rugged features to perfection.

Dear Lady, she'd never dreamed his battered saddlebags held such finery, or that a man of his holy discipline would condescend to such worldly garb. Only the high boots were familiar, beneath the dark luster of trunk hose clinging to sinewed thighs. He made her breathless; no doubt her stomacher was laced too tightly, which was why she felt like sinking into a maiden's swoon. Vaguely she wondered whether she might be succumbing to some mortal fever.

Or perhaps she merely feared him. When she used her Sight, she could see the great winged form looming over him like a shadow, beautiful and brooding, a banner of shimmering white-gold hair streaming over the silver scales of his armor.

Surely even these mortals could sense that dread Presence, though they hadn't the Sight to see it. They quailed visibly before him—or was it only that his reputation preceded him?

For Beltran's part, barely contained impatience simmered in his piercing eyes as they dismissed the fluttering courtiers. When his gaze locked on her, an intensity leaped into his sun-bronzed features that arrested her breath. His eyes moved over her body, encased in tissue-thin sarcenet, and a muscle flexed in his jaw. Those glacier-blue eyes heated to flame. With a hooded gaze, he strode into the banqueting hall and made straight for her.

Rhiannon felt faint, overheated. The sun burning her back was far too warm. Surely that explained the butterfly flutter in her belly—not the lithe, barely leashed power in his gait as he closed the distance between them. And the way her heartbeat quickened, liquid warmth pooling low in her core. Merciful Goddess, what was happening to her?

Drawing a swift breath, she opened her mouth to address him. *You see, Lord Beltran, I have not fled. Even a Faerie must honor her oath.*

Before she could utter a syllable, he pivoted away, leaving her startled and uncertain. He descended upon the elegant Sir Henry, whose lean figure was instantly dwarfed by Beltran's muscled frame. As she struggled to master her unsteady pulse, Rhiannon hardly knew whether she felt irritated or relieved to be abandoned.

"Lady Rhiannon!" Elizabeth Tudor's commanding voice brought her spinning toward her royal hostess.

Among the strained mortal faces surrounding them, the daughter of King Henry VIII glowed like the sun in splendor, flaming hair vivid against a stylish gown of sage-green velvet. Surely this Dudley business had placed her under intolerable strain, but the lady disguised it magnificently.

"Mercy, I would scarce recognize you!" Elizabeth declared with satisfaction. "The bath has done you worlds of good."

"I'm profoundly grateful for thy hospitality, Your Grace."

Rhiannon dipped into a curtsey as Linnet had taught her, not a difficult obeisance to perform before this woman, though Rhiannon herself was styled a princess. The artful tilt to her ruddy head, the mischief dancing in those glimmering silver eyes, the vitality that crackled from her slender form—all proclaimed the wild Fae blood Elizabeth shared with Rhiannon and no other in this vast echoing chamber.

Again she felt that sneaking sense of kinship—royal bastards, both of them, despised and distrusted, belonging nowhere. But she mustn't be seduced by this illusion of likeness, the alluring prospect of easing her own loneliness. The Fae required a treaty with the English sovereign, and that was her only purpose.

Blithely Elizabeth said, "I've instructed my steward you'll remain until tomorrow, to effect a full recovery."

"Oh?" This was welcome news, yet she hesitated. "Has Lord Beltran—?"

"We shall inform him shortly. I wished also to assure you I've dispatched men to search for your missing comrades."

"Oh, I'm so grateful!" Despite the certain prospect of Beltran's reaction to the delay, Rhiannon beamed at her. If only she could locate Ansgar! Her retinue had been utterly decimated, but surely he would know what to do.

"Indeed, 'tis I who am grateful." Elizabeth slipped effortlessly into the Roman tongue—Latin, these mortals called it. "Sir Henry would have run me to earth like a rabbit if you and your...protector...hadn't intervened."

Rhiannon couldn't help glancing at Beltran, who stood with his broad back to her, consulting with Sir Henry in muffled tones.

"Lady Elizabeth, I think you overstate your peril." The Roman tongue came to her effortlessly, unlike the new English. And she couldn't help smiling at the drama. The Tudor princess was twenty-three, so Linnet said, yet she frolicked beneath the shadow of the block with all the reckless fire of thirteen. "Surely Sir Henry seeks only your protection."

Elizabeth continued to smile, but her silver eyes hardened to steel. She looped her arm through Rhiannon's. "Come. Walk with me."

Rhiannon was familiar enough with royalty to recognize a command when she heard one. Still she hesitated, glancing again at Beltran. Suddenly she wanted to slip up behind him, spread her hands across his shoulders, and knead the tension from them. A healer's impulse, surely, and one he wouldn't welcome.

Elizabeth's quick eyes followed hers, and those reddish brows arched. "Or perhaps you don't wish to be parted? Are you in love with him?"

Rhiannon blurted a startled laugh, face heating. Such an outlandish notion had never occurred to her, and she held no doubt the mere utterance would shock the man they called God's Vengeance. With his stubborn sense of duty toward the Inquisition, Lord Beltran Nemesto was the closest thing to an adversary she confronted in this realm.

Besides, no man had ever desired her in that way. She'd lived a thousand years by mortal reckoning, though time flowed differently in Faerie. Yet she'd never been so much as kissed. To men of the Fair Folk, her mortal blood tainted her.

Firmly, she quelled a flicker of self-pity. She was what she was, and ever would be. No sense pining for the girlish dreams of love she'd long since resigned herself to abandon.

These thoughts raced through her mind in a flash. Elizabeth was still watching her expectantly, a quizzical smile curving her lips. Rhiannon found herself still blushing.

"I—I've never been in love, Your Grace," she stammered. "And he…he is sworn to the Church."

Elizabeth glanced toward his averted form, gaze flickering over his broad back and corded thighs. "In that case, what a pity."

Arms linked, the two women strolled along the banqueting hall. Shafts of sunlight spilled through the leaded glass windows, gleamed on the wood-paneled walls, glittered on the fortune in gold and silver plate that dazzled the eye on table and sideboards.

"Tell me," Elizabeth said casually, still in Latin, "what business brings you out in the Godforsaken weather we've suffered this spring? You've journeyed long, have you not?"

Rhiannon's heart quickened. Here was her opportunity, fallen into her lap like a Midwinter gift, the chance to win over Queen Mary's closest kin— though the two were hardly intimates. Still, if Protestant Elizabeth championed her cause, it could damage her chances with Mary rather than the reverse.

Yet she was reluctant to utter a falsehood. Her father had been renowned throughout England for his honesty, his integrity, his sense of chivalry. She was Arthur's only daughter. Her father might never open his eyes and look upon her face as she'd always yearned for, but she would not sully his name with falsehoods.

She tried for a light laugh, not very convincing. "How do you know I'm long traveled? Was the state of my gear and garments so desperate?"

Clever as a fox at scenting avoidance, Elizabeth shot her a keen glance. "You looked as though you fled a battlefield—that desperate indeed, that bedraggled, with almost no baggage, no maid or governess for chaperone though your station clearly warrants it. Your escort mysteriously lost, and a Blade of God hardly qualifies as a suitable replacement, no matter how fearsome with a sword he's rumored to be."

Well, no one had ever called Elizabeth Tudor a fool, that much was certain. Pausing, Rhiannon turned toward the window and lifted one hand to the glass. Inches away, bathed in sunlight on the sill, an early primrose quivered, its folded petals trembling.

"As for Lord Beltran, Your Grace, you're correct that he's no protector of mine, though he surely saved my life. He happened upon us in the forest and rescued me from bandits."

She'd resolved to say nothing of the fiery Being he'd channeled, for who on earth would believe her? She hardly understood what had happened herself.

"Chivalrous of him," Elizabeth murmured, eyeing the trembling primrose. Pale yellow petals began to unfurl from the leaves. "Although that is not his reputation. Nor is it generally considered chivalrous to bind a lady's hands."

Rhiannon could hardly refute that. "As you've rightly concluded, I'm a foreigner in these lands and no fervent Catholic. My lord has determined I should be questioned, and I've given my word of honor not to plot escape within these walls. So you need fear no disturbance beneath your roof. You may be certain I would do nothing to compromise you, or worsen your uncertain situation."

"God-a-mercy, I had no thought of it!" Elizabeth said lightly. Unlike Rhiannon, her hostess appeared to have no such fine sensibilities where honesty was concerned. "I wondered only how I might assist you. I've great sympathy for a woman alone in the world, pushed hither and yon by the whims of men."

Rhiannon absorbed this in silence, while the primrose unfolded into yellow glory beneath her fingers. In her world, the Faerie Queene ruled supreme, balanced only by the cruelty and caprice of her daughter Morrigan. Yet Rhiannon had been warned, by Ansgar and Linnet both, that the mortal realm was ruled by men.

It was a lesson Elizabeth herself must have learned quickly, with her first love—reckless Lord Admiral Seymour—dead on the block for wooing her without the council's permission. Reportedly, he'd all but seduced the smitten girl when she was barely fourteen, and Elizabeth had lost her heart to him.

Yet this mortal history could not help Rhiannon. The question before her, both pressing and dangerous, was whether she dared trust the disgraced Tudor princess. The fate of both their nations could depend upon her choice.

"I...am indebted for your assistance." Thinking furiously, she dipped a little curtsey to buy a few moments. "My lady Elizabeth, have you ever heard of the Convergence?"

Her hostess blinked, the only sign of recognition Rhiannon could detect. Otherwise, Elizabeth's face remained carefully blank. She was still watching the primrose that opened now into full-throated splendor, its petals stroking the glass where Rhiannon's fingers rested. Realizing what she'd caused, this flowering of wild Fae magick she could no more control than her own heartbeat, Rhiannon dropped her hand swiftly.

"Let us take the air, my lady." Abruptly, Elizabeth turned toward the door that opened onto the gardens.

Rhiannon was quite certain Beltran wouldn't care for this plan—neither her intimate congress with their royal hostess and her Lutheran leanings, nor her escape from his vigilance. Uneasily she glanced toward the high table, where servants were carefully laying trenchers of white manchet bread before each place.

"Your Grace, the dinner…"

"Will not be on the table for another thirty minutes," the lady said dismissively. "At this very moment, my cook and my governess—my own dear Kat—are being questioned in the solar by another of the Lord Privy Seal's bloodhounds over this damnable Dudley business. They've done nothing, of course, just as I've done nothing. We're all utterly loyal and devoted to the Queen's Grace here."

Elizabeth paused to invite her agreement. But Rhiannon was exclaiming with delight as they emerged into the clipped green hedges of an elegant knot garden, leaves sparkling with rain in the sunlight beneath spring skies of eggshell blue. Well-tended grass wove a carpet of emerald velvet underfoot, tan ribbons of raked soil unfurling in paths before them. The delicate buds

of mauve and lilac crocuses, newly opened, quivered
in rows beside the path.

The rigid order of these English gardens was foreign to one who'd grown up running barefoot through
the moss-draped forests of Faerie. Still, to feel sunlight
on her face and breathe clean air after the wretched
stench of perfume, roast meat and sweating fear inside! Her anxious spirits rose and spread like a sail
before the wind.

"Do our gardens please you?" Elizabeth too was
smiling, face raised to the sky, the brisk wind whipping color into her pale cheeks. The Tudor princess
stepped lightly as a wood-sprite along the path—joy-
ful as any soul with a drop of Faerie blood in the open
outdoors. "I was raised here, you know, and I love this
old manor, but sometimes one does long for an hour
of freedom…"

Casually Elizabeth glanced around them. The green-
walled paths were unoccupied, classical statues and
fountains standing sentinel.

"You'd mentioned something inside, Lady Rhiannon? We'd best finish sharing our girlish secrets
quickly, or we'll have Sir Henry and God's Vengeance
breathing down our necks."

Recalled to her purpose, Rhiannon glanced back
toward the russet brick manor. The sun reflected bril-
liantly from its rows of lead-glassed windows. Any one
of them could conceal unfriendly eyes.

"I mentioned the Convergence, Lady Elizabeth. Perhaps you've heard this term?"

"I cannot recall," the other said vaguely, leading
them ever farther from the house. When they rounded

a corner, the high hedges rose up on either side to conceal them.

Rhiannon approached the matter cautiously. "'Tis said you're a student of history, my lady. You must know the tale of Arthur, King of Britain, who fought the Celts and Picts and Saxons to bring peace to these shores after the Romans left."

"He's a legend to every English schoolchild. They say Arthur is merely sleeping, and will return again when his people need him." Elizabeth arched her brows. "But that was a thousand years past. Surely you'll not tell me this ancient history has somehow propelled you onto the road?"

Rhiannon reached to caress the hedges as they strolled and wondered how much time she had before Beltran noticed her absence. Minutes at best, surely. She quickened her stride.

"There is another legend about Arthur, Your Grace. According to folklore, he sleeps in another realm—a hidden realm, a shadow land that lies alongside the Christian lands like an estranged lover—lying in the same bed, but never touching. A Veil hangs between the worlds, concealing and protecting them from one another, so that any travel or congress between them is difficult."

"You speak of the Faerie realm, I suppose." Elizabeth laughed lightly. "Of toadstool rings and standing stones and goblins who grant wishes. Children's tales."

Rhiannon crossed her fingers and took a chance. "Are you so skeptical of the Faerie realm?"

For an instant, Elizabeth's level stride faltered. Something fluttered in her face. Then her burnished head regained its regal tilt.

For certain she knows something, though Goddess knows from where. But she's going to deny it. The instinct for self-protection was too strong in Elizabeth Tudor. She'd learned to deny everything, to lie about everything, just to keep her head off the block.

Faintly, over the rustling wind, a man's voice rose from the manor. "My lady Elizabeth?"

"Every thousand years," Rhiannon hurried on, "the two realms draw close, and eventually intersect. When this occurs the Veil thins, and creatures from both sides can cross the barrier at will, or even blunder across by accident. This event is called the Convergence, my lady. It last happened one thousand years ago, in the dark days after the Romans left—and it's happening again very soon."

"Lady Rhiannon!" There was no mistaking the commanding bellow of that rumbling baritone. She shivered, although not precisely with chill, a tingle racing across her skin.

"Hurry," Elizabeth said briefly, not wasting time with foolish questions. She tugged Rhiannon around another corner, winding deeper into the garden, the high hedges still concealing them.

"When the Convergence occurs, Your Grace, there is great suffering in both realms—for they are not meant to occupy the same space and time. Their energies are too different, and their respective natures too hostile to one another. The drawing-near causes famine, flood, pestilence, rebellion. When the two realms touch, it means full-blown war."

"In other words, precisely the circumstances that currently confront this realm," Lady Elizabeth murmured. "Last time it was Arthur's son Mordred, was it not, who's said to have led the revolt against Arthur that ended his realm? At least, that was Sir Thomas Malory's claim in his *Morte d'Arthur.*"

"Yes. Mordred." Rhiannon shivered. The spring wind had roughened from playful caress to a raw slap. "He was my half brother, but I never really knew him. I was just a child…too young for him to bother with."

Elizabeth's startled gaze flickered toward her, the only indication this revelation had surprised her.

"You must share your beauty secrets," she said lightly. "For you appear even younger than I."

"Things are not always as they appear, Lady Elizabeth. Surely you, of all women, have learned the truth of that."

Elizabeth laughed, low and grimly. Her stride lengthened, a fierce light burning in her silver eyes. "This time it's the damned Spanish, isn't it, and that fanatic Philip my sister's taken into her bed."

Rhiannon released her held breath. *Merciful Lady, thank you. She may not be prepared to believe me, and certainly not to acknowledge it. But at least she doesn't dismiss my words out of hand as a lunatic's ravings.*

"'Tis more than the Spaniards who threaten your realm. 'Tis the Scots on your very border, and the Catholic Church with its Inquisition, its instruments of torture and oppression and burning."

"Have a care," Elizabeth murmured. "For those events of which you speak are now my sister's life work. She is convinced she'll never bear a son until she purges this land of heresy."

"Her very barrenness is a symbol of this divided land—"

"*Rhiannon.*" Beltran's shout was nearer now. "Where are you? Return at once!"

Elizabeth pulled her through the garden until they were nearly running. The confining cage of her stomacher dug into Rhiannon's ribs; the accursed farthingale swayed wildly around her legs. Desperately she longed for the graceful flowing garments of home, but her native garb would shock these prudish mortals speechless.

"Quickly," Elizabeth said. "How much time do we have before this... Convergence?"

"Very little," Rhiannon panted, clinging to her arm. "Time flows differently in the Faerie realm. We misjudged the year by a full generation. My mother, the Faerie Queene, seeks to avert this disaster. She charged me to bring before your sister a treaty of perpetual peace between England and Faerie, and to persuade your sister by any means necessary to sign it. But Lord Beltran has taken the document. Without it, I cannot—"

Rushing breathlessly around a hedge, she collided against a hard body. She gasped and staggered, but hard hands closed around her shoulders to hold her upright. Her eyes flew upward, over a broad chest encased in sapphire brocade and glittering with gold, to meet the blazing blue fury of Beltran Nemesto.

Instinctively, she tried to retreat, but his hands still gripped her. Heat radiated from his touch through the thin fabric of her sleeves. As she stared riveted into his gaze, wildfire spread through her, making her tingle, raising the fine hairs along her forearms. Her heart fluttered against her ribcage like a startled bird.

"Lord Beltran," she whispered. Dimly she sensed

Elizabeth falling back, slipping between the hedges—
driven by her honed survivor's instinct to avoid interrogation.

And leaving Rhiannon to face him alone.

SIX

HE'D FOUND HER. She hadn't fled him after all. Beltran's first reaction was sweeping relief, just as he'd felt when he found her in the banqueting hall. When she'd vanished five minutes later, he'd turned the entire hall upside down—aided by an annoyed Sir Henry, who'd clearly gone through the exercise for his own wayward charge too often—before they thought to search the gardens.

Now, as he held her slight form between his hands—hands that hacked and butchered in God's name—every thought of duty and piety and virtue was dissolving. He thought only that her wide green eyes matched her gown and the fresh spring garden surrounding them. That her lips were the pale pink of the primroses blooming, improbably out of season, from the hedge he'd backed her into.

That the tender curve of her upper lip, with its ripe bow, was made for kissing.

"Lord Beltran," she whispered, hands rising to his chest as though she sensed the turmoil raging there. Her voice was as trusting as a child's, despite what she knew of him. The movement brought her that fatal inch closer. The faint haunting sweetness of violets rose to fill his head.

Barely knowing what he did, driven by the need to really feel her—all that softness and warmth and innocence, all her unspoiled sweetness—he closed the remaining distance between them. A carpet of pale snowdrops was blooming somehow under their very feet. When his boot crushed the fragile petals, their elusive fragrance added to the sensory onslaught.

His advance brought her slender frame up against him, the soft curve of her breasts encased in fabric thin as parchment, nipples brushing his chest like burning coals. His hands slid from her shoulders to her waist, eased the gentle swell of her hips against his. His blood surged beneath his codpiece, making him swell and harden.

And still she stared up at him, wide-eyed, with the same trusting sweetness. When he pulled her against him, her lips parted. The battered armor of his self-control shattered.

"Rhiannon," he said hoarsely. "My God."

Beneath his hands, she shivered. "Don't, my lord. That Name—"

At that moment, he would have sworn to the Devil himself if that was what it took to keep her in his arms. Because nothing under Heaven was going to stop him from kissing her. His arm wrapped around her waist—his sword-arm, he must remember to be gentle. He cradled her head in his hardened palm, silver-gilt tendrils slipping from their knot to cascade around his fingers.

"So sweet and warm and innocent," he groaned. "You'll be my undoing, Rhiannon."

"Just as thou art mine," she whispered.

Then she couldn't speak because her mouth was under his, sweet and soft and melting. She knew nothing of kissing, that much was obvious, and the knowledge only made him crave more. He, who strictly confined his infrequent liaisons to experienced widows and worldly women, felt his heart hammer at the unmistakable proof of purity. She didn't even know what to do except clutch his shoulders. But her lips were pliant and yielding against his, opening beneath him when he pressed her.

Christ, she tasted like candied violets. He was never going to have enough of kissing her.

Until a woman's cold mocking laughter rippled in his ear, rising from the hedge beside them.

RHIANNON OPENED HER eyes to a flat gray landscape—lead and steel and somber slate. The knot garden's hoary hedges rose around her, tangled and ragged, dagger-sharp thorns protruding from waxen leaves. Beyond the hedges, skeletal orchards rattled in a sobbing wind, winter-white against a pewter sky. In a gap between the hedgerows, the manor house at Hatfield loomed gray as death—tiles tumbled from the roof, chimneys crumbling, shutters hanging from broken windows.

It looked as though a hundred years had passed since she'd closed her eyes and surrendered to the swimming pleasure of Beltran's kiss. Now she stood alone in that colorless garden, the world gripped in stillness like a fist, while bone-colored snowflakes swirled down and stung her unprotected skin.

No doubt of it, this was witchery. She must keep her composure, untangle the enchantment and snip the thread. But Beltran knew nothing of witchcraft; he would require her aid.

"My lord?" Rhiannon spun in a slow circle, or perhaps the garden revolved around her. "Where art thou?"

There, a flash of color—a splash of blood-red in the winter landscape. Red roses blooming out of season, a tall lady gowned in black-and-red, rising gracefully on tiptoe to gather the brilliant blossoms. A cloud of ebony hair swirled around her shoulders. Fearless among the wicked thorns, she sliced the stems with a dagger and piled the blood-dark roses in the basket over her arm.

Somehow Rhiannon was moving toward her, or the world was sliding backward around her, until she stood near the solitary figure. The wind moaned in the trees and lashed the tattered rags of her leaf-green sarcenet—moth-eaten and dusty with cobwebs.

Morrigan turned toward her, glowing white skin, red-black eyes smoldering like embers, ruby lips curved in a cruel little smile. "Good morrow, my sister. How like you this future?"

"This is no future of mine. 'Tis a mortal future—naught but illusion." Rhiannon struggled to conceal her sinking dread, the barely leashed panic that fluttered in her heart. *She's found me, Lady save me.*

Brazening it out, she tilted her chin defiantly. "Why do you weave such lies?"

"Illusion, is it?" Smiling, her sister caressed crimson petals with a scarlet-tipped nail. "Any spell must be woven with a thread of truth. You know that very well."

"A slender thread indeed! Am I to exclaim in dread and wonder, or applaud your spell-craft like a child? You've folded time forward in the mortal realm, nothing more—merely shown a glimpse of what will come. All things made by men must fade."

Rhiannon pretended to a boldness she was far from feeling. Morrigan's power might be weakened in the mortal realm while the sun shone—at least until the

Convergence, when the vengeful Fae and her shining legions would be unleashed. Still, the full-blooded princess was Queene Maeve's heir, lethal and rancid with malice. The mortal Beltran would be powerless against her, unless that strange holy magick of his reared up to protect him, the dark angel he seemed unable either to summon or control.

"Are you wondering what I've done with your mortal?" Unerringly, Morrigan followed her thoughts.

Rhiannon clenched her fists within her ragged skirts. Her knees were weak with fear, her stomach turning to water, and not merely for her own sake. Beltran's best hope of safety lay in pretending she cared nothing for his fate. Indeed, he was the Church inquisitor, bane of witches, God's Vengeance. Why should she feel concern for him?

But oh, she felt it.

"I don't care what lies you utter, Morrigan. You've no power here and can do nothing to me."

"Oh, I wasn't threatening you." The wind groaned in the branches, fluttering Rhiannon's skirts and unraveling her hair behind her with icy fingers, yet Morrigan's black hair and gown were untouched. "I've had a vision, and spoken a prophecy. Poor sweet sister, you'll be the instrument of your own downfall. You and your Church enforcer."

Rhiannon fought to say nothing, show nothing, but a flicker of worry in her face must have betrayed her. Her sister looked so certain, gloating with secret knowledge. Surely Morrigan wouldn't expend the substantial energy this enchantment required, folding time forward on itself, unless it served some purpose Rhiannon wouldn't care for.

Disdainful, Rhiannon flung back her head. "A blind man could see you're longing to tell me. Very well then, what is it? How will I become the instrument of my own downfall?"

"Truly, I'm amazed our doting mother never told you." Idly, Morrigan strolled along the rosebushes, leaving Rhiannon to follow. "A cat would make a better mother. Still, no doubt she thought it would never be needed—if she thought of you at all. You've lived a thousand years and never had a lover. No man in Faerie would even look at you. Why should she believe you would acquire one on your valiant quest?"

"What foolishness is this? I have no lover." *Nor ever thought to, until now.*

Until Lord Beltran Nemesto strode through carnage to save her life, until she'd looked into that piercing gaze burning with cobalt fire, felt the hard controlled strength of his hands spanning her waist, the hungry heat of his mouth on hers. Suddenly she understood the dizzying passion the bards sang of, the yearning to soar reckless into the sun's consuming fire. She'd felt the molten warmth that melted her maiden womb and quickened her innocent heart.

Morrigan watched with knowing eyes. "You ache for him, don't you? That flat little girl's body of yours has kindled at last. You'll let him peel those stiff mortal garments from your tiny breasts, caress you and suckle you until you pulse for him, stroke and fondle your little pearl until he makes you whimper and beg him to slide that great throbbing man-root of his between your thighs, won't you?"

Breathless, her face burning, Rhiannon could say nothing that wouldn't betray her utterly. As if the words conjured his hands and mouth upon her, her nipples hardened to pebbles beneath her thin gown. As the heated images flared in her mind, she felt the sudden dampness between her thighs.

Embarrassed by these wayward sensations, she shook her head fiercely, gilded curls tumbling around her shoulders. "Nay!"

"Not very convincing, are you?" Morrigan laughed.

"Even if I did fancy him," Rhiannon cried, "love is hardly a crime. Sharing the gift of life between man and woman honors the Mother. Goddess knows *you've* honored her often enough. Why should I have nothing and no one?"

"Why, no reason at all, sister. Except that your situation and mine differ in one critical regard." Morrigan plucked a red rose and twirled it between her fingers. "You're half mortal, my dear. If you sacrifice your maidenhood to couple with a mortal man, you'll become one of them forever."

"I—I don't understand." *What new trickery is this*?

"Lord and Lady, it's hardly a great mystery. You'll become fully mortal, live a brief mortal life, age and wither into a hunchbacked old crone no man will ever touch—and die a mortal death." Cheerfully Morrigan swung her basket. "Steep price to pay for one night of pleasure in a man's arms…although, for such a man, I'll admit I understand why you're tempted. Still, your Vengeance must inevitably repudiate you and loathe himself forever for his moment of weakness."

"I don't believe you." In a thousand years, her mother had never hinted at such a thing! Of course, they'd hardly spent enough time together for Queene Maeve to tell her anything, since Rhiannon avoided the Faerie court with its subtle slurs and intrigues so fervently. Surely Morrigan was lying to disconcert or distract her.

Yet she felt a hollow sensation in the pit of her belly. She'd always known she was never fully Fae, that she lived among them on sufferance, barely tolerated for her mother's sake. Always friendless and alone, except for the forest creatures who loved her—and now the Faerie Queene was sickening.

And Rhiannon had learned enough spell-craft to know powerful magick could be worked when maiden blood was spilled. Lives could be saved or lost by it. Only human sacrifice invoked stronger magick, and she left those dark powers strictly alone.

"Ask our mother, if you think I lie." Her sister shrugged. "Forsooth, I hardly know why I'm doing you the favor of telling you. Seeing you stripped of your immortality and your place in Faerie would serve my purpose admirably well."

"You want him for yourself!" Rhiannon flashed, with a sudden fury that surprised her. "You're a pathetic, spiteful old witch—you've ever wanted what others have. You can't bear it when a man looks at any woman but you."

"I don't deny I'd enjoy having your Vengeance in my bed for a moon or two." Morrigan's rich contralto deepened. Languorous as a cat with cream, she licked her lips and laughed as though she felt the jealous pang that twisted Rhiannon's heart. "I'd make him burn for me, as a virginal child like yourself could never do. I can feel him already, that hard warrior's body pinning me to the bed, thrusting into me until he floods me with his seed, cursing himself and his impotent God with every breath…"

Clearly, her sister sought to provoke her as she'd always done. Yet the knowledge did nothing to combat the flare of white-hot fire of pain and envy that obliterated all reason. Perhaps no man had ever wanted her; certainly no man who'd ever had a chance with Morrigan had wasted a moment of his time with Rhiannon. No doubt Beltran would prefer her sister, like all the rest did, if Morrigan contrived to put herself before him. Rhiannon might be a woman grown among the mortals, but she was scarcely more than a child in Faerie.

She would have liked to slap her sister's face, but even in extremis, the healer in her shrank from violence. Instead, deliberate as a man hurling glass to the floor, she clenched her stomach muscles hard against the pain and cried the words she'd heard Beltran wield like a weapon in the wood. Her half-mortal blood allowed her—barely—to utter them.

"Morrigan le Fay, be gone and banished, by the power of Christ!"

The agony of the shattered spell tore at her like jagged glass, ripping a gasp from her lips and driving her to her knees. Beside her, Morrigan screamed and shattered the dream-world silence.

Rhiannon grasped her sister's heaping basket and wrenched it away. The basket tipped, spilling blood-hued roses in a shower of thorns and crimson. They tumbled down around her, petals fluttering free, the ghost-wind whirling them through the air in a frenzy.

"Beltran Nemesto would never soil his hands with a harlot like you!" she flared.

Although the illusion wavered around them, Morrigan was still gripping the rose she'd cut. As Rhiannon knelt before her, trembling and incandescent with rage, her sister stroked her flushed cheek with the silken petals.

"Red is for heartbreak," Morrigan said softly. "That is my gift to you, sister. I wish you much joy of it."

Then the gray world was swirling around her, tattered skirts and hair lashing her skin, snow stinging her cheeks like tears. As she tumbled endlessly into the void, Rhiannon realized she was weeping.

BELTRAN OPENED HIS eyes to find Rhiannon had vanished. Blinking, he stepped back, turning swiftly to find her. His blood still simmered from the sweet warmth of her kiss, his cock aching in his codpiece. God's fury, he *must* find her...

He stopped short. In place of the verdant spring, the knot garden around him blazed gold and bronze and crimson with the full glory of autumn. Against the shattering blue sky, gray stone turrets rose where the manor had stood—a fairy-tale castle of high walls and crenellations and green-capped towers, ivy twining over the crumbling stone. A crisp wind, scented with the tang of apples, snapped and fluttered the cape around his shoulders.

Christ's Blood, was he dreaming?

"What the Devil?" He started to sign himself with the Cross against enchantment—but there! Among the copper-leaved hedges, a woman was running, slender and light-footed as a child, leaf-green skirts trailing behind her, silver-gilt curls swinging free down her back.

"Rhiannon?"

As she fled, she glanced over one shoulder. The silver chime of her laughter floated back to him.

"Rhiannon!" Cursing, Beltran broke into a run. Pursuing her, of course, and she had to know he wouldn't stop until he caught her. "Wait, damn it!"

As he closed the distance between himself and her fleeing figure, details niggled at his brain—the eerie stillness of autumn splendor around them, the castle's abandoned air. And surely Rhiannon's leaf-green gown seemed subtly different. In place of a farthingale and English hood, he thought he saw long trailing sleeves and a kirtle, fashioned in a style he'd seen on ancient tapestries and carved on the tombs of queens.

When she glanced back at him, laughing, he'd drawn close enough to glimpse the silver circlet that banded her brow like a coronet.

As her running form flashed from sunlight into shadow, passing from hedgerows to the ordered ranks of an apple orchard, the green gown seemed to flicker black for an instant, her pale curls to ebony, as though the world reversed itself.

A nameless dread tightened his chest, and he launched into a fresh burst of speed. The whole damn world had gone topsy-turvy. Though his thoughts seemed oddly muddied, he knew he needed to reach her, pull her into his arms and claim her for himself, more than he'd ever needed anything.

He brought her to bay beneath an apple tree laden with gleaming crimson fruit. Laughing and breathless, she spun to face him, her elfin face alight with mischief.

"Damn it, Rhiannon." Breathing heavily, heart thumping hard in his chest, he imprisoned her against the tree's broad trunk. When she darted playfully to one side, he braced his arms against the wood on either side. "Why do you run from me? I'd never force you—never harm you."

"But what of thy Inquisition?" she murmured, a fringe of black silk lashes falling to veil her gaze.

Aye, he'd vowed to turn her over to the Inquisition's tender mercies readily enough. The heretical documents he'd found among her possessions, paired with her own rash admissions, would sign her death sentence. His chest knotted hard at the thought.

Jewel-bright apples swung from the branches above them. Rhiannon rose on tiptoe to pluck one, her breasts brushing his chest—fuller than he recalled somehow, her curves voluptuous and womanly beneath the antique gown. The cloying sweetness of apple-blossoms rose from her hair. Her dark brows winged upward as she laughed up at him, daring him without words to do what she knew he wanted.

"Never run from me," he muttered, catching her raised chin gently in his sword-hardened palm. Her skin was soft damask against his calloused fingers, stretched over a delicate curve of bone.

Careful with her, man. She's fragile. She could shatter like glass under your careless touch. Still, she'd demonstrated reserves of inner strength and resilience and courage in captivity that won his reluctant admiration. She was far less delicate than she appeared, but the world in these dark days was a dangerous place.

"Promise me you'll never run, Rhiannon." Fired by a strange urgency, he gripped her shoulders.

Her little teeth nipped daintily into the apple, blood-red skin and white flesh, tart aroma filling the air. In a daze, he watched her tongue sweep across the tender pink curve of her upper lip where droplets of juice glistened. Again, that sense of wrongness tugged at him. Where had she acquired this blatant carnality, so unlike the innocent freshness of the girl he'd begun to know?

"Kiss me, Vengeance," she whispered, her sweet voice husky with a note of passion he'd never heard there. As if she'd spoken a spell, his cock stirred and tightened.

Growling, he lowered his head and claimed her mouth with his.

Instead of the candied-violet sweetness he expected, she tasted sharp and spicy as apple cider. Instead of winding her arms around his neck and yielding sweetly to his strength as she'd done before, her little hands slid boldly down his back and snaked around his buttocks—the knowing touch of a practiced seductress. Heated thoughts darted through his mind—what she'd let him do to her, forbidden deeds he'd never dreamed of doing with a Christian woman, perversions she seemed more than willing to encourage. His manhood throbbed as the blood surged through him.

Yet that niggling sense of wrongness deepened.

"Oh, that's right," she breathed into his mouth, hips undulating against him. "You want me on my knees before you, don't you, Vengeance? Licking and sucking your man-root, over and over, working you with my lips and tongue until you buck and moan with the pleasure of it..."

The image seared through him, his cock so full he felt like bursting, spilling his seed into his codpiece like a boy with his first erotic dream. Grimly he fought with it, swift-rising lust set against deepening confusion.

Not right, this isn't bloody right! I don't want her like this...

Her suggestive little tongue darted deep in his mouth, stroked and tasted hungrily. One knowing hand slipped his codpiece aside and dipped beneath it. Eager fingers closed around his hardened shaft and began working him, swift and skillful as any whore—

"Stop." Rougher than he'd meant, Beltran pushed her hand away. "What's happening here?"

Lips cherry-red from kissing, flushed and heavy-lidded with passion, Rhiannon smiled.

"What's happening," she said throatily, in that other voice, "is that a princess of Faerie is fucking one of the Christian God's premier angels—he who watches over thunder and terror and guards the gates of hell with his fiery sword, pitiless as any demon. Is this what He wanted for you, Uriel?"

Beltran felt the ground dissolve beneath him. The world shifted and blurred around him. He thrust free from her and staggered back, winded as though from a blow to the belly. The name she'd spoken was echoing through his skull like the tolling of a great bell, like the blast of trumpets—familiar as his own skin, and not merely because he knew his Scripture.

Uriel was the Angel of Vengeance, known as the Flame of God, one of four archangels in the Holy Book who were closest to God. But why under Heaven should the woman apply that name to Beltran...?

He fell to hands and knees, the earth quaking beneath him. The skin of his back was burning, the cloth of his shirt and doublet splitting wide and falling in shreds around him. For the first time in his mortal memory, unhidden by the bright blaze of holy madness that had protected his conscious mind from the knowledge and thus preserved his sanity, the Presence born to flesh as Lord Beltran Nemesto unfurled the mighty span of his wings. With a single powerful beat, he soared aloft.

Rhiannon le Fay stood beneath the tree, surrounded by blood-red apples, no longer laughing as she stared up at him, bathed in the dazzling light of his transformation.

"Nay, Vengeance," she murmured, low and thrumming with power, "this is my world. I am the only Deity here."

Uriel threw back his head and roared. "The only God is—"

"Nay." The world of blazing fall foliage and crumbling gray castle dissolved around him. "*Do not remember.*"

Then Uriel was falling through flame-streaked darkness, endless and terrifying as the plummet from grace that had plunged him into this mortal body a lifetime ago. He had fallen before, fallen and then forgotten, fallen like a flaming comet from divinity into the womb of a Yorkshire whore bearing the fragile spark of life.

Now the witchcraft of a woman's curse was erasing that memory anew, drawing the curtain of oblivion before his eyes.

In an explosion of feathers his wings disintegrated, leaving him flightless and forgotten once more.

SEVEN

SLOWLY RHIANNON RETURNED to her senses, the green English spring coalescing around her. Beltran's strong arms surrounded her. Gratefully she clung to his powerful shoulders, her face wet with tears, dizzy with the speed of hurtling from illusion into reality in Morrigan's reckless grip.

Only heartbeats had passed in mortal time. Her lips were still moist and tingling from his kiss. Dear Lady, the way he'd kissed her! Through the thin sarcenet, her nipples brushed his chest. Tendrils of pleasure snaked through her, making her woman's channel run with honey.

Arousal. This is what makes the troubadours sing. To think she'd lived a thousand years and never felt it, never guessed what she was missing. She sighed and nestled against his hard body.

"Damn it, Rhiannon," Beltran growled, thrusting her away. His abruptness made her stumble. If he hadn't gripped her shoulders, she would have fallen. "What are you trying to do to me?"

She raised her face and smiled at him through the tears. "I might ask thee the same, Lord Beltran Nemesto."

His eyes blazed cobalt in his chiseled features as he scowled down at her, a muscle flexing in his jaw.

Against his sinewed bronze throat, a pulse beat hard and fast.

Well, no wonder he was unsettled. Morrigan's illusions would unsettle anyone. Lord and Lady knew what tapestry of harrowing images her sister must have woven, unspooling the thread from his deepest soul.

"Goddess be praised, Beltran! Thou art whole and well—"

"Don't speak to me of your pagan Goddess and her wanton ways." Abruptly he released her, as though he couldn't bear soiling his hands with her. "How many men have you lured into your bed with your tricks? Your hands, your tongue, your obscene little whispers?"

"I..." Stunned by his sudden wrath, the air of violence barely leashed, Rhiannon dashed a hand across her wet face and struggled to collect herself. "If I've wronged thee in some manner or caused some offense, I crave thy pardon. I—I've never been—"

His nostrils flared. "You were ready to couple with me right here in broad daylight, Rhiannon. Do you seek to destroy my reputation, so the Church will question my judgment?"

"Why...destroy *thy* reputation? That is a right dishonorable notion. I vow it never crossed my mind!" Beneath his accusations and his inexplicable anger, a tide of mounting indignation swept through her, obliterating the tingling desire his mouth and hands had roused.

She'd done nothing wrong, as usual. But as usual, he bullied and threatened and accused her of all manner of crimes!

Despite her rising temper, she struggled to see his

side of it. "Beltran, what befell thee? My sister Morrigan—"

"Silence!" One hand slashed through the air, the seal of Justice flashing in the sunlight. Again he was the Inquisitor, the stern-voiced enforcer, heartless and devoid of mercy.

She fought down a rising sense of hopelessness and tried again. "Beltran, if thou would only *listen*—"

"Nay. I'll listen to no more of your lies and witchery."

"My lies?" Outrage crackled through her, burning away the last of her patience. "I'll have thee know I've never in my life soiled my tongue with a falsehood! I'm the daughter of the Dreaming King."

"You're the daughter of Lucifer," he muttered, scrubbing a hard hand over his face. Briefly he peered at the green hedges around them, the mass of snowdrops blooming at her feet. A cloud of confusion dimmed his piercing gaze.

He shook his head, as though to clear his thoughts. "There's something you said… I'm not recalling. God's Blood, I feel half-bewitched!"

His holy oath made her stagger beneath a surge of weakness—a skipped heartbeat, a breathless moment, the brief dizzying pitch of earth beneath her.

But she'd spoken that Name herself, hadn't she, to banish Morrigan and shatter her enchantment? She'd done it by instinct, given her mortal blood free rein, cried words no proper Faerie could bear to utter. Now, through the fog of illusion, her sister's odd prophecy seeped into memory.

If you sacrifice your maidenhood to couple with a mortal man, you'll become one of them forever.

Red is for heartbreak.

Of course, her sister could have lied. Morrigan was
always capable of that. But she'd called it a prophecy,
and those were Goddess-sent. Her sister was a priestess, among other less savory vocations, and surely
would not defile a holy vision by lying about it. When
she spoke of divinity at least, Morrigan would have
spoken truly.

A clammy tide of fear rolled through her. With new
eyes, she watched Beltran's restless pacing. He could
do it, she knew, after that searing kiss. He could seduce her into his bed. He could make her burn for
him, until she flung caution to the wind and risked
everything—her mother's life, her mission, her painful hope for acceptance, even her immortality. Until
she'd dare anything to feel his hard hands on her body
and drink the spiced wine of his kisses, setting her
drunk with passion.

What was it Morrigan had crooned? *You'll let him
peel those stiff garments from you, caress you and
suckle you until you pulse for him, stroke and fondle
your little pearl until he makes you whimper and beg
him to slide that great throbbing man-root of his between your thighs…*

Even now, the image made her woman's place ache
with longing. Oh, she wanted him there, she *burned*
for him there. But not enough, not nearly enough to
risk losing her immortality and becoming that thing
the Fae despised.

Mortal.

In midstride Beltran halted, tawny head lifting, caution invading his features. She heard it too—the snatch
of mortal voices carried on the wind. Sir Henry Bed-

ingfield's elegant drawl, Elizabeth Tudor's crisp voice crackling with Faerie magick. Their arrival would mean rescue from this humiliating interview and Beltran's wrathful presence.

Do I require rescue from this narrow-minded mortal? Her chin tilted proudly.

Snared by her movement, his keen gaze fixed her— so clearly attuned to her nearness, his nerves strung tight with it, just as she was attuned to him.

Rhiannon gathered her wits and dipped him a stiff curtsey.

"If I'm the daughter of Lucifer, the Father of Lies, as I am now named," she said coolly, "thou should be more than pleased to be quit of me. I'll relieve thee of my vexing presence, unless that too is forbidden me."

His jaw knotted. "Damnation, Rhiannon. I know I spoke harshly—"

"As always!" she said lightly. "Why apologize? Passing judgment comes natural as breathing to you. Have I your leave to withdraw?"

"You're the most maddening woman I've ever met," he muttered. "Withdraw then, if it please you, and stay out of trouble. I'll send a tray to your chamber."

"While you feast?" she said pointedly. "I believe Lady Elizabeth mentioned a masque. No doubt I may enjoy the music through the walls."

"Oh, for the love of Heaven!" he snorted. "I'll do no feasting this night, believe me. My sins call for Vespers and a vigil—and penance."

PALE MOONLIGHT SPILLED through the row of windows across the long gallery of Hatfield House. The light gleamed pearlescent on the watchful faces painted on canvas, mortal art, stiff and unnatural, figures unsmiling and surrounded by symbols of mortal power.

Pensively Rhiannon roamed the gallery, the gay lilt of a galliard floating upward from the banquet hall below. Head tilted, she paused to study another splendid canvas—monstrous and bloated, the ruin of a man glittering with jewels and brocade, sturdy legs braced as though he meant to claim the whole world. Lifting her candle, she peered at the title scrolled across the frame.

Ah, this was Elizabeth's father, the magnificent Henry. Linnet had spoken of him. The king who slaughtered his own queens when he tired of them, like cattle too old for breeding. The mad king whose own gluttony had driven him to his grave.

Now, eyeing his prim little mouth and the slab of a face quivering above his jeweled collar, Rhiannon shivered. Clearly, whatever Faerie blood coursed through Elizabeth's veins hadn't come from him. Her mother must have carried it, the bewitching Anne Boleyn, but Rhiannon knew better than to seek that doomed lady's image among these hallowed ranks.

In her precarious situation, Elizabeth would do nothing to remind her furious sister of the mother who'd borne her. That upstart Protestant with her dazzling wit and her flashing temper who'd done all within her power to see Catholic Mary and her ailing mother destroyed.

Such heedless passions these mortals had! Such stormy hearts, such violent impulse that flung them into disastrous affairs and wars that spanned continents with a speed and frenzy the Fae—lost in the slow drift of time—could never hope to match.

Beltran himself had been heedless that day, the fortress of his rigid discipline cracking at last. She understood he was spending the night on his knees, doing penance for whatever sins he fancied he'd committed.

If she lived among mortals a thousand years, she would never understand them, or the harsh dictates of their vengeful and pitiless God.

Yet the man called Vengeance was not always vengeful. She'd seen his compassion toward the dying bandit he'd comforted, seen him show empathy and deference to her touchy royal pride when he sliced her bonds and presented her to Hatfield as a noblewoman rather than an ignoble captive. Even after that fiasco in the garden, he'd left her at liberty, trusting her sworn oath to hold her.

The Church might demand ruthlessness from its enforcer, but she knew he was capable of more.

Again she wondered what Morrigan had shown him. Better to wait until he calmed, sometime on the road tomorrow, before she asked. For certain, she dared not venture to the consecrated ground where he kept his vigil—terrain the Fair Folk could never bear to tread.

Sighing, Rhiannon resumed her prowl through the gallery. Tendrils of crisp night air raised gooseflesh beneath her gown and set her shivering.

The scuff of a footfall stopped her in her tracks, heart rearing and racing like a runaway horse. Her mouth dried to dust. If Morrigan descended upon her here, wrathful as any Christian demon from banishment, after hearing the Christian God invoked full in her face…

Clammy with fear, Rhiannon lifted her candle. But the tiny circle of light did nothing to lift the thick

darkness surrounding her. Senses honed by a lifetime
among the swift-footed forest creatures, she could hear
someone breathing in the darkness.

"Who is there?" She assumed her most imperious
tone and pitched her voice to carry. If men came running, she'd feel foolish, but at least she'd be safe. "Show
thyself!"

"Oh, hush, dearie!" someone hissed. "D'you want to
bring half the castle down on our heads? Put out that
candle, if ye please."

Not a chance of it. Stubbornly she held it higher.
"I am unaccustomed to disobedience. Show thyself,
I say!"

Her unseen visitant uttered a snort. "You're handy
as my mistress hurling commands hither and yon, milady. Maybe she should've come herself."

A stout woman of middle years pushed into the light,
round face plain and homely beneath her English hood,
her gown of gray damask somber but fine. No servant
this, nor any fine court lady.

"Thou art from Elizabeth?" Rhiannon searched the
shadows. "And alone?"

"Aye and aye." The woman smiled, brown eyes
creasing. "Be a love and douse that light, dearie, unless ye want to bring Sir Henry down on our heads."

Still Rhiannon hesitated, using ears and nose and
eyes to search for treachery, but somehow she couldn't
fear this motherly figure. She blew out the tiny flame,
and the velvet night enveloped them.

"There's a good girl." A work-worn hand clasped
hers. "Come along now."

"Who art thou?" Curious, Rhiannon followed her
through a little door set in the oak-paneled wall.

"Oh, I'm Kat Ashley—Lady Elizabeth's governess. Just mind yer footing 'round this bend. This stair hasn't been repaired since before the Great Harry—milady's father. One of these days I'm afraid I'll tread wrong and go plunging through to the cellar."

Despite the peculiar circumstances, Rhiannon warmed to the spirit of mischief she'd seen twinkling from Kat Ashley's dancing eyes. "Mistress Kat, is it? I thought thee detained over this Dudley business."

"Oh, *that*. They've not enough to hold me. Sir William Paget will need to rise early to get the better of an Ashley, and that you may tie to."

"Thou art a redoubtable woman," Rhiannon murmured, unable to repress a smile.

Kat Ashley halted before a door, barely visible in the darkness. The cold breath of outdoors fluttered her skirts around her ankles.

"Quiet now if ye please, dearie. We'll need to step quick past Sir Henry's watchdog, in case that little something I slipped into his ale hasn't done the trick."

This nocturnal odyssey had acquired the feel of a forbidden adventure. Beltran would certainly disapprove, but she hadn't sworn not to walk the grounds. Besides, she was in no mood after his harsh words to pay any heed to Beltran's preferences.

Daughter to the Father of Lies indeed!

Lifting her chin with a flash of defiance, Rhiannon stepped boldly into the night.

THE GAMEKEEPER'S COTTAGE nestled deep in the wooded deer park on Hatfield lands. In the soft purple dusk she slipped among the rustling spruces, silent as the red deer whose gentle presence she sensed nearby. Her passage didn't startle them, for they sensed her affinity and accepted her among them.

Not so the drugged guard; him she had feared. But Kat Ashley led her unerringly past danger to this sway-backed cottage, shuttered and sleeping among the deer. A thin seam of golden light spilled beneath the door.

Mistress Kat bustled up to the portal and tapped—a signal to whoever waited within. Then she beckoned kindly to Rhiannon.

"Come along, dearie. Here's someone right glad to see ye. I'll just step back along the path and raise a ruckus if someone comes."

Within, the snug room was white-plastered and wood-floored. Overhead, sides of cured meat swung from smoke-stained beams. A merry fire crackled and danced, shedding its friendly light over the trundle bed before the hearth. With a pang, Rhiannon recalled the cozy nook snuggled deep in the Faerie wood where she'd made her home. A surge of homesickness swelled up, making her eyes sting and her throat thicken.

Then she beheld the familiar form propped on pillows in the trundle bed—gray-streaked dark curls clipped in the Roman fashion, features drawn with weariness, but his beloved eyes steady as a guiding hand.

"Welcome, dear heart," her foster-father said gently.

"Oh, Ansgar!" With full heart and brimming eyes, Rhiannon flew across the chamber to his side. "How I prayed Her Grace's searchers would find you! I've been so dreadfully worried. I should never have left you, but Lord Beltran would heed nothing I told him. I intended to return…"

At her captor's name, a frown darkened Ansgar's

pain-worn features, but his grip on her hands was strong. "I tracked you and the priest as well as I might, but this accursed shoulder slowed my pace. 'Tis grateful I am to find you safe and well here, child."

"He's kept me safe enough," she allowed. "My lord is a capable guardian—too capable—and he's no priest. How are you feeling, love?"

Even while her heart overflowed with joy, her mind catalogued his pallor and breathing, the white bandages binding his arm to his chest, the pungent odor of healing herbs. Marigold probably, a poultice plastered on the open wound to prevent festering...

"At least you're well tended, Lady be praised." She nodded satisfaction. "You've no fever and the wound smells clean. How did you manage?"

"Lady Linnet has been a most devoted caretaker." Ansgar smiled. "She's just a slip of a girl, but faithful, and her heart is kind. She could have gone to her own kin here in the mortal realm, who must surely mourn her for dead. But somehow she seems less than eager to return to them, and no knight would press a lady to act against her wishes. Rather than abandon us to our fate, she returned to the battleground and found me."

Rhiannon forbore to comment upon Linnet's kindness. Ansgar the divine spear might be the greatest knight England had ever known, the hero of countless lays and legends, but he was naïve as a child where matters of the heart were concerned. His own heart had been buried with Arthur's long-dead Queen Guinevere. He'd dwelled alone and celibate in Faerie ever since, oathbound to Rhiannon's defense by a vow he'd sworn to Arthur on his deathbed. But he'd saved Linnet from her wrathful pursuer the day she blundered through the mists into the Summer Lands. Small wonder, then, the girl clove to him as her protector.

Now that she'd been returned to her own kind, her wits no longer befuddled by Faerie magick, Rhiannon hoped the girl's love for him would fade. Otherwise, the poor child was destined for heartbreak.

Red is for heartbreak…

Briskly she shook off the chilling memory of Morrigan's malice. "And where is Lady Linnet now? I'll be pleased indeed to see her well."

"Mistress Kat smuggled her into the house for a clean gown and provisions. I gather the lady of the manor does not intend that her captor or yours discover our presence," he said dryly. "Which is all to the good. Rhiannon, we must flee tonight."

In the midst of checking his bandages, she lifted her startled gaze. "That has certainly been my goal. But I gave my parole to Lord Beltran."

His dark brows drew together. "That was unwise, child. You must reach the Tudor Queen."

"I know the Veil is thinning and my mother is—is failing—"

"Your mother is dying," he said flatly.

Rhiannon's heart swooped like a sparrow fleeing the hawk. Never had anyone dared to speak those words aloud in Faerie, though the bitter truth was guessed by all. Queene Maeve had ruled for millennia before the Romans came to the isle they called Britannia. But even the Fae faded in time, and the strife and strain of the looming Convergence merely hastened her fall.

And when the Queene passed, her heir Morrigan would take up the crown.

The Faerie Queene had never claimed to love her

mixed-blood daughter. But despite a lifetime of her benign neglect, Rhiannon would not stand tamely watching while her mother died and two realms plunged headlong into war.

"We still have time to save her, Ansgar. I *will* save her—that I swear to you."

"Time flows swiftly in the Summer Lands," he murmured. "As mortals reckon it, we've been gone a sennight."

She heard the words he did not speak. *Your mother may be dead by now, or nearly so. The Convergence may have already begun.*

A fist of panic squeezed her chest. Suddenly, she was struggling for breath to fill her lungs. "I'll reach the Tudor Queen in time."

"How? I doubt very much this inquisitor fellow intends to take you."

"Nor does he." Renewed annoyance with Beltran's high-handed treatment made her voice crisp. "He intends to leave me somewhere for questioning…a church in Yardley, I think he said…and continue his journey alone. If I hadn't given my parole, I would have been locked in a dungeon, treated far less honorably and unable to leave in any event."

"Damn." He frowned. "I suppose he plans to do this shortly? He'd the look of a man in a hurry during our brief acquaintance."

"He intends to leave Hatfield on the morrow." Somehow Rhiannon felt uncomfortable discussing Lord Beltran Nemesto beneath her foster-father's perceptive gaze. Restless, she wandered to the hearth, where a kettle hung over the flames, and busied herself there. At least the fire would justify the uncontrollable heat rising in her cheeks. If he guessed the way Beltran had kissed her...the way she'd kissed him back...

"Be logical, child, and clear your mind," Ansgar urged. "What exactly did you swear?"

Rhiannon paused to recall the words, which she'd crafted with some care for precisely this reason. Every Faerie ever born knew how to shape vows to her advantage. "I gave my word...as the Dreaming King's daughter...not to seek escape while I rest beneath that roof."

"There! Well spoken, child. You didn't seek to escape, but left the manor honestly. Beneath this roof, no oath binds you."

She voiced an incredulous laugh. "That's slicing the thing rather fine, don't you think? My lord's clear belief was that I'd bound myself not to escape at all."

"Ah, but that isn't what you said." Ansgar watched her keenly. "For the Lady's sake, you're one of the Fair Folk, child, and our need is most dire. He should have bound you more carefully than that. Likely he doesn't believe you, thinks you some foolish girl playing at fantasies, doesn't he?"

Face averted, she nodded. Indeed that was what Beltran believed or tried to believe—his skepticism being one of his more maddening qualities.

"Let this be a learning experience for him." Her foster-father shrugged, then paled as the careless movement jarred his shoulder. "I only wish I could journey with you. But as matters stand, I'd only delay you. I must needs follow at a more sedate pace. Your best hope is to reach the Tudor Queen at speed, if you think he's likely to pursue you."

"Oh, he'll pursue me, that you may believe." Somehow Rhiannon never doubted it, despite the pressing business he'd cited. "Though he seems passionately to want nothing to do with me, he'd consider it an affront to his own honor if I escaped his vigilance and his Catholic judgment. But, my dear, I can't flee now."

"Why not?" Suddenly his eyes narrowed. "Rhiannon—tell me he hasn't…"

Her foster-father paused delicately. To her irritation, she flamed crimson and busied herself brushing earth from her bottle-green slippers. "He's done nothing. He's an honorable man, Ansgar, despite his calling."

Aye, he's honorable and brave and stalwart. He can even be gentle. But the harsh strictures of his faith have twisted him.

And he consumes my thoughts beyond reason.

Still, she'd resolved to bury those feelings, after Morrigan's terrible prophecy. Perhaps her sister was lying, but Rhiannon would not risk her immortality for that.

She must never let him close to her again, and Goddess knew she wanted no other man in her bed. If she fled Beltran, the curse could never come true.

"You may believe, foster-father, I would be more than glad to escape him." She quashed the odd little pang of regret that stabbed through her. "The reason I say there's no purpose to it is because *he has the treaty.* He took it from me, remember? Without the treaty to trigger the spell when Mary Tudor signs it, there's naught to bind either the Fae or the mortals."

They fell silent, impaled on the horns of the dilemma she'd been wrestling with since yesterday. Rhiannon sat on the floor beside his low bed and slipped her hand into his worn grip for comfort.

Their silence held until Kat Ashley bustled in with kindling for the hearth.

"What's this now? Cat got your tongue?" the stout woman said cheerfully, lowering her burden with a grunt.

Exchanging a glance with Ansgar, Rhiannon sketched the broad outlines of their predicament. Uncertain how much Elizabeth shared with her governess, she said nothing of the Convergence or the Faerie realm, but spoke in general terms about her urgent need to speak with Mary Tudor and the life-and-death document she must deliver.

"I would not mind so much the delay if—if I knew the Church's questions would only be—questions," she faltered, steeling herself against the fearful images that reared up in her mind. "But my mother's health is failing, Mistress Kat, and we've precious little time. Still, without that document…"

"Oh, posh! Is that all that's holding ye, dearie?" the older woman exclaimed. "Is my mistress a Boleyn and the Great Harry's daughter for nothing? She has her father's stubbornness and her mother's wits, and that you may tie to. Besides which, milady, I daresay there's something she wants from *you*."

EIGHT

BELTRAN STRUGGLED BACK to consciousness as the first spears of sunrise stabbed against his closed lids. He stirred against the icy flagstones where he lay face-down before the altar, arms spread in a cruciform shape. Sharp blades of pain pierced his stiffened joints. He bit back a groan by habit, conditioned to ignore the agony of a lifetime of such vigils.

He'd discharged his penance for the momentary lapse of reason that left him kissing Rhiannon le Fay in a public garden as though he'd devour her, all but fumbling with eagerness to raise her skirts.

So much for the Blades of God and his vow of chastity. He'd tumbled from grace once more. Why the hell was he so clearly ill-suited for this—the only life he'd ever wanted?

But soon the bell must toll for Lauds. Elizabeth's chaplain would be wanting his chapel back.

Grimly ignoring the white-hot needles of agony piercing his shoulders, Beltran pushed to hands and knees, then climbed stiffly to his feet. Around him the chapel coalesced—the old Catholic relics he'd always loved, which Hatfield's Protestant mistress so reluctantly displayed: the golden monstrance blazing on the altar; the holy table draped with crimson damask. Beeswax candles burned to stubs around the figure of sorrowful St. Sebastian, bound to his post and pierced with arrows, slain at the Emperor Diocletian's command, his eyes raised soulfully toward Heaven. Nearby stood the haloed figure of St. Catherine, who'd famously consecrated her virginity to Christ rather than wed a pagan Caesar, and looming behind her the breaking wheel.

The Inquisitors still used the Catherine wheel at San Miguel to break the bones of condemned witches and others who flouted God's authority. God had broken the wheel to save Catherine, but He seemed disinclined to intervene for the Inquisition's victims. Beltran had seen it used himself, though never yet by his command. The Cardinal claimed his reluctance to torture in God's name was the sole obstacle preventing his rise to a far greater station.

Beneath the penitent's robe of undyed wool, his muscles knotted tight with sudden spasms. After his nightlong vigil in the unheated chapel, the air was cold enough to freeze the wine in the chalice.

Not so young as I used to be—nor yet a mumbling fool gumming your porridge, man. Brace up.

Briskly he rubbed his arms and slapped his chest for warmth. His hands tingled as hot blood rushed painfully back to the frozen limbs. Finding the shirt and hose he'd left folded on a pew, he shrugged into them. Despite his aching bones and the gnawing hunger in his gut, his mind was blessedly clear, the clamoring voices of guilt and unworthiness silenced by the purifying rite of contrition.

When he knelt before the altar last night, his body had been burning for her. *Rhiannon.* Now, in retrospect, their encounter had acquired an air of unreality, like a dream. He blamed himself for kissing her, for yielding to the temptation of silver-gilt curls and leaf-green eyes and pert breasts he'd been aching to cup for two days.

Yet the girl was indisputably different from the discreet widows of means who customarily slaked his lust, or the mistress he'd left behind in Rome. Unwedded and innocent, for one thing—barely more than a child, her beauty fresh and unspoiled as dew sparkling at dawn. Or so he'd thought.

The way she'd warmed under his kisses, the winsome sweetness that made his heart ache…he'd been so careful not to hurt or frighten her. Though some primitive part of him had wanted to roar in triumph like a beast when he claimed her and she yielded.

Then the way she'd arched against him and purred like a cat, the knowing slide of her fingers, the matter-of-fact way she'd moved his codpiece aside and eagerly worked his throbbing length, crooning for him to spill in her hand—the woman who'd touched him then was no innocent.

Almost as though she'd been a different woman entirely.

You were wrong about her, clearly, beguiled and befuddled by her witchcraft.

And something else was bothering him, something he'd almost forgotten. Something she'd said or done that reminded him of a dream he had sometimes, whose details he could never quite recall.

That dream was pure sensation, the feeling of plummeting through an endless abyss, wind howling around him, tattered wings fluttering in his wake. Falling away from the incandescent light of Heaven, away from all consolation, away from the source of life and warmth and grace into harsh and lonely exile, his heart twisted with bitterness and simmering with inconsolable rage.

Inevitably he woke aching with loss, feeling as though he'd been stabbed in the back by his closest friend. In fact, now he thought of it, he'd had the dream again last night, while he lay as though crucified before the altar. Yet he understood it now no better than before. Why should any God-fearing man dream of fallen angels, unless the dream was devil-sent to test his faith?

The half-remembered images nagged at him like a sore tooth as he shrugged his doublet around his warming body, stomped his feet into his boots and strapped the sword called Judgment across his back. The solid feel of the leather-wrapped hilt restored him fully to himself. The assurance and authority of God's Vengeance settled around him like the cape he swirled around his shoulders.

No more dallying in gardens, man. You'll confess your lapse to the Cardinal as usual, and take your punishment like a proper Blade. The girl—Rhiannon— goes to the church at Yardley, and with hard riding you'll see the walls of London tonight.

Muttering a word of thanks to the hovering chaplain, Beltran strode from the chapel.

THE GIRL WASN'T at Lauds, which made him frown as he sang his psalms and said his prayers with Elizabeth's carefully devout courtiers ranked behind him. Despite the ordeal looming before her, she hadn't troubled to attend Mass since he'd met her, nor made any pretense to seek the solace of prayer. Probably a heretic as well as a witch—but the latter would be easier to prove.

And the Tudor princess herself was absent. But that he'd half expected.

Beltran skipped breakfast, as he often did; he'd been taught to make the hollow ache of an empty belly a gift to God. He was arranging their departure when he discovered Rhiannon's mist-gray mare was missing.

Now here he stood, cooling his heels in the corridor like a damn pageboy, while Lady Elizabeth's moon-faced governess explained—patient but resolute—why the mistress of the house was unavailable. Her Grace was suffering one of her megrims, Kat Ashley said firmly, and would likely be indisposed all day. Not even the daunting prospect of God's Vengeance in a fury would sway Mistress Kat to admit him.

Beltran contained his mounting ire and stalked off to find Bedingfield, whom he threw into dismay and stiff-worded apologies with a few well-chosen threats. Elizabeth's guardian seemed perplexed by his agitation, which was understandable, since Sir Henry had been laboring under the impression Rhiannon was free to do as she pleased. He could hardly share the bitter realization breaking over Beltran—the girl had cast aside her oath and slipped away beneath his very nose, no doubt laughing at his gullibility all the way to London.

Beltran struggled against an unexpected sting of disappointment. So much for her shining mantle of honor, her noble manner, the promise of grace and purity he'd longed to believe in. The lady was a liar, an opportunist, either a fool or a charlatan. And evidently a harlot to boot.

He bit out a vicious curse and pivoted toward the stables, an annoyed Sir Henry hurrying in his wake.

The groom Beltran had bribed to mind her mare

was, unsurprisingly, nowhere to be found. He fired off a barrage of questions to the night guard, a poor stammering lad who couldn't recall seeing a pale-haired lady on a gray mare. Was he supposed to have seen and detained such a person? Pale with dread, the youth swore on his mother's soul he'd received no such orders.

Judging by the woody bite of ale on his breath, Beltran suspected the lad had slept through his watch—a dereliction that would, at San Miguel, have earned him a flogging until the blood ran down his back. But flogging derelict boys for minor failings was not Beltran's business. If Sir Henry couldn't compel better discipline from his lackeys, that was his problem.

"Why not leave her to her own devices, my lord?" Sir Henry urged. "As I understand the matter, there is no real connection between you, and you have said you're overdue in London. One does not wish to keep the Archbishop of Canterbury waiting."

Beltran's mouth twisted in a cynical smile. Briefly, he pondered the notion of leaving Rhiannon le Fay to her fate. Whatever her dubious business with the Queen, surely her welfare or lack of it was no concern of his. How much damage could that slip of a girl possibly wreak? Pious Mary would make short work of her heathenish claims. Like as not, the girl would end up in Bishop Bonner's pitiless hands—and thence to the pyre—with no intervention on his part.

Still, he'd come to England to support the Inquisition. More, he'd assumed responsibility for Rhiannon when he took her into custody, and Beltran Nemesto was no man to leave a job undone. The girl was his duty, nothing more. It was not as though he'd come to know her personally, not that he'd miss the imperious tilt of her chin when he imposed upon some prerogative she claimed as her due. Not that he'd hide a smile at the quick flare of her temper as she rode haughtily beside him, her emerald eyes incandescent with spirit, perched delicate as…well, a Faerie in her saddle.

Nor would he miss the smile that lit her elfin face, the chime of her laughter like silver bells, the faint sweetness of violets that floated around her, or the trusting way she'd yielded when he kissed—

He jerked these unsuitable musings to an abrupt halt.

God's body, here he stood daydreaming about the chit like a lovesick maid, while every minute that ticked past opened more distance between them. Clearly the thing to do was depart for London forthwith. If he encountered the girl on the road—or word of her, for he'd question those who might have seen her—then he'd reclaim her. If not, he'd be sitting at the Archbishop's fire by nightfall.

In either case, his business with the ethereal and unsettling Rhiannon le Fay was finished.

Beltran was swinging into his saddle when it occurred to him to check the cache of heretical documents stowed in his saddlebag. It rather surprised him she would have left those behind…

When he realized they were missing—his sole evidence of her witchcraft—a red fury filmed his vision. In a heartbeat, his intent shifted. The blood began burning in his veins, unmistakable precursor to the holy madness. Clenching his teeth against the inevitable, he fought the onslaught with every particle of resolve, until smoke all but rose from his skin.

"Ride hard, Rhiannon," he whispered hoarsely, the low rumble of a lion's growl. "And pray to your pagan Goddess I don't find you now."

NINE

THE FRENCH WERE invading the Tudor court.

"Alas, we are come too late," Rhiannon murmured to Lady Linnet Norwood as they edged through the roistering throng at Hampton Court. "Clearly, war has already commenced."

On a hastily erected stage in the Great Hall, some sort of elaborate pageant was rollicking along with gusto. Fortunately, the gallants of the invading force—mallard ducks sporting French colors—were armed with nothing more lethal than balloons filled with lavender water that drenched the hall in sweetness.

Behind the painted cliffs of Dover, England's female protectors shrieked beneath the onslaught and rained showers of spring blossoms upon their assailants.

Lady Linnet held her ground bravely as a pair of drunken lords jostled past, leering at the ladies. Lord of Light, the girl looked nervous enough to jump from her skin, plunged into intimate congress with her own kind after the dreamlike drift of a year or more through the lavender mists of Faerie.

Of course, these mortals were Rhiannon's kith also, little kinship though she felt with them. Disconcerting—the sheer din of these mortal hordes, reeking of sweat and stale perfume, so crude and alien, so removed from the sun-dappled green bowers and brooks of home.

Now she was drowning in a sea of brocade and taffeta and silk stretched over whalebone farthingales that bumped and poked her with every step. Her slippers pinched her feet; her toes were trodden on twice while they pressed through the crush. Her eyes were dazzled and blinded by the glitter of gemstones on hats and hems and borders, ears deafened by the roar of laughter. The ragged cacophony of lute and pipe that passed for music made her head ache.

And every man present, except the scurrying servants, was wearing steel.

In Linnet's wake, she threaded among them, skin itching and burning at the nearness of daggers the length of her forearm. Nervously she fiddled with her silver rings. If they should slip off, or be stripped from her, she would convulse in agony...

Despite her own anxiety, Linnet seemed to sense the desperate unease that made Rhiannon long to flee this hellish inferno.

"Don't fash yerself. It's only a pageant, my lady. The Tudors are famous for them." The familiar Scottish lilt of the girl's voice reassured her as Linnet looped a slim arm through Rhiannon's for a steadying squeeze. "No one here will harm ye."

Unless Lord Beltran has managed to arrive before us. The thought sent legions of butterflies cartwheeling through Rhiannon's belly. Again she prayed the Blade of God had washed his hands of her. She doubted Kat Ashley would have been able to conceal her flight for long, even with clever Elizabeth's connivance.

But somehow Rhiannon knew he would pursue her. She could almost sense his wrathful presence, that stern-faced Being with flaming eyes and garnet wings, sweeping down the Queen's Highway. He would have known instantly where she'd fled, grasping the treaty stolen from his very chamber while he prayed in the Hatfield chapel.

Hurry! The voice of instinct quickened her step. *Find the Queen quickly.*

Pushing back the clamoring tide of panic, Rhiannon summoned a shaky smile. For the faithful child beside her also required reassurance.

"Dear heart, how would I manage without thee? I bless thee a thousand times for thy constancy, Linnet."

Reluctant to leave the wounded Ansgar yet more reluctant still to return to her Scottish kin, Linnet had gamely accepted his charge to guide Rhiannon through the Tudor court. Without her escort, Rhiannon could scarcely have managed to advance even this far. She must be very careful not to lose the girl in this teeming horde of mortals.

Despite the frantic gaiety that permeated this half-Spanish court, the very air seethed with rumors. The French were massing under Dudley in Elizabeth's name…they'd risen to capture the outpost of Calais… the Scots were arming over the border and would murder them all in their beds….

Despite the stifling heat of the Great Hall, her hands were ice.

Hurry, you must hurry. God's Vengeance is coming.

She'd prepared so carefully for this moment, striven so desperately to reach this place, pleaded and struggled and suffered. She'd sacrificed the lives of precious friends—Caedmon, Cynyr, Nineve, so many others. Dear Goddess, would she never cease grieving them?

Too much hung in the balance to be less than starkly terrified.

"The Watching Chamber lies yonder, if ye're still intent on approaching the Queen tonight." Glancing cautiously toward a knot of cassocked priests who scowled nearby, Linnet pitched her words beneath gusts of laughter that rang from the hammered beams.

"Forsooth, I'm determined," Rhiannon murmured. "We dare not wait."

"We'll not manage our wee peek at her without a bit of luck," the girl warned. "Only senior courtiers are permitted past the Yeomen without invitation. It needs more than a bonnie gown to broach the Queen's privy chambers."

"We've a message from the Queen's own sister—the Lady Elizabeth herself." Rhiannon lifted her chin. "If that will not suffice, perhaps a silver crown will prove persuasive. I've some coin left from our travel-purse."

"I'd like to see ye pay a crown to those rogues in livery!" Linnet gasped. "Mercy, have ye no sense of money?"

"Forsooth, I suppose I have none. Easy come, easy go, do these mortals not say?"

For Queene Maeve had filled her purse with Faerie gold, which always returned to its mistress. Little though she liked the deception, all Rhiannon could do was urge her vendors to spend it quickly.

They'd gained the Great Hall without resort to bribery; a lady's finery and Linnet's childhood court memories proved sufficient for that. How easily the court's gaze skimmed over Linnet's demure figure in her rose damask, her sherry-gold eyes downcast, her riot of fire-streaked mahogany curls coiffed smooth beneath her

Spanish hood. The ease of their passage had steadied Rhiannon's nerves—until she noticed how the mortals looked at her.

Uneasy, she toyed with her moonstone pendant, the fragile charm all that stood between her and inevitable disaster if she were unveiled—an otherworldly being with glowing alabaster skin and hair like moonlight.

Thankfully, Rhiannon need not contend with Philip of Spain, away on the continent about the Holy Roman Emperor's business. But lovesick Mary rarely emerged from her privy chambers as she pined for her missing lord.

A fresh commotion drew Rhiannon's gaze to the oak-paneled doors of the Watching Chamber. Something was happening, a sudden disturbance among the blue-and-green liveried ranks of the Queen's personal guard. Serving-folk scurried with trays and cushions. Then the door swung wide to disgorge an influx of black-haired lords and ladies, encrusted with gemstones, sallow-skinned and exotic to Rhiannon's eyes.

Her heart beat swift with excitement. "What's happening, Linnet? Are those the Spanish grandees?"

"Aye, some of them—though wearing French fashions." Disdainfully Linnet tossed her loyal head. "Ruffs the size of dinner plates."

But Rhiannon cared naught for fashion, despite the stiffened ruff edged with silver lace whose constant itch at her own throat nearly maddened her. Tightly she gripped Linnet's fingers, the world narrowing around her until she heard nothing but the stern voice trumpeting:

"Make way for Mary, by God's grace Queen of England, Spain, Sicily, Naples, Jerusalem and Ireland,

Defender of the Faith, Duchess of Milan and Brabant,
Countess of Habsburg, Flanders and Tyrol!"

Around her, every head bowed. Every knee bent low
in homage before the glittering figure commanding
the doorway. Belatedly Rhiannon sank into her curtsey, her head swirling. *Dear Lady, grant me strength.*
If I should fail...

Slowly her vision cleared. She focused on the rich
luster of her own skirts, black brocade divided over
ivory taffeta, billowing around her bent knees like an
ocean of moon-crossed midnight. The colors symbol-
ized eternal virginity—an irony not lost on her, after
Morrigan's prophecy. With shaking hands she straightened the rope of fat black pearls that girdled her hips—
pearls for maidenhood, pearls for sorrow. The tang of
clove-studded citrus from her pomander revived her.

Before her neighbors could rise, she floated to her
feet, stately as a queen herself. Head lifting proudly,
she looked straight into the eyes of a startled Mary
Tudor.

The daughter of King Henry VIII and Queen Katherine of Aragon was a woman of forty, no taller than
Rhiannon, face lined and haggard with a lifetime of
hardship. Boleyn caprice had torn her away from the
mother she adored, then left her to languish in lonely
penury while Katherine sickened and died. She'd been
threatened with beating and worse for defying the ty-
rannical father who established his own Church of
England and placed himself at its head. She'd suffered
through Henry's six wives, bastardized and removed
from succession, clung stubbornly to the mainstay of
her Catholic faith while her father died and a boy of

eleven replaced him, though his Protestant Council threatened and bullied her.

Then her brother Edward coughed out his lungs and died in wasting agony at the tender age of fifteen. And his greedy council scorned Mary to crown her heretic cousin Jane Grey. At last Mary Tudor had flung off the fetters of injustice and risen, sweeping into London with magnificent courage to face down her oppressors, bringing the entire nation with her to tumble Lady Jane from her nine days' throne.

But those triumphant events were years behind her. Now the Queen's auburn hair was faded, thin lips pinched with pain, small shoulders stooped beneath the crimson-and-gold train that dragged at her like a disappointment she could never cast aside. Her eyesight was failing; her red-rimmed eyes squinted against the blaze of light, as though she'd been weeping.

Now those weary eyes skimmed over her kneeling court to find the woman who'd boldly risen too soon—a slim moonbeam in black pearls and damask, bareheaded but for a coronet of silver-gilt hair, face framed in silver lace that violated the sumptuary laws for any lady who lacked a Maid of Honor's status.

Suddenly Rhiannon feared she'd dressed too richly, that the paranoid Queen who burned heretics alive must view her pride and boldness as an unforgivable challenge.

The Queen of England's gaze pierced her like an Inquisition. "God in Heaven, *is it you*?"

Rhiannon swayed before the Holy Name, but refused to drop her gaze. She was a princess of the Fair Folk, daughter of the Dreaming King; this sister mon-

arch must be made to acknowledge it. Suddenly she
was alive and tingling with energy.

"Majesty," she said steadily, ignoring the court's
straining ears, "I bear thee tribute and greeting from
thy fellow sovereign on this blessed isle. Wilt thou
speak with me?"

Mary Tudor's mud-colored eyes narrowed. "Are you
an emissary from Scotland? From that brazen strumpet
Mary Stuart who seeks to supplant me as England's
Queen?"

"Nay, not from Scotland. And well do thou know
it." Rhiannon put steel in her spine and assumed her
mother's commanding tone. On the edge of this moment she would rise or fall, her life forfeit in a Catholic
dungeon if she failed. Already the Queen's attention
was flickering over the eagle-eyed Spaniards who hovered, avidly absorbing every word.

Bold action was called for, or Rhiannon would miss
her moment. Swiftly, she unclasped the moonstone
pendant from her throat.

Just for a breath, she stood revealed. An astral wind
stirred her garments—stiff damask no longer, but the
shining pearlescent draperies of a Faerie princess,
the star of evening flashing in her fingers. Moonlight
poured from her skin to stream over Mary Tudor's lined
face. The Queen's pupils shrank to pinpricks against
it as she gasped.

From those nearby swelled a murmur of shock and
wonder. Beside her, a pale-haired youth gripping a lyre
sank to his knees and gazed worshipfully at Rhiannon.

"Oh Goddess," he breathed.

With unsteady fingers, Rhiannon replaced the pendant. The cool weight settled against her breasts and

the magickal glow subsided, leaving her soaring spirit shackled and earthbound once more.

"Majesty," she whispered, beneath a tide of superstitious mutters, "I am Rhiannon le Fay, daughter of the Faerie Queene."

An odd recognition flickered in the Queen's sunken eyes. "So the test of my faith is come upon me. Jesu grant me strength for the trial."

The Queen's invocation, echoed by her Catholic followers, demanded its painful toll. Darkness nibbled around the edge of her vision, but Rhiannon blinked it back. When she swayed on her feet, faithful Linnet bore her up.

But Mary Tudor's wondering gaze had narrowed on her courtiers' curious faces. She stood stiffly under their scrutiny, with none of her sister Elizabeth's natural ease. In the crush and din of the crowded hall, most could not have witnessed the vision she'd beheld, and surely this embattled Queen knew it. Already her Protestant subjects whispered in secret that the King's abandonment had left her mad with grief. She would not wish to add fuel to those fires.

Watching the older woman compose herself and draw a mask of chilly hauteur over her careworn features, an unexpected stab of compassion pierced Rhiannon's heart.

Mary Tudor played out her life on a public stage— her brief unhappy marriage to a husband who despised her, her barrenness, her faltering health, the bitter discord over faith and disputed succession that divided her kingdom, and the doubt that tore her heart.

Rhiannon's tidings from the Summer Lands could only worsen her lot.

Even as she watched, the Queen pressed a ringed hand to her stomach. With her healer's instinct, Rhiannon sensed the deep-rooted ache in the other woman's womb, where the stiffened bodice dug into tender flesh. The Queen was bloated and cramping with one of her infrequent moon flows, and a vicious headache stabbed cruelly behind her eyes.

In a heartbeat, both treaty and Convergence were forgotten as concern for a suffering patient surged to the fore. Heedless of any insult of *lèse majesté*, Rhiannon sprang forward to slip a supporting arm around the faltering Queen. Mary sagged against her, fingers kneading ineffectually at the dull throbbing in her belly.

"Leave her alone, sorceress!" a voice hissed. One of the Queen's companions—an older woman, plain-faced, garbed in somber finery—scrabbled at Rhiannon's arm. Spite and envy radiated from her like heat from an open hearth. Greedy eyes darted over her, counting every jewel to calculate her worth.

What can I get from this one, the woman was thinking, *if I grant her access to the Queen?*

Rhiannon shrank from the creature in distaste, but never lessened her grip on Mary, whose discreet clutch on her arm was all that held the Queen upright.

"Be thou at ease, lady, I am doing thy Queen no harm," Rhiannon murmured.

"Who are you to handle her so familiar?" the woman spat. *And without seeking my favor first.*

"I'm a healer," Rhiannon said quietly, not to aggravate the sharp pain flaring behind her patient's eyes. "Thy Queen requires a private refuge, a stool to elevate her feet, wine with herbs to quicken her blood. I shall mix her a potion—"

"No doubt you'll mix a potion that sends her straight to her grave! Always her enemies seek to poison her."

Mary Tudor lifted a ringed hand to stay the flood of venomous spite, but the Queen was beyond speaking. Whatever ailed her was beyond the megrims of a woman's moon-time. In a moment she'd be fainting, and Goddess knew what they'd say if the Queen of England fell insensate at Rhiannon's feet!

Dreading the cost her healing would demand, she met Mary Tudor's tortured gaze.

"Be at peace, Mary," she whispered, spreading her fingers over the dagger-sharp point of the Queen's stomacher. Deliberately she blocked out her surroundings—the hostile faces, the hissing malice, the dreadful clamor of music and the stink of soiled rushes.

Dimly she sensed Linnet's capable hands coaxing the spiteful woman from her side.

"Come away, Susan Clarencius. I know ye love yer Queen, so come away now and let my lady Rhiannon assist her…"

Rhiannon opened the floodgates of her heart, and a lifetime of dammed-up love burst forth. The life-energy poured through her fingers into the ailing Queen.

Deep in her own womb, she felt the ripples of the Queen's anguish gradually subside, soothed by the warm torrent of healing energy that bathed her.

At last, Rhiannon drew an unsteady breath and opened her eyes. The colorful walls with their jewel-bright tapestries blurred around her. Through sheer will, she stayed upright.

Mary Tudor stared at her raptly, the deep grooves of pain easing between her eyes.

"You're an angel descended from Heaven," the Queen breathed. "God be praised who sent you to me."

"I'm no angel, I assure thee." Swaying, Rhiannon raised a hand to stop this flood of ardent prayer, the words a rain of blows she could no longer withstand. Unexpectedly, an image of Beltran Nemesto intruded upon her—that great Presence of stern and terrible beauty, opal and cobalt and ruby flashing as his wings unfolded.

"Your coming was shown to me in a holy vision." Mary Tudor clasped her hands in prayer and lifted rapturous eyes toward Heaven. "While I kept vigil and prayed for my husband's safe return. Oh divine Spirit, what message from Heaven do you bear?"

Rhiannon's head was swirling, senses dulled by the outpouring of healing energy that had drained her to exhaustion. Now she must sit quietly and sip a cup of wine, like her patient, before she could broach the delicate subject of the Convergence to this Queen's devout ears.

But the opportunity before her was Goddess-sent. Who knew when she might be offered another such opening?

Gathering her wits, she detached the belt-pouch from her girdle. "If thou art prepared to hear my message, I pray we may withdraw to some quiet place. Forsooth, I bear a treaty from Queene Maeve of the Faeries, that I would implore thee sign—"

Across the Great Hall, words rang out like the blast of trumpets, making the earth tremble beneath her slippers.

"If you love your soul, madame, do not sign."

Rhiannon felt a sinking sense of inevitability. She needed no oracle's Sight to know who spoke. She'd sensed his nearness all evening, trembled at the thought of his demon or angel ravening down on her. Fear of him had driven her to expose herself too rashly.

Belly quivering, heartbeat fluttering like a frantic sparrow, she raised a hand to her dry throat. Before her the Spaniards were falling back, opening a passage in the bright sea of bodies.

Through their midst he bore down on her—an austere and terrifying figure clad in mud-spattered sable, the blade of judgment jutting over his shoulder, cape sweeping behind him like oncoming night. Torchlight burned like a holy aura in his dark gold hair and flashed on the flaming cross that swung over his heart. His chiseled face was thunderous, jaw knotted with contained anger.

She trembled with a forest creature's blind urge for flight. But his blazing eyes transfixed her where she stood. Divine wrath rooted her in place. That and the desperate knowledge that if she fled now, she would never have another chance to sway this pious Queen.

Already Mary Tudor was wavering between them, gaping at this force of nature. In a moment, her opportunity would be lost. Thoughts jostled through Rhiannon's brain in a tumbled rush. The Queen had spoken of a holy vision—an angel who somehow resembled Rhiannon—and that could be no coincidence. The Faerie Queene wove mortal dreams and visions easy as wool upon her loom.

Rhiannon's skin tingled as she sensed her mother's hand in this business.

Tearing her eyes away from Beltran Nemesto's imposing frame, Rhiannon captured the Queen's distracted gaze.

"In the name of the Deity thou serve, and thy sainted mother before thee, in the name of Him who is called Prince of Peace, I implore thee receive this treaty of perpetual harmony, and grant me audience this night."

Then she seized Mary Tudor's slack hand and pressed the enchanted scroll into it.

TEN

By the time he'd withdrawn with Rhiannon to the Queen's Privy Chamber at Mary's command, alone and away from the prying eyes of court and commoner, Beltran's rage had dwindled to a cold fire that simmered in his gut. His blood no longer burned with the dangerous prelude to holy madness he'd been fighting all day, jaw clenched, as he thundered down the long road from Hatfield.

God's Blood, he hadn't even stopped to shave or shift his linen, just leaped straight from Serafin's saddle in the courtyard to invade the Great Hall. If not for the badges of his office, the ring and medallion that won a Blade of God instant *entrée* to any Christian court, he would have come too late.

"Thou might as well cease pacing about like a caged lion," Rhiannon said from the high chair where she perched, her slender form nearly lost in its gilded depths. Cool as a spring morn, damn the woman, as she sipped the sweet hippocras and nibbled steadily at the plate of sugar wafers a servant had brought.

How she'd paled when she saw him bearing down on her—as she bloody well should!—but the refreshment had brought the wild-rose color back to her cheeks. As she watched him over the rim of her goblet, her leaf-green eyes were huge. But the scornful tilt of her chin proclaimed defiance like a trumpet-blast.

"'Tis likely we'll be waiting some while for this audience with thy Queen." Her brows winged up—all wide-eyed innocence, with an imp of mischief winking in her gaze. "To pass the time, thou may wish to scrape the road-mud from thy boots."

Despite his simmering wrath, he was seized with an inappropriate urge to grin. Frightened though the girl clearly was, still her irrepressible spirit blazed forth to challenge him. Instead he slung the cape from his shoulders, tugged straight his black grosgrain doublet, and threw her a dark look.

Of course she was flawless in that stately court gown, slim and fair as a lily gleaming against ebony damask. The high ruff framed her delicate features, crowned by a torrent of moon-pale hair. The way her gown clung to the sweet curve of her breasts was indecent. Enough to make any man burn to unlace the stiff cage of her bodice—

Neatly Beltran cut off that dangerous thought. Perhaps some chilled wine would be wise after all.

"I should offer my compliments," he said roughly. "That was quick work at Hatfield. In the course of a single day you lied to me, pilfered my possessions while I prayed, beguiled a royal princess to abet your deception, and delayed—though not escaped—the Church's judgment."

Her incandescent eyes darkened to emerald. "I took nothing from thee save mine own property which thou had stolen. And thou had *no right* to detain me, nor thy Deity to judge me. I am not under thy Church's jurisdiction."

"And what of your duplicity? Haven't you some

ready excuse to justify that? You swore an oath on your honor, else I'd never have granted your parole."

For the first time he saw her hesitate, white teeth nibbling the pink curve of her lip. A blush warmed her creamy skin. *Caught her on the raw, did I?*

"Well am I rebuked for that," she said softly. A fringe of silken lashes dropped over her mutinous gaze. "I could argue niceties with thee, that I swore precisely thus-and-such. But the truth is that I wronged thee and sullied my own honor. Yet our need is so dire— my mother's need, my people's need. Even thine own folk need this peace, though they know it not. Don't you see? I *had* to reach Mary."

"Well, so you've done. Your blasphemous treaty's in her hands now. Still, a lie is a lie, Rhiannon, and you are forsworn. Pray God is merciful in his judgment."

So Beltran had always believed—that black was black and white was white, like the stark pattern of her gown. Why then did he find the sharp blade of his anger blunted by this show of remorse? Repentance was well and good for a sinner, but judging her soul was God's business. His own grim duty was to render Rome's judgment, and nothing she said now could prevent it.

No doubt she sensed his choler. In her high-backed chair she seemed lost, a wide-eyed waif in a world too large for her.

"As thou have said, the matter lies in the Queen's hands." Her pointed chin rose. "Now that I'm recaptured—if captured I am—what is thine intent?"

Unexpectedly, he hesitated. Before the level courage in her gaze, he pivoted and strode to the hearth. A servant had stirred the fire and it crackled briskly, but he caught up the poker and thrust it vigorously into the kindling.

He'd settled on his course during his day-long gallop. Her fate lay in his hands; she must be tried and condemned like any other witch. Indeed, she'd added thievery to her list of offenses. Why was he so reluctant to denounce her?

Was he growing soft in his dotage, neglecting the sacred calling he'd devoted his life to uphold? For the good of his own soul as well as hers, the girl must be made to recant.

A torrent of gruesome images flashed through his mind—the manacles, the rack, the Catherine wheel. They loomed before him like his own destiny, the tools of his trade he'd been ordered to use. Instruments of salvation, the Blades called them. Still, every particle of his being reared up against the monstrous thought of using them to break the stubborn spirit of the girl before him.

How the Cardinal would mock him for these weak-minded fancies.

"You're in London now, or as good as," he said curtly, scowling into the flames. "You've shown yourself before the Queen and her Spanish dons. I'd have left you with a gentler gaoler in Yardley, but your own willful deeds have removed that option from the table. Now I've no choice but to deliver you to St. Paul's. Given the Queen's involvement in this business, I've no doubt Bishop Bonner will wish to deal with you personally."

Beneath the mournful dirge of a pavane in the Great Hall, he heard her breath hitch. Viciously he thrust the poker in its stand and pivoted to confront her.

*Are you a man or a mouse? If you're going to con-
demn her, at least look her in the eye.*

He found her pale as milk, trembling but composed,
more composed than any woman facing the Bloody
Bishop's attentions had a right to be.

"If only she signs the treaty, thy bishop may do as
he likes," she said quietly. "I am but one woman. If
spending my life buys peace for this isle, then the coin
is well spent."

"Christ, Rhiannon! Don't be a damn fool—"

The rattle of the door brought him spinning around,
battle-ready, dropping by instinct into a crouch. He
barely restrained himself from drawing his sword.

*Easy, man. Draw steel before the Queen, and it'll
be you in the dungeon with the questioner.*

He hadn't expected Mary Tudor to return. He'd been
certain she'd pass the matter to some minor councilor,
one of Sir William Paget's lackeys or even the Lord
Chancellor himself—given the girl's unfortunate mention of the disgraced Elizabeth.

Yet the Queen herself rejoined them, quietly and
without fanfare, attended by two of her ladies.

Swallowing his astonishment, Beltran swept her a
leg. Rhiannon had sprung to her feet like a deer startling into flight, but she sank into a pretty curtsey.

Mary Tudor nodded gravely. Her voice was deep
and guttural as a man's, her gaze as direct. "We regret
the necessity to keep you waiting—Mother Church's
own enforcer and a foreign emissary. Under such extraordinary circumstances as you present, we felt it
meet to pray for guidance."

Beltran reached for the courtly manners he'd learned
in San Miguel and wore like a second skin in Rome.

"Your Majesty, all men know you as God's faithful handmaiden. You're wise to seek His guidance. Rome is ever grateful for your devotion."

"I am rather grateful myself," Mary murmured, "for the opportunity to behold with my own eyes one of the Pope's holy knights, a Blade of God. My blessed husband the King has spoken of your order, but this court has not been honored by a visit since my father's time."

Rhiannon stepped forward, hands clasped, all decorum and humility—rare for her, Beltran thought dryly—her elfin face alight with expectation. The hope he saw shining in her eyes, despite any conceivable chance for a good outcome, made his gut twist.

"Most Gracious Majesty," she began, "for the gift of thy welcome, I bear the gratitude of thy sister sovereign, Queene Maeve of the Summer Lands. When last the Fair Folk petitioned mortals for peace, I was a babe in swaddling. At that time, the King with whom the Faerie Queene treated was Arthur Pendragon."

Her voice wavered over the name, as though it held some deep meaning for her. Gaping like an idiot, Beltran swung toward her. Before he could speak, the dark-gowned woman near the Queen pushed forward, her hatchet face blazing with spite.

"Majesty, here's filthy witchery and accursed blasphemy! I told you this one's from the Devil."

"Peace, Susan." Mary Tudor raised a regal hand. "This matter cannot be so easy dismissed. You, Jane Dormer, stand at the door and ensure we are undisturbed from the Presence."

The younger attendant, a slender dark-eyed beauty who moved with willowy grace, bowed and glided to her station.

The elder Susan was forced to subside. Still her eyes darted over them, lingering covetously over jewels and fabrics. He'd seen her type often enough at the papal court—a grasper who sought her own profit by controlling access to the monarch. If Rhiannon wished to triumph over this one, she must buy her off. Then would the woman's greed take precedence over any religious sentiment she proclaimed.

At the head of the oaken table, Mary settled into her thronelike chair. Beltran mastered his towering impatience and forced himself to sit. Begrudgingly, the one called Susan poured the chilled hippocras. He waved the cup past without tasting.

Rhiannon pressed the goblet into his hand. "My lord, thou must take sustenance. Thou art exhausted from thy pursuit."

From habit, he started to refuse, then realized he was indeed parched and famished from hard riding, fueled only by a few bites of bread and cheese wolfed in the saddle. Thirstily, he downed a few swallows of the chilled wine. An encouraging smile lit the girl's face as she pressed a plate of wafers into his resisting hand.

"God's body, woman!" he muttered irritably and saw her flinch. "I'm no invalid or doddering grandsire to be cosseted. Look to your own welfare."

Mary Tudor was watching their byplay, her deep-set eyes shadowed with weariness. Thoughtfully she fingered the glittering rubies of a rosary she'd drawn from her girdle.

Beltran itched with unease. He hadn't expected this audience. Already she ought to have dispatched Rhiannon to the Tower for sedition—for aiding the

Queen's disgraced sister. Foreboding balled his fists on the table.

Her fate is in God's hands now. If the Queen turns against her, I can do naught in a civil court to aid her.

"So, it is Rhiannon of the Faeries, is it?" the Queen murmured. "Yesterday I would have sent you straight to the bishop, and thence to the fires at Smithfield. We're about grave business here, ridding this land of heresy—as you, Lord Beltran, can doubtless attest."

"No charge could be more serious." He leaned forward. "England's restoration to the Church is of prime importance. His Holiness ordered me here to support the Archbishop of Canterbury and Bishop Bonner in their work, to bring the Inquisition to England and serve as God's enforcer against the heretics. King Henry, God assoil him, imperiled the souls of all good Englishmen by his willful rebellion against Rome's authority."

"And all for the sake of that harlot—she who was Elizabeth's mother." A note of steel entered the Queen's mannish voice. "I do not call her my sister even now, for I'm all but certain my father is not her sire. She has the look of her mother's lowborn lutanist, Mark Smeaton."

Beltran recalled the musician who'd been convicted of adultery with the unfortunate Anne Boleyn. But, hearing the rosary beads rattle as Mary Tudor trembled with wrath, he judged this no time to indulge her jaunt over this lurid history. Truth be told, he'd admired Elizabeth Tudor's wit and spirit, but the lady was an undoubted heretic. If the Pope had his way, he'd be using the instruments of salvation against her own unruly soul.

But Rhiannon had fired up in defense of the woman who'd sheltered her.

"Majesty, I know thy quarrel with Her Grace is an old one, but she regrets so heartily how her conduct has displeased thee! Why, she charged me with this very message, to recall her tender love and devotion to thee, her sweet sister, and her submission to thee as her sovereign. Majesty, she is utterly ignorant and innocent of the Dudley plot—"

"Silence, you fool!" Susan uncoiled like a serpent from the shadows behind the throne. "Her Majesty has decreed no man or woman speak to her of the whore's daughter. Any message you bear must pass through the proper channels."

Meaning through you, or some accomplice on the Lord Steward's staff. Beltran eyed the vile creature with contempt. He thought less of Mary Tudor for tolerating such a woman among her ladies, despite whatever years of faithful service she claimed.

"Susan Clarencius speaks the truth." The Queen nodded grimly.

"But if Thy Majesty would only *listen*. She is thine heir—"

"Nay!" Mary's pain-rimmed eyes flashed with the dangerous Tudor temper. "We shall bear many strong sons to succeed us. One more word on that harlot's behalf, and you'll spend this night in the Tower for treason!"

If the Queen thought Rhiannon a foreign emissary—for surely she was no common Englishwoman, fashioned of moonbeams and starlight—she could not be accused of treason. Still, Beltran touched the girl's wrist and squeezed lightly in warning. Her bones were fragile as a sparrow's under his sword-hardened grip.

God save her, the breaking wheel would snap her limbs like kindling.

He sensed Rhiannon struggling to contain her own royal temper. Her color had risen, but she dropped her lashes over her angry eyes and said nothing. Beneath the Clarencius woman's gimlet gaze, he released her.

"The two of you make a rather unlikely pair," the Queen mused. "But the Lord works in mysterious ways. Perhaps, God's Vengeance, you will extend us your spiritual counsel."

"I'm no priest. Surely Reginald Pole or your own chaplain—"

"They dismiss this business as the sick fancy of a woman desperate to fill her womb. And so I am." The Queen's worn fingers trembled around her rosary. "But the truth has been shown to me. Like the Holy Virgin when the angel Gabriel descended unto her with his precious message, I too have been blessed with a vision."

"A holy vision?" Christ, the woman was demented. Beltran no more believed in holy visions than in goblins and Faeries.

And yet they existed.

The realization that he was entertaining Rhiannon's bizarre claims annoyed him. But the Queen's burning eyes—the passionate flush of the fanatic in her sunken cheeks—made him bite off the cynical dismissal he wanted to utter.

"While I kept vigil last night," the Queen said raptly, words tumbling forth in a gush, "I prayed for the strength to stay the course, to root out the heresy that has sprouted like a vile weed in our good English earth. For it was given me to know I must destroy it, and bring all heretics to repentance, before God will bless me with the son I must have.

"Until now, we have allowed Lutherans and Lollards and Anabaptists to recant before the fires are lit, and thus they are spared the flames. But so many return there, tumbling again into the Devil's snare, that Bishop Bonner has advised us to deny any soul convicted of heresy this chance for mercy…"

There was more in this vein. Beltran listened with the grave respect of a man indulging a child's fantasy. Inwardly, he was appalled. The Church needed a monarch on the English throne with a clear head on her shoulders—unclouded by delusions and holy visions—far more than the damn Lutherans needed more bloody martyrs.

But Rhiannon looked upon the raving old woman without shrinking, her face soft and glowing with compassion.

When Mary Tudor paused to draw a shaking breath, the girl said gently, "My dear lady, thou must not excite thyself in this way. Surely thy Maker knows thy devotion. Thou may be devout as any saint and yet parlay for peace with my kin."

This sympathy seemed to restore the Queen to some semblance of calm. Irritably she brushed off the Clarencius woman's anxious hovering. "God sent me a vision while I prayed. And in my vision, Rhiannon le Fay, I saw *you*."

Beltran frowned. What was this new madness? He distrusted the pious conviction that rang through the Queen's gruff voice.

"Nay, it is true! I saw you in a blue mantle with your silver hair unbound, bearing a scroll, and God's holy light streaming down around you. And behind you in the shadows...a guardian angel, wings spread and glittering with every hue under Heaven—oh, it was a glorious sight! I knew then you would come before me, bearing a missive from our Savior."

Under her breath, Rhiannon whispered, "Mother, this is too cruel. To play so upon her desperation..."

The Queen's lined features were foolish with hope and religious fervor. "Forsooth, I never expected your missive to take this form. My councilors are calling it witchcraft. But so it says in Scripture, that blessed are those who believe—"

Beltran could no longer keep silent. "If I heard this claim anywhere else, I'd call it outright blasphemy. This girl is no Virgin Mary incarnate, nor yet some holy messenger. At first I thought her a pure charlatan or a fool, or possibly mad. Now I confess I'm not certain *what* the Devil she is. But to claim—"

"I am astonished, Lord Beltran," the Queen said coldly, "to hear you say so—you who are sworn to defend the faith. Yet I know you too are sent to me from Him."

Shifting uncomfortably, he clamped down on an urge to pace. "I'm no saint or holy man."

"Why, to the contrary." Mary smiled beatifically. "You were part of my vision. For the angel who guarded the Virgin wore *your* face."

RHIANNON WAS WATCHING Beltran when the Queen uttered her surprising statement. She saw it hit him, low and hard, like a blow to the belly. A muscle flexed in his temple as he ground his jaw.

Even now, he seemed unaware of the shadowy Presence brooding over him, hands folded over the cruciform sword standing blade-down before him. The Being was watching her, clear eyes pulsing with banked fire.

Just as clearly, Mary Tudor was stone-blind to that looming Presence. Rhiannon doubted the Queen's vision came from her God. Nay, this was the work of Queene Maeve, weaving her magick over a weak-minded mortal to smooth the way for Rhiannon's arrival.

Yet her mother too had the Sight. If she'd seen Beltran Nemesto as an angel of the Christian God, Rhiannon could not discount it. But could he truly be so heedless of his own nature?

Now, the man himself struck silent by the lightning bolt the Queen had hurled with this pronouncement, Rhiannon seized her moment and stepped into the breach.

"Majesty, hast thou read the treaty?"

"I read it as an allegory, or a parable from Scripture." The Queen crossed herself, and behind her Susan Clarencius mirrored the motion. Rhiannon averted her gaze. "This Convergence is the Judgment Day, the end of time, when our Savior shall return, and all lands drown in blood and fire."

Rhiannon hesitated, reluctant to take advantage of the sick woman's delusions. But her words held a kind of truth, as a simple Christian soul might comprehend it.

Clearly, the Blade of God felt differently. His sun-bronzed hand crashed against the table, making the goblets jump. The gold ring with its scales of justice flashed.

"Damnation, I'll tolerate no more of this blasphemous talk! God does not speak through vagabond spitfires who appear in the wilderness spouting wild tales of Faeries and angels and some damned Convergence. If her claims have swayed even you, a God-fearing monarch, it merely proves how dangerous this young woman is. In the name of all that's holy, I demand she be remanded to my custody."

So unyielding, he condemned her, his face chiseled granite, steely eyes flashing as he pronounced her doom.

"I can have her in London before dawn," he said flatly. "There she may be questioned at length and leisure. Turn her over to me, and I swear I'll see her judged fairly."

"I'm afraid we've gone beyond that," the Queen said, faith shining from her sunken eyes. "I must follow my conscience in all things."

Beltran had gone silent and grim. His words, uttered low, echoed like a growl against the oak-paneled walls. "Madam, I forbid this. The Church forbids it. Your own councilors and bishops will forbid it. Don't let your hunger for a child lead you astray, and plunge your precious soul into jeopardy."

Despite her conviction, Mary Tudor paled. Scarcely able to breathe, Rhiannon watched the Queen wrestle with her misgivings.

"As the Pope's own emissary and his voice in this court, I cannot disregard your council." Mary sighed. "Nor yet can I dismiss this holy vision or the dictates of my conscience. It comes to this. The two of you must parlay, one with the other, and together advise me which course to take."

"Parlay—with him?" Rhiannon exclaimed. "Already I've talked myself hoarse in a vain effort to persuade this man to reason. If we parlayed a year and a day, still would he be blind and stubborn and pedantic as he is this very moment! There's nothing more I can say to him."

Nostrils flared, he eyed her coldly. "One does not *parlay* with God. Your own bishops will affirm that much, Your Majesty."

"Nonetheless, we have chosen this course." As if by magick, the frail woman with her shattered dreams and personal tragedies had vanished. Suddenly the Great Harry's daughter looked upon them, narrow-eyed and resolute, the famous Tudor temper burning in her cheeks.

"We shall instruct our Lord Chamberlain to assign you chambers at court through May Day festival, four days hence. You have so long to negotiate the terms of any treaty, so long to recommend some common course. Based upon your counsel and God's wisdom, which I seek daily through prayer, we shall determine England's best interests at that time."

The Queen's gaze faltered, grandeur dissolving as her thin shoulders slumped. "In that time, also, we shall consult with Spain and send word to our husband King Philip abroad. No doubt he will advise me of his wishes."

Tensely Rhiannon perched in her chair, warring impulses jostling in her heart. Philip of Spain would view a treaty with the Fair Folk as the Devil's bargain. He was Rome's creature, and peace ran counter to the goal of subjugating this unhappy isle.

Nor could it be coincidence that the Queen fixed her deadline upon the spring equinox, on a night when the Beltane fires would flare the length of Britain, when the door between the worlds opened and high magick could be wrought. Tingling from head to foot, she sensed enchantment at play. She could almost see it swirling in the air, like flecks of gold glittering in the candlelight.

Somewhere, the haunting sweetness of apple blossoms perfumed the air. She heard the husky chime of her sister's laughter. Suddenly Rhiannon was shivering, her slight frame trembling like a wind-kissed leaf.

"So be it, Majesty," she whispered. "I shall inform my companion, Lady Linnet Norwood. I pray she may be accommodated as well."

Abruptly Beltran thrust to his feet. Catching up his sable cloak, he swirled the heavy garment across her shoulders. She started to refuse it, the smooth fur and velvet lining warm with his body heat. The rich dark spice of frankincense filled her head.

"Take the damn cloak," he said curtly. "This room's drafty as a tomb. I'll find the Archbishop, and explain why our business must again be delayed. The Inquisition will simply have to wait."

Rhiannon knew she'd won a minor victory. At least the Queen hadn't dismissed her claim outright! She should be gracious in her triumph. Still, irritation prickled through her at his grudging tone.

"Lady grant me patience, sir, I hardly obliged thee to forsake thine affairs and harry me across the length of Britain, scolding and lecturing all the while."

"This island's spiritual welfare and the salvation of souls is God's business—and therefore mine," he muttered.

Regally Mary Tudor rose, signaling the royal audience ended. "I shall summon you both to account on May Day. My lady Jane Dormer will conduct you to the Chamberlain."

Recalling her court manners, Rhiannon swooped into her curtsey. She was grateful to follow the soft-voiced Lady Jane rather than Susan Clarencius, who threw her a baleful look as the Queen swept out. No doubt she'd have problems with that one before this business was through.

But her greatest problem was looming over her, hard and unsmiling, his unyielding grip steering her through the Privy Chamber. Sternly she rebuked herself for trembling beneath his touch. For all his dire threats and bullying, his overwhelming physical presence, he'd done nothing yet to harm her, even when his stubborn insistence on duty and virtue drove her nearly mad.

Warm beneath the seductive softness of his heavy warm cape against her bare shoulders, she glanced at him sidelong as he strode beside her. Firelight gleamed on his short-cropped hair and glittered gold along his unshaven jaw. From somewhere, the impulse seized her to run her fingers along that stern chin, feel his whiskers bristling against sun-browned skin, soften the mouth that had kissed her—was it only yesterday?

She wondered if he too sensed the potent magick simmering between them. Goddess knew he showed only seething impatience as they followed the demure Lady Jane through the Presence Chamber. Here they paused as mortal custom demanded to bow before the empty throne, under the sly and speculative gazes of the lingering courtiers.

He leaned close as he raised her up, voice low and intimate. "Satisfied with your work tonight, are you, my lady? You've managed to beguile both this most Catholic Queen *and* her heretic sister—which is no small feat. Are none of us poor mortals immune to your charms?"

Rhiannon knew she should guard her tongue, as she must beguile him too before Mary would sign the treaty. Yet his clear disapproval made her crackle with annoyance.

"No decent, warm-blooded woman could be satisfied with her entire escort slaughtered to a man, merely because they believed in me and followed me."

Thankfully, Ansgar lived. He was coming to court as soon as he regained his strength. But she had no intention of betraying that knowledge to Beltran.

"Thou seem to believe I act merely for mine own amusement, sir. I hardly know what else I may do to convince thee."

She could do what she'd done before he arrived, and lower the magickal veil that disguised her from mortal eyes. But then he'd be crying witch again.

His hand tightened beneath her elbow—an unsettling touch, oddly intimate since he'd stripped off his gauntlets—his sword-toughened palm warm with the divine fire coursing through his blood. Her skin tingled and the fine hairs on her arm lifted beneath the current of energy that surged between them.

Sweet with hippocras, his warm breath tickled her ear. "I don't know what to believe anymore, Rhiannon. Half this court fancies the Blessed Virgin appeared here tonight, fair and shining with silver light. If you don't come from God, you must come from the Devil. You've woven your spell over all of us."

At the head of the oak-paneled stair, with Linnet and Jane Dormer descending before them, she paused to glance up at him. Behind them a quartet of guards, bristling with halberds in the Queen's blue-and-green livery, shouldered past in a fast-moving block. Beltran backed her up against the wall to let them pass, while the ladies moved onward, unaware.

The movement brought him far too close, his broad chest and shoulders filling her vision. She backed away by instinct, almost stumbling into a page's alcove. She glimpsed whitewashed walls and a trestle table, benches empty, as her spine brushed the wall.

Still he loomed over her. Suddenly her heart was fluttering in her throat, breath quick and shallow. Heat coursed through her as she tipped back her head to look up into the burning cobalt fire of his gaze. Imposed like a bright shadow over his rugged features, the cold beauty of his angel stared down on her, a banner of golden hair streaming in the celestial wind.

Aye, *he* saw her, no doubt of it. Even while Beltran himself remained in stubborn denial of the supernatural Being that shared his flesh.

Yet the hard body against hers was mortal, taut with muscle, powerful heart thudding against her palm. Through the open door behind him, the world tramped past, while he stood so close his codpiece nudged her belly. And her own blood caught fire, the soft folds of her woman's place swelling like a ripe peach, tantalizingly bare beneath her skirts.

He need only gather those layers of damask and

muslin, lift the whalebone cage of her farthingale, skim his calloused fingers past the garters that bound her stockings to her thighs, to find bare skin and heat and the dampness of arousal collecting like dew in her womb.

Now she was blushing, on fire with the secret, lips parted as she stared breathless into his gaze.

"Damn," he said roughly, one hand rising to capture her jaw. His thumb brushed the tender curve of her lower lip. Possessed by the imp of mischief, she let her tongue flicker out to taste him—salt mingled with sugar from the wafers they'd nibbled. His breath rasped, a harsh catch that made her flush with sudden knowledge of her own feminine power.

"Rhiannon, this is madness." His thumb stroked her lip. "Wherever we're lodged tonight, I need to see you."

"Oh, but why?" That playful spirit still seized her. Her lips curved in a teasing smile.

"You know why, God help us." His eyes were hooded, watching her parted lips. A breath and he'd be close enough to kiss.

His invocation made her shudder, breaking the spell of madness that held her. Morrigan's curse echoed in her head.

If you couple with a mortal man, you'll become one of them forever.

"Dear Lady!" she cried softly. Her grip tightened on his doublet, holding them apart. "I can't. What shall come of this lunacy between us?"

"The Devil if I know," he muttered, bending toward her.

She could taste the wine-scented sweetness of his breath. A powerful lassitude swept over her, making

her knees weaken. Helpless as a floating leaf in the rising tide of passion, she leaned toward him. Her eyelids
fluttered closed.

The shock of his mouth on hers made her gasp, a
man's hard driving hunger spiced with the sweet bite
of hippocras. She clung to his broad shoulders for pur-
chase as the world shifted around her, felt powerful
muscle flex under her desperate grip. When her mouth
opened beneath the fierce possession of his kiss as
though he had every right to claim her, a low groan
rumbled through him.

"My God, Rhiannon…"

Beyond words, she moaned softly in reply.

His arms swept around her and dragged her hard
against his body, overwhelming her with the searing
heat of the divine Presence that crackled like brush-
fire within him. The dizzying spice of frankincense
rose from his travel-stained doublet and made her head
spin. Yet she met him kiss for kiss, the slow burn of
passion building like magick between them. The deep
pulse of pleasure made her arch against the hot bulge of
aroused male flesh that jutted against her belly, barely
contained by his codpiece.

When his big hands gripped her buttocks and
snugged her closer, she surrendered to the sweet ache
between her thighs and undulated slowly against him.

Beneath the noisy bustle of the staircase and the
muted din of the great hall, she barely heard the coarse
comment as someone stumbled past. But she felt Beltran stiffen, heard the low curse that exploded from
him. Dragged back to awareness of their surroundings—hardly private for a tryst—she caught the tail
end of the ugly exchange.

"...so much for chastity! They're supposed to be fighting priests. His blade will be swiving that sweet sheath tonight."

In a blur of motion, Beltran released her and spun toward the offending voice. Rhiannon blurted a protest, hand flying to her tingling lips, fearful any moment she'd see the great sword of Judgment flashing down. Was it only she who heard the lion's roar of rage blasting forth from his angel, felt the floor tremble beneath her feet?

Beltran's fist shot outward and cracked into a man's sneering face. Here and there along the stair, scattered cries rose as the gold-clad gallant reeled back, sprawling on his rump across the stairs.

"Merciful Goddess!" Seeing Beltran tower over the luckless lad, Rhiannon leaped forward and seized his arm. Tendons stood taut beneath her grip, but he contained himself and stood glaring down on the fellow.

The gallant pressed a handkerchief against his bleeding nose and glared back. A torrent of heated words in a foreign tongue spilled out.

"Hell." Beltran heaved a sigh and dragged a hand roughly through his hair. "One of the Queen's Spaniards."

Rhiannon eyed the astonished spectators ranked on the stairs—a gaping Linnet and Jane Dormer among them. "I fear thou may have a greater problem."

Halfway down the stair, arrested in midconversation, an authoritative figure with a flowing russet beard stood riveted, bright in crimson robes and cap. A gold cross swung from his belt that made her avert her burning eyes.

Beltran followed her gaze and bit out an oath that

had no business on the lips of a Church enforcer. Then
his shoulders straightened as he made a leg. "*Bene-
dicite*, my lord Archbishop."

ELEVEN

AT DAWN, BELTRAN threw down his quill and rolled the kinks out of his knotted shoulders. Sometime during his interminable session in the confessional with the Archbishop, a band of pain had clamped down around his brow.

Healthy as a horse under most circumstances, he rarely suffered headaches or any physical malady. He'd always boasted a robust constitution and miraculous rate of healing from his rare battle wounds.

But if anything could give a man the megrims, last night would do it. Groaning, he rose and swung his arms vigorously across his chest.

The chambers assigned him were comfortable, the dayroom furnished in the somber splendor of Spain, but cold as a damn tomb. He hadn't paused to build a fire before penning this explanatory epistle to his mentor Cardinal Calvino. He needed to dispatch it quickly, before the news of last night's spectacle reached Rome through other means.

Now the rising sun, streaming between the curtains, scalded his tired eyes like fire.

Grimly enduring this added penance, he sanded the parchment, then pressed his signet ring into the soft wax. Let it go to Rome with his report on the Inquisition's progress in England before he dove into the rest of his work.

A courteous missive to the infamous Bishop Bonner was the next order of business.

A soft scuff made him swing toward the interior door. Ever since he'd stormed irritably back after Matins, feeling somehow less eased by the rite of Confession than usual, he'd been trying to forget *two* bedchambers shared this dayroom. The damn Chamberlain had assigned Rhiannon the other.

He couldn't seem to rid his mind of her tempting nearness. She flickered and danced in his mind like a lit candle, beckoning him with her glowing light—the promise of warmth and life and grace he'd never found in the cold comfort of his religion, or in the harsh exigencies of its discipline.

Even now, the only constraint holding him on *this* side of that door was the knowledge Rhiannon wasn't alone. Her mysterious companion, that demure dark-haired beauty from God knew where, shared her chamber and her bed.

He could imagine the disturbance he'd cause if he strode through those doors, randy as a stallion in mating season, and flung back the curtains. Deep in the feather-tick the two girls would cower, screaming until the servants came running. Then would Beltran have a greater scandal to contend with.

Whatever's left of my name after last night would be shredded. The Blades would throw me out of their sainted order. And the prospect should alarm me, damn it.

It was growing harder to pretend the fire of faith that once burned in his belly hadn't guttered and dimmed. Where the hot ember of devotion should glow, his heart and soul stood cold as an unlit forge.

*God has betrayed you, Vengeance. He lost all claim
to your devotion when He cast you out.*

This bleak shell of service to a distant and unfeel-
ing Master was what God had left him instead of—

A tentative knock jerked him awake. The fog of
half-recalled dreams rolled back.

If he loved his soul, he should pretend he'd never
heard that sound. The thought of Rhiannon le Fay tightened his groin, set his heart hammering like a schoolboy.

"Enter," he called gruffly, running a hand over his
bristling jaw. After the night he'd had, he must look
like a pirate.

Light as a wood-sprite or the spirit of spring, she
slipped into the dayroom. A shaft of sunlight bathed
her in radiant light.

Hungrily his eyes devoured her—silver hair twisted
into a chignon at her nape, dainty frame encased in
blush-rose velvet, the tiny waist he could span with
his hands, the sweet curve of her breasts like ripe
peaches against the fabric. The gown brought color
to her creamy cheeks and deepened her bewitching
eyes to emerald.

Yet his keen eyes didn't miss her pallor or the violet
shadows beneath her eyes. The strain of her mission,
the hostile scrutiny of this Catholic court, was already
taking its toll.

Beneath his regard, her lashes dropped. She dipped
into a small curtsey.

"I know thou slept but poorly, for I heard thee pacing
to and fro. Is there any use to bid thee good morrow?"

"I find little that's good about it." Abruptly he
turned away from this new temptation. He wanted to

stride across the chamber and crush her in his arms, pluck the pins from her hair until it tumbled in gilded ringlets around her shoulders. He wanted to haul her against his throbbing length as he'd done last night and kiss her until she turned wanton.

Instead he gathered his correspondence for the courier. "I'm busy. What do you want here?"

"I regret disturbing thy crowded schedule." Her edged tone told him she resented his brusque dismissal—unsuited to her royal dignity. Yet she clung to her temper. "But we've much to discuss, my lord. Thy Queen has commanded it."

"Not my Queen, and I'm not hers to command." Impatient, he tossed down the documents and strode to the window. In the cobbled courtyard, a cluster of mounted nobles gathered. Off for a morning jaunt, he supposed, with nothing better to occupy them.

Her skirts rustled as she swept after him, quick steps betraying her agitation. "Would thy Church have thee yield, and leave me unopposed to court the Queen's favor?"

Aye, there's the rub—and she's clever enough to know it. Acknowledging her thrust, he barked a laugh and gripped the lintel, shoulders bunching beneath his doublet. The hellish pain in his head gave another nasty throb. Behind him, her steps halted.

Senses heightened by her nearness, he heard her quickened breath—a tribute to the awareness thrumming between them. The haunting sweetness of violets teased his nose. He'd never smell that fragrance again without thinking of her.

Lightly, her hand touched his shoulder. "Thou art in pain. Let me ease thy suffering."

"More of your magick? I think not." He pivoted to confront her, hooking his hands in his belt to keep his resolve. Otherwise he'd close his hands around her waist, slender and pliant as a sapling birch, and drag her into his arms.

Her upturned face chided him, ash-dark brows winging up. "Art thou afraid of me, Vengeance?"

That tore it. With a growl, he caught her waist, pulled her hard up against the throbbing length that pressed behind his codpiece. "Is this what you want, princess? Shall we resume where we left off last night?"

A gasp slipped past her parted lips. Yet she flung back her haughty head, eyes blazing green fire. "A bit importunate for a Church enforcer, but this will do."

Butterfly-light, her fingers grazed his temples, then cupped his head with both hands. Mesmerized, he stared into her determined gaze. *I wanted her wanton…*

The rising sun streamed through the window around them. The light tricked his eyes, lit her skin with an alabaster glow, until her radiant beauty shone like moonlight. Her touch made him tingle, sent shivers sparking over his skin. All the blood rushed to his groin.

God's fury, he wanted to tear aside the thrice-bedamned codpiece between them. Wanted to gather her skirts above her waist to expose her pouting mound of Venus…wanted to make her moan for him, drench his fingers in her salty cream…wanted to sheathe his aching length in her heat. He burned to tug down her bodice, bare her succulent little breasts, suckle her impudent nipples until she writhed against him.

As though she could read the dangerous images smoldering in his eyes, she jerked her hands away.

The glow behind her elfin features flickered wildly. A rosy blush suffused her; she moistened her pink lips.

Gradually, as that otherworldly glow faded, the abominable hammering in his skull receded.

"I'll be damned," he said hoarsely. "I don't know whether you've healed me or merely distracted me."

She gazed into his eyes, her lips parted. "I healed thee, Beltran. When wilt thou open thine eyes?"

He shook his head. "Either way, I'm not complaining. Kiss me, Rhiannon."

A frown flickered between her brows. She stirred against him, small hands rising to grip his biceps. "My lord, we can't do this."

Modest as a damn virgin once more, something like fear mingled with arousal in her eyes. Well, no doubt that was for the best.

Beltran dragged in a breath and ordered his hands to release her. They obeyed him, but one rose to cup her cheek. Her silken skin was warm beneath his calloused palm.

For a heartbeat, her face turned into his touch, lids fluttering closed. Her lips brushed his palm.

"Please, Beltran," she whispered. Begging him to keep his distance. Did she lack the will to pull away of her own accord?

Frustration knotted his gut. With a low oath, he released her and strode off, leaving her alone at the window.

"Why did you come here, Rhiannon?"

She remained near the window, facing away from him. "My lord, we must talk, and time is short. I am summoned to ride with the court this morn. Wilt thou accompany me?"

That was the last damn thing he needed after last night's scandal—to trail after Rhiannon le Fay like a besotted schoolboy.

But he'd told the Archbishop he would spend time in her presence to collect evidence against her. Good Catholic that she was, Mary Tudor would never sign that infernal treaty if the Church stood against it—no matter what her fool's vision told her.

Reginald Pole the Archbishop had been unequivocal during their session in the confessional last night. If Beltran intended to continue rising despite his recent slip—as he surely did—convicting and condemning Rhiannon le Fay for witchcraft was the swiftest way to do it.

"How do you find Lord Beltran Nemesto, my lady?"

The unexpected question brought Rhiannon alert, her heart speeding suddenly, shredding the dreamlike daze where she'd floated all morning. Awareness returned of the gray mare's supple stride beneath her, the soft murmur and creak of the royal hunting party threaded through the forest all around, a spring breeze stirring the boughs and blowing a silver ringlet loose from her chignon to tickle her cheek.

Ever since she'd unwisely taunted him—*Art thou afraid of me, Vengeance?*—ever since he'd retaliated by dragging her into his arms. Despite her certain knowledge of the consequences if she weakened and tumbled into his bed, the smoldering blue heat of his gaze had nearly melted her knees.

Even now, a good hour later, the memory of that swift rising passion left her almost swooning. Heat flooded her tingling body and pooled where her thighs gripped the saddle.

"As bad as that, my lady?" the speaker asked wryly.

Rhiannon dragged her scattered wits together before the Queen of England's probing gaze. "I'm honored by thy concern for mine affairs."

"Ah, but they're also England's affairs...or so you tell me."

Overhead, dappled green-gold light spilled through the tapestry of budding branches above the Honour— the wild, wooded deer park that bordered Hampton Court. Beneath it, Mary's skin appeared sallow, the auburn hair under her Spanish hood thin and lifeless. With a healer's instinct, Rhiannon knew the aging Queen had slept poorly. The throbbing ache and bloating of her moon flow had returned.

In truth, this morning ride was the last thing she needed.

But Mary was a hardy soul; she'd endured far worse in her solitary life. Physical suffering was nothing to her, set against the bitter knowledge that her womb remained barren, her women's courses drying up within her, the moon tides of life and passion no longer flowing. Now the winter of life crept upon her, freezing her soul and body.

While Mary despaired, the royal husband she adored frolicked through Europe with the beautiful Christina of Denmark, his acknowledged mistress.

Soft with compassion, Rhiannon replied to Mary's words.

"The welfare of thy realm and mine are inextricably linked, Majesty—though thy Church enforcer seems determined not to see it." With a flash of spirit, she tossed her head. "Still, I've not yet finished with him."

Behind her, she knew Beltran rode, corded thighs gripping his white stallion, his hooded gaze vigilant as he followed the Queen's retinue. He appeared utterly unaware of her, Rhiannon saw irritably, absorbed in conversation with Spain's representative at this most Catholic court—the Spanish ambassador, the Duke of Feria, whose dark flashing eyes strayed so often to the winsome Jane Dormer.

A fine group we make. The ambassador makes sheep's eyes at the Queen's most chaste and seemly lady, while the Faerie emissary sits dreaming of the Church enforcer…

Without turning her head, she kept Beltran at the edge of vision. Yet she remained keenly aware of his precise location among the party. Just as he was attuned to hers.

Catholic chastity or not, wherever his duty might lie, he wanted her. She wondered if he lay wakeful at night as she did, her body aching for his touch. Would he slide both hands under the bedclothes to grip the hard length of his manhood and think of her?

The image left her breathless and flustered. A scalding tide of warmth swept her cheeks.

Beside her, Mary Tudor chafed her swollen belly.

"The Blades of God are Heaven's most vigilant servants, Lady Rhiannon. If you can persuade Lord Beltran your cause is right and holy, the Pope himself will surely bless it."

Unlikely, she thought dryly. The Catholic pope would rather see her burning in the Christian hell.

The Church had ever been the Fair Folk's most implacable foe.

"Be assured I shall do my level best to persuade him," she said neutrally.

Still the Queen seemed preoccupied, her old bones aching until Rhiannon's throbbed in sympathy. Ceaselessly, the older woman rubbed her belly beneath its blood crimson stomacher. The color filled Rhiannon with foreboding.

Red is for heartbreak.

Abruptly Mary gestured her courtiers to fall back. Rhiannon drew rein, but Mary signaled her to keep pace. Together, they rode on.

Dainty Astolat picked her way along a wooded bank carpeted with ivy and leaped a little streamlet. Mary's blood bay courser vaulted the barrier as easily, but a grimace of pain twisted the Queen's features under the jarring impact of landing.

Impulsively Rhiannon reached toward her. "Dear madam, let me mix thee a posset to ease thy pain."

"I was born to suffer pain," the Queen said dispassionately. "It began when I was a little maid of twelve, when That Woman appeared at court with her French fashions and her harlot's ways to tempt my father from my mother's side—she, Katherine of Aragon, daughter to Isabella of Castile, and never less than a very saint."

"Majesty, pray do not distress thyself…"

"Not long afterward he banished my mother to the drafty castle where she met her death. I never saw her again. When he married That Woman, I was exiled from court, my household dissolved, and sent to serve her bastard Elizabeth."

By now the Queen's dispassion had vanished. The

venom that dripped from Mary's voice made Rhiannon prickle with foreboding. A hectic flush rose in the Queen's sunken cheeks; her eyes glittered with a zealot's fervor.

"Once my sister was a sweet child, despite her blood, and I was fond of her. After my father's death, her heretical leanings developed and she became the scandal of this kingdom. I've always known she whored for her own stepfather. I speak of that devil Queen Katherine Parr wedded when she outlived my father—Lord Admiral Tom Seymour, an intemperate rogue with dangerous ambitions. Elizabeth spread her legs for him at the tender age of fourteen, if you can credit that. And him lusting for this girl whose breasts had barely budded, like a man possessed—or bewitched. If you'd seen the way she flaunted herself before anything with a codpiece, the way she swayed her hips and smiled, goading men to tumble her and do it roughly—"

Appalled, Rhiannon tried to staunch this sickening flood of poison.

But the poison must come out. Spittle glistened on the Queen's pitiless lips. "I have it from a reliable source that she was seen…by the laundress or the gardener or something like, perhaps some tradesman visiting the house, I don't recall…seen backed against a tree, with her bodice open and skirts pushed above her waist, moaning against her lover's fingers. And this is the Jezebel you would champion, Rhiannon le Fay, the serpent you would have me welcome to my bosom!"

The urge to defend Elizabeth from this shameful slander burned in her heart and trembled on her lips. Yet, before the Queen's virulent hatred and envy of her lovely young sister, Rhiannon dared to say nothing. Defending Elizabeth now would only poison her own cause in Mary's eyes. Still, she couldn't bear to listen to the ugly diatribe.

"If indeed that event took place, Majesty, she was so young..."

"Then I knew she was no king's daughter." Mary went on relentlessly. "She is That Woman's bastard by her lute player, Mark Smeaton, just as I've always maintained. And rest assured he went to the gallows for it. My father came to his senses and lopped off That Woman's head. If true justice had been served, she would have burned for the vile adulteress she was."

The Queen swiveled toward her, nearsighted eyes squinting, as though sensing the white outrage that blazed through Rhiannon. Elizabeth was part-Fae and a king's daughter, just as she was herself. She had to remind herself forcibly that Mary Tudor was ill and old and weary, that her vitriol wasn't aimed at her.

"I relate you this sad history so you may understand, my lady, that I will tolerate no intervention or meddling on her behalf. Whatever may come, Elizabeth has earned her fate thrice over." The Queen drew an unsteady breath. "I shall overlook your ignorance, as a foreigner to this land, so long as it goes no further. That blessed vision of mine was God's command to give you fair hearing. Nonetheless, my councilor the Archbishop warns me not to presume I know God's will."

Mary paused. "I tell you frankly, Rhiannon le Fay, that unseemly business on the stairs last night did not advance your cause."

Rhiannon would not abandon Elizabeth to her fate, but recognized she must turn now to her own defense. "Last night's occurrence was—unfortunate, that I grant. My lord sought only to defend me from vile slander. Any knight or gentleman would have done the same."

"He spilled blood within the Verge of the Court." Mary frowned. "Some would call that a hanging offense. The usual penalty in my reign is imprisonment. My father would have had his hand off."

Rhiannon recoiled in horror. *Dear Lady, these mortals are savages, just as my sister always said.*

The Queen sighed. "Unfortunately, the man my lord struck is a member of the Duke of Feria's household, and he is bringing a formal complaint."

"Perhaps I should bring my own complaint against the Duke's man." Rhiannon tossed her head, heat blazing in her cheeks. "He insulted me most foully."

The older woman's face darkened. "I would not wish to be compelled to delve too deeply into the conduct of those involved—not least your own behavior."

"I tell thee I did *nothing.*"

"I'm granting you a favor, Rhiannon le Fay, by refusing to hear the matter." The Queen's voice hardened. "At least until your business here is finished. As for your so-called defender, he should count himself fortunate to get off with a reprimand and steep fine."

A fine? Well, no doubt his Church can afford it. Rhiannon exhaled, a tide of relief sweeping through her. She couldn't have borne seeing Beltran suffer, merely for defending her from a foul-tongued rogue.

"Majesty, thou art merciful," she murmured. Queens liked their small favors to be received with fawning gratitude. The words were as close as Rhiannon could bring herself to it.

The dangerous color receded from Mary's sallow

cheeks as she accepted the accolade. "Have a care for him, my lady. Lord Beltran Nemesto is a protégé and favorite of Cardinal Calvino, one of the Inquisition's most fervent champions, and known to the Pope himself. His Grace the Archbishop tells me Nemesto stands on the brink of a great promotion and a glorious future."

"Why, is it so?" Rhiannon slanted a glance over her shoulder.

Beltran's white stallion paced nearly within earshot, his rider no doubt burning to know what Mary was telling her. When their gazes locked, his keen eyes seared through her like blue flames. With difficulty, she broke the heated contact and turned away.

Mary toyed with her reins. "He's a man of ambition, your protector. Risen from collier's brat to nobleman in a single generation, and I'm told he intends to lead his order. Likely to succeed as well. These continental wars have thinned their ranks, and the Don's post stands vacant."

Rhiannon spoke carefully. "Certainly he's a formidable man—pious and constant, and fearsome in battle. No doubt he has earned the honor."

"I'm informed he lacks but one credential. He's zealous in rooting out witches and heretics, thorough and ruthless in his interrogations. His preferred outcome is for the accused to recant, though he condemns those damned souls he cannot save." The Queen's mouth thinned. "But he's never yet sent one to the stake. Some view that as a sign of squeamishness. Burn a witch or heretic, prove his devotion to the Inquisition, and his rise is assured."

Rhiannon battled a surge of dizziness, the green-

wood swirling around her. Swaying in the saddle, she
breathed deeply to clear her head. Could this require-
ment explain his fervent pursuit of her, his dogged insistence on her interrogation? Was he seeking a good
candidate for burning?

Nay, surely he could not intend that fate for her.
Despite his orthodox views and rigid thinking, she'd
believed him a decent man, an honorable man. Even a
knight in shining armor from a troubadour's lay, like
her foster-father had been.

But the Catholic Queen was watching her too
closely, that narrowed gaze too suspicious for comfort. Rhiannon dared not betray fear, which the fanatical woman beside her would consider proof of guilt.

"Surely my lord would never condemn an—an innocent woman to such a gruesome end." Carefully she
steadied her voice. "I'm certain he will follow his conscience."

Mary waved that away, the signet ring of England
flashing on her bony finger. "To speak plainly, Lady
Rhiannon, Mother Rome would suffer a great loss if
God's Vengeance ever faltered in his faith. Of course,
he's a red-blooded male, prone to temptation like any
man living—including my own dear husband."

The bitter rage of a woman spurned hardened the
Queen's voice. Her words sliced into Rhiannon like
a sharp-edged blade. "Your uncommon beauty has
stirred discord in this court, like mythical Paris with
his golden apple. Like Aphrodite who won the prize,
you beguile my lords—even those sworn to Christ. You
spawn spite and envy among my ladies."

Rhiannon shook her head in disbelief. She must
be speaking of some other woman, some mortal not

tainted by mixed blood. Either that, or it was Susan Clarencius's malice. "Surely thou art mistaken. I am no great beauty."

"Hear me well, Rhiannon le Fay," the Queen of England warned, "and tax not my patience with false claims of modesty. Tempt the greatest Blade of God in a generation to stray from his holy duty, now when the Church needs his service the most, and I swear I'll send you to the stake myself."

TWELVE

RHIANNON MANAGED HER escape by remaining behind when one of the Queen's courtiers spied a fox. The entire party went thundering after the poor creature in exuberant high spirits. Stomach churning with nausea, nerves humming with fear, heart skipping with the fox's desperate terror, Rhiannon slipped into the trees and slid from her saddle.

She sank to her knees and pressed her hands against the loamy soil. Eyes closed, she poured a stream of faltering life-energy into the good earth, imploring the Goddess to lend speed to the fox's limbs and strength to his panicked heart.

Run hard and fast, my friend. Find your earth and burrow deep...deep...where these cruel mortals cannot find you.

Dear Lady, if only she could do the same. The Queen's blind zeal terrified her, that poisonous hatred of her own kin, her virulent jealousy of all women younger and fairer than she. Whatever advantage Queene Maeve's magick had won for Rhiannon, that so-called vision that had prised open the dark closet of Mary Tudor's narrow soul, the Catholic priests were working hard to undo it. Without Beltran's support— and she knew how likely that was—the English Queen would turn on her like a rabid dog.

What was one more heretic screaming in the fires at Smithfield?

Gradually the peace of earth and growing things settled into her soul. Her panicked heartbeat slowed. Hearing the gentle gurgle of water, she led Astolat along a narrow tongue of land, between the river and an inlet's still green glimmer. A thick stand of greensward hemmed the water, hiding from view the gentle stretch of the Thames beyond. Protected by water on three sides, she felt her clamoring panic fade to a whisper.

Gratefully, the mare dipped her nose to the inlet. Rhiannon knelt alongside, rose-pink skirts billowing around her. Though the still water was carpeted with emerald moss, fear had parched her throat.

When the mare's head lifted, ears swiveling forward, the breath hitched in Rhiannon's lungs. When a horse whickered, her chest tightened.

A moment later Beltran strode into view, brow furrowed, reins gripped in a gloved fist. As he glimpsed her kneeling form, his grim features eased. Loosing his stallion with a friendly slap, he circled the inlet, closing the distance between them. She tingled with anticipation.

He'd resumed the stark black garments of an almost-priest, severe and foreboding, the double-handed sword jutting over his shoulder. A stray shaft of sunlight pierced the thick-woven branches to blaze in his tawny hair. Fire flashed on the gold-and-steel medallion against his heart—his badge of service, token of his holy vow.

What was it worth to him, that emblem of militant Christianity? Enough to see her burn for it?

From his towering height, he frowned down on her, gaze inscrutable as he searched her upturned features.

"Are you well?" he said abruptly.

Not precisely. She managed a shaky laugh. "Pray do not trouble thyself. Thou art not my keeper."

"The hell I'm not, at this court," he said grimly. "What's amiss?"

"'Tis nothing." She swept a hand outward, a shadow of her usual imperious self. "Return to thine own kind, my lord. While my business at this court remains undone, thou need not fear I'll fly from it."

Or from you, badly though I might yearn to.

An involuntary shiver raced through her, raising goosebumps on her skin. His tawny brows drew together.

"Rhiannon, what did the Queen say to you?"

"Rather I might ask what the Spanish Ambassador said to thee," she countered, rash and heedless with unstrung nerves. "Some new command from thy holy stronghold at San Miguel? Thou wished to be in London, and here thou art—or nearly so. Why trouble me any further when thine Inquisition beckons?"

In part, she said it to draw him out. He'd never said precisely what brought him, save that it concerned the Queen's closest counselor, the Archbishop. And he'd thrown around easily enough the name of Bloody Bonner, the Archbishop's lackey who did the Inquisition's burning.

"I've spoken to the Archbishop, and I'll dispatch a note to Bonner before dinner. It's Inquisition business." Irritably he shrugged that aside, dropping to his knees beside her. "The Queen—has she ruled against you?"

"That would please thee, would it not?" she flashed.

"Nay, she is undecided, and not inclined to rush to judgment until May Day, three day hence. She continues to insist I must persuade *thee*. If I loved my people even a little less, cared even a little less for peace, I would quite have given up on thee—"

To her shame, her voice cracked. Eyes stinging, she bit her lip and ordered her tongue silent. In a moment she'd be weeping, and that her pride would not tolerate.

Despite her resolve, a single traitorous tear spilled from her brimming eyes.

"Rhiannon," he murmured, more tender than was his wont. Hunkered on one knee, he gripped her chin gently. "Let us have a moment's peace. For once, let's not talk about my God or your Faeries."

"In that case, I suppose we must be silent." Fiercely she blinked the tears back.

Through her blurred vision, she saw not the Blade of God's strong-hewn features—marked by the slow hand of time—but the brooding tenderness of the Presence, stern and beautiful, shadowy wings curved over them.

"What else have we to discuss, my lord?" she asked both of them—this hard-faced warrior of unflinching duty, and the celestial Being that was somehow part of him.

One finger caught her defiant tear as it spilled, his leather glove brushing her skin so soft it made her shiver.

"You know what lies between us." Eyes hooded by gold-tipped lashes, he raised the sparkling tear to his lips. "Don't you?"

She knew what he made her feel, this alarming and contradictory creature, marriage of mortal and divine. He made her flesh weaken, her heart flutter, her body burn beneath his touch. If she surrendered she was lost...her immortality, her dream of belonging somewhere, anywhere. But surely there was no harm in touching him, brushing the crisp golden stubble that glittered against his hard jaw.

At the touch, his eyes flashed open, summer-blue. She was drowning in them. Casting aside caution with both hands, she reached for him, arms winding around his neck.

"I crave thee like a very wanton," she whispered, astonished by her own boldness. "I've never known anything like thee—despite everything in me that warns me away. Wilt thou kiss me once?"

He uttered a laugh, a groan of despair, she hardly knew what. His arms closed around her, strong and certain, hauling her hard against him. Then he kissed her as he'd done before, his mouth hot and fierce and hungry. Senses reeling, her mouth flooded with rich claret and tart red apples.

Ah, what was it about apples...?

The thought slid away as she yielded to the seductive lure of him. Like a blind woman her hands sought the bulging power of his muscled shoulders, flexing under smooth brocade. The short spikes of his hair curled around her fingers, the hot skin of his nape burned her. He made quick work of her hood, plucked the pins from her hair until it tumbled down around them in a cloud of violet scent.

"I've wanted to do that for days," he muttered, cradling her head, plunging his hard warrior's hands into the heavy tendrils. "You should never wear it up."

She gasped a little laugh. "That would hardly be convenient."

Oh, this was more, much more than she'd dreamed, more than she knew was prudent. As she gasped for breath, his lips found her throat, rough whiskers rasping against tender skin. His kisses made her shiver with a strange fever.

Surely that was why she didn't protest—silent for just a moment longer, one moment more of this swooning pleasure—as he eased her to the earth. The fresh scent of spring rose around them, mingled with frankincense from his hair and clothing. A bulwark of solid earth lay under her, steadied her. Yet she was drunk from his breath and lips and tongue plundering the fragile hollow of her throat, his hard length pressing into her.

When his hands found her breasts, her eyes fluttered open. The stiffened busk of her English bodice was a carapace between them; she could hardly feel his touch. She could have wept with frustration. Her breasts ached for him to touch her, really touch her.

The deft tug of his fingers loosened her laces. A voice of caution whispered in her brain.

"Dear Goddess," she breathed, clinging to his shoulders, anchoring herself as the world revolved around them. "I never expected this."

"I'll never harm you, I swear it," he said huskily, lips moving against the upper swell of her breast. Heat ignited along her skin. "If you knew how I've dreamed of this. Let me see you, princess."

Nay, we mustn't, because… But she couldn't quite recall why they mustn't. While he dealt with her laces, she thrilled and tingled. The shell of her bodice opened, cool air raising shivers on her skin. The sleeves slid

from her shoulders as he brushed aside layers of velvet
and muslin, baring her body to his touch.

At last his hands were on her breasts—the hard calloused hands that had once saved her life. She was
melting and tingling and floating all at once. The wet
heat of his mouth…merciful Goddess, his tongue…
teased her exquisitely sensitive nipples. As he nuzzled
and tasted, heat pooled between her thighs.

No doubt a Christian maid would have blushed and
hidden her face. But Rhiannon felt no shame in her
woman's body or her passion, new and wondrous as
it was.

When she hoisted her heavy lids, her breath escaped
in a rush. For it was *he*—the Presence—light spilling
like water from his cobalt eyes, silver locks streaming
in the astral wind, opal-and-garnet wings unfurled to
shelter them.

"So beautiful," she marveled. Those eyes of light,
like wheels of fire, seared into her. "Who *art* thou?"

The Being's lips brushed her brow. He whispered
something—a word—

But she heard nothing save a thunderous hiss, like
liquid sizzling against hot stones, as a massive dark
shape erupted from the mossy inlet beside them.

BELTRAN'S WORLD NARROWED to the woman who lay beneath him—at last!—on the leaf-carpeted earth. As he
wrestled with the impenetrable armor of her thrice-
damned bodice, he thought his head would explode
with frustration. Finally, he managed to unlace her.
God's fury, she was everything he'd imagined and
more.

Creamy skin flawless as damask, flushed with passion from his touch. Breasts pert and perfect as ripe peaches, just enough to fill a man's hand. Any more would be wasted. Pale pink nipples jutting under his hungry gaze. Her sighs and murmurs had him aching behind his codpiece, longing to tear the damn thing off.

When he tasted her at last, teasing her nipples, suckling them to hardened buds between his lips, her soft cries nearly drove him mad.

Christ on the Cross, did she even realize the way she was moving under him, thighs parting beneath her velvet skirts, letting him lodge so sweetly between them? He should give her more time—if he could stand it—before he eased his hands under her skirts, past the ribboned garters around her thighs to stroke her virgin-soft skin.

The thought of Rhiannon, warm and willing for his touch, beckoned him like a dream of Heaven. This very hour, he'd stake his claim and make her his.

And then he'd take her…somewhere…away from the poisonous intrigue of the Tudor court, the odious instruments of torture the Church would wield against her tender flesh. To a cozy little inn by the sea perhaps, someplace her safety would be assured—

Suddenly a rattling hiss split the air. A jet of water fountained beside them, a geyser erupting from the placid pond. Moving on instinct, he spun free of Rhiannon and thrust her behind him. Then he was rolling to his feet.

Beneath his hand, the sword of Judgment cleared his sheath. He stationed himself before Rhiannon and slanted it defensively before them. Then he gaped at the nightmare rearing from the depths.

It towered above them like a demon vomited from

the pit of Hell—long neck thick and muscled under
obsidian scales, horse's head ropy with black mane,
slitted eyes glaring red. The rest of the creature was
submerged, water bubbling and smoking around it.
The muzzle split to reveal wicked fangs and a forked
tongue as the thing hissed.

"Lady preserve us!" Rhiannon cried, somewhere
behind him. "'Tis a dragon."

"Nonsense," he muttered. "There's no such creature.
Stand back, Rhiannon!"

The head was snaking down, striking at him with
serpentine swiftness.

"God and St. Michael!" Fiercely Beltran swung his
blade, cleaving sideways in a two-handed stroke. His
sword bit into the mighty neck and glanced off the
scaled armor.

Rearing back, the creature screamed, venom dripping from its jaws to spatter the earth. Where each
droplet struck, leaves curled and blackened, steam rising from the acid.

Beltran risked a glance behind him and cursed.
Rhiannon huddled desperately on the ground, hands
pressed to her ears as she grimaced in pain. Beyond,
their panicked horses were vanishing in the trees—
their fastest means of escape now forfeit.

"Christ," he roared at her. "If you love life, *run*!"

Another rattling hiss from the weaving serpent
drowned out his command. Rhiannon writhed on the
ground. He stared between them, uncomprehending.

"The Name of thy God," she gasped. "It wounds
both of us! 'Tis a Faerie creature."

A flicker of movement made him leap aside as
the beast struck like a monstrous adder. His sword

screamed through the air to deflect, slashing open the snarling muzzle. Steaming ichor sprayed from the wound.

Skirts flashing, Rhiannon scrambled back from the deadly rain. The snakelike head tracked her, an impossible length of scaled body uncoiling from the depths. Wildly Beltran wondered if its length was endless, spiraling down and down into the Abyss. Its gyrations drove Rhiannon fleeing down the spit of land between the inlet and the Thames—a refuge too narrow to offer shelter.

"Not that way," he shouted, despairing.

"There's no other way!" Rhiannon cried. "Invoke thy Deity."

The creature was still uncoiling, arrowing after her with a speed no human could match. Beltran pelted after them, hacking at the sinuous column as he ran. Harmlessly, his blows glanced off the onyx scales.

Barely believing it would help, he bellowed, "The power of Christ compels you. *Begone!*"

The thing erupted into an agony of thrashing coils, whipping to and fro. Beltran flung himself flat, the head striking him a glancing blow that made pain explode across his back. Rhiannon dropped and curled tight, arms wrapped around her head—a heartbeat from those lethal jaws.

His back was on fire, but Beltran hardly felt it. He gathered his limbs beneath him and launched toward her, pelting hard, screaming words of warning he knew came too late.

Then his skin began to smoke. His blood turned to fire in his veins; the world went red around him. Despair and exultation whirled through his brain—the holy madness he'd fought all his life. He loathed and dreaded it. Yet it might be the only thing that could save her.

And he must save her. He knew that beyond question, beyond the flicker of a doubt.

Barely in time, Rhiannon scrambled to her feet. She raced along the shore, light-footed as a young deer, silver curls streaming behind her. But she could never outrun the maddened monster that streaked after her.

Beltran felt his jaws stretch wide, voicing a deafening howl of anguish. Gold-and-white flames ignited along his sword. Fueled by the fearsome might of his holy rage, he brought the flaming sword hurtling down like a meteor against the iron-hard coils.

Green ichor exploded as the blade bit deep. A spray of smoking acid arced through the air to splatter him. Scorched holes opened in his doublet, droplets stinging his skin like hornets. Now the infernal beast was turning on him—

A rippling note, like a harp touched by God, reverberated through the air. Beltran faltered, blinking. The red fog of rage receded. In midlunge the serpent froze, its onyx coils quivering.

Beyond the evil head, Rhiannon stood with arms outflung, her slim hands spread, fearlessly touching the wicked scales. And Beltran knew that resonant melody arose from her.

As he watched, astonished, silver light flared around her. It limned her slight frame, streamed through her like the Blessed Virgin or the pagan moon-Goddess. The light flowed through her fingers into the shuddering monster, spread like water over its armored form.

Rhiannon whispered words in an unknown tongue. Somehow his soul grasped their essence:

"Ease thy rage, great serpent, Father of Dragons. Cool the fire of thy wounds in the watery depths. This mortal world is not thy place. Return thee hence to Faerie in peace, peace, peace…"

The serpent shivered along its length, ichor seeping from its wounds. The savage jaws parted to emit a low croon that was almost a purr.

As Beltran stared in disbelief, the creature began to withdraw, coils sliding into the mossy inlet. Under his breath he prayed, adding his voice to hers. Down and down beneath their mingled words the serpent sank, until the hideous head with its slitted eyes sank beneath the waves. The waters stilled. Silence settled upon the wood.

Rhiannon heaved a shuddering sigh and crumpled to the earth. Her pure silver light dimmed and vanished. Gradually Beltran felt his killing rage evaporate, the world resuming its everyday hues of green and brown and gold.

He crouched on hands and knees, panting and drained, muscles burning with fatigue.

His brain reeled, scrambling to make sense of what he'd seen. A creature of legend risen from the tame waters of Hampton Court? And she… Rhiannon… that maddening, impossible girl he burned to bed, who could bring everything the Church strove to accomplish in England crashing down around his ears.

That healing light had poured from her like a miracle. Yet she was no saint, no God-fearing Christian.

The voice of recognition whispered through his shocked brain.

She's telling the truth. All of it—the Faerie Queene, this mystical Convergence, her pagan magick and the danger that threatens.

The world was nothing he'd believed it to be, no orderly realm of sinful souls queuing for Hell or Heaven or Purgatory, their deeds weighed by God, shepherded by a stern omniscient Church.

And if that world was illusion, his entire life was based upon a fallacy.

Blindly he pushed to his feet, tortured muscles screaming in protest. Absently he fingered the smoking holes in his doublet. His wounds still smarted, but the white flare of pain had faded. He was already healing, as he ever did, with the uncanny swiftness he'd attributed to divine favor—God's reward to his faithful servant for suffering in His name.

What if that, too, is mistaken?

What manner of creature am I?

THIRTEEN

CONSCIOUSNESS SEEPED THROUGH Rhiannon slowly—
the faint sweetness of blooming celandines, blossoms
crushed beneath her curled form, a warm blanket of
sunlight across her legs, the tickle of grass against her
cheek. In the distance, the strains of a gay melody
floated across the hedgerows of the palace gardens.

Memory coalesced around her of last night's arrival
at the Tudor queen's palace, the Queen's threats that
morning. That searing encounter with Beltran beside
the river, the way her breasts had kindled and her body
caught fire at his touch, his solid strength pressing her
into the greensward.

The dragon rearing, acid dripping from its jaws.
The calm certainty that thrummed in her blood like a
well-tuned lute as she released the evil spell and banished the beast.

No doubt of it, every day the Convergence drew
closer, and her sister was growing stronger. Only the
combined power of Beltran's invocations, his angel's
flaming sword and her own unpredictable magick had
saved the day.

Again she heard Morrigan's laughing voice, that
taunting whisper in her ear, as her creature sank beneath the waves.

I've done you a favor, sister. I saved your maiden-

head. Your lover's mighty lance would have skewered you this day. Remember what I told you?

Shivering, Rhiannon pushed to a sitting position. She'd sought solace in this green bower because the looming walls, the endless racket, the noisome stench of the palace confined her even worse than these tortuous mortal garments.

Stunned by the attack, her sister's mocking words still ringing in her ears, she'd said little to Beltran during their silent return. He'd been wrapped in his own dark musings, gaze turned inward, hard features hewn in a forbidding mask.

'Tis a wonder I didn't awaken in the Tower. For surely he knows for certain that I'm a witch now.

With a mounting anxiety that bordered on panic, she wondered what he would do with the knowledge.

Unable to remain still, Rhiannon sprang up and hurried through the peaceful garden. Unwilling to return to the hostile scrutiny of the manor, she followed the galliard's distant strains. The sounds of revelry led her to the Banqueting House—a free-standing bower between the gardens and the Thames.

Hesitating beside a hedgerow, she straightened her hood and brushed the pale gold silk of her skirts. She plucked a stray celandine from the hair tumbling loose down her back. Flowing hair was considered a banner of virginity among mortals, she'd learned.

Well, that was fitting enough. Evidently she'd be wearing her hair loose forever. Unless Morrigan had lied to her about the penalty of love.

She tasted bitterness in her throat. Since when had her virgin state troubled her? She'd never found it burdensome, nor been tempted to alter it. Until the day

Lord Beltran Nemesto came striding into her life—
and her heart.

"Lady Rhiannon?"

The words made her pivot, heart rising in her throat.

"I was told ye'd passed this way." Linnet Norwood
arched inquiring brows, framing her perceptive gaze.
"I thought perhaps ye'd come to attend this gathering?
'Tis the Earl of Arundel's natal day, a Catholic crowd...
my father's crowd while he lived." Briefly, a shadow
darkened her gold-flecked gaze. "A likely place to seek
new allies, aye, which ye may need if ye're having a
wee stramash with Lord Beltran?"

Rhiannon glanced toward the bower—wicker roof
woven with ivy, white-draped tables groaning beneath the gilded swans and full-plumed peacocks and
sculpted subtleties these mortals favored. A double row
of colorful forms romped along the floor, gentlemen
leaping high, ladies retreating coyly before them. Involuntarily, she smiled at the sight.

"A fine notion, Linnet! We should show ourselves
among the Queen's faction, show sympathy with their
interests..."

Her voice trailed away. For the Queen's faction
was the Church faction, and therefore Beltran's. Her
heart quickened as she searched the frolicking throng,
seeking broad shoulders encased in black and a proud
golden head that towered over lesser mortals. Several
dark-frocked clergymen huddled in one corner like a
murder of crows, but the Blade of God was not among
them.

From henceforth, she'd steer clear of him. She'd resolved herself on that much. She couldn't seem to refrain from swooning into his arms when they were

private, and that course could only end in downfall.
Their future discussions must occur in public, when
she was fully in command of her senses.

Linnet shot her a sidelong glance. "Don't fash yerself—he isn't here. He's planted on his knees in the
chapel for Nones."

"Again?" Relief and disappointment warred within
her. "Well, we shall find another champion to advance
our cause. Beltran Nemesto is hardly the only Catholic at this court, and another may well prove more
tractable."

Fresh hope unfurled within her breast. Rhiannon
lifted her chin and pinned a bright smile to her lips.
She could dissemble with a right good will after a lifetime on the fringes of the Faerie court, pretending not
to mind her exclusion.

Linnet squeezed her hand and summoned her own
shy smile. "There stands the man of the hour—Arundel
himself. My father knew him…once. Would ye fancy
an introduction?"

BELTRAN EMERGED FROM the chapel in an uneasy mood.
Prayer seemed less and less the comfort it used to be;
surely it had done nothing to settle him after the day's
ungodly events. His thoughts seethed like stew in a
boiling cauldron—like the innocent English waters
that had vomited a demon from the depths.

One lesson he'd learned. He'd hired a man to follow Rhiannon. She'd not slip away again without his
knowledge.

Tonight she was keeping company he'd never expected—no less a man than Henry FitzAlan, the Earl

of Arundel. And the Archbishop of Canterbury himself in attendance. A fist of foreboding knotted his gut.

The sun hovered low and burning, slanting through the Banqueting House. Music floated through the air, punctuated with chimes of laughter. The linkboys were lighting the first torches, the Sewers broaching a fresh cask of Burgundy as Beltran vaulted the stairs. Some instinct held him on the threshold, unseen in the gathering shadows, while he searched for his quarry.

Before him, the dancers swirled into pairs for the Italian dance called *la volta*. Laughing cries rose from the ladies as their partners flung them into the air.

It was an unseemly dance, almost lecherous, and Beltran was frowning when an ethereal figure in pale gold floated into view, light as thistledown in her partner's hands.

There. Even in this colorful throng, he would have found her anywhere. There was nowhere on earth she could hide from him.

A blaze of sunset lit the cloud of gilded ringlets that swirled around her, like the aura that appeared when she summoned her strange magick. The incandescent joy lighting her winsome face snared him, green eyes flashing like a cat's in the twilight.

Her partner lowered her from view. Beltran knotted his fists as a pang of loss tightened his chest. *Ridiculous! Moping after her like a lovesick swain.*

When she soared aloft again, a lithe form clad in shimmering gold, head flung back with innocent joy, he couldn't tear his eyes away.

What the Devil was that fellow doing holding her like that, hands lodged just under the sweet curve of her breasts? The man was too bloody forward. The sight of a sinewed thigh clad in burgundy hose, planted so snugly under her derriere to lift her, made Beltran grind his teeth.

When he wrenched his eyes from their intertwined bodies and glimpsed her partner's face, Beltran suffered another unpleasant blow. The man whose embrace Rhiannon was so transparently enjoying was none other than the man of the hour—His Grace, the Earl of Arundel.

Beltran cursed under his breath. Rhiannon had set her sights on the Lord Steward himself, a premier peer of England, one of the highest Catholic nobles in the whole sodding court.

And there wasn't a thing he could do about it.

Pivoting away, he gestured impatiently for a cup. The crisp bite of ale washed the bitter taste of jealousy from his throat and restored him to something like sanity. Glimpsing a flash of red among the black-frocked clergy, he took himself firmly in hand and strode forward to greet the Archbishop.

Reginald Pole inclined his head coolly. Beltran hadn't made a stellar first impression on the man during last night's imbroglio. Likewise, the Archbishop's companion eyed him without warmth—a square, blocky figure with a bulbous nose, fleshy lips arranged in a permanent sneer.

"Lord Beltran," the Archbishop murmured. "Are you acquainted with His Lordship Bishop Bonner?"

So this brutish fellow was Bloody Bonner, the terror of English Protestants. Beltran concealed his distaste and swept a proper bow. "Lordship. I dispatched a missive to you this morning. I'm here under orders from Cardinal Calvino to enforce your efforts on the Inquisition's behalf."

Edmund Bonner pursed his lips. "Indeed, I petitioned the Pope for a Blade of God with zeal to act as my unflinching rod of punishment in this holy work. At the time, I was gratified to hear he'd dispatched so legendary a warrior as God's Vengeance to persecute these unrepentant heretics. We expected your arrival weeks ago."

"Foul weather postponed my Channel crossing." Beltran itched to see what Rhiannon was doing, but dared not draw the bishop's gaze toward her by looking. "You may be certain I chafed at the delay. No man could be more eager to advance the Lord's work."

"Indeed?" Bonner's hooded eyes followed the dancers. "I heard of last night's unfortunate business with that unusual young woman. This... Rhiannon le Fay. Mistress Susan Clarencius, a good Catholic of excellent standing, says much that I find disturbing."

The cold precision with which he uttered Rhiannon's name made Beltran's blood run cold. He bit off a curse. "Aye, the Queen asked me to examine Lady Rhiannon's petition. I'll conclude the matter by May Day, never fear, then devote my full attention to your efforts."

"You won't be overhasty, I trust." The bishop studied him. "It's said that you know the woman?"

"Not in the Biblical sense." Beltran bared his teeth in a cold smile. His mentor Calvino might praise Edmund Bonner, but something about the man set his teeth on edge. "Purely by chance, I encountered her on the road."

"Then you had some opportunity to observe her?" Bonner's black brows lifted.

"Somewhat." Beltran wondered at his own reticence. Not long ago he'd planned to turn Rhiannon over to the bishop's tender keeping and wash his hands of the troublesome minx. Now that the opportunity to condemn her was staring him in the face, he couldn't force the words past his lips.

He couldn't turn her over to this butcher and his instruments of salvation.

"What a pity." The bishop was watching her again. His gaze drawn like a magnet, Beltran found her laughing up at Arundel—still with the old satyr, damn the man, though the dance had ended.

"Based on Mistress Susan's rather unorthodox report," Bonner pressed, "and the unwholesome effect she's had upon the Queen, I'm convinced the girl warrants questioning."

His nerves prickled with alarm. Hell would freeze before he saw Rhiannon turned over to this monster for questioning. The words that would protect her sprang to his lips as though divinely inspired.

"I'll interrogate her myself, Lordship. If I detect the merest whiff of witchcraft or heresy, you can be certain I'll deal with it."

Now Reginald Pole too was watching Rhiannon, far too interested for Beltran's peace of mind. "Her Majesty seems convinced she saw the woman in a vision, but I've warned her that is unlikely. The Queen may be admirably devout, but she's only a woman and hence a flawed vessel. As you know, a woman's husband is ordained by God to tend her spiritual welfare. It's regrettable hers is occupied elsewhere."

Beltran barely contained a snort. He'd seen the Spanish King's royal mistress, the fair Christina of Denmark. If he were Philip of Spain, he too would prefer her alluring beauty to Mary Tudor's faded charms.

"I trust you understand the importance of this case, Lord Beltran?" Bonner murmured. "I speak not only of the Queen's spiritual welfare, but the affair's personal importance to you. The Blades of God will shortly choose a new master, I am told?"

Beltran absorbed the significance of that connection. Delayed on the road these many weeks, he hadn't realized his name was bruited about so openly for the Don's post. Could he be so close to achieving this signal honor? The thought of his mentor's approval made a flicker of satisfaction curl through him.

"Your reputation in battle is formidable," Reginald Pole was saying. "Lutherans and Huguenots and Anabaptists all dread your name."

Aye, I'm a hired blade—a butcher with a title. A surge of self-loathing rose in his gullet, sweeping away the warm glow of satisfaction.

"I do my duty, no more," he said curtly.

The bishop leaned toward him. "Certain members of the ruling council have asked whether you are equally willing to exact God's judgment against the frailer sex. The dons require only this final act of faith—some convincing demonstration of your commitment—to resolve the matter in your favor. I put to you that the case before you, the case of this Rhiannon le Fay, arises at a critical juncture in your career. Handle the matter properly and you'll be proclaimed Don within a month."

Beltran stared into the bishop's burning gaze. A slow tide of disbelief churned through him. Aye, he'd considered the timing and the personal implications when this girl who styled herself a Faerie princess stumbled across his path. But he'd intended to see her treated fairly, given an even chance to prove her innocence, not condemned out of hand!

He would rush no hapless innocent to the stake, merely to win a title. Christ, he barely wanted the one they'd already forced on him.

But if he declined the honor, the man they called Bloody Bonner would find some other, less principled rogue to do the deed. If the bishop didn't clamp the thumbscrews on her slender fingers himself.

A crimson tide of fury washed across his vision. Breathing hard through his nose, he fought down the whisper of holy madness before it rose to a roar that deafened him. Grimly he forced each word through gritted teeth.

"Never fear, my lord bishop. I'll attend to the matter personally. You may be certain Lady Rhiannon will be treated as she deserves."

The bishop smiled and sipped his wine.

RHIANNON FELT PLEASANTLY surprised by the success of her new stratagem. She'd been expecting a cool reception, akin to the way she was treated behind the Veil. But she'd forgotten—these mortals didn't know of her mixed heritage, the taint that left her barely tolerated in the Summer Lands.

Here, she need only allow her natural interest and curiosity about these bluff, exuberant, extravagant males to surface, and they seemed flattered by it. They smiled, kissed her hand, uttered witticisms and murmured compliments in the most agreeable manner. And the music! The grand romps and leaps of these English dances brought her genuine delight.

How balmy was the twilight, how soft with dusk the purple sky, how friendly the evening star rising in the west. She could almost have forgotten the dire mission that brought her here, and the danger that loomed over them all.

Almost, until she glimpsed the gleam of torchlight on golden hair rich as butter, the lithe rippling prowl of a powerful black-clad figure stalking into the Banqueting House with lethal grace. There in the midst of the dance, a strange fever swept over her. A hectic flush rose in her cheeks.

This is Beltran's magick, though he wields it unknowing. Far more fatal to me than any enchantment.

Distracted by his entrance, she stumbled over her partner's feet and gasped an apology. Through the jewel-bright lines of courtiers, she caught flickering glimpses of Beltran, huddled in low-voiced discussion with the mighty Archbishop, every line of him etched and bristling with intent. When he wheeled and strode decisively toward her, she murmured a hasty excuse and slipped away, leaving her startled escort protesting in her wake.

Light-footed as a sprite, she slipped among the laughing mortals, the stench of sweat and heavy-sauced food rising up to choke her. Suddenly her corset was biting into her ribs, her lungs fighting for air, a faint dizzy panic rising in her brain.

Surrender your maidenhood to a mortal man, and you'll become one of them forever...

A slender figure in buttercup yellow came hurrying to intercept her, smooth brow puckered with worry.

"Saints preserve us, ye look as though ye've seen yer own fetch."

"Nothing so dire, I assure thee." Rhiannon's brittle attempt at flippancy fell flat. "Linnet, I can no longer court Lord Beltran's interest. I beseech thee, tell him I'm exhausted and have gone to bed."

"He sleeps in the next chamber, barely a wall between us," Linnet murmured. "If he truly wishes to see ye, I doubt anything I say will keep him out."

Fresh panic sparked through her. "Then I won't retire until he's gone to Vespers or whatever he does to pass the night."

"A wee bit late for evasion, my lady. He's nearly upon us and in a rare swivet."

"For pity's sake, deflect him if he follows!" Fleeing, Rhiannon scrambled down the stairs into the fragrant night.

The soft lavender gloaming drifted down like mist around her. An ethereal moon floated in a cloudy sea, one familiar friend in this bewildering mortal world. She drew strength and resolve from it, the symbol of the Goddess these mortals would burn her for worshipping. She absorbed tranquility from the still green hedges and banks of blossoms breathing gently in the night, exuding their pale perfume.

Torchlight bobbed and flared around the Banqueting House, and she gave it a wide berth, slipping on cat's feet along the graveled paths. She'd wend her way to her chambers circuitously—the same way she navigated through Faerie, by pretending to go someplace else, ever turning away and away from her goal.

Beneath the distant music, a soft cry pierced the silent night. Her footsteps faltered, healer's instincts aroused to tingling alert. An echo of fear rippled through her, the start and stumble of a small panicked heart. A boy was jeering in the darkness, crowing with high-pitched laughter whose spite curdled her blood. Unnervingly like the way Mordred had laughed when he taunted her long ago, before their father defeated him.

Another soft cry pierced her heart. Without conscious decision she was running toward it, kicking her farthingale aside to free her steps, breath sharp as splintered glass in her lungs. She burst into a secluded glade, where a pale statue of some barefoot maiden gripped a bow. Moonlight softened the darkness to reveal the scene—two half-grown youths in satin and velvet, stranded somewhere on the uncertain threshold between boy and man, faces twisted as they slung pebbles at the marble Goddess. But nay.

A piteous mew rose from the terrified white scrap of a kitten clinging to the marble maiden, just beyond reach of its tormentors.

Outraged comprehension rushed through Rhiannon in an icy flood. Sparing no thought for her own safety, she sprinted across the clearing and flung herself between the frightened kitten and its oppressors. A late-slung pebble stung her arm as she deflected the missile.

"How dare thee!" she raged. "Is there no shame in thy hearts, no scrap of conscience nor decency?"

Her sudden arrival and the ferocity of her defense seemed to startle the aggressors. The pair faltered. Then the larger of the two—a big black-haired lad, nearly a man—checked their retreat with a hoot of contempt.

"Who are you to command us? You're naught but a girl yourself."

Making the most of her slight frame, Rhiannon straightened her shoulders and planted her hands on her hips. "If thou would know my name, run and ask thy Queen to provide it. Or find better sport somewhere, I care not where."

The younger boy, wiry and sallow-skinned with the look of Spain, bent to scoop a handful of gravel from the path. "The sport here's good enough."

"I command thee *desist*!" Her voice rang with all the authority of a queen's daughter. This time they barely hesitated, but spread to flank her. Caution prickled through her. If they both came at her together, she could never fend them off.

Lightning-quick, she spun and gathered the kitten into her arms. Protectively she cuddled it against her breast. The poor creature clung to her, tiny claws digging into her bodice like needles. Feeling its swift frantic heartbeat beneath her fingers, a scalding flood of anger surged through her.

"Oh, thou art mighty knights, bold as the great Lancelot himself, to set thyself against a woman and a mewling kitten! What great foe wilt thou challenge next—a babe in the cradle?" she cried.

At this, the younger lad shuffled his feet and glanced away, some latent spark of chivalry firing. A shoot of hope unfurled within her.

But the older jeered. "I know you now, by your queer speech! My father spoke of you. He says you're a witch and a heretic."

"What, a Protestant?" The younger boy took heart—Spain in his voice, for certain. "Don't you know they burn girls like you at Smithfield? We'll see how proud you are then, dancing hotfoot on the kindling!"

Rhiannon felt sickened, as much by their naked malice as the ugly threat. Warily she glanced around the shadowy garden, hoping for some passerby whose arrival would startle them into flight.

But she'd given the torchlit areas a wide berth to make her own escape. She glanced at the moon to get her bearings, then at the palace's distant chimneys dark against the heavens. She could outrun them in a twinkling, even with the kitten clutched to her breast...if not for her heavy skirts and the cumbersome farthingale.

A sharp hail stung her cheek and bosom—a handful of gravel slung by the younger boy, growing ever bolder as they realized her vulnerable placement.

"Nay, wait!" said the elder, voice deepening with intent, a new note of cruelty that made him nearly a man, albeit one any mother would weep to claim. "She's a pretty little thing, isn't she, Rodrigo? Fair enough for what we're planning, any rate. Why hie ourselves all the way to the Southwark stews when we can find our bit o' muslin right here at Hampton?"

Although some of his references escaped her grasp, Rhiannon grasped his meaning well enough. Cold fear sheeted over her, but she knew better than to show it. Men and boys, they were all like wolves. Let them scent her terror and they'd be at her throat.

Or under her skirts, which seemed now their intent.

"Ha! Thou claim to wield a man's blade and do a man's business?" She laced her voice with derision. "Against an unwilling woman?"

"You'll be willing by the time I'm ready." Her opponent leered and loosened his codpiece. "You'll bloody be begging me for it. Watch here, Rodrigo, and see how a man does his business."

Gripping the kitten against her chest with one hand, Rhiannon cast about desperately for some means of defense. Her legs weakened with sickening fear. Had she overcome bandits and a dragon and Morrigan's malice, only to lose her precious shield of maidenhood to this half-grown braggart?

"What the Devil is going on here?" A man's voice, cold and pitiless as revenge, brought them all spinning around. A black-clad figure strode into the clearing, sable cloak unfurling like great wings in his wake. His aura blazed fire to Rhiannon's Sight—the white heat of divine rage.

She closed her eyes, strength and hope flooding her trembling limbs. A few minutes ago she would have done anything to avoid him. Now she could have wept with relief to see him.

"Lord Beltran." She fought to steady her voice. "What is happening here is that I found these...*gentlemen*...tormenting this poor helpless creature for sport. Perhaps now they find the sport less to their liking."

His keen gaze swept from the trembling kitten clutched to her chest to the youth's loosened codpiece. A terrifying coldness hardened his features to granite.

"Best retie that codpiece, boy," he growled. "And find yourself another diversion—at once."

Moonlight flashed on his gold-and-steel medallion, no less cold or hard than the menace in his narrowed gaze. Perhaps the younger lad recognized the symbol. Or perhaps he sensed the blazing image of the wrathful angel that burned in Rhiannon's vision.

The boy called Rodrigo scuttled back from danger. "*Madre de Dios*! It's *him*."

"Who?" the elder asked uneasily, hand twitching near the hilt of his sword.

"The wrath of God, *amigo*." The younger boy crossed himself. "God's Vengeance."

She watched fear infect the elder like a creeping plague. Her would-be assailant adjusted his codpiece and grumbled an oath.

The young Rodrigo fell to his knees, hands clasped, his sallow features rapturous as he gazed up at Beltran. "Will you give me your blessing, *senor*?"

"I'm no priest," Beltran muttered, shifting. "Off with you, *chico*. And best take your intemperate friend with you."

Unsurprised, she watched the pair retreat, Rodrigo dragging his unnamed comrade behind. The elder shrugged him off, but at least he went.

Rhiannon's breath escaped in a shuddering rush. Trembling, she crossed to a stone bench and sank down, cradling the kitten to her breast. The little creature had stopped shivering and nestled into her warm bosom as though it belonged there.

"Damn it to hell, why did you run from me, Rhiannon?"

She tingled with wariness as the Blade of God stalked toward her, darkness cloaking his features.

"Thou knowest why, Lord Beltran."

His voice deepened with purpose. "I would have taken nothing you weren't more than willing to give."

"Perhaps that's why I was running," she said softly.

Now he towered over her, close enough to touch. The sweet spice of frankincense made her dizzy. She

glanced aside, struggling to show nothing of the al-
chemical reaction his presence evoked—not her breathless excitement, nor her melting yearning, nor the
confusion and alarm her vulnerability provoked.

*You must keep him at a distance if you value your
immortality. You could lose everything in his arms.*

She bent over the kitten, cupped carefully between
her hands, hair falling forward to curtain her features.

"Thou could have let them have me just now," she
said lightly. "Another missed opportunity to be quit
of me."

"Devil take it, Rhiannon! I may be a butcher but I'm
no rogue," he said roughly, hunkering on his heels before her. "I'd no more abandon an innocent woman to
random brutality than I would that dumb beast you've
rescued, poor mite."

Still avoiding his probing gaze, she stroked the kitten's milky forehead with a gentle finger. The little
creature dissolved into purrs.

"Thou art a decent man," she allowed, "despite the
harsh and unforgiving God thou choose to serve, and
thy Church's bloody dictates."

The breath chuffed from his lungs. "God doesn't
look to me for leniency, Rhiannon. I'm His unflinching sword-arm, His judge and executioner, His wrath
and His rod of punishment."

"Justice may be blind," she murmured. "But it
should also be merciful. This grieving, strife-torn land
cries out for God's mercy and thine. Why wilt thou
not see it?"

Restless, he thrust to his feet and paced the clearing.
"I'm a Blade of God. It's not my place to show mercy."

"Why must thou be so stubborn?" Seized by a feverish urgency, she placed the kitten carefully on the grass beneath the bench, safe from harm, and rose. "After such evidence as thou have seen today, thou can no longer deny I speak the truth! The Convergence is nearly upon us, Beltran, or that dragon could never have passed the Veil. My sister is growing stronger, and the Veil thin as cobwebs."

"That creature was a demon, vomited up from Hell." The lion's growl reverberated through his voice as he pivoted and stalked toward her. "The Name of God caused it mortal anguish, but it was your witchcraft that banished it. These are strange events, Rhiannon, and I assure you the Church won't tolerate them. If anyone should testify to your peculiar magick, the bishop will see you burn."

"And still I must strive unaided—nay, opposed by thee!" Exhausted and overwrought, she surrendered to a flash of temper and stamped her foot. "I vow I have reached my limit. I'll waste no more time dallying with a narrow-minded, pigheaded doddypol who lacks the wit to see the truth before his own eyes."

"Doddypol?" His tawny brows hoisted.

"It means fool, fool, fool!" Furious, she clenched her fists and glared at him. "I tell thee I've had enough of thee."

He halted, dangerously still. "Unfortunately you've no choice but to tolerate me. The Queen has placed your fate in my hands."

"I'm not so certain, Beltran. The Queen doubts thy virtue after that outburst on the stairs. Any staunch Catholic with status at this court would serve my purpose better than thee. Why, I found half a dozen men at that fete tonight who would champion me and gladly!"

"No doubt they would," he said, low and menacing. "In exchange for such sweet pleasures as I savored today, with you all but naked beneath me. Will you lure FitzAlan and his cronies the same way?"

She burned with outrage. "How dare thou imply I used woman's wiles to lure thee? Thou art the one who cannot seem to keep thy distance, no matter thy political ambitions—"

Hearing her outraged voice ringing through the garden, Rhiannon tumbled to a halt. Over the echo of their quarrel, the stately strains of a pavane lilted through the night. This was no place for a rousing row on such dire matters as these, no matter how he vexed her.

Besides, she'd resolved to spend her efforts elsewhere. She only hoped Beltran wouldn't denounce her outright or arrest her, as she knew was still a danger. Beyond that, she need no longer waste her breath on the provoking man.

"My ambitions?" Deliberately he stalked toward her. "Now what would a Faerie princess know of such business?"

"I haven't been living in a cave," she said irritably. "I know thou art being considered to head thine order. Besides which, I'm told thou art sworn to chastity, which I assure thee matches mine interests to perfection. 'Tis best for both our sakes to keep our distance."

Now he looked distinctly dangerous. "Is that so?"

Rhiannon knew little of men, either mortal or otherwise, but she was learning to know this one. Nervously she glanced around the glade. For all she knew, Morrigan herself could be lurking, though the day's mighty effort must have exhausted her.

Beneath the bench, the kitten mewed plaintively.

Grateful for the diversion, she hurried past the scowling man to scoop it up.

"'Tis growing chilly. I'd best take this kitten inside where it's warm, and see if I cannot find its mother."

"So we intend to keep our distance?" His warm breath licked her ear, and she jumped. Keen though her senses were, his tread was silent as mist when he wished.

"Precisely so," she said briskly, starting past him.

His hand closed beneath her elbow, drawing her close. Another wave of weakness assailed her. "I don't intend to seduce you, Rhiannon, if that's what worries you. What you said about my vows, at least, was accurate."

She stifled an odd flicker of disappointment. "I thought thou might agree."

His grip tightened, making her heartbeat quicken. "But I do intend to escort you chastely to your chamber, before you stumble into some new mischief. You have a habit of finding trouble, girl."

She gritted her teeth and raised her chin. "Beyond a doubt, Lord Beltran, the worst trouble I've found since I passed beyond the Veil is *thee*."

FOURTEEN

ANOTHER ENGLISH DAWN, cold and clammy as a tomb. Who'd believe May Day was nearly upon them, a scant two days hence?

Beltran heaved a breath and rose stiffly from his knees. He'd fallen asleep before the little reliquary in his dayroom sometime after the bells rang Matins. It wasn't the first time he'd failed to keep his eyes propped open through a night-long vigil. Now he was staring forty in the face, his lapses appeared to be growing more frequent.

Groaning, he rolled his head on his neck, wondering dully why he drove himself this way. Why did he flog himself more relentlessly than he'd ever hounded any witch or heretic?

The old rituals had mattered to him once, when the stronghold of San Miguel seemed a haven of order and cleanliness. Of course, the Southwark stews would have seemed that way to the boy he was, compared to the hell on earth of his Da's smithy, and the filthy crib where his Mam whored on her back for any man with a groat to pay her.

He'd wanted to punish the whole world for his parents' failings—his father's dumb unthinking violence, his mother's apathy to their misery. He'd settled for wielding the hammer of justice to smite God's enemies.

He'd thought any inkling of compassion or forgiveness had been knocked from his head by his father's fists.

In those early years of fervent devotion, he'd never dreamed a woman like Rhiannon le Fay could exist. Her gentle touch, her lilting voice, her gaiety and compassion had been revelations to him. The way life and love surrounded her, flowering wherever she walked like the Holy Thorn on Glastonbury when Joseph of Arimathea planted his staff. She watered the barren soil of this wretched world.

She made him want to believe his life could be something more than the bleak desert he'd made it. She made him long to breathe clean air, unsullied by the pyre's bitter ash.

She would be utterly wasted on a man like Arundel.

Last night Beltran had deferred to cold duty and left Rhiannon to her solitude, though he burned with unholy fire to possess her.

Today he'd resolved on a different course. He'd spirit Rhiannon away from the hostile eyes and dangerous intrigue of the Tudor court, take her someplace safe and private. There he'd ask her again to explain this jumbled business of the Veil and the Convergence and her vengeful sister. And this time, he'd actually *listen*—

The rough thunder of a fist on wood brought him wheeling around, reaching for the sword he'd left nearby. He didn't draw it, but checked to ensure Rhiannon's door was securely bolted before he answered.

"Who goes?" he called roughly.

A page's youthful voice piped faintly through the wood. "Make way for the Bishop of London!"

A warning whispered in his head.

"The hour is early, Your Lordship," Beltran called softly. "What's amiss?"

"Holy Mother Church needs your service, Vengeance," the bishop said calmly. "Will you answer?"

Gripping his blade, Beltran rubbed a hand against his bristling jaw, then unlatched the door.

His first glimpse of Edmund Bonner redoubled his warning whisper to a roar. The Inquisitor's fleshy face was arranged in somber lines, but his eyes glittered with suppressed excitement. Beltran noted the parchment gripped in his fist, its broken seals and ribbons dangling. His skin prickled as he recognized his mentor's distinctive seal.

"Lord Beltran Nemesto, Blade of God," the bishop said formally, "I have here the latest dispatch from your order's ruling council in Rome. A new Don of San Miguel has been nominated."

Automatically Beltran shifted the sword to his left hand and signed himself, murmuring the proper benediction. But his mind was racing. His fingers tingled with anticipation. There was but one reason the bishop would rouse Beltran from his bed, unwashed and unshaven, to deliver the news personally.

The bishop's eyes never strayed from Beltran's face. "His Eminence the Cardinal reports that the council—at his suggestion—is prepared to appoint you Don of the Blades."

Beltran absorbed the words, turned them over in his mind and waited for the soaring elation to hit him. He'd been dreaming of this moment all his life, hadn't he, this gesture of acknowledgement and recognition from the Church he'd devoted his life to serving?

Instead of the sweet tang of triumph, bursting like

a ripe grape on his tongue, he tasted the bitter salt of regret.

When he said nothing, the bishop frowned. "As the Inquisition's ruling voice in the nation where you're currently posted, Lord Beltran, I am requested to second the appointment. I'm prepared to confirm you immediately—under one condition."

Beltran gripped the sword, his gut knotting. "Best speak plainly, Lordship. I don't wish to mistake your meaning."

"As you will." Edmund Bonner inclined his head. "I understand your chambers adjoin those assigned to the lady known as Rhiannon le Fay. Based on Mistress Susan's testimony and the other evidence I'm certain you have amassed, I'm ordering you to arrest the lady on charges of witchcraft. The gesture will serve as adequate demonstration of your unfaltering commitment to the Inquisition. I expect to see Lady Rhiannon chained in a cell at St. Paul's awaiting my interrogation tonight."

The bishop eyed him. "Is that speech plain enough for you?"

RHIANNON WAS DRIFTING uneasily on the river of dreams when a hand shook her awake. She startled upright in bed, heart leaping, frantic eyes combing the pearly dawn. For an unsettling moment she recognized none of her surroundings. Then her modest bedchamber at Hampton Court took shape. Above her floated the pale oval of Linnet Norwood's features, mahogany hair streaming down in a sleep-tossed tangle.

Goddess save her, the poor girl looked terrified.

"My dear child." Swiftly Rhiannon caught the cold hands and squeezed. "What is wrong?"

Never had she seen the girl look thus, even when she'd stumbled through the Veil into Faerie. Her face was chalk, eyes rimmed with white like a frightened mare's. The muscles in her throat moved as she tried to swallow.

"Ye must wake, Rhiannon!"

"Wait, don't try to speak." Gently Rhiannon lifted from her lap the warm weight of the sleeping kitten— its mother not yet found—and reached for the pewter pitcher. "Have some of this ale to hearten you."

Linnet shook her head, eyes frantic, but her hands curled around Rhiannon's and held the cup to her lips. The girl managed to choke some of it down. Color crept back to her pallid cheeks.

"There now." Despite her mounting concern, Rhiannon managed a reassuring smile and stroked the girl's tumbled ringlets from a brow damp with sweat. "My dear, thou art fevered."

"For pity's sake, Rhiannon, let me speak!" Linnet brushed her hands aside. "I was coming back from the garderobe when I heard a wee skelloch near our door. Lord Beltran was there, thick as thieves with someone. I think it was Bishop Bonner."

A cold shaft of foreboding pierced Rhiannon's heart, but she kept her voice level. "Well, what of it? The two are cronies, both henchmen of the Christian God. I'm certain they have much to discuss."

A frustrated sound escaped Linnet's lips, and the girl caught her throat with both hands as though to hold the sound inside. "I heard him say our laddie Lord Beltran is appointed to lead the Blades of God! The bishop need only confirm it."

Though she'd half expected the news, Rhiannon felt as though she were falling. Regret and disappointment clenched her heart and twisted. Once made master of his order, Beltran would never turn against it, never choose her over the Church's interests.

Not that she'd dared hope for that, not truly.

Blinking back the stinging tears, she hurried to the little window. In the soft gray dawn, mist hung over the river and shrouded the quay. Only a few early craft, the little cockleboats that served as couriers and ferries for coin, bobbed amid the swells.

But the household was stirring, carts rumbling into the Fish Court, servants stoking the fires in the great kitchens. Soon the bells would toll—a sound to make any Faerie quail—and the household would come streaming forth to Mass.

Linnet twined loosened ringlets around her fingers, a nervous habit Rhiannon recognized from the girl's time in Faerie. "I heard my lord say—"

"That he accepts the honor with all humility and rides at once for Rome?" Rhiannon swallowed against the aching lump that swelled in her throat.

Fool—fool—ten kinds of fool! You should have prepared for this, as the Queen herself prepared.

"Sweet Jesus, don't interrupt! We've no time." By this, she judged the depth of Linnet's disturbance, when this sweet child who'd dwelled behind the Veil cried the Name that deafened Faerie ears like trumpets.

Linnet drew a shaking breath. "Rhiannon, that wee brute of a bishop vowed to confirm the appointment under one condition."

Rhiannon gripped the sill, white-knuckled, her heart knowing what must come next.

"Lord Beltran is ordered to arrest ye. The bishop plans to question ye himself."

The shock of it nearly set her swooning. Somehow she kept her feet, though her limbs were ice, though she floated in the gray mist of perfect despair. Dear Lady, she'd known this was coming! How not, when Beltran had threatened her with it the very night they met?

Surely she'd never been fool enough to fancy he'd spare her for the sake of whatever passion burned between them. That he could find in the stews, and likely not even need to pay for it.

Her tongue swept over her lips—bone-dry. Somehow she forced out the words. "What said my lord to that?"

"Oh, they plunged right into their plotting, the wicked devils! My lord said something to the pageboy about seizing yer horse, and then I took to my heels. I was that afraid they'd see me if I stood there gaping witless like a gomerel."

"When will he come for me?" Rhiannon's voice sounded pale and distant in her ears.

"I don't know! He could be coming this instant. If only yer Ansgar were here. My lady, what should we do?"

Bleakly Rhiannon shook her head, shivering as the chill struck through her linen nightgown. "It matters not. Ansgar hasn't come, and I can't flee with the treaty unsigned, Linnet. If I leave here now, slipping out by night like some thief or vagabond, Mary Tudor will never trust me and never sign."

"Gentle Mother, she'll never sign now!" Linnet's

voice rose. "Yer mission here is finished. Ye must save yerself, for pity's sake! Find some other way."

"There is no other way. The Convergence will descend, and then Fae and mortals will be at one another's throat. Queene Maeve will fall and Morrigan rise in her place. And yet…"

She paused, thoughts racing like mice through a mill. The habit of defeat sat poorly with her. "Morrigan has only been defeated once—by my father, King Arthur. 'Tis prophesied he'll awaken when England's need is greatest. How can the need be greater than now, at this time, with my sister ascendant, my mother dying, and England torn to bloody shreds by the Spaniards?"

"For mercy, Rhiannon, we've no time for this! Here, I'll pack ye a wee bundle—this bread and cheese, a pouch of healing herbs, some small jewels ye can sell for coin. Wear yer warmest gown and cloak—"

The threads of a desperate scheme wove together in her mind. "Nay, Linnet, let me wear yours. For I must appear nothing beyond the ordinary to leave these chambers by the servants' way." Slowly she worked through it. "But how can I flee? He's seized my poor Astolat."

Even in extremis, Rhiannon suffered a pang of loss. She'd loved that mare from a foal. Surely when Ansgar arrived—for he would never fail her, unless his wound took fever and killed him—he could retrieve the mare.

Now she faced a more immediate crisis.

Blindly her gaze searched the riverbank—a flock of geese waddling toward the water, the goose-boy fisting his eyes and stumbling after, a gallant in rumpled finery clambering from a wherry to stumble up the quay.

She could never hope to flee on foot and outdistance any sort of pursuit. But the river…

BELTRAN STOOD AT the threshold of her bedchamber—the sanctuary he'd used all his resolve not to violate—and catalogued the signs of a hasty departure. Morning sun streamed through the mullioned window over the four-poster bed, blankets tangled, Rhiannon's sumptuous gowns flung willy-nilly in bright swaths of green and rose and azure. Nearby her trunk stood open, a froth of petticoats and ribboned stockings trailing over the rim. A hint of violet fragrance teased his nostrils. On the table a small casket of jewels lay open. Peridot and pearl and tourmaline threw dazzling sprays of color in the sunlight.

She was gone. Of course she was gone. And her Scottish lady-in-waiting was nowhere to be found. Even the damn kitten she'd rescued was missing.

Mingled with gnawing worry, Beltran was grimly aware of his sneaking sense of relief. Witch and heretic she might be, and he sworn to perform a duty for which he'd developed an active loathing, but he could dredge up no enthusiasm for the task.

Indeed, some might say his reluctance had aided her escape. For certain, he'd taken his time about the business, doing naught to conceal his intent…

Beside him, the Archbishop of Canterbury surveyed the scene. "So she is gone. I fear you were not prompt enough to seize her."

"Arrangements had to be made," Beltran said curtly, "and the Queen's permission secured. We can't simply lay hands on a foreign emissary, one with whom England has opened diplomatic negotiations, and drag her screaming from her chambers. She's no halfwit milk-maid or mumbling granddam, accused by her neighbors of cursing a cow or chicken."

He felt the Archbishop looking askance at him and bit off the words before he said worse. He'd sounded censorious, critical of the Church even to his own ears.

"You might have placed a guard upon her door, at least," the Archbishop pointed out.

"I've had her under surveillance since yesterday. Evidently the lady donned a disguise and slipped out the servants' way." Admiration rose within him for her courage and resourcefulness. "Her lady-in-waiting, a devout Catholic, had already left for Mass and knew nothing."

"The companion is nothing to us." Reginald Pole stroked his russet beard. "You'll pursue the girl and bring her back, I presume?"

Beltran grunted. Aye, he'd ride after her, or Bloody Bonner would dispatch a constable or some common thug in his place. Fiercely he quelled the misgivings that sprouted like mushrooms in his brain, the teeming doubts about his faith and calling that had never crossed his mind before an elfin beauty named Rhiannon le Fay danced into his life.

If I don't bring her back, if I choose a woman over my sworn duty, I can no longer call myself a Blade of God. And if I'm not God's Vengeance, then what am I?

In that case, he was nothing—a Yorkshire collier's brat with a fancy sword. Without even the flickering candle of faith to hold the darkness in his soul at bay.

Secretly he was relieved when the Archbishop was summoned away, one fewer witness to his black musings. Grimly, with the sparse economy of experience,

he made his own travel preparations. Riding out after
Rhiannon had become a veritable habit. He was arranging storage of the jewels and finery Rhiannon had
left—a handsome haul for the Church if she were found
guilty—when the patter of running feet sent him spinning toward the door, hand hovering near the dagger
at his belt.

The panting pageboy had to catch his breath before he could speak, hands planted on his knees as
he panted.

"Nay, lad, throw back your chest and make room
for the air." Beltran set him erect with a brisk shake.
"Now what is it?"

"Message," the boy gasped, "from milord bishop.
Your guard—is mounted and—awaits your command."

"My command? But I gave no orders for such."

"The hounds are—restless—so the huntsman said.
And hungry."

Swiftly his mind made the leap.

His so-called guard would be no better than a mob,
thrown together to capture the fugitive and drag her
back to judgment. This was Bonner's doing, his way
of ensuring Beltran did his duty.

And if he refused for any reason—even if he threw
the Church another bone, some poor maid guilty of
casting a love-spell for the butcher's boy—he could
bid farewell to his place and ambitions.

He'd seen the loathing in the bishop's eyes when he
watched Rhiannon frolic, the premier Catholic peer
of England dancing attendance upon her. Rhiannon's
mission, her claims, most of all her influence posed
a direct threat to Rome's authority over the Queen. If

Beltran refused to hunt her down and haul her in for judgment, Bloody Bonner would probably go himself.

"BLESSED GODDESS GRANT me strength."

Mired to her knees in an unknown bog thirty miles from London, Rhiannon bent and fought for breath. Her frozen legs and feet were numb, her sturdy shoes and skirts soaked through with marsh water. She'd been shivering since yesterday, when she crept from the wherry she'd hired to row her swiftly from court and the dungeon that waited.

Now the Thames was far behind her, the terrain so treacherous she doubted she'd ever be able to retrace her steps. And that was all to the good, because Edmund Bonner would have dispatched someone to bring her back.

What she didn't know, what she'd give anything to know, was whether he'd sent Beltran. Or if he had, whether she stood any chance of dissuading the Blade of God from his duty. Was it a woman's foolish fancy, or had her escape from beneath his vigilant nose seemed oddly convenient?

Behind her, the strange horse balked—exhausted and terrified, the poor creature, wading into a quagmire whose sucking sands threatened constantly to give way beneath them and pull them to a watery death. She thought longingly of Astolat, tears stinging her eyes. Leaving the faithful mare behind was one of the worst parts of this wretched business.

"Come along now, my good fellow," she coaxed the brown gelding. "I know you're cold and hungry and frightened. But I need you, my friend. We'll come to open ground soon, I know we will, and then we'll have a nice gallop. Just a little farther, I swear to you, then we'll rest a little."

The cob whickered a protest and trudged forward without enthusiasm. Rhiannon hauled the reluctant animal with one hand and clutched her muddy cloak with the other. She blessed Linnet for the warm garb she'd lent her—good serviceable wool, far better for desperate flight through this treacherous bog than her cream velvet riding habit, slashed with cloth-of-silver...

But her thoughts were wandering again. She straggled to a halt, straining to see through the thickening dusk that shrouded the gnarled roots and moss-draped trunks.

No sun and no moon, just this miserable drizzle, so she couldn't navigate by the heavens. She needed the stars to find the place—one of the ancient nodes of power from long before the Romans came to the land they'd called Britannia. A place where the old earth magick was strong enough for even a mixed blood Faerie like Rhiannon to summon the mists and cross the Veil.

No good. The old horse was balking again, and she lacked the stomach to force him. Wearily she dragged him up a hillock into the lee of a weathered oak, bent and twisted, and let him forage where he would. Digging into her bundle, she found the wineskin of cheap red and swallowed a mouthful of the raw vintage—tart as vinegar, but all she had to warm her. She dared not kindle a fire to hold her fear at bay.

A mournful cry echoed through the marsh, stopping her in her tracks. Wolves, was it? Bright Lady guard her, she'd never encountered a wild creature she couldn't tame. Why was she suddenly so uneasy?

Another long howl soared over the gray waters, rising and falling, echoed dimly by the baying of the pack, already a little closer. Well, in the worst case, she could free the gelding and climb a tree. She needn't fear being devoured in the wilderness—

Abruptly she froze, her blood turning to ice water. She hadn't thought she could be any colder, but now she clenched her jaw to keep her teeth from knocking together. It wasn't wolves she was hearing on the desolate moor.

It was hounds.

Hunting her.

An elemental fear brought her leaping to her feet. Terror arced through her, as though she'd been struck by lightning. Her white gasping breaths came hard and fast, just short of sobbing. The gelding shied, and she fought to hold him.

He was only a beast, yet he sensed the cruel malice of the men who stalked them.

Gripping her courage in both hands, she bound her bundle to the saddle. For a moment she listened in the slate-gray twilight, all her senses searching for the magickal pulse of the ancient earth.

What does it matter? she thought in despair. *Even if somehow you find the place, there's no mist tonight.* She'd never been strong enough to summon it. She could only cross the Veil through fog that nature had already woven, and only from a place of power.

Mist or no mist, if she couldn't find the node she was stranded—trapped on the mortal plane, at the mercy of those who hunted her.

"Lady of Light," she whispered, trembling with resolve. "I'm a daughter of kings. I swear they shall not have me without the mother of all battles."

Clutching her sodden garments, she urged the reluctant gelding deeper into the treacherous bog.

FIFTEEN

BELTRAN HAD NEVER cared for hounds. The ones in his Yorkshire hovel had been vicious brutes, with an unpleasant penchant for turning on weaker members of the pack. He'd far rather have left the beasts behind when he rode out with this hunting party, twenty men strong—if not for one unfortunate fact.

Edmund Bonner had ridden out with them.

The bishop trotted purposefully beside him through the twilight, his sturdy cob plodding through muck to his hocks. Hardly an amiable companion, given the air of malice he exuded as he stalked Rhiannon—relentless as the Devil himself.

As far as Beltran knew, Rhiannon had never met him. But the moment the bishop laid eyes on her, harmlessly romping in the Banqueting House, he'd seemed to recognize a mortal enemy.

Driven by necessity, Beltran broke the silence of hours.

"It'll be full dark soon, Lordship. We'll never manage to track her through this slop at night. We'll make camp on the high ground and resume the hunt at first light."

"No," Bonner said quietly, his hooded head turned forward, intent as the hounds that snarled and fought at his heels. "The witch is close, Vengeance. I can

smell her. We'll hunt her to ground like the foul vermin she is."

Despite his grim resolve to see the wretched business through to its bitter end, Beltran's hackles rose.
"Christ, she's only a harmless girl."

"Harmless? She spreads the disease of heresy wherever she goes, even into the Queen's very presence!
She's far too dangerous to remain at large."

"I don't advise pressing on by night," Beltran said
doggedly, fists clenching at the thought of Rhiannon
roaming the wilderness alone. "The horses will trip
on these damned roots and break a leg, or blunder into
quicksand and send us all straight to Hell."

"The hounds won't lead us astray. We're doing
God's work here, bringing the purifying fire of truth
to scald England clean of heresy." The bishop cast him
a sidelong glance. "Have a little faith, Lord Beltran."

"Faith or folly, I'm putting a stop to this madness!
The safety of these men rests in my hands."

Beltran hailed the fewterer, a sullen brute with a
harelip, scarcely less bestial than the dogs he tended.
"You there, man! Whistle down the hounds. We'll
make camp on dry ground—"

A high-pitched howl nearly dislodged him from the
saddle. His white Serafin reared high, forelegs paw-
ing the air. The rest of the pack took up the cry, the ly-
mers with their keen noses surging ahead, the mastiffs
growling and lunging on their leashes, horses snorting
and plunging all around.

Thighs clamped around his saddle, Beltran settled
his stallion and chivvied his men into order, a task
grown more complicated by the worsening drizzle. At
last, impatient, he ordered torches lit.

Gripping a flaming brand in one fist, he spurred ahead to survey the terrain. A low hillock rose above the surrounding wetlands. He urged Serafin to vault upward to its summit.

Now the savage belling of hounds filled the air, echoing over the silent waters and brooding reaches of the bog.

No doubt of it, they have the scent. Damn it to Hell! He'd hoped their eager noses had been confused by the wet ground. But that lout of a fewterer had given them Rhiannon's scent, straight from her rose-red mantle. Just as the waterman who'd ferried her had scented a fugitive's desperation. He'd taken her coin, wished her well, then sailed straight back to report where he'd left her. With the Devil's own luck, the wretch had encountered Beltran's party *en route*.

Before him the marsh spread, pink sun sinking behind a lowering mass of clouds. Its watery rays cast shadows behind the twisted trees, picked out every hillock and reed-choked shore and straggling spray of cattails—an utterly bleak and barren landscape.

Briefly he took heart. No force under Heaven could find a lone wanderer in all that vast wilderness, not even Edmund Bonner.

Brandishing his torch, Beltran cast a last glance over the landscape as he prepared to wheel away. A flicker of movement caught his eye, and an incongruous flash of silver. His chest tightened. One gauntleted fist clenched his reins.

Swinging the torch behind him so the light wouldn't blind him, he peered intently into the setting sun. There, struggling along a distant tree-lined shore, a slim cloaked figure waded through the reeds, haul-

ing a balking horse. If not for the tangle of silver curls
cascading down her back, her drab garments would
have concealed her.

Rhiannon.

It seemed God had intervened after all. Unless he
wished to violate his oath outright, he'd have to lead the
malevolent bishop and those slavering hounds straight
toward her.

RHIANNON SOBBED AS she struggled through the reeds,
heart laboring, her lungs aching. Every muscle in her
chilled body burned with fatigue. But the hounds—
blessed Lady—they sounded so close! If they came
upon her, how would she guard her precious flesh
against savage teeth that could rend her limb from
limb?

I must rest, just for a moment, must catch my breath.

Clinging to the gelding, she cast a wild glance
backward. There rose the low tableland she'd slid and
scrambled down an hour ago, dimly silhouetted against
the dying light.

A tongue of fire blazed suddenly against the dark-
ening sky. Her breath snared in her lungs. A mounted
figure was etched against a canvas of brooding clouds,
flaming torch brandished high, cloak swirling around
his powerful frame like ink spilled from a bottle.

Though her pursuer was too distant to discern his
features, she knew beyond doubt it was he.

Beltran.

His nearness squeezed her heart in a fist of despair
and fury—the same painful tangle of emotions he always inspired. Couldn't he merely have let her go?

Breath catching painfully, she hoisted her muddy skirts around her knees and began to run.

Behind her, the hungry cry of the hounds arose.

Icy water swirled around her knees, stones turning underfoot as she waded desperately through the muck, racing parallel to the dark shore. She sensed the proximity of that pulsing nexus where powerful magick could be summoned; it called to her like a raised voice, a physical tug that pulled her forward. Overhead the moon was rising, a ghostly orb floating among the clouds. Near the shore, thin eddies of mist were rising.

Behind her, the frenzied barking rose in pitch. They'd seen their quarry, those starving beasts, raised to gorge their hunger on heretic flesh. Goddess save her, they were close enough now that she sensed their fierce craving for spurting blood to fill their aching bellies. Her own stomach knotted and heaved.

Of his own accord, the gelding plunged past her, as the hunters herded them away from the reed-choked shore where they might hide. The siren call of power pulsed and ebbed, still maddeningly out of reach, nothing she could grasp to pull them free.

Frantic, she glanced back. Fresh panic seized her in its grip.

A dozen dark shapes were hurtling toward her, water spraying around flying legs, all gleaming eyes and slavering mouths in the night. The huntsmen had loosed them. No force on earth could save her…except one.

Merciful Goddess, Mother, I beg you. Show me the way!

Like a miracle, the answer to a prayer, torchlight flared in the darkness behind them. A massive shape was bearing down on her like a juggernaut—white charger cantering through the waves, black rider on his back, firelight flashing on the sword of Judgment whirling overhead.

Beltran bellowed at the hounds, cursing when his commands fell upon deaf ears. She caught a wild glimpse of his chiseled face, contorted, desperate as he leaned from the saddle. Then he called upon his God, the words streaking like meteors through the darkness.

The night ignited with holy fire.

Above the laboring figures of horse and rider, the mighty shadow of wings unfolded, garnet-red and emerald-green in the torchlight.

Still too distant, just a few breaths too late, to reach Rhiannon in time.

The lead hound—a woolly mastiff half her size, eyes red with hunger and hate, was lunging at her. Desperately she raised her pack between them, anything to fend off the rending jaws.

Then Beltran roared a word—a hail of syllables in a tongue that knotted her stomach. Thunder shook the heavens as a coil of shining platinum light arced from his pointing finger. Divine fire seared into the foremost mastiff as it leaped for her throat.

Before her very eyes, the snarling beast charred black and shriveled into ash.

All around her hounds were lunging, savage growls filling the air. Rhiannon stumbled blindly back, swinging her bundle to keep them at bay. Another coil of silver light exploded from the mounted figure bearing down on her, seared across the surging pack. Mastiffs scattered left and right, yelping, to avoid the spray of fire.

Desperately Rhiannon reached for the earth magick that lay so close, hidden beneath the featureless waves, glimmering in the moonlight.

Almost upon her, the towering Presence unleashed a resonant roar. "*Rhiannon—get down!*"

Obeying by instinct, she crouched. Heat singed her hair as a brand swung through the air, too close. A hulking giant of a man afoot had somehow circled behind her, driving her toward the hounds. He loomed over her, face twisted—the hideous maw split by a harelip, rotting teeth bared like one of his hounds.

Then Serafin thundered past, sheets of water spraying from his hooves. The Blade of God hurtled from his saddle and collided with her assailant. A flailing arm clipped her shoulder as their tangled forms went flying. She lost her footing and slipped to one knee, plunged to her waist in icy water. Pain shafted through her ankle, wrenched violently as she landed.

Around her, the world was noise and chaos. Hounds growled and slavered, turning on their fellows, maddened by the white fire whose afterimage lingered pale in the air. A circle of men on horseback spread out from the shore, surrounding her, appearing and vanishing in the tendrils of mist that swirled over the water.

Beltran and the harelip thrashed in the water. Somehow he'd lost his sword, his prized blade, and he seemed unable to summon another bolt of the purifying fire.

Even the Christian God must have His limits, she thought wildly. *Here in this place.*

For the tide of magick was rising at last, strong and sweet as salvation, a sea of liquid light that turned the world cloudy and gray. Her pack tumbled heedless from her fingers as she straightened, face lifted gladly toward the rising moon.

Beside her, steel flashed—serrated blade smeared black with foulness, gripped in the harelip's raised fist. As the two men grappled, the blade drove down... down...

The winged Presence roared in agony. The world shifted beneath her feet. Anguish flooded her healer's senses, exploded between her shoulder blades, as though the blade plunged into her own tender flesh, where the mighty wings joined the muscle of back and shoulders.

Beltran. Mortally wounded.

Possibly dying.

Body and heart and soul, every particle of life that formed Rhiannon's essence rose up in fierce denial. A surge of strength more potent than she'd ever known rolled through her, nearly lifting her feet from the earth. Soul fired by despair, her arms swept up and plunged into the heavens, head tilting back as she cried out the ancient words of power.

A curtain of mist fell like a blanket around them. With her last flicker of rational thought, she reached blindly to grip Beltran's sinewed forearm. Even in extremis, that vital current of awareness arced between them. His calloused hand closed over hers, the hard band of his ring pressing her flesh.

Then the silver light of magick washed over them. The pale remnants of the mortal world faded. Dizzy with the rush of power, Rhiannon smelled the sudden sweetness of apple blossoms.

He was burning. He was freezing. The white heat of agony seared through him, swelling and receding like the tide. Yet his hands and feet were numb, as if plunged in icy water. The red inferno of pain between his shoulders was a swirling vortex that threatened to drag him into its hungry maw and consume him.

Dimly, in the corner of his mind that remained his, Beltran knew what had befallen him.

Poison.

He'd been stabbed with a poisoned blade.

Sometimes the tide of pain receded. The swirling darkness parted to reveal a vision, pure and clear as redemption. A girl whose elfin features were sweet and grave, her face screened by curtains of silver hair, brows furrowed over leaf-green eyes that shimmered with tears.

And her gentle voice, begging him to rest quiet— please, they weren't safe here, they mustn't draw attention—was the essence of love.

She was desperately frightened of something—his healer, his angel, his heart. For her sake, he pushed back the darkness and lifted his heavy head. Briefly the world took shape. He glimpsed a low cubby warmed by ruddy coals, neat coils of herbs and roots hung to dry, mortar and pestle and a pile of red-stained linen on the trestle table, woven rugs adding flashes of warmth to the earthen floor. Around him, wooden walls bowed in a smooth curve that had never known axe or adze.

Somehow, he thought bemused, they were *inside* a tree.

"Please, Beltran," his angel whispered, cradling his head, pressing a steaming cup to his lips. The bitter odor of willow bark curled in his nostrils.

He preferred the sweet fragrance of violets. Fretful, he pushed the cup away.

"*Please*. Thou art consumed with fever."

"Good," he rasped, the word scraping his tender throat. God's body, his gullet felt as though he'd swallowed liquid fire. He must have been screaming.

He forced words past the pain. "Do God a favor, Rhiannon. Let me die. It's what He wanted—when he cast me out."

"Goddess! Thou art raving." Her sweet voice sounded choked. "I pray thee, drink the potion."

"Don't waste your tears…on me." For her sake, to still her weeping, he gulped a few mouthfuls of the scalding brew, sharp as acid on his tongue. Then the world went spinning away, and he sank back into darkness.

He kneeled with head bowed before his Father's blinding light, his body schooled into lines of contrition. But his soul was a seething stew of resentment and outraged pride. He'd done his duty, nothing more, and done it well. No creature in Heaven could deny that much.

Yet the resonant Voice that made oceans rise and mountains quake rolled on, remorseless as the march of time, discounting one by one the honors he'd earned in an eternity of service.

"Prince of Lights, Regent of the Sun, Destroyer of Hosts, Flame of God…you who were Wrath of Jacob and Mine own Angel of Vengeance. I trusted your sense of justice and defended the hard fairness of your judgments even when all others doubted you. Yet in your

pride you ignored all My warnings. Finally, your severity has shaken My faith."

Sullen anger burned like embers in his belly and made his skin smoke. "I'm Your punisher, Father. I'm Heaven's necessary evil—the corollary to Your endless capacity to forgive. Your grace leads them to love You, but my chastisements make mortal souls fear You."

"You are proud and heedless, my Vengeance. Proud as Lucifer, my Son of the Morning, before his insurrection." The bright Light dimmed. "For your own sake, Uriel, you must learn compassion."

"I'll try, Father." Yet he brooded without remorse, a powerful sense of injustice chewing at him. For eternity, he'd served in unfaltering loyalty, despite the shower of reprimands and recriminations that rained down on his head...

The Light breathed and watched him; Heaven sighed around them.

"I love you, Uriel." Now the murmured Voice throbbed low and rich. Uriel's chest ached with his own love, despite the resentment that seemed always to simmer in his blood. "It is because I love you that I grant you this chance, this sole prospect for redemption."

Now the Words rolled out like thunder, like the slow knell of doom, as the world slowly darkened around him.

"I consign you, Vengeance, to a mortal life—to birth from a mortal womb and life as a mortal man, with no knowledge or memory of your divine station. I grant you the same free will I give to all souls, the same power to learn, to temper your severe justice with mercy. Be taught this precious lesson, and you *are restored to Me, first among Mine own archangels, beloved servant of the Presence once more.*

"Fail to learn this lesson, and your soul will pass as mortals do, to whatever place the merits of your mortal life may warrant."

Slow comprehension broke over him. He was exiled from Heaven, from the Light, cast down like faithless Lucifer from the beloved Presence. Consumed by grief and rage, Uriel flung back his head and howled.

But the firmament of Heaven was dissolving beneath him, the celestial wind shredding his mighty wings to useless tatters.

And then he was falling...

RHIANNON SPONGED THE fever-sweat from Beltran's furrowed brow, and wished she could sponge away the grooves of pain as easily. He was raving again, wild and thrashing, shouting despite all her desperate efforts to quiet him. Ravaged by poison and the corrosive fury that seemed to be eating him away from inside, her patient was slipping from her.

And she knew she could not bear it.

She couldn't comprehend how Beltran Nemesto, Blade of God, had acquired such central importance to her existence. Perhaps when he'd saved her life, flinging himself so recklessly between her and the jaws of death. Perhaps when he'd made love to her—for it had been nearly that—on the forest floor.

Whenever it happened, however it happened, watching all his tireless strength and blazing courage and unwavering conviction rot away from inside was killing her.

If he died, it would save Morrigan the trouble of slaying her.

Sighing, Rhiannon unfolded her cramped limbs and rose. He'd sent the bucket flying in one of his thrashing fits. Now she must draw water before his fever peaked again. Gripping the bucket, she hurried through the little cubby she called home—the den beneath an ancient oak that was her secret sanctuary in the Faerie realm. She slipped through a round wooden door into the copper light of sunset.

A cruel wind knifed through her travel-stained gown, and she shivered. Only balmy breezes had ever caressed her skin in the Summer Lands, warmed by banners of honey-colored sunlight, pollen drifting like summer snow through the perfumed air. Now the leaves burned gold and crimson on the boughs and scudded on the autumn wind.

Nearby, hidden among the trees, a brook gurgled. Deliberately she turned her back and walked away from it, letting her thoughts skip from worry to worry, thinking of everything except her destination.

Although she'd never been adept at navigating the shifting terrain of Faerie, she was fortunate today. Soon the trees parted before her, and the brook trickled past.

Quickly Rhiannon drew water and lugged the heavy bucket back, glancing fearfully left and right through the shadowy forest. Every footfall she placed with care. Aye, she shared an affinity with the green growing things and gentle creatures that inhabited her wood; they'd known her since childhood. She prayed they would keep silent to protect her, that no whisper of her presence would reach Morrigan in Camelot. But she dared not count on it.

The coming of winter to the Summer Lands could mean only one thing. Her mother's strength was failing, and her sister's star was rising. Soon Morrigan must learn of her return. Here among the Fair Folk, where her power was nearly absolute, it would be child's play for Morrigan to kill her.

Consumed with worry, she hastened through the round door and latched the portal behind her. She'd descended the curving wooden stair and approached Beltran's pallet when she realized her patient wasn't alone.

On the stool sat a man, chin propped on fists, staring broodingly at Beltran as he tossed and mumbled with fever. In the brazier's flickering light, the stranger's skin shone pale as starlight against a doublet of blood-dark crimson. A gleaming mane of raven hair, glinting with indigo light, spilled over slender shoulders and poured halfway down his back.

As she stared in alarm, his head turned toward her. His violet eyes glowed and pulsed with divine fire.

"Don't be alarmed," the stranger said, a melodious tenor to set any bard weeping. "I'm a friend of his."

Rhiannon dragged a few wits together and lowered her heavy bucket. "How—how did you enter here? You're no Faerie, and the Summer Lands are well warded."

In her confusion, she'd spoken Latin. He answered in kind, his mouth curving wryly. "Let's just say I have connections."

"Whatever connections you may have, sir, you shouldn't be here! It isn't safe for a mortal, particularly now."

"Surely you don't mistake me for one of those." With inhuman grace, he flowed to his feet. For a heartbeat, gleaming jet-black wings flickered into view. When she blinked, the effect vanished.

Only once had she seen anything like—on the Blade of God who tossed restless in the bed. "You're...like Beltran."

"Well, not exactly." He offered a fluid shrug. "Our friend here is bound to a mortal body. Thankfully, I'm not. Although if I keep on the way I'm headed, I may indeed find myself wrenched from celestial bliss and stuffed willy-nilly into a body by Someone in a fit of pique, just like our friend here."

Swift recollections hurtled through her brain—the Presence who materialized during Beltran's holy rages, the divine fire he'd hurled to save her, the wild ravings he'd shouted in his delirium.

"Tell me the truth." Blindly she gripped the table. "Who is he?"

"He *was* Uriel, Flame of God—one of our leading archangels up there, one of the favored four who guard You-Know-Who. Until he fell."

She stared into those violet orbs, glowing with heavenly light. "And...you?"

"I'm Zamiel." He swept her a careless bow, flicking his gleaming mane aside with one gauntlet. "Angel in disgrace, at your service."

A hundred questions jostled on her tongue, but Beltran convulsed and cried out in his sleep. Renewed fear gripped her chest. Brushing past the visitor, who obligingly stepped aside, she kneeled and laid her hand against Beltran's sweating brow.

"Dear Lady, he's burning up," she whispered. "I've tried every remedy to bring down this fever."

"He's dying," Zamiel said calmly.

"*Dying!*" she cried, in horror. "But he—he can't die, not him. I won't allow it!"

"That blade was poisoned, with a little magick from the bishop thrown in. No healing simples are going to cure that. Meaning no offense to your formidable talents."

Rhiannon barely heard him, her entire being absorbed in the unconscious man before her. Her heart reeled with discovery. Her entire essence rose up to voice a great shout whose echoes rang through her soul.

She loved him.

She, Rhiannon le Fay—outcast and misfit, mocked and reviled, more than half an orphan—had found the one man whose presence made her feel safe. This revelation of his identity as an exiled angel of the Christian God did nothing to alter her heart. She loved him for the traits his divine origins could not blunt—his unyielding resolve, his coolheaded competence in the teeth of any crisis, his lion's heart and his angel's conscience. She craved the leaping heat his touch ignited in her blood.

Riveted by disbelief, seized with sudden euphoria, she laughed.

"That hardly strikes me as appropriate," Zamiel murmured, one wicked brow arching.

"I swear to you, I won't let him die." Thoughts whirling, she pushed to her feet and paced the chamber. "Think! Did your God send you here to help him?"

"Him?" The angel's lip curled in scorn. "Oh, hardly. He's fretting madly over Uriel here—I mean Beltran— it *is* Beltran, right? But He can't go changing the script in midact. If it were up to Him, our suffering friend could die in lingering agony and He wouldn't lift a finger to intervene. Believe me."

"Surely there's *something* that can be done," she urged. "If he was poisoned by the bishop's magick, by Christian magick and Christian prayer, there must be some spell or invocation that can heal him."

"Oh, there is." Zamiel shrugged. "But it's risky, Rhiannon—*may* I call you Rhiannon?"

"Risky to him?"

"Nothing worse can happen to him than what's happening right now," he pointed out. "He's dying unconfessed with his sins unshriven, including a few to make any priest quail. He's made decent progress toward his…rehabilitation, shall we say?…which I attribute to your wholesome influence. But I fear it's not enough, in Christian parlance, to save his soul."

Zamiel paused. "When I said the spell was risky, I meant it's risky for you."

Impatiently she brushed that aside. "All magick carries risks. My lord—Zamiel—"

"'My lord' will do nicely," he murmured. "Though I've always felt 'Angel of Death' has a certain ring."

She stifled a strong urge to grasp the Angel of Death by his doublet and shake him. "Whatever the risk, I'll take it. Tell me what must be done."

Thoughtfully he studied the restless Beltran. "He's under the influence of powerful death magick—trust me to know. To reverse the spell, you must invoke the power of life. There's a ritual whose outlines I can describe for you, but you must make haste. The ritual must be performed at moonrise. If you miss your moment, he won't last the night."

He paused, his violet gaze turning toward her, clearly measuring her resolve.

"As you surely know, or would know in time—which our friend is rather short of at the moment—the most powerful life-force in the world is the power of creation. Or in this case, the power of *procreation*."

"I beg your pardon?"

He arched a brow. "To speak plainly, we're talking about intercourse, but not just any tumble in the hay. If the witch who casts the healing spell were, say, a maiden? And if her maiden state were immeasurably precious to her? I'd say that should do the trick."

Halfway through the explanation, Rhiannon had grasped where he was headed. She halted in her tracks and stared at him, torn between suspicion and denial. Then sudden anger seared through her.

Was he playing games with her? Was this a vile trick of some kind? Was this uncanny and beautiful young immortal some deception of Morrigan's?

The dream she'd had in the mortal realm surfaced in her mind. Her sister clipped crimson roses with pruning shears, the blossoms red as virgin blood.

Red is for heartbreak, she'd whispered.

Lose your virginity to a mortal man…

Her sister could have been lying. But if the Goddess had shown her a vision, she would surely have told the truth.

Her first wild impulse was to cry that she wouldn't do it. There must be another way. But she knew in her heart Zamiel's words held the ring of truth.

Still, she'd survived a lifetime of trickery through constant suspicion. She was unwilling to accept this complete stranger and his dangerous advice on faith.

"Tell me this, my lord. If your God refuses to intervene, then why are *you* here? Are you and Beltran such intimate friends?"

"Intimate? Not as I'd define the term." Again that wicked brow lifted. "He isn't really my type, Rhiannon. But intervening in this little crisis that has the Fellow upstairs in such a delightful dither? Stirring the pot, as they say? How could I possibly resist?"

SIXTEEN

RHIANNON SUPPOSED SHE should thank the Goddess for the Angel of Death, odd as that notion sounded. But she decided to hold her gratitude in reserve until she saw whether this exotic ritual he'd described truly worked.

And whether she had the nerve to perform it.

Carefully she made her preparations, focusing on the moment to avoid dwelling upon what would come. If she'd harbored any other hope, any rare herb or treatment or prayer she'd thought could work...but she'd exhausted every remedy her healer's knowledge and instinct could imagine.

Without this desperate sacrifice, Beltran would not survive the night.

He'd risked his own life and his immortal soul to save her. She loved him for it. And she would not allow him to pay the ultimate penalty for that sacrifice.

Instead, she chose to pay that penalty herself.

His wound had been severe, deep enough that she feared the knife had pierced a lung. But his flesh had closed and knitted like a miracle, healed with supernatural speed, the only remnant of that injury a fading pink scar across his muscled back.

Nay, it was the poison that was killing him—the bishop's death magick, which Bonner had certainly meant for her.

Briefly she paused in her preparations to examine

her patient, hoping against hope for some sign of improvement. Beltran had ceased tossing and mumbling, and lay still as a man already dead. His chiseled face was etched with lines of pain, his burnished hair dark with sweat. Golden stubble rasped against her fingers as she touched his hard jaw, felt his pulse flutter faint and fast.

No doubt of it, he was dying.

Except that Rhiannon had no intention of allowing that to happen.

Blessed Lady, how is it possible that I've grown to love him utterly, and in so little time?

Torn between marvel and dread, anticipation humming in her blood, she finished her preparations swiftly. She performed her ritual bath, while the unknown incense Zamiel had left smoldered and blackened in the brazier, its queer bittersweet smoke curling thick as mist through the cubby.

Gratefully she cast aside her muddy mortal gown, clad herself in a gossamer milk-white robe of spidersilk, and brushed the silver tangle of her hair until it swirled loose around her shoulders.

Barefooted, she padded to the brazier, where she brewed a potent tea from the forked root of mandrake. Deadly nightshade, and too much would kill him. But for this spell its hallucinatory and aphrodisiac qualities were essential.

Carefully she measured out a few sips for Beltran, who was beyond even swallowing, forcing her to pour the dangerous potion directly down his throat. The potent dregs she drained herself, with an anxious glance through her shuttered window.

In the Summer Lands one rarely saw the sun, but the

russet light of sunset was fading in the sky. Beneath the boughs, the lavender shadows of twilight thickened.

Less than an hour till moonrise. She must act now or never, and live with the consequences.

Seized in a terrible paralysis of indecision, she caught up her bronze mirror and searched its depths. Her own familiar face stared back at her, eyes enormous with trepidation, smudged with violet shadows of exhaustion. She should have been white with dread, yet a wild-rose blush bloomed in her cheeks. Her breasts rose and fell swiftly, and that hum of excitement was mounting. The mandrake was working its magick, she supposed.

The next time I look into this glass, I'll no longer be a maiden. Perhaps I'll no longer be a Faerie princess, blessed with immortality, but a mortal woman cursed to wither and die.

Would they exile her from the Summer Lands or let her live like a shadow among the Fair Folk? Would she be anything more than a nameless face, just another mortal who'd stumbled through the Veil by mischance?

A low groan from the bed dragged her back to the present. Straightening her shoulders, tilting her chin with resolve, she laid the mirror aside and took up her silver lute. Standing before the brazier, while Beltran lay senseless, she touched the strings. A glissade of liquid notes rippled through the air.

For a time she merely played, letting the cascade of music soothe her desperate fears and ease her anxious heart. When the music led her to it, she wove her voice into the melody, spinning a song of sweet repose.

Beltran lay unresponsive, bedclothes twisted around his naked hips, sweat gleaming like oil on the broad planes of his chest. Muscles twitched in his bulging biceps and shoulders, in the sinewed column of his abdomen. His warrior's hands lay curled on the blanket, strong and calloused, infinitely capable of both kindness and cruelty. The gold seal of Justice glinted in the firelight.

She thought of those hands on her body, hard and sure. Heat kindled in her blood and pulsed in her womb.

Now her song deepened and slowed, the low croon of a woman in love, flesh tingling and aching for her lover's touch. She closed her eyes and swayed with the rhythm, her silken garment whispering around her.

When the spirit moved her, she began to dance, spinning slowly, breath quickening, hair flying free in a scented cloud around her. Her fingers caressed the strings; her tongue caressed the words. The fire's heat built against her skin and pooled deep within her.

She was no longer herself, no more the shy maiden.

Yet she'd never felt more free.

She was floating across the floor, eyes closed, entranced...

Warm hands closed around her waist and pulled her back against a man's tensile heat. Her eyes flew open to find the bed empty, blankets flung to the floor.

The ritual had begun to weave its magick, turning her love from the threshold of death to a last flickering glimpse of life.

Soul and body, she recognized the touch of the man behind her, though she could not see him. Strong brown hands spread over her ribcage, just beneath her breasts, as though he had every right to claim her. Naked beneath the whisper-thin silk, she felt his fever-heat seep into her, his chest scorching her back.

One hand gathered her loosened hair and smoothed it aside. The warm flutter of his breath teased her neck, there at the vulnerable nexus where neck and shoulder joined. Then the brand of his mouth seared her.

A tingling pleasure raced through her. She gasped and shivered beneath his kiss—surely the mandrake doing its work. When his hands closed around her breasts, she voiced a low cry.

Dear Goddess, the way he claimed her, weighing her breasts in his palms, fingers circling and teasing her nipples until she ached for him. As he brushed the tingling peaks, low pulses of pleasure throbbed in her belly. Moisture gathered like dew between her thighs. Wickedly skilled, he played her like the lute that dangled from her fingers. He touched her with a certainty that had no business in a man sworn to chastity.

"Rhiannon," he breathed, low and husky, breath tickling her ear. A flicker of relief made her sag against him. Between the magick and the mandrake, she hadn't been certain he would know her, or be capable of any more than mindless rutting.

Still she knew he was deeply drugged and far from waking, else he'd never have the strength to stand.

"Do you want to know what I intend to do to you?" he whispered against her skin, voice thick with mandrake and desire. "You who made me wait for you? Made me burn for you? I plan to undress you, princess—one layer at a time. I want to tease and suckle your perfect pink nipples until you moan and rise against me, just as you did in the forest. Until I smell the musk of your arousal, until I spread your thighs and drink the sweet cream of your desire, until you arch into my tongue and tighten around my fingers and beg me to take you."

Surely if he'd been himself, he would have known she needed a maid's patient wooing. Instead his words left her breathless, half-fainting against him.

"Beltran, for the love of all Gods! We must do this slowly…"

"I want you to take my cock in your warm little hands and fit me against you, princess," he murmured, "so both of us know what you want me to do."

Heedless of her plea, his hands slid down her body, a liquid caress that left her languid and melting against him. One hardened palm stroked down her belly, until he found the heat burning between her legs. The lute slipped from her fingers.

"And then, Rhiannon," he whispered, "I'm going to mount you slowly. And you're going to beg me for every inch."

"Merciful Lady," she whispered, on a scrap of breath. Her mind was reeling, her thoughts dazed and clouded. Yet her thighs eased apart to grant him the access he demanded. Her head tipped back against his shoulder, face turning into his neck, the sweet spice of frankincense mingled with male arousal.

She was an aching void of craving, her skin chafed by the gossamer silk between them. She was arching into his seeking touch, just as he'd promised she would. His fingers slipped between her folds, only the cobweb silk between her flesh and his.

Yet even that barrier between them was intolerable.

With a low curse he released her, but only for a heartbeat. He caught the thin fabric in his fevered hands and swept it upward, baring her body to his unfettered heat. Reflexively she grabbed for it, a last flash of defiance against her fate. But he moved with a fighting man's quickness. The silk settled to the floor in a cloud, and the fire's heat encased her naked skin.

Like a physical touch his gaze swept over her—the arch of her spine cloaked by the fall of hair, the curve of her naked bottom beneath.

"God in Heaven, Rhiannon," he muttered.

The world of Faerie turned gray and shivered around them. But the enchantment gripped him too tightly to notice. The shadow of death blotted out the world around him; he saw and heard and smelled nothing but her.

"Please don't," she whispered, a tendril of fear snaking through her. Any attempt to call upon the Christian God within the bounds of the Summer Lands was blasphemy. It made the entire realm tremble like an insect struggling in cobwebs. Inevitably, the dissonance must pluck at Morrigan's attention.

And then she would send her hordes to deal with them, or be upon them herself.

"Too late," he said roughly. Clearly his senses were clouded by magick, mistaking her fear for sexual reluctance.

His warm mouth blazed a trail of fire across her shoulders. His hands claimed her breasts once more, calloused thumbs teasing her upright nipples until they thrust eagerly against his touch. Her senses reeled beneath the assault.

When his fingers sought her warm core, slipping between sensitive folds to find the honey of passion that coated her, her body melted against him. Unerringly he found the pulsing pearl that swelled and ached with her yearning for him. His fingers teased her, swirling around that tender bit of flesh, stroking her own cream over her, massaging her flesh until she moaned and writhed against his touch.

"You'll let him peel those stiff garments from you, caress you and suckle you until you pulse for him, stroke and fondle your little pearl until he makes you whimper and beg him to slide that great throbbing man-root between your thighs…"

She thrust away the unwelcome echo of her sister's warning. She cared for nothing but that rhythmic friction, *there*, this breathless excitement that squeezed her chest and made her breath hard and fast, the mounting excitement that fluttered in her belly and pulsed against his touch. Tingles raced down her thighs, her toes curling into cool earth.

Blindly her hands sought him. His corded thighs seared her palms. Burning with a sudden hunger to know all of him, she caressed his hard lines, her hands curving to find the clenched muscle of his buttocks. He groaned and thrust against her, the stiffened blade of his arousal nudging her spine. Relentlessly he teased her nipple, making fire arc through her. A vortex of heat swirled at her core. Her body, burning like a brand, kindled to a bonfire by his touch.

She turned her face into the tendons of his neck, tasting salt on her lips—the sweat of his craving, or the salt of her tears? Moaning, she rubbed against that maddening friction between her thighs. All the blood in her body was collecting in that little pearl of flesh, making it swell and harden beneath his touch. In another moment, she would explode…

Abruptly, he nudged her forward, strong hands

steering her progress. When the front of her thighs brushed the bed, her eyes flew open, arms stretching to catch herself as she tumbled forward. Deftly he caught her, cradling her hips, bending her forward at the waist. Hair spilled around her hot face, blinding her. His hands slid up the backs of her thighs and parted her, spreading her wet channel wide for him.

Now the potent magick they'd kindled could not be turned aside. He'd forgotten her lack of experience—made her forget herself—abandoned both of them to the sweeping force of this unstoppable seduction. Again he found her throbbing pearl and she thrust into his touch, her body moving with the rhythm she could no longer contain. Her tight channel opened to the finger that eased into her virgin depths. Her face burrowed into the bed, linen sheets still hot from the fever that consumed him. She panted as the unbearable tension built and spiraled into a tight coil of need.

His rampant lance seared her thighs like a white-hot iron as he bent over her. The heat of his body enclosed her, cradling her, steadying her for what was to come.

Deep within, a last futile warning rang like a bell, the slow peals tolling through her soul. Bright Lady, she couldn't do this! How could she surrender everything she was, her dream of acceptance among her people, her identity, the only life and home she'd ever known?

But if she didn't, he would die. The notion was monstrous, unbearable, worse than all the rest.

If she didn't, she would die herself. Surely no living creature could suffer this pounding craving and survive it. For her own sake, for the love of him that burned like a candle within her, she closed her ears to that warning tocsin.

Afire, restless, fretful, she managed to roll over. She needed the reassurance of *seeing* him, her own eyes showing her she wasn't alone, that he too burned for her. For the magick was strong in him now. His manhood was probing her, sliding into the slick channel her desire had readied for him. Surely he was far too large, would never fit there—

Afloat and drowning in a sea of pleasure, she saw the bloom of pain like a crimson rose.

…Red is for heartbreak…

A moment of perfect clarity shimmered around her. Her eyes fluttered open to drink in the erotic tableau—his powerful crusader's body taut and rippling with muscle, sun-gold skin glistening with fever-sweat, thrusting against her slight fair-skinned form, her hair flung across the bedclothes like a tangled silver banner.

Then a glowing shaft of moonlight streamed through the window to pour across the bed. Her skin glowed alabaster, bathing their entwined bodies with a pure nimbus of white light. The lightning charge of magick lifted the hair on her forearms.

But it was more than moon magick that swept through her, tingling along her skin, building into a tight spiral of need between her thighs. She soared beneath another kind of magick entirely—the enchantment of sweat-slick skin and the rhythmic clench of his buttocks under her desperate grip, the rush of hot breath as he gasped words of command and endearment in her ear, the sweet shock of need as the friction against her woman's pearl drove her mad with wanting.

Still the thrust of his manhood filled her aching

depths, slippery with her own desire. Shameless, her body arched to meet him, found the driving rhythm of passion and matched it. Deep within, the low, delicious ripples of pleasure built and spread. She wrapped her legs tight around his hips and surrendered to him.

The climax tossed them high, to the very pinnacle of passion. It crashed over and through them, arcing from one to the other. Together they shuddered, voices mingling as they cried out. Her woman's channel pulsed with spasms of pleasure, rippling outward until her fingers curled and tingled. When he convulsed atop her, the spurt of life flooded her womb like spring rain.

Slowly her vision cleared. She found him collapsed against her, his raspy jaw cradled against her shoulder, face buried in her tumbled hair. His weight pressed her deep into the straw-filled mattress. She felt the slow rise and fall of his chest, the deep rhythm of a restful and healthy sleep.

His skin had cooled, his fever broken, sweat drying on both their limbs. Weak with relief and gratitude, swamped by the knowledge of her loss, Rhiannon turned her face into the mattress and wept.

SLOWLY BELTRAN RETURNED to himself, though the journey was far from easy. His memories of the previous days—weeks?—had kinked into a maddening tangle: the baying of hounds, the glimpse of Rhiannon's terrified face that turned his heart and obliterated all his godly intentions in a heartbeat, the burning prelude to the killing rage dropping over him like a curtain wreathed in flames.

Clear as his faith in God, he recalled the intense

pounding pleasure of climax, a paroxysm more powerful than he'd ever known.

"Christ, what a dream," he muttered. The earth quaked beneath him.

His eyes flew open.

A half-remembered scene coalesced around him—a cozy chamber walled in red-gold wood, beams hung with bundles of dried herbs. A bright banner of sunlight streamed through the window, across a trestle table littered with mortar and pestle, wooden cups and a pile of bloody bandages.

Nestled in bed beside him lay Rhiannon, tucked into the curve of his arm as though she'd never belonged anywhere else. Her sleeping face was turned into his shoulder, her delicate profile like white damask against his sun-browned chest. Her mane of gilded curls wrapped around their entangled limbs.

Both of them naked as newborns beneath the supple deerskin tossed over them.

In a scalding rush, a torrent of images and sensations tumbled through his brain.

"*Not* a dream after all. God save me." Again the world trembled like a strummed harp. Overhead, the hanging roots swayed.

Against him Rhiannon stirred, dark lashes fluttering up to reveal sleep-clouded eyes. For a moment she blinked at him, gloriously tousled and bewildered. Then comprehension rushed into her face.

Swiftly she sat up, clutching an armful of deerskin to her bare breasts. *And wasn't that a pity?*

Swift with urgency, her words tumbled out. "Beltran, for pity's sake, don't invoke thy Deity in this place. 'Tis like dropping a stone into a still pond. It causes ripples, as thou hast seen. Above all else, we must pass unnoticed here."

His mind groped to make sense of this chaotic speech. Carefully he spaced his words. "Where are we?"

"At my house in the Summer Lands." She paused when his brow furrowed, demanding more. "In the Faerie realm."

Superstitious dread flared within him, but he quashed it.

"Don't be absurd," he said roughly.

Caution invaded her features. Glancing down, she nibbled her lower lip. "Thou remember nothing?"

Of course he remembered. How not? Until the day he died, he'd remember her bewitching grace, spinning in the dance, her lithe shape silhouetted against the fire. He'd remember the warmth of her pert breasts cupped in his palms, nipples hard and tight as cherries with desire for him. He'd remember the hot wet slide of his fingers through her cream-soaked cleft, the way she'd arched into his caress, her low throaty moans as he massaged her throbbing quim.

God, the way she'd looked when he bent her over, her sweet bottom upturned, back arched, legs spread to expose her swollen folds, flushed and glistening with dew. The way she'd *smelled*, the perfumed musk of arousal mingled with the fragrance of violets.

The intense surge of satisfaction that made him roar like a lion when her tight channel gripped him.

The tremors of her climax milking him until he spurted inside her.

"I remember everything," he growled, voice thick with passion. Already he was hard and aching.

But her green eyes were troubled as they lingered upon him. "Beltran, there's something I should tell thee. Last night…there was a visitor here. Do thou remember?"

Absently, he shook his head. Christ, the pope himself could have been here last night and it wouldn't have stopped him. He'd been burning to tumble her. And now that he'd given in to the impulse and flung himself headlong into sin, he intended to stay there a while, damn it.

"Beltran," she began, resolute.

"Not now, princess. Let me see you." Before she could think to protest, he tugged the deerskin down.

Breasts lush and silken as peaches, God save him, her pink nipples already peaking beneath his stare. Navel tucked like a jewel against her tiny waist. Her cross-legged position, like a Yuletide gift, exposed her beautifully to his hungry gaze. The plump petals and deep rose cleft of her cunny blushed under his attention.

God, she was perfectly formed. And she fit him like a glove. He remembered that well enough.

Then he glimpsed a spot of crimson, like a rose petal, staining the bedclothes. The knowledge hit him like a fist.

"Damnation, Rhiannon!" he blurted, dismayed.

She'd been a virgin, and he'd all but raped her last night.

He'd given in to lust before in his life. But he made it a rule never to deflower an innocent, just as he never trifled with a woman who belonged to another.

Confused, he rubbed his forehead, forcing order to his thoughts. "I thought—that day in the garden at

Hatfield, the way you touched me, the things you whispered in my ear…"

Suddenly, with startling clarity, the pieces fell into place. The sorcerous fog that shrouded his memory, the ripe curves of the woman wearing Rhiannon's face, too voluptuous for a girl of her slimness—the full figure of a mature woman. The way she'd undulated against him like a cat in heat, the bold words she'd breathed, her hot little tongue darting into his ear as she described exactly how she was going to suckle him.

Not Rhiannon.

No doubt it was more trickery from that malignant sister of hers, like the monstrous serpent that reared from the water, like the magick that swept them through the mists into this other realm.

Slowly he shook his head. "Rhiannon, I was out of my mind last night. I make no excuse for it. I should have realized…"

Realized you were a virgin.

"I would have stopped, if I'd known," he said lamely.

More likely, I would have seduced you properly, damn it.

"Thou need not speak of it," she said quickly, her lashes falling. Rose color stained her downturned face. "Thou art a Blade of God, sworn to serve thy Deity. If not for the magick, I know well what happened between us would not have been thy choice."

That wasn't it at all. God's fury, he'd been craving her like wine since the day they'd met. But he could hardly tell her that. What could he offer her? Nothing but shame and dishonor—a few days of stolen pleasure with a renegade apostate who'd turned his back on his obligations, chosen sin and damnation over duty. He'd taken from her, roughly and without consideration for a maid's tender state, the virtue she must have preferred to save for the lucky bastard she'd marry some day.

He'd brought the bishop down on her. And on himself. If he abandoned his vocation and his vows for her sake, the Blades would hunt him down like an animal, like the villain he was.

Summoning all his discipline, he pushed those worries aside and went straight for the immediate issue. He braced against the unpleasant truths she might tell him.

"Rhiannon, did I hurt you?"

"A little." Her head lifted with the swift pride of a princess. "But I'm no coward to quail from a bee-sting. The pain was naught compared to the…the pleasure of it. Of course I knew women enjoy the business in the natural way, just as all living creatures must. But I never dreamed it could feel like *that*."

Again her lashes swept down, demure as any virgin. But the low throb of passion in her voice told the tale of what he'd made her feel. The knowledge made triumph surge through him, a primitive male satisfaction that made him want to roar like a lion.

"I'm glad to know you enjoyed it." Idly he wound a gilded tendril of her hair around his fingers. "As the more experienced one between us, I feel obliged to point out that, if I'd been in my right mind, I would've made you feel more than mere pleasure. I would have had you begging me, just as I promised."

Her rosy blush deepened, but her chin tilted mutinously. "I'm a royal princess, Beltran. I'm not in the habit of begging a man for anything."

The wicked impulse seized him to prove it was no idle boast. No doubt she was tender, after last night's indulgences. But if he put his mind to it, he could make her burn for him.

"Do you question my ability?" he murmured. "You're challenging me to prove it."

Cat-quick, she leaped to her feet and whirled to snatch a shift. The movement treated him to a flashing glimpse of her lissome back and the sweet bottom he'd gripped when he mounted her, now maddeningly out of reach.

Christ, she was made for loving. For *his* loving, and he wanted to hear her admit it.

He pushed to a sitting position and reached for her.

A surge of dizziness rolled through him. The world blurred around him. He cursed and gripped his aching head. He wouldn't be sprinting like a satyr through the house after her or anyone else in this condition.

When his vision cleared, she was bending over him—barely decent, Lord save him—slender limbs spilling from her muslin shift. She pressed a cup upon him, leaf-green eyes warm with concern.

"Thou mustn't try to rise so swiftly," she rebuked him. Her soft hands folded his fingers around the cup, cool and dripping between them. "Goddess, thou nearly died last night! Now sip this slowly."

"Don't coddle me, girl," he said irritably. But he couldn't deny his mouth was dry as dust and tasted worse. He sipped the crisp brown beer and found it ambrosia. As the cold wetness slid down his throat, he grunted approval at the nutty taste.

She looked modestly pleased by his appreciation. "'Tis my own brewing from the summer wheat. I enjoy such household pastimes, the brewing and baking and spinning, when I can. Rest here awhile, and I'll fetch thee a rich rabbit broth with herbs to build thy blood."

Already she was bustling about, her steps quick and light. To his eternal disappointment, she slipped on a gown of fine-woven brown wool, then twisted her hair into a thick loose braid. It was a crime to cover all that beguiling beauty. But he supposed it was for the best, unless he wanted to violate her again.

Suddenly he cursed. "What of the bishop? What of Edmund Bonner and my men? Did they follow us through the mist?"

"Nay, we left them behind, combing the shores for us. No doubt they're convinced thy Lucifer spirited us away."

In the midst of rigging a tripod over the brazier, she hesitated. "We must return thee to the mortal realm as soon as we may. Time flows differently here in the Summer Lands, and we've already lingered far too long. If we wait much longer, thou may return to find a hundred years or more have passed beyond the Veil. It's happened thus before."

Normally he would challenge this pagan nonsense, but suddenly he was no longer certain what he believed. And that would be a problem, wouldn't it, when he returned to the fold?

The world wasn't what he'd believed—what he'd been arrogantly certain it was. Did other creatures like Rhiannon dwell peacefully in the hidden places of the earth, more women and men and children with her innocent beauty, their souls brimful with love and compassion like hers? If they did, he no longer had the stomach to bring the Inquisition roaring down on them.

Grimly he mastered his chaotic thoughts. He swung

his legs out of bed and reached for his hose. His head ached, but his vision stayed clear.

"How soon can we leave?" he asked.

"The sooner the better, as I've said." She busied herself strewing herbs into the stewpot, the savory aroma making his empty belly growl. "Morrigan will know we're here, if she doesn't already. We lack the strength to fight her in this place where she's strongest, and where thy God holds little sway."

She paused, her countenance grave and troubled. Keenly attuned to her moods as he was to his own body, his instincts prickled in warning.

"What is it, Rhiannon?"

Her gaze flickered toward him. "It's merely—I'm hoping I have the power now to bring you through the Veil. 'Tis possible I could no longer pass unaided from the mortal realm to this one. But I may still be able to pass the other way, with help."

Frowning, he pushed to his feet, only a little unsteady. Refusing to indulge the floor's annoying tendency to sway beneath him, he scooped up shirt and doublet. "Why would you be unable? You managed well enough last time."

She nibbled at her lip, considering. "I might as well tell thee the truth, since thy welfare may hinge upon it. There is great power bound up with the virgin state, which is why it was so valuable for the healing spell. When I surrendered…what I surrendered… I lost that maiden power. I'm only half-Fae to begin, and my magick has never been great. I fear I may have lost what little I possessed."

Undeceived by her light tone, he stared at her and felt his heart turn over in his chest. That she'd made such a sacrifice for him was astounding. Her selfless-ness touched him in a way he hadn't expected and was ill prepared to deal with.

Impatiently he brushed aside the implications for himself. He ought to be considering what it meant for her. Tossing his garments aside, he strode bare-chested to her side. Gently he gripped her arm to draw her away from the bubbling stewpot, and tilted her chin to meet his gaze.

"I'm humbled and honored by your gift to me, Rhi-annon. I scarcely know what I've done to merit your generosity, after the way I've hounded and persecuted you."

Again that wild-rose blush tinged her cheeks. Her eyes seemed to glimmer with some vast and secret knowledge that saddened her. "I'm a king's daughter, Beltran. My honor is life itself to me. Thou saved me, didn't thou, not once but twice? Last night I merely returned the favor."

Her simple logic should have reassured him. But for some reason he didn't like hearing that she'd given herself to him for honor's sake, to repay a bloody debt.

With a smile, she slipped from his grasp, and he quashed a pang of loss. He scowled but let her go. He had to resign himself to letting her go, somehow.

"You mentioned getting help from some quarter," he said when they were seated at the table, hungrily devouring the succulent stew and sopping up the juices with a hunk of fresh barley bread. "Do you have many allies at your court?"

"At Camelot?" Her ash-dark brows winged up in surprise. "Where my sister is? We shan't pass a hundred leagues from there if I can avoid it. Nay, I'm thinking of the hallows."

He looked at her blankly.

"Those who worship the Goddess revere four sacred hallows, one for each element—dish of earth, spear of air, the sacred cup of water mortals call the Grail, and the sword of fire, which last appeared in England as King Arthur's blade Excalibur. Both dish and spear are well beyond our reach. And the Grail too is beyond Morrigan's reach. She cannot hope to claim it while Queene Maeve lives."

He struggled to subdue raw disbelief. She had no reason to lie to him, and he'd learned Rhiannon never lied. Her actions had earned her the right to be trusted—or at least not mocked for her beliefs, whether they were Christian or nay. He swallowed a mouthful of bread and spoke with what calm he could muster.

"That leaves the sword of fire. Excalibur."

As he spoke the name, an odd tingle swept over him, as though a ghostly wind had stirred his hair and garments. With difficulty, he focused on her words.

"Of the four relics, the only one within our reach is Excalibur—and only if its guardian will lend us its magick." She paused, face solemn, her bright eyes fixed upon him. "I shall never lie to thee, Beltran. The way is risky. Even if we succeed, I'm not certain 'twill be sufficient. It may be I still cannot part the Veil. But we must try, and quickly, before Morrigan tracks us here."

Frowning, he gripped the dagger belted at his waist. The loss of his prized sword had dismayed him—and alarmed him, if danger threatened. Could this be a message from God, the Lord's way of telling him he should

pursue this mad quest for a legendary blade to replace
the one he'd lost? He'd be mad as a loon to think so.

"You say the way is risky." He studied her. "How
so?"

"Distance is an odd thing in the Summer Lands.
The Faerie Queene rules at Camelot, the place my sister schemes to fill. Once it was a mortal keep, the court
where Arthur ruled with his Queen Guinevere, but it
slipped behind the Veil during the last Convergence.
The Grail resides in Camelot—the Cup of Truth, sacred to the Goddess—though Morrigan cannot touch it.

"But Excalibur rests in Avalon, the holy isle, which
was once the Christian Isle of Glass. Sometimes the
mists lie thick between these sacred places, and the
distance between them is vast indeed. But…"

She paused. "As thou have witnessed, the mists are
thinning as the Convergence draws near. The distance
between places in Faerie is shifting. Possibly, without
my magick, I won't be able to find the sacred isle. Possibly we'll blunder through the mists to find ourselves
someplace else entirely.

"If we can't find Avalon, we may come to Camelot
instead—and Morrigan. Though we fly from peril, we
may be walking straight into her arms."

SEVENTEEN

THE MIST ROLLED thick over the Summer Sea, somber white swirling over the slate-gray surface. Rhiannon sat in the prow of the little coracle, bleached smooth and silver with age, and felt her senses tingling, alert for any whiff of magick.

She should be utterly riveted on their desperate goal. She must devote whatever minor magick she retained to steer their course—not toward the high cliff where Camelot perched like an eagle, rampant and mantling for blood, but toward the green meadows and golden orchards of the sacred isle of Avalon.

Instead her gaze lingered on the powerful black-clad figure, hood flung back from his tawny head, seated midship with oars gripped in his fists. Smoothly he pulled and drew, pulled and drew, putting his back into the chore of propelling them through the still waters. Strain though she might, she heard nothing but the susurrus of water slipping past the hull, the rhythmic splash of oars digging deep, and Beltran's steady breath like a bellows. Tirelessly his keen blue gaze scanned the mist.

"How much farther do you reckon?" He pitched his voice low, for she'd warned him that sound carried on the Summer Sea, and theirs might not be the only craft plying these waters. "We've rowed a good hour."

"Longer than that." Shivering, she chafed her arms

beneath her woolen mantle. "As to how much farther we may drift, I cannot say."

She paused. "Remember well what I told thee—think not of Avalon, nor the sword, or for certain we'll never come there. Wish thyself anywhere else. If we fail, we may wander the Summer Sea forever."

"What manner of unholy place is this?" Frowning, Beltran started to cross himself, but stopped the motion in time. "Forsooth, I can scarcely credit what you've told me—that we wander between worlds, outside the realm of men."

"Thou must choose thine own beliefs," she said shortly, quelling a flicker of impatience. "If, like the Nazarene's Thomas, thou must see to believe, I trust what we witness shall persuade thee. Believe firmly enough in the world of men, believe I'm a fraud or a poor deluded fool, and perhaps we'll come indeed to Ynys Witrin, the Isle of Glass, which is Avalon's shadow in the mortal world."

What will it take to make him believe? For the man called God's Vengeance possessed a will so formidable that he'd wiped out all knowledge of his own divinity.

What had Zamiel called him? The Flame of God, one of four archangels who guarded the Presence. If Beltran had managed to deny even that, how could he ever believe in the gods who ruled this place?

His sharp gaze lingered on her struggling face. "What of you, Rhiannon? What befalls you when we return to my world? Are you still hell-bent on persuading Mary Tudor to sign your infernal treaty? Surely you know if you show your face in London, the bishop will have your head. If you're lucky."

Rhiannon shivered and looked away, hugging herself for warmth. Goddess knew, revealing herself so rashly before the Tudor court had been a fatal error. She'd been too heedless and indiscreet, and roused the Catholic faction to full alert against her. The thought of returning to wild-eyed Mary and her Romish henchmen was enough to ice her blood.

"I can't shrug my shoulders and turn back, Beltran, merely because the way has grown difficult. I've seen with mine own eyes the coming of winter to the Summer Lands. Truly, the Convergence is upon us. My mother…"

Her voice wavered. "Queene Maeve, the Faerie Queene, must hover on death's doorstep. When snow flies in the land of the Fair Folk, I'll know she is gone. My only hope of saving her and defeating my sister is not the lion who rules England, but the cub in waiting."

"Elizabeth?" Grunting with exasperation, he pulled at the oars. "That can never be. Spain will tear England to bloody shreds before Philip allows a heretic to sit the throne. Never hope for it."

"Who art thou to tell me what to hope? I *do* hope for it," she said stubbornly. "If a path through the Veil is revealed, I shall make for Hatfield."

"Better to make for the Tower if you wish to find Elizabeth, with the way this Dudley business is unfolding."

His voice was rising, echoing over the water. She gestured urgently for silence.

"Please try to remember, Beltran," she whispered, searching the wall of mist, thicker now, the light so diffuse she could no longer steer by the sun. "If we return—*when* we return—to the mortal realm, anything may be possible—the Tudors cast down, French or Spaniards on the throne, Rome ascendant or utterly eclipsed by whatever Gods men will worship when yours is forgotten."

"Damnation! I won't listen to this blasphemy."

"I merely wish to prepare thee for all eventualities! When wilt thou open thy mind?"

Uneasily he glanced away, and she knew he would cross himself again if she hadn't cautioned against it. As his gaze slid past her, his face altered. The oars stilled as he leaned forward.

Heart lodging in her throat, she twisted to search the mist. There for an instant, like a ghost or a mirage, the dark shadow of land appeared. When a curtain of fog swirled across the view, she clasped her hands and prayed for the fortitude to survive whatever waited.

Dear Goddess, please…please let it not be Camelot… let us come anywhere but there.

As though the Goddess listened, the mist parted and rolled away to reveal a sun-drenched shore. Golden apples gleamed among russet leaves—for here, too, the creeping hand of frost had brushed. Above the wooded hills rose the Tor's whale-shaped bulk, bisected by the path that snaked toward the summit. There against the blue heavens, amid a circle of standing stones, rose a temple of pale marble.

Rhiannon squeezed her eyes closed, her heart overflowing with gratitude and relief, tears stinging her lids. "Lord and Lady be praised! This is Avalon."

How long had it been since she'd set foot on this shore? For too long she'd shirked these dutiful visits to her father's tomb, for they'd grown so painful and seemed so pointless. Arthur of Camelot would never wake on her account, no matter how she prayed for it.

This visit, too, might prove pointless. They'd reached the silent shores of Avalon, aye, but she saw no sign their desperate need would be heeded.

How could she hope, when every tear-choked plea she'd ever uttered on this isle had fallen on deaf ears? She'd come only because she knew no other choice.

But what of Beltran, whose orderly God-fearing brain was already balking at where they were and what they must attempt? He'd come farther down the road toward acceptance of her and this place than she'd ever dreamed possible. Yet still he wore his allegiance pinned to his sleeve, or more truly above his heart—the gold-and-steel medallion of a Blade of God.

He wavered on the brink of some great crisis, and his choice would determine both their fates. He would either fall back to the narrow dictates of the militant path he'd always trodden, the very harshness for which his God had cast him out. Or else he'd embrace her way, the path of peace and mercy and forgiveness.

Which way would he choose when the choice lay before him?

BELTRAN CLIMBED THE steep path in a daze, trudging across ancient terraces cut into the slope, barely aware of the burn in his thighs or the rower's blisters stinging his palms. When he glimpsed the angry red swelling, he recalled Rhiannon's caution about the passage of time. Christ, judging by the look of him, he could have been rowing for days.

Before him, Rhiannon scrambled lightly as a fawn, unencumbered by her simple gown the color of rich brown earth and her cream-colored mantle. When her foot slipped on the slope, he leaped to catch her, one arm circling her waist to steady her.

God's fury, the feel of her supple warmth beneath his hand.

She glanced up with an absent smile and slipped away. She'd seemed preoccupied since they set out… whenever they'd set out…and her distraction was mounting as they climbed. He wondered if she too was dreading the inevitable farewell that loomed before them.

He needed to return to London, set things right with the Archbishop, mollify the Catholic Queen and placate his order. As for Rhiannon, she'd stated her clear intent to go to Hatfield and cast her lot with the Queen's Protestant heir.

No force under Heaven would induce him to drag her back to the bishop.

Hence their parting was imminent and unavoidable. She was no fool; she knew it as well as he.

How could she ignore so blithely the hum of sensual tension between them? Did she truly believe she'd gone to his bed for honor's sake? He'd felt how she shuddered beneath him when she climaxed, heard her sharp cry of rapture when he claimed her. The torrid memories set his cock throbbing beneath his codpiece. Grimly he ordered himself back to the business at hand.

He planted his boot on a jumble of rocks, gripped a protruding root and hauled himself over the last rise. Abruptly the grassy summit opened before them—a circle of brooding gray dolmens, the standing stones crumbling with age. Beyond rose the slender columns of a temple in the Greek fashion, the long porticoes silent and abandoned, strewn with a carpet of fallen leaves.

Above soared the vault of heaven, cerulean blue, wisps of cloud scudding before the brisk wind that rippled the long grass. Beneath the wind's low whistle the world was hushed, as though gripped in enchantment.

They were utterly alone on this island.

Slowly he turned to scan the view. The rolling orchards and meadows of Avalon spread beneath him, blazing in autumn splendor, hemmed by the reed-choked waters of the Summer Sea. Beyond rose a curtain of fog, blocking any glimpse of what lay beyond.

He saw nothing to threaten them, yet his nape tingled. Somehow, he knew they were being watched. Shrugging uneasily, he turned away from the panorama below and strode onto the summit.

"Wait," Rhiannon breathed, placing a light hand on his arm. "Listen."

Impatient, he shook his head—then stilled, arrested. Beneath the wind, the faint echo of chanting rose and fell. Too distant to make out the words, but it sounded like Latin.

"Aye," she whispered. "'Tis the hour of prayer for the monks on Ynys Witrin, which the mortals call Glastonbury. It lies like a shadow over Avalon. We must wait a little, or we'll find nothing but an empty tomb."

Beltran quashed the urge to cross himself. He didn't like waiting here, exposed and alone beneath the vast sky, where anyone could see them.

"How long?" he said tersely.

"Only a little." Deftly she untied the belt-pouch from

her waist. "Sit and rest here on this stone, and I'll bandage thy hands."

"It's nothing, Rhiannon—a trifle." But she'd kept her distance all day, and it was slowly driving him mad. If she wanted to touch him now for whatever reason, he'd seize the opportunity and make the most of it.

He strode to the fallen column half-buried in knee-high grass. Before sitting, he scanned the horizon once more, assuring himself nothing was out of place. She knelt beside him, graceful as a willow, and unscrewed the lid of a little stone pot. The pungent aroma stung his nostrils, but he barely noticed. All his attention was riveted on her light touch as she caught his hands in hers.

"'Tis a poultice made from marigold," she said quickly, as though to fill the pregnant silence. "I'm sorry about the smell."

"I've smelled worse." Before she could anoint him with the stuff, he captured her hands. "Rhiannon."

His voice sounded foreign in his ears, husky with the craving for her that burned in his blood. Startled, she glanced up at him, eyes wide and wondering beneath her dark brows. Under his heated gaze, color rose beneath her creamy skin.

Nay, you're not nearly as indifferent to me as you pretend.

"What is it?" Her voice was breathless, breasts rising too swiftly beneath her brown woolen gown. No corset or farthingale, nothing but a shift underneath, and he'd thought of nothing else since he watched her dress. Easy enough to get her out of it.

"You seem flustered, princess," he murmured, thumbs stroking her soft palms. "Are you remembering the last time I held you?"

"I'm perfectly well. Why should I be otherwise?" Her chin tilted in swift pride. But he tightened his grip and drew her forward, until she knelt between his spread legs. The pale sweetness of violets rose from her skin to surround him.

"Why indeed, Rhiannon? You claim to feel nothing and care nothing for me—for the way your blood sings when you burn in my arms." He spread her palms over the hard sinew of his thighs, her light touch searing through his hose. "Isn't that true, princess?"

"I'm no princess any longer." Her hands fluttered like trapped moths beneath his. "Beltran, there's no purpose to this. Thou have chosen thy God above any woman."

A spark of dangerous anger ignited within him. "I've failed God and failed my order. I've cast them both aside for your sake. Just as you sacrificed your innocence for me."

The words burst from him, fired by a mad hope he hadn't realized he was entertaining. "Rhiannon, listen to me. I've been thinking about Elizabeth Tudor. Perhaps she can yet be saved from heresy. If I draw her into the true Church, if I persuade her to join her sister's crusade, we can bring the light of God to this benighted isle. The Archbishop would overlook anything for that, and my order would hail my return. We could go to Hatfield together!"

But she was shaking her head, face poignant with regret, eyes shimmering with tears he despised himself for causing. "Nay, Beltran, I won't join thy crusade. Thou must abandon this militant struggle, this relentless persecution of the good English people. Last night, I told thee, someone—"

"I can't give it up. I won't give it up. And you're going to admit you want me anyway."

He hauled her against him and claimed her the only way he could, with the fierce driving hunger of his mouth on hers. Clearly furious at his peremptory handling, she struggled to wrench away, but posed no match for his strength.

He trapped her between his thighs, arms closing hard around her, tongue plunging deep into her honeyed mouth. She was proud and angry, hissing like a cat, gripping his doublet in her small fists but meeting him kiss for kiss. Her tongue dueled with his, sharp teeth nipping his lip in a declaration of war. It was all the challenge he needed to subdue her as he deepened the kiss, crushing her soft breasts against his chest.

She sighed into his mouth and yielded, as she always did for him, arms twining around his neck in surrender. A fierce surge of triumph rolled through him. Swiftly he rose, lifting her slight weight without effort. Her legs wound around his waist, fitting her snug against his codpiece. All at once, he wanted to be inside her, and he didn't intend to wait.

But first, he'd make her beg for him. He'd demand her confession of how he made her feel. As her mouth clung to his, drinking his kisses like wine, he lowered her to the fallen stone, nudging her legs apart and kneeling between them so their positions were reversed. Swiftly he pushed the soft folds of her skirts aside, hands skimming past her stockings to find the soft bare skin of her thighs. She moaned into his mouth and opened for him, hands clutching his shoulders as though she'd never let go.

"Tell me you want this, princess," he muttered, calloused palms sweeping over her warm skin, pushing her skirts up around her hips. "Show me your beauty. Tell me you never want me to stop."

"I don't," she whispered, shifting restlessly on the stone as he spread her wide. "Merciful Goddess, don't stop. Please don't stop."

With a growl of conquest, he surveyed her, a sight so wanton it sent the blood straight to his groin. She sprawled in abandon beneath the open sky, skirts pushed around her waist, her slender thighs parted to expose the plump peach of her cunny, framed by his sun-browned hands. Starving for the sight of her, he spread her wider, creamy moisture glistening on her folds. Her musky scent filled his nostrils. His cock jerked beneath his codpiece like a living creature.

He barely recognized his own deep-throated voice. "Open your gown, princess. I want to see your gorgeous breasts."

"Oh, yes," she whispered. Feverishly her hands fluttered to her bodice, tore at the simple laces, pushing the gown open with a boldness that delighted him. Her breasts spilled out, pink nipples tight as if begging for his touch. He couldn't resist tonguing them, teasing the sensitive peaks to hear her gasp, feel her arch against his mouth. But he wanted much more from her, and he intended to have it.

He lifted his head and surveyed his handiwork—her face flushed, eyes lidded and gleaming with passion, nipples hard and glistening from his kisses, back arched, thighs spread wide to offer her cunny for his inspection. His heart thudded hard at the sight, blood pounding through his veins, his cock more than ready to thrust into her wet quim.

"I'm going to taste you now, princess," he said gruffly. "You want that, don't you?"

"Yes…yes…"

"Beg me."

For a moment, he thought he'd misjudged his moment, pushed her too hard. He thought the proud royal would leap to her feet, eyes flashing, and put him in his place.

Instead her eyes fluttered closed, head falling back in a gesture of complete trust that made his chest tighten.

"Oh, Beltran… I want you to taste me. My dearest love…"

Blood roaring in his ears, he bent forward and swept his tongue along her deep cleft. Softly she cried out, her salty sweetness flooding his mouth, her little pearl quivering for his attention. He circled and teased her, drawing forth more of her exquisite cream, until she raised her hips and pleaded with him never to stop.

Her responsiveness, the frank eroticism of her innocent desires amazed him. She had none of the shyness and self-consciousness he'd expect from an almost-virgin. Indeed, if he weren't restraining her with his hands, drawing back to prolong her pleasure as she writhed beneath his tongue, she would have climaxed for him already.

"What a treasure you are," he murmured, tongue dipping into her channel to gather more of her musk. Her gorgeous quim was weeping for him. "Cup your beautiful breasts for me, princess. Go on—I want to see you do it."

He raised his head long enough to ensure she complied. She moved as though delirious, cupping her pert

breasts in both hands. Of her own volition, her fingers
strayed to her nipples, toying with them as he'd done.
Her breath escaped her parted lips in desperate gasps.
Unable to tear his eyes away, he flicked her hard little
pearl with his thumb. Suddenly she was calling out,
hips thrusting into his touch, squeezing her nipples
rhythmically as her pleasure peaked.

"Oh, my love…my love…!" She was crying out for
him, abandoning herself utterly to rapture and release,
entrusting herself utterly to his keeping.

Beneath his codpiece, his aching balls tightened
and clenched. The shuddering force of his own release
roared through him. Beltran flung back his head and
groaned her name as his seed spurted. He squeezed
his eyes shut and prayed to God the moment would
never end.

THE MOMENT HAD the feel of farewell. After the dizzying
rush of orgasm left them both spent and trembling, Rhiannon had gathered her wits and restored her clothing
without a word. It had taken him another long moment
to realize the echo of chanting had faded into silence.
The world waited for them to complete their journey.

While he stepped aside to attend his own necessary
business, she waited for him as calmly as though she'd
never writhed beneath his touch, never shattered in his
arms or cried his name in passion.

My dearest love, she'd called him. And his world
had turned sideways.

Could she possibly have meant it? Surely she was
a woman, of all women living, who knew what love
meant, both the joy and the pain of it.

Now Rhiannon glanced toward him as though she

would speak, a tangle of emotions he couldn't decipher flickering across her winsome features. He waited, breath hitching in his lungs.

Would she admit she loved him? He mustn't hope for it, not when he wasn't free to return the sentiment, not while he was promised to God. And yet...

Instead she sighed and waded through the knee-length grasses toward the vault. Silently he stalked after her, calling upon all his hard-won discipline to put their extraordinary encounter behind them and focus on the business at hand.

But he was acutely conscious of the empty sheath strapped across his back.

At first she seemed hesitant, steps tentative as she entered the standing stones. Now her stride quickened as though she squared herself for what lay ahead. Resolutely she mounted the cracked marble steps and crossed the portico.

Beyond, the temple was open to the elements, rows of pillars holding aloft the carved roof. In the center reared the massive bulk of a sarcophagus, its four corners guarded by tall black candles that flickered with flames no mortal hand had lit. The lid lay propped against its side, exposing whatever lay within to the open air.

"Beltran." Her warm hand stole into his, and he squeezed to comfort her. "I have not visited this place for many lifetimes of men. But one truth I know has not changed. Whatever thou may see here, whatever may befall, I beseech thee not to invoke thy God, nor make any Christian sign or symbol. It would be sacrilege in this place, which is sacred to the Goddess."

So she'd strip his greatest weapon—the power of

prayer—from him. He didn't like the edict, but she knew what to fear in this place. Hell, he hardly knew what he expected to find. Not Excalibur, surely?

Curtly he nodded. "I swear it."

Her throat rippled as she swallowed. Gently she tugged him forward. He sensed her apprehension. Somehow, this serene sanctuary posed a painful ordeal for her. She was trembling, but his touch seemed to lend her strength.

She squared her slim shoulders and marched ahead, until they could see into the tomb.

In the vault, a knight lay sleeping.

Scaled armor of steel and silver encased his chest and shoulders, glittering as if alive. A double circlet of gold and silver banded his high brow, long fair locks streaming beneath. A gray-threaded beard shadowed his gaunt face. Folded over his chest, his gauntleted hands gripped the hilt of his greatsword, sheathed in a scabbard of crimson velvet stitched with gold and silver runes.

A sword made for a king, no doubt of it.

Nobility rested on his brow like a second crown. Unearthly peace shone like a white light from his still face. But the mailed chest rose and sank slowly, so slowly, with the rhythm of slumber.

Rhiannon clutched Beltran's hand as though she were drowning, her entire body trembling as she stared down on the vault.

"Behold the Dreaming King," she whispered. "He who sleeps until the trumpet winds and the land has need of him once again." Her fingers tightened. "Behold my father."

A gulf yawned beneath his feet. Beltran gripped

the tomb to anchor himself. Hoarsely he spoke a single word.

"Arthur."

Sadly she smiled. "Yes, I am his, though I've never seen him move nor speak. I was but an infant when my brother Mordred waged war against him. Their armies fought on the shore of the Summer Sea, and each of them struck a mortal blow.

"Mordred went…to another place, and Morrigan was banished from the mortal realm for aiding him. Queene Maeve kept her throne but worked a great magick, summoning the Veil to protect the realm of Faerie. As for Arthur, she wove a spell to protect him from death until England's need should summon once more."

"She loved your father then?" The word *love* caught strangely in his throat.

"Aye, she loved him. But as the Faerie Queene, she may never wed, except for the sacred marriage with the Horned God she makes each year to bless the land. For a time, she made it with Arthur. When he fell, his sacrifice ended the last Convergence, a thousand years past."

She paused, her voice thickening. "Often I've wondered whether this new Convergence means my father will waken. Will he open his eyes and look upon my face? Will he recognize me as his—the child of his love for the Faerie Queene?"

Beltran wrenched his eyes from Arthur, the Dreaming King, whose high cheekbones were indeed a faded mirror of Rhiannon's. A sparkling tear spilled over her pale cheek. A great shuddering tenderness for her squeezed his chest.

Cursing, he pulled her into his arms. Briefly she resisted, but lacked the will to fight him. Sighing, she turned her face into his shoulder.

He stroked her trembling back, pressed his chin to her crown to anchor her. His embrace sought to shelter her from everything that could ever hurt her.

"You long for him," he said gruffly. "You must feel half an orphan."

"Oh, I'm an orphan." Her bitter voice was muffled in his doublet. "An orphan twice over, with both parents still breathing. My mother wanted a son who could wear the double crown and rule both realms, like Arthur. Or failing that, another great sorceress like Morrigan, who could queen it over the Fair Folk at least. I disappointed her on both counts. And my father never knew me as more than a mewling babe."

"You called yourself an outcast, a misfit," he recalled.

You were a misfit like I was at San Miguel. And like me, you rose beyond your origins by your own strength. Admiration for her courage swelled as he cradled her shaking frame in his arms. She was no less brave or determined than the legendary king who'd sired her.

How easily she could have grown bitter and cold and joyless, as he did. Yet she'd found room in her heart for compassion, for the tender care that healed others. She'd opened herself to the love that drew living things to her, as a flower turns to the life-giving sun.

Too soon she stirred in his arms, and abruptly he recalled their danger. Warily he scanned the empty porticoes and the rippling green summit. Alone, but for how long?

"The sword," he said curtly. "Do I simply take it?"

The notion seemed like blasphemy—snatching that shining sword from the peaceful hands that gripped it, with the pettiness of robbing the dead thrown in. Nor did the task seem likely to prove simple, else the witch Morrigan would already have seized the precious blade.

Rhiannon shook her head. "There are powerful spells woven into the hollows. 'Tis death to touch them unprepared."

"How then? Time is pressing."

She hesitated. "It's never been done before, Beltran. I've only instinct and half-remembered lore to go by. It's said that when England's need is greatest, Excalibur will return. If thou wish to wield it, even only to pass through the Veil, thou must petition its master."

"Petition Arthur?" he asked, incredulous.

"Explain thy need, and ask him."

Meeting his skeptical gaze, she shrugged, eyes flashing with mingled irritation and apology. "What harm will it do to address him? The worst that can happen is what's happened all my life when I brought him my own fears and upsets—and that is nothing."

His first impulse was to mock the mad, absurd, impossible notion. But he quashed it. Whether the sleeping king was Arthur of Camelot, whether this blade was the legendary Excalibur or a costly fraud he couldn't say. But Rhiannon believed they needed the sword, and she'd proven a reliable ally.

He trusted her.

And she loved him.

Shaking his head in disbelief, he scrubbed a hand over his face. Good Christ, he must be wearing three days of stubble. They'd set forth from her cottage mere hours ago—no more than a day ago, surely? He cleared his thoughts and looked down at the sleeping king.

Was it his imagination, or did Arthur's hands grip the hilt more loosely? He could almost have slid the sword free, except that Rhiannon said it meant death to touch it.

"Don't question thyself," she urged, standing close at his side. "My father was a godly man, crowned king in a Christian church. Excalibur is the sword of fire. If any creature can break the spell, surely the Flame of God has that power."

Flame of God...

The phrase echoed oddly in his head, like the tolling of a great bell. Where had he heard those words?

His voice sounded strange in his ears. "Why do you call me this?"

She glanced at him askance, as if belatedly realizing what she'd said. A strange urgency seized him like a terrier shaking a rat.

"Rhiannon, I asked you a question. *Tell me why you called me this.*"

Her worried eyes surveyed him, then she gestured helplessly. "When thou were fevered and raving, thou said many strange things. I thought nothing of them until Zamiel appeared."

"Zamiel?" Again the word tolled in his ear. That odd sense of familiarity...at least in this case, he recalled how he knew it. "In Bible lore, he's a dark angel. He's the Angel of Death. You're saying you had a *holy vision*?"

Her stubborn chin tilted. "Not a vision. Zamiel appeared in the cottage while you were raving."

"I must have been close to death indeed." He tried to joke, but it fell flat. That strange urgency was mounting, his skin tightening with a rictus of anticipation and dread. "Did you wrestle with him as Jacob did?"

The mockery was a mistake. He saw her eyes turn mutinous. "He told me how to save thy life. He told me thy ravings were no mere fever-dream. Thou will scarcely heed it coming from my lips, but Goddess knows that is nothing new."

She hurled the words at him like stones, color rising in her cheeks. "He said thou art an archangel, exiled from Heaven, cursed by thy Deity to a mortal life to learn mercy. Now thou may accuse me again of lying and heresy and witchcraft and all the rest."

He barely heard her now, for the words she'd spoken drowned out all the rest. They vibrated through his skull like ripples in a barrel.

Thou art an archangel…cursed by thy Deity to a mortal life…

A hot tide of rage bubbled through his blood, turning his vision red. His killing fury was mounting, the outrage of insult spiked with the sharp sting of betrayal. Dimly he knew the woman before him must not be the target of that deadly rage.

His words scraped out as though gouged from his very bones, voice distorted by the growling prelude to his madness.

"Which angel am I supposed to be?" When she hesitated, he roared the words. "*Tell me my name!*"

She squared her shoulders and answered through gritted teeth. "Thy name is Uriel."

Uriel.

The name blasted through him like a warhorn, like a thousand lifted trumpets that shredded his eardrums and deafened him.

Thy name is Uriel.

"*Prince of Lights, Regent of the Sun, Destroyer of Hosts, Flame of God… I consign you, Vengeance, to a mortal life…*"

Remnants of a dream flickered through his brain—the sickening sensation of falling, tumbling through a howling abyss, shredded wings fluttering useless in his wake. He was more than mortal, his malady more than human. And the God he'd devoted eternity to serving had betrayed him, betrayed him, betrayed him…

Uriel threw back his head and roared.

Rhiannon stumbled back from the tomb as the deafening blast of Beltran's fury echoed through the vault. The pillars trembled and the earth pitched beneath her, sending her stumbling to her knees.

She scrambled back from the vision before her—the black-garbed figure with arms flung wide, back arched, face contorted in a paroxysm of rage. Where Beltran had stood, a fiery Being burst into existence, blinding bright. Crying out, she covered her eyes.

The afterimage seared across her brain—the towering form of Uriel, Angel of Vengeance, mighty jet-and-garnet wings outspread, silver hair streaming in the astral gale that howled around him. His flaming sword thrust into heaven as though to pierce the heart of God himself.

Goddess save me, and save Beltran from himself.

Skull splitting, white lights flaring before her eyes,

Rhiannon pried her lids open and peered through her fingers. The Being lowered his head and looked straight at her.

Her heart nearly stopped.

His eyes were pools of rage, twin maelstroms of swirling cobalt with lightning flashing in their depths. His gaze transfixed her and pierced her soul.

No doubt of it, he saw *her*—Rhiannon—crouching terrified on the flagstones.

For a breath, the heart-stopping fury that froze his chiseled face seemed to soften. The lightning dimmed in his rage-filled eyes.

Then his terrifying gaze lifted toward Heaven, his head tilting, as though he heard the whisper of a distant call. That stern and beautiful countenance hardened. He roared words in an unknown language—a challenge toward the Christian God whose meaning she could well surmise.

The archangel hurtled into motion, earth quaking with every stride as he vaulted toward the open air. As soon as he cleared the portico, he launched into space, wings spreading to catch the air in a powerful downbeat. He soared aloft, tendrils of fire streaming in his wake.

She blinked, and he was gone.

The man she loved was gone, obliterated as if he'd never existed.

She fought to fill her lungs, lump swelling in her throat, tears burning in her light-stabbed eyes. Somehow she gathered her trembling limbs and struggled to her feet.

Gradually her vision cleared. As she stood shattered

and raw in Arthur of Camelot's vault, tears scalding her stricken face, she lifted her head and gasped.

Here in the temple between the worlds, she was no longer alone.

HE'D BEEN IN this place before, surely, stumbling alone through the wilderness, blinded by tears of rage. Every muscle in his body screamed with familiar agony, a remnant of the holy madness. But something more was driving him.

He couldn't wander forever through this desolate bog, soaked through and shivering in the thickening mist, staggering blindly through the shadows as he'd done for hours, days, a lifetime…

And he couldn't soar free of the mist because he'd lost his wings again. Clearly God didn't intend for him to keep them.

He inhabited a mortal body, however unwillingly. Beltran Nemesto, Blade of God, now recalled his exile from paradise with stunning clarity.

His Father had punished him merely for doing his job too well. And when the moment of discovery passed, that first dizzying rush of exultation faded, he found himself still locked in this mortal shell— alone and wandering through this God-cursed marsh. Unless he'd soared over the Summer Sea, which he greatly doubted, he was lost somewhere in the slough that linked the isle of Avalon with the mainland.

In his madness, he'd left Rhiannon behind at the temple. He must have been mad indeed to do that. Through the swirling chaos of images, he was haunted by her stricken face, upturned and bathed in glowing white light, tears streaking her lovely features.

He'd abandoned her, abandoned Excalibur, abandoned his duty to return to the world of men. Abandoned them all willfully, burning with the need to confront and defy the God who'd condemned him.

But no man could look upon the face of God. Encumbered by this mortal flesh, his wings had shredded and driven him to ground. Now Beltran found himself wingless and earthbound once more, condemned to a mortal life until this body failed him. Then would God judge him and determine his fate.

For now, he'd no wish to hasten His judgment. Self-slaughter was a mortal sin that would send his soul plummeting straight to Hell. And he had unfinished business on the mortal plane.

Wrapped in a shroud of angry memories, he didn't see the gnarled root until he stumbled over it and measured his length in the shallows. Murky water seeped through his garments and closed over his head. Sputtering, he reeled upright and stood panting, breath raw and rasping in the unnatural silence.

God's body, I need to take hold of myself. I could wander lost forever here, until this mortal body dies and my soul lies at Heaven's mercy once more. First I need to find Rhiannon, ensure her safety, do what I should have done long before.

His gut twisted and his heart seized at the thought of losing her. Somehow he'd become entwined body and soul with the ethereal beauty, enthralled by her core of shining valor and hidden steel, beguiled by her compassion and capacity to love. But the best way to help her was to set her free.

Then I'll return to the Church and start anew, be the fairest enforcer the Inquisition has ever seen. I'll

*show Him I've taken whatever lesson He wanted me
to learn, that I've changed, that I can grant mercy as
well as punishment.*

Christ, what was happening to Rhiannon?

Fighting to clear his head, he took stock grimly—his
hose and doublet drenched, boots fouled with mud, his
prized stallion God alone knew where. He hadn't seen
Serafin since the night he'd been stabbed. No provisions, not even a water-skin.

At least he was wearing his thick hooded cloak and
his good boots. He could walk to Jerusalem in these
boots if he had to. His dagger was strapped to his belt,
the sheath across his back still empty. For the loss of
the sword called Judgment, given him by the Cardinal
when he took his oath, he grieved.

Still, his body was sound—no injuries beyond the
debilitating fatigue caused by his madness, the understandable protest of a mortal body unsuited to provide
a vessel for his angelic form. His belly rumbled with
hunger, but he'd endured worse. He could forage for
something, berries or mushrooms, set snares for wa-
terfowl or fashion a throwing stick.

He glanced around, taking his bearings, seeking
stars or moon to steer his course. But the mist shrouded
everything. The black trees stood wet and gleaming in
the twilight, boughs draped with curtains of moss, and
everywhere the glimmering gray water.

Beltran chose a direction at random and strode forward, planting each foot with care on the uncertain
ground. If he blundered into a quagmire or tripped
and broke a leg, he'd be no good to anyone—neither
the Church nor Rhiannon.

There.

Dimly through the trees, the moon was rising, its silver glow pouring through the marsh. It turned the mist to pearl and painted a shimmering path across the water to his feet. With renewed vigor, he waded toward the light. If he emerged from the fen near where he'd entered with the bishop, he could find a boat and make for London. He'd meet first with the Archbishop, Reginald Pole, to set matters right.

But it wasn't the moonrise that was the source of the light. Instead the uncanny glow emanated from the surface of a still pool, from *beneath* the surface. Raising an arm to shield his eyes, he vaulted onto a hillock of solid earth and dropped to his knees. Leaning forward, he peered down into the water.

An exclamation burst from his lips. There, beneath the mirrored surface, wavered an image not reflected from above—a floating figure, hands clasped on her still breast, slim as a moonbeam and fair as starlight, pale draperies drifting like mist around her. A banner of nut-brown hair streamed around her, rippling as the water rippled. A ring flashed like the star of evening on her pale hand.

The Lady's face shone with light, so bright it burned his eyes, yet somehow she bore the look of Rhiannon— pointed chin, high cheekbones, brows winging from tilted eyes to lend her a mischievous air. Her lashes lay against her cheeks though she slept.

Then her eyes flashed open, blue as the Virgin's mantle, or the heart of heaven. Beltran gazed into their depths and was lost. The world around him vanished behind a curtain of swirling fog. He saw nothing and heard nothing but the words inside his heart.

"Why have you turned your back on your heart's desire?"

He jerked back in surprise, sensing no mortal ear could discern the rich, resonant voice that echoed through his thoughts. But her gaze held him like a net.

"Who are you?" he said hoarsely, half convinced he was dreaming the entire encounter. But he'd just learned to believe in dreams, hadn't he, and the truths they could reveal?

Her serene blue eyes smiled. *"I am the Lady of the Lake."*

Once Beltran would have snorted to hear this woman name herself the mainstay of Arthurian legend: the high priestess of Avalon in Arthur's time, who'd placed Excalibur in his hand and ushered in the dawn of his kingship. Now, he was surprised at nothing.

Firmly he applied himself to her question.

"I haven't turned my back on anything. I'm trying to find my way home."

"You have no home, you who are Prince of Lights and Regent of the Sun. No home in the mortal realm like other men. Yet your heart found a home-in-exile, a hearth to warm you from your lonely journey."

An image of Rhiannon as he'd first seen her flickered in his memory. Her beauty glowing through travel-stained finery, kneeling gracefully over her wounded comrade, elfin features alight with compassion as healing energy poured from her fingers. Her proud and angry eyes as she rode with wrists bound before her, every inch the princess even in captivity, blazing with undaunted spirit. The grave vulnerability in her leaf-green eyes the first time he'd kissed her.

And God, the way she'd felt trembling with passion

beneath him, the sound of his name on her lips when she cried out her climax

Oh, my love…my love…!

What the hell am I doing? he wondered suddenly, in a moment of crystalline clarity. *I'm headed the wrong way, away from the woman I…the woman I love.* His place was at Rhiannon's side, then and always, not pursuing some misguided campaign against a country that had suffered more than enough under the lash of religious persecution.

"*So then.*" Beneath the waves, the Lady smiled. "*You recognize your soul's destiny. Will you embrace love at last?*"

He gripped the wet soil under his hands and leaned forward. "Show me the way back to Avalon."

Her smile dimmed. "*What you seek is no longer there.*"

His thoughts flew to the little coracle they'd left on the shore. Had Rhiannon gone already?

"Damnation! How much time has passed in the world outside while I blundered about here? A week? A month?"

"*Beyond the Veil, two years and more have fled. On the sacred isle of Avalon, moments only. Still, your absence was long enough for Morrigan.*"

"Rhiannon's sister?" His gut clenched, cold sweat breaking out on his brow.

"*She sees very far, Uriel. Part of her gift is prophecy. Long ago Morrigan foresaw that you and Rhiannon, united in love, would bring about her downfall. Thus, all her efforts are bent upon keeping you apart. Only adrift and alone is Rhiannon vulnerable—as your rage left her on the holy isle.*"

"Rhiannon." He cursed his failure of discipline, the heedless fury that had left her undefended. A fist of dread squeezed his throat. "Is she taken?"

"Taken and delivered into the hands of her enemies, where she does Morrigan and her cause the most good. For Morrigan's Sight has shown her the Convergence will begin in London. And it must begin through Rhiannon."

"*Through* her? Rhiannon would die rather than open the door to that!"

The Lady nodded sadly. *"That is why she will confess to the litany of so-called sins the Roman Church has charged her with. Her grief and fear for you left her helpless against Morrigan's witchcraft. Rhiannon is now convinced the Convergence can only be averted through sacrifice—the sacrifice of a woman who walks both realms, mortal and Fae, who carries the blood of both races. A woman whose womb even now carries the seed of both races. Rhiannon believes she has become the door through which the Convergence must occur.*

"But Morrigan has bewitched her to believe this lie. In truth, the crisis will not be averted by Rhiannon's sacrifice, but commenced. When Rhiannon dies, the Veil will tear, and her sister's hordes will pour through to the mortal realm."

Beltran had long since pushed past his sense of unreality at finding himself crouched in the mud, passionately conversing with a mirage. Still he fisted his eyes, shaking his head hard to clear it. If he gave in to the mounting panic that scrabbled at him like rats in a sewer, he would never be able to help Rhiannon.

Only the cold and heartless logic of God's Vengeance could save her.

"Lady, tell me, where is she?" he said hoarsely.

"*She is held in the dungeon beneath the cathedral of your Roman saint—the one who was stricken blind and later beheaded by Nero.*"

Horror twisted his gut. "St. Paul's? That means the bishop has her."

He leaped to his feet, ready to charge through Hell itself to save her.

"*Hear me, Vengeance. The Veil cannot part on consecrated ground. You must go to the burning ground on the day of Samhain and arrive before Tierce, or you shall arrive too late.*"

The burning ground—Christ, she must mean Smithfield. Bloody Bonner's favorite place for a public burning.

Wildly he searched the mist-wreathed heavens. The moon rode high and round overhead, but the constellations were none he'd ever seen.

"How can I get there in time?" he cried, fists clenching as he battled despair. "We must be days from London!"

If only he could summon his divine form, the wings that punched through his mortal flesh, rending and tearing until he screamed with anguish, he would launch into the half-recalled rapture of flight.

But he'd never been able to summon the killing rage at will. It was God's impenetrable will that governed the change.

"*On that count, you need not fear. You shall be given a token.*"

Beneath the mirrored surface, the Lady's head turned as though she viewed some distant vision, nut-brown hair swirling around her. The silver light intensified, piercing his skull like white-hot daggers. The evening star flashed like the eye of God on her finger.

Some blind instinct made him stumble back from the pool as the light poured from it. Something pierced the surface, a pale meteor of blinding metal, curlicues of fire etched on its flat surface and sparking along its fine-honed edge. The water rippled as a hilt broke the surface, gripped in a woman's hand that glittered, as though scaled with diamonds.

A pure high note hummed through Beltran's brain. It pierced him like a sword. The scent of apple blossoms flooded his senses.

Beneath the onslaught of sound and impossible beauty, he fell heavily to his knees.

"Uriel," the Lady said gently, inside his pulsating skull. "Someone wants you to have this."

EIGHTEEN

THE RAT WAS back again. Rhiannon thought it the same one who'd been making these nightly forays from the sewer into her cell over the fortnight she'd been kept here. But she couldn't be certain.

Once she would have relied on magick to befriend the creature. He was the only living thing beyond her odious jailer who ever visited, and she valued the company. But she'd learned the dismal truth when she woke in this cell with Morrigan's mocking laughter echoing in her ears.

Her wild Faerie magick had deserted her. When she traded her immortality for Beltran's life, she must have forfeited that too.

"Come along now, Finnegan," she coaxed. The rat perched on its hind legs in the filthy straw to observe her, whiskers twitching. "I know thou art hungry. I've saved this crust especially for thee. 'Tisn't much, but I won't be needing bread after tomorrow."

A black gulf of panic yawned before her. They would burn her tomorrow, so the jailer had warned her. She thought he'd meant it as a twisted sort of kindness, believing she'd welcome the chance to prepare her soul before they came for her.

The important thing now was not to think of it. Just as she'd avoided thinking of it since she'd returned to the mortal realm and known what her fate would be.

Indeed, she was fortunate, blessed by the Goddess with both knowledge and means to avert the Convergence and save the Faerie Queene. She was utterly certain of it, beyond any doubt or hesitation, the firm decision made to sacrifice herself for that worthy end.

Although in truth, she could not quite recall how she knew it. Someone on Avalon, she thought, must have told her...

She'd avoided the rack with her ready confession—another blessing to be thankful for. With her signed confession of witchcraft in hand, the Church's macabre machine had ground toward judgment and sentence more briskly than she'd dared to hope.

Still, she went to her death barely in time. For time indeed had flown here while she lingered in Faerie—spring evidently leaped to autumn in a day. Tomorrow was Samhain, the day the dead walked. Tomorrow at midnight the Veil would fall, and her sister's howling hordes would break into the mortal realm. Rhiannon's sacrifice would avert that fate for all of them.

All except me.

"Come, Finnegan, thou blessed beast!" she whispered. If only she weren't so terrified. Nostrils quivering, the rat crept toward her outstretched hand.

Praise the Lady for this whiskered visitant and his stubborn reluctance to yield to her overtures! How she dreaded these lonely vigils as she waited for the end, shivering and quietly sobbing her way through the dreadful nights.

But worse, far worse, were the nights she dreamed of Beltran.

In her dreams he was her protector once more, planting himself and his sword between her and the outlaws, pitting his strength against the slavering hounds, his wits against the grief-stricken Tudor Queen and her fanatical henchmen. His unflinching valor had been her shield. He'd never abandoned her, even when his faith demanded it.

Until the day he was torn apart by his savage rage toward the God who betrayed him.

Then he'd taken wing—fashioned of mortal clay no more, but limned by the divine fire of Heaven. And so, she presumed, returned to his Maker for a reckoning.

She prayed for his contentment through the slow eons of eternity, prayed to her Gods and his. He'd been the best of men. Despite his harsh and loveless upbringing, he'd shown her what it meant to love. She would never cease blessing him for that.

The heavy tramp of boots jerked her from her reverie. Beyond the filth-crusted bars of her cell, the red glow of torchlight was approaching. Reflexively she shrank from the light, her pupils constricting painfully, and dashed away the tears that streaked her face.

The low murmur of men echoed from the damp stone walls, punctuated by jingling keys. A smothering blanket of dread fell over the cells around her. When they came for these prisoners, holed up in the bowels of St. Paul's, it meant either torture or execution.

Perhaps tonight they were coming for her.

In the straw at her feet, Finnegan squeaked and scurried back to his hole. Trembling, she watched him go and felt her only friend had abandoned her.

She curled tighter on the stone floor, arms wrapped around her knees, and shivered in her threadbare gown. Her bare toes curled apprehensively—filthy despite her best efforts with her meager allotment of brackish water.

In the cell beside her, unseen, a boy started to whimper. He would burn with her tomorrow. But she'd heard that brute of a jailer tell him they might rack him first, to get a better confession. Heresy, the charge was. He'd failed to affirm that the bread and wine they raised at Mass were transformed to the Body and Blood of Christ. Both his parents had already fed the flames, but the bishop was hoping for a better haul.

Shaking herself free of paralysis, Rhiannon scrambled to her feet and laced her fingers through the grate.

"Courage, young John!" she cried softly, beneath the mounting tramp of boots. "Thou art not alone. We are here with thee. Pray to thy God now."

Far better the boy pray than dissolve into babbling terror. When she heard the child's unsteady voice gabbling the paternoster, she nodded approval. Since she'd sacrificed her maidenhood for Beltran's life, Christian prayer no longer hurt her—the clearest evidence she'd found that, indeed, both her immortality and her fickle magick must surely have deserted her. Sometimes she liked hearing the holy words now, when they were spoken in faith. The prayers reminded her of Beltran.

The torch burst into view, but she refused to cringe like vermin from the light. Refused even when she saw the Archbishop of Canterbury's red-and-black robed form sweeping behind the jailer. Instead she lifted her chin and surveyed him, proud in her rags as a princess on royal progress.

The jailer didn't scurry past, but crouched to unlock her cell. The cold seed of fear in her gut blossomed into terror.

Quaking, she stood while the jailer brought a chair for the Archbishop—though none for her, of course—and locked the cell again behind him. Locking her in with Reginald Pole—architect, with his executioner Bonner, of the Tudor Inquisition.

Seating himself comfortably, the Archbishop stroked his long brown beard and surveyed her. She stood barefoot and straight-backed, resisting the impulse to brush her tattered skirts or smooth the tangle of hair that spilled down her back.

Fae or mortal, you are still a king's daughter, she told the terrified quiver in her belly. She'd heard the man before her carried Plantagenet blood, the old royal line of England. He would respect a composed demeanor. She demanded respect from her butchers, even if she had nothing else.

"Rhiannon le Fay?" Reginald Pole nodded, as if acknowledging her composure. "I've come to hear your confession."

"My confession?" Her voice trembled with anger, but she steadied it. "I've made my confession, signed and witnessed, to thy toad of a bishop. He's assured me 'tis more than sufficient to burn me. What more can thou desire?"

"Tomorrow you feed the flames at Smithfield, no matter what you say now," the Archbishop agreed calmly. Despite her resolve, a black cloud darkened her vision.

Through the darkness, a thread of sound trickled to her ears. Young John next door, whistling a few bars of music—a way to hearten their fellow captives, letting Rhiannon know she was not alone. Comforting her as she'd comforted him.

She drew a shaking breath and opened her eyes.

"What more must I confess?" she asked.

"His Lordship the bishop believes, as I myself believe, that you've withheld certain information that would aid our sacred mission to root out heresy in England," Pole said smoothly. "We must have it, mistress, to rip up the Protestant fallacy root, branch and tree. I'd like you to tell me again about the fate of Lord Beltran Nemesto, the former Blade of God."

Rhiannon started, heat flaming in her cold cheeks. *This again? I'll give them no such pleasure. Beltran is safe with his God, safe beyond their grasp, no matter what evidence they think to wrest from me.*

"I've told thee all I know. I barely knew Lord Beltran when Queen Mary named him my counterpart at court."

"Ah yes, to ascertain the validity of your claim to be royal emissary for the so-called Faeries." Contempt dripped from each punctilious word, but he didn't linger here—no need, for she'd already "confessed" to these so-called crimes. "What interests me, mistress, is what befell him in the fens on the night he disappeared."

"I haven't seen him," she said honestly, pain constricting her chest. "I believe he's left England, never to return."

Reginald Pole leaned forward, dark eyes intent upon her face. "His Lordship the bishop believes you're lying."

Her temper sparked, and she welcomed the tincture of strength coursing through her. "I, Rhiannon le Fay, do *not* lie. Why would I lie about such a thing?"

"To protect your paramour, who forsook his oath

to follow you into sin and damnation! We know either your feminine charms or your witchcraft led him astray." His voice lowered. "Confess to this, mistress, and it will go easier for you tomorrow."

A flicker of hope leaped in her heart, but she knew it for false hope and cold comfort. Mary Tudor was convinced she would never bear the heir England must have while a single witch or heretic drew breath in her realm. No force under Heaven could save Rhiannon from the stake.

Besides, there was the Convergence. If the Goddess were denied her sacrifice, both realms would burn.

Briefly something niggled at her, a vague confusion. She could never quite recall why she felt so certain her death would avert that evil. Surely, it was enough that she knew.

To keep from breaking down and begging for her life, she summoned all her scorn and flung it at him. "What, if I condemn him, wilt thou refrain from burning me after all? I tell thee, Lord Beltran is innocent."

His eyes blazed with wrath, yet his tone held reasonable. "Think now, mistress! What harm will it do to confess this last? You're condemned to burn, as you know, but there's more than one way to roast. Confess your blasphemous union with Lord Beltran, confess he defiled his vow of chastity in your bed, and you'll know the mercy of the garrote before ever your flesh feels the flames.

"Strangle instead of burning, mistress—it's a far kinder death. Or if that end's not to your taste, a mercy-pouch of gunpowder hung round your neck will serve the same purpose when the sparks fly upward."

He paused. "But hold to your stubborn denials,

protect this failed priest and failed enforcer—who abandoned you after all, did he not, when he tired of you?—and my passionate friend the bishop will pile your pyre with greenwood and ensure you feel every flame. Sometimes it takes hours to die. That fate you may still avert."

A surge of dizziness made her sway on her feet, half-fainting. Somehow she kept upright, determined to deny her tormentor that final satisfaction. Like a holy talisman, she held a vision of Beltran in her mind.

"He did not *abandon* me," she said, furious. "Thou and thy bishop know nothing of him."

The Archbishop stroked his beard and leaned forward gravely. "Oh, but mistress, we know more of him than you. Did you know he was denied the honor of a priest's ordination because he couldn't contain his lust for female flesh? Much has emerged about Lord Beltran in the two years and more since he's vanished."

Two years and more. Blindly she groped behind her for the wall to hold herself upright. She'd seen the autumn leaves scudding through her tiny grate and assumed they'd lost six months in Faerie. It had been spring when they crossed the Veil.

Three springs ago.

Clearly mistaking her shock, Reginald Pole nodded satisfaction. "You were merely the latest of his paramours, you see? This is a man who swerved from the path of virtue more than once. After he vanished, his steward in Rome declared him dead. Regretfully, the Dons had already nominated him to head their order, though he wasn't yet confirmed in the post. The Blades of God live by their own archaic rules, and his death must be proven before they can name a successor. Either we must know how he died—knowledge only *you* can provide—or we must see him discredited and expelled from his order. Give us that, mistress, and I'll give you the merciful end you crave."

"Your Queen can discredit him," Rhiannon said dully, staring at the red robes pooling like blood on the flagstones.

Red is for heartbreak.

She'd fancied she was somehow special to Beltran, even if he could never love her. Even though he'd abandoned her when he discovered his divine origins. Was she only one of many he'd dallied with, after all, no more than a casual tumble?

"I'm of no mind to trouble the Queen with this trifle," Pole said briskly. "She is ill these many months and has taken to her bed."

Regardless of whether Beltran abandoned her at the end, he'd saved her life more than once. She owed him a debt of honor, and she loved him. She would do nothing to malign him. She'd go to her death with a loyal heart, at least.

Wearily she leaned her head against the wall. "I've told thee, he no longer resides in England. For thy purpose, he is dead. I'll sign whatever statement thou wish to that effect, but I have a demand of my own."

"You hardly negotiate from a place of strength." But Pole's voice hummed with satisfaction, and she knew she had him. "You know I can't release you. The Queen herself signed your death warrant, and those of all the heretics who die with you tomorrow."

"I'm not asking to be released." Grimly she thought of the Convergence. "Nay, I'll take thy mercy-pouch of gunpowder, and go to my death singing. There's a boy in the next cell who's also condemned. If thou wish to have my testimony, the final price is a mercy-pouch for him."

HIGH NOON AT Smithfield was a burning day, fine as a Midsummer fair for the jaded citizens of London. Pasty vendors, apple girls, peddlers and prophets, beggars and whores, all thronged to the open field beyond the city walls. The jostling crowd made Rhiannon shrink as her procession of unfortunates stumbled forward, bare feet bruised from the long walk through the streets, arms and shoulders burning from the weight of the heavy penance candle.

Despite her utter certainty that this sacrifice was necessary—*but why am I so certain?*—that niggling sense of wrongness still worried at her tired brain. If she dwelled upon it, her resolve would crumble to shrieking hysteria. Desperate to hold panic at bay, she touched the trembling shoulder of the boy beside her.

She reached deep for strength and mustered a wobbly smile. "Fear not, Young John. Thy mercy-pouch awaits thee. Thou have been very brave."

Though his gamin face was streaked with tears, Young John managed to smile back at her. Rhiannon stayed close to him as their guards pushed back the gaping crowd—oddly grim and muted for an execution, with none of the bawdy mockery she'd been braced to expect. For that much, at least, she was thankful.

Roughly the guards thrust them forward. When the crowd parted to reveal the pyre, Rhiannon closed her eyes and fought back a surge of terror.

Drop the candle, push through the guards, run for the alley. Run anywhere!

Above the heaped kindling, bare stakes jutted toward heaven, piercing the mass of leaden clouds that roiled overhead. Ominous thunder rumbled in those clouds, and lightning flashed among them.

The foul weather of Rhiannon's lost spring had lingered. London at Samhain was bracing for the mother of all storms.

No doubt the threat of rain dampened the spirits of its denizens. That, and the plague and the famine and the war with France, all the grim handmaidens that heralded the Convergence. Mary Tudor's illness, too, must cast a pall over her people. The jailor had said the Queen's condition was worsening. If the Queen's ailment kept Reginald Pole and his toady Bonner at the royal bedside rather than attending Rhiannon's funeral pyre, well, she would thank the Goddess for that too.

A biting wind knifed over the field, making the spectators curse and clutch their cloaks. With the other poor souls condemned to death, Rhiannon huddled into her threadbare gown and shivered.

At the pyre, confusion reigned. With brutal efficiency, the guards wrested away the penance candles and roughly began sorting the prisoners for burning. Sick and shaking, longing for the ordeal to be over yet dreading it, Rhiannon searched the dull faces of the observers who ringed them.

She remembered what the Archbishop had said about Beltran. Could it be possible he still lived? A flicker of hope stirred within her. If the archangel Uriel walked the mortal plane, surely he would do what he could to save her.

Yet she glimpsed no burning figure hurtling down from Heaven, no familiar tawny head or flash of cobalt eyes in the uneasy crowd around them. Tears stung her eyes, and fiercely she brushed them away. Not for worlds would she have these Popish bullies believe she wept with fear!

Hard hands seized her shoulders and thrust her toward the pyre. Clinging to courage with both hands, she reached for Young John.

"Please, sir, the boy. He's to have a mercy-pouch."

The guard, an unshaven lout with greasy hair, hawked and spat in the dirt. "No mercy for heretics."

Horrified, she twisted toward him. "But we paid! The Archbishop himself promised—"

"Well, His Grace ain't here, is he?" The lout propelled her toward the pyre, Young John stumbling and struggling in their wake. "He's too fine for the likes of this."

Now the poor boy was sobbing. Rhiannon burned with the urge to comfort him, to run this fat bully through with his own spear. Panic and outrage and steely defiance mingled in a heady brew that set her drunker than any wine. Planting her feet, she flung off the guard's bruising grip. For a dizzying instant, she stood straight and free.

Why have I been so docile, so blindly certain this sacrifice is required?

"Here now, go where you're told!" Jowly face twisting with rage, the guard cocked back a meaty fist.

She hissed defiance and braced for the blow.

Abruptly a hooded figure loomed over them, commanding the pyre like God on his mountain. A heartbeat from striking her, the guard faltered and fell back, crossing himself with superstitious dread. Rhiannon tipped her head back and gazed into the eyeholes of the executioner's dark hood.

Here, then, was the man who would light the pyre. A tall man, chest and shoulders solid with muscle—strong enough to swing the axe, she supposed, on the days that was called for. Within the hood, his cold eyes glittered.

A peculiar blend of dread and anticipation launched butterflies in her stomach. Blindly, she reached to draw Young John closer.

In silence the executioner extended a gloved hand, a surprising courtesy. Responding to this, the only civility she'd known since her sentencing, she placed her hand in his. Strong fingers closed around hers and lifted her to the pyre with ease. Desperate to stay with her, Young John scrambled up behind.

She gazed up and up into the executioner's hooded gaze. "Please, sir, the boy. The Archbishop promised him a mercy-pouch."

The hooded figure gazed at her, still amid the scuffle as cursing guards muscled the last struggling captives toward the stakes. Her skin prickled with curious awareness. At last the executioner spoke in a hoarse whisper.

"Never fear, my lady. God's a Being of infinite mercy. Today you'll see the depth of His love."

As she stared up at him, riveted by this odd pronouncement, the lowering skies opened. The dry rattle of hailstones, tiny and hard as pebbles, hissed across the pyre and stung her bare skin. Below, the Smithfield crowd scurried for cover beneath trees and carts and market-stalls.

As for the condemned, most stood like sleepwalkers

beneath the stinging pellets, lips moving in prayer, staring hollow-eyed at the surging crowds. A few struggled madly as the guards braced them against the stakes and shouted for rope. A sudden crash of thunder raised scattered screams.

Abruptly the guard with greasy hair loomed beside her. Brutally he seized Young John and dragged him toward a stake. Frantically the lad fought him, crying out for Rhiannon.

The sound of her name on the child's lips pierced her heart—she, the healer, who lived to bring aid and comfort to others. That piteous plea shredded the veil of delusion and witchcraft that had blinded her since she woke in her captors' keeping.

A child's need shattered the wicked illusion, and the unmistakable tingle of Avalon magick that flared into life, radiating tangible heat from the executioner's hooded figure.

"Goddess!" she gasped, making the warding sign against evil. "This is Morrigan's doing. Merciful Lady, I was bewitched."

A lightning rush of energy arced through her tingling limbs, banishing the lassitude that had gripped her for so long. Every nerve in her body fired for flight or a deathly struggle for life. She glanced wildly at the scene around them—the menacing guards, the panicked captives, the crowd running for cover as the hail slashed down. Another flash of lightning pierced the deepening gloom, limning the executioner in silver fire.

As if dreaming, she watched him fling aside his black cloak to reveal the sword strapped to his back. In a single motion, he unsheathed it. Lightning flashed

long the tapered blade etched with curling flame, the
ilt fashioned like an upraised hand thrusting a torch
nto Heaven.

Lady of Light, she knew that sword. She'd seen it a
housand times, clasped to her father's breast.

Arching back, legs braced, the executioner plunged
he sword straight up toward the roiling clouds. At the
ame moment, he dragged the hood from his head.
An aura of unearthly fire burst into life around his
owerful frame, cloaking his short tawny hair with
he streaming white-gold mane of the archangel Uriel.

But she knew him by another name.

"Beltran," she whispered, one hand rising to her
hroat. Somehow, blessed Goddess, she'd known he
vould come.

But the blade gripped in his fist was no Christian
word of Judgment. As lightning forked down to en-
elop the sword with cobalt fire, she breathed the word.
Excalibur.

The archangel lowered his head and gazed at her,
lue flame pulsing around his body. A warm torrent
f tears blurred her vision.

"Thou art restored to divinity. Why did thou remain
n the mortal world?" she said, numb with disbelief.
he rising wind tore at her gown and lashed stream-
ng tendrils of hair around her.

The lion's roar that could shred eardrums like the
last of trumpets rumbled so low it made her bones
ibrate.

"Rhiannon, my treasure, do you not know?"

A human voice pierced the storm, a great bellow
f rage. Movement flickered at the edge of vision—

her beefy guard, his arm cocked. His spear whistled toward her.

Beside her, Beltran's arm swept up, palm raised toward her attacker in a halting motion. The lightning channeled through his upraised sword and burst from his palm in a cascade of fire. The blast incinerated the flying missile to ash. The guard's contorted face vanished behind a wall of flame.

Fresh screams filled the air as spectators, guards, captives scattered wildly in all directions. The poor unfortunates bound to their stakes struggled as scattered fires kindled in the pyre all around.

Driven into action, Rhiannon darted through the smoke to the nearest stake and began working madly at the ropes. Beside her, Young John leaped over a tongue of fire and began tugging at the cords that restrained a second captive.

A fresh torrent of blue fire scorched through the open air, whelming a knot of guardsmen who were charging toward them. Howling bodies scattered in all directions. Blindly Rhiannon darted from captive to captive, pausing only to snatch up a dagger from a fallen guard to saw at the ropes. Young John flitted like an imp through the smoke, herding the stunned prisoners toward open air.

At last they'd freed them all, sent them all stumbling toward safety. Now fire roared up around her, the acrid smoke stinging her eyes, setting her lungs ablaze. Bent double with coughing, swiping her streaming eyes, she reeled toward open ground. Goddess save her, the smoke had grown so thick she couldn't see.

Before her terrified eyes, the flames parted. Beltran's black-clad form emerged, Excalibur held up-

right like a cross before him. She voiced a glad cry
and rushed toward him—her hope, her guide, her love.

With one strong arm he caught her around the
waist, sweeping her effortlessly from the burning pyre.
Coughing, she wound her arms around his neck and
clung to him as the flames crackled around them, the
intense heat singeing her hair.

Like a miracle there was a horse before her, a saddle beneath her, strong hands boosting her forward to
straddle the pommel as he swung up behind.

"Wait," she said hoarsely. "The others! We can't
leave them."

"We won't," he said grimly, arms closing around her
to grasp the reins. The coal-black stallion—a strange
mount, not Serafin—sidled and snorted. "Some have
already scattered. The others are bundled in a wagon.
We'll have to lead them out, but I fear we won't get far."

Above them the skies opened, the dry sting of hail
now mixed with sleeting rain. Rhiannon was drenched
between one breath and the next, as though someone
had overturned a basin of icy water on her head. She
stripped back her wet hair and squinted into the gale,
straining to see through the billowing smoke.

There. A brewer's wagon, its barrels heaved over
the side and staved against the earth, a dozen sooty
captives crowded within. Young John perched on the
seat beside a graybeard prisoner with fierce eyes. The
graybeard raised the brewer's whip and lashed the carthorses into a clumsy gallop.

She and Beltran thundered past, leading the way
over the storm-lashed field, the flaming pyre falling
away behind them.

Blinded and deafened by the tempest, Rhiannon

clung to the saddle, gasping for air as her burning lungs slowly cleared. When Beltran flung his cloak around her, she huddled gratefully in its folds, still warm from his body, and inhaled the familiar spice of frankincense. Still trembling, she leaned back against his broad chest and closed her eyes.

She could hardly believe he was here, she was saved, they were together—for however long. She could scarcely believe she wouldn't wake screaming in her cell.

But she mustn't go to pieces now. Thanks to Uriel and the storm—and hadn't there been a hint of Faerie magick, her mother's weather magick about that?—they'd escaped the immediate threat. But plenty of survivors had watched them flee, seen them bowling along the road from the city.

She'd lay odds this great black stallion with his noble heart galloping beneath them could have outrun any horse in Britain. But the heavy-laden wagon was already slowing. A dozen fleeing heretics with death warrants signed by the Queen herself—pursuit would not be long in coming. The Archbishop and Bloody Bonner would see to that.

She twisted to look up at Beltran, chiseled features intent as he scanned the horizon. The rain had eased to a steady downpour, but the road was a sucking sea of mud that slowed their flight.

Rhiannon gave herself a moment, just a moment to embrace him with her eyes—his strong jaw, his firm mouth, his beloved brow furrowed with determination. His piercing eyes flickered with wrathful lightning. Then she applied her wits to the business at hand.

"Beltran," she said huskily, throat scratched and raw

from coughing. "This headlong flight is folly. That wagon will be mired in mud in no time. We must get off the road."

Reluctantly he nodded, his gaze flickering toward her. When their eyes met, his hard face softened.

"God's body, Rhiannon!" he said, low and intent. "I prayed I didn't come too late. If I had—if they'd burned you—I swear to Christ I would have climbed on that pyre myself."

She managed a wobbly smile of reassurance and lifted a trembling hand to brush his jaw, raspy with stubble. "I doubt thy God would have allowed that."

His cobalt eyes creased in a thoughtful smile. "We've called an armistice, He and I. I'm beginning to learn to channel this holy wrath. And it seems my earthly exile has some…compensations."

"You've seen firsthand thy God's capacity for mercy," she said softly. "All those poor souls who were condemned to burn, myself among them—"

"Never," he growled.

"Thou could have let thy Church carry out its sentence, and yet thou chose to save them," she marveled. "And the sword! Excalibur. My father allowed you to…?"

"He seemed to want me to have it." He shook his head in wonder. "Or so claimed the Lady of the Lake. But I've the feeling I'm not meant to keep it."

"Nay, it must return to my father's hand. The magick that binds it to him is very powerful." Her eyes lingered on the hilt thrust over his shoulder—a hand gripping a golden torch. "'Tis more than a weapon, that blade. Especially in thy hands, with the double magick of the sword and thy God flowing through it."

"It burned like a torch indeed, and showed me a way through the Veil. Without it, I would never have reached you in time." Protectively his arms tightened around her. "Your father loves you, Rhiannon."

She sighed and leaned into his strong embrace. "The blade is a guiding light, a guide through the mists..." She trailed off. Then inspiration seized her, and a gasp spilled out.

"Beltran, stop the horse!"

"What is it?" In a heartbeat he shifted to battle-readiness, tension crackling through him. Excalibur seemed to leap to his gauntleted hand as he surveyed the rain-swept fields and hedges.

Gray stubble shimmered with pools of standing water. Coils of smoke rose from the wattle-and-daub chimneys of a handful of cottages scattered like dice across the fields. The foul weather had kept them all indoors—all save themselves, and the laden wagon churning through the mud in their wake.

Hastily she scanned the view. "We need some-place...a little hollow or valley, a freshwater spring. There!"

Not far from the road rose a spinney of rowan trees, with water glimmering beneath. Rowan, which her people called witch wood. Precisely the sort of place they wanted.

Frowning, Beltran eyed the terrain. "The wagon will never make it over that plowed field."

"We can walk." Tingling with excitement, breath-less with a blend of anticipation and fear that somehow her instincts were wrong, Rhiannon jumped down from the saddle before he could stop her.

He cursed, but reined in and swung down. She was

already running to the wagon, words of reassurance and explanation bubbling from her lips. In the sea of tired and dirty faces turned toward her, worried eyes swung between her and Beltran's stern features.

Although he must have thought she'd run mad, he backed her up, bless the man. Beneath his calm authority the wagon was halted beside the road, the exhausted carthorses cut free at Rhiannon's insistence. Soon the small cavalcade of smoke-stained men, women and children went straggling across the plowed field. Beltran gripped the black's reins and strode along beside her, the sword held loosely in his fist.

"I hope to Christ you know what you're doing," he muttered. "Those guards will have organized and ridden after us by now."

She knew she should share his concern, but a strange ebullience buoyed her up. Incongruously, she wanted to skip and laugh with it. "Don't you trust me *yet*, Beltran?"

His eyes seared into her. "With my life. I'd follow you through Hell itself."

She heard his words and her soul thrilled. All the love in her heart welled up, bringing tears to her eyes. Wordlessly gazing up at him, she slipped her hand into his. Their fingers twined together around the stallion's reins. On the other side, Young John came quietly forward and linked his thin hand through hers.

Behind them, taking heart from their serene certainty, their companions drew closer, hands finding hands, the strong helping the weak over the rutted earth.

Now the spinney rose around them, green and brown, a floating carpet of leaves coating the still pool inside. Swiftly she glanced about, taking stock. Even with all her lost magick, Rhiannon could never have raised the mists and summoned the Veil unaided, far from the ancient nodes of power. A brief flicker of worry furrowed her brow.

Then she glimpsed her father's sword, gleaming pure silver in the shadows, and took heart. Through narrowed eyes, Beltran watched her. Their companions clustered around, forming a circle without her guidance, hands linking in a chain.

A deep stillness settled over and inside them, the low thrum of expectation she recognized as the prelude to powerful magick.

Barely whispering, she instructed Beltran to hold her father's sword upright between them. Lightly she wrapped her hands over his and gripped the hilt. The blade brightened, a low hum rising from the steel, making her bones vibrate. Calm and certain, Beltran's gaze locked on hers like a steadying hand.

She swallowed past a throat gone dry with nerves.

"I'm not certain how to make this work," she whispered.

"When you summoned the Veil, you cried out something," he urged, brow furrowed as he fought to recall the event. "I was praying, begging God for your life."

As though he too felt the growing compulsion, he began murmuring a prayer to Christ in the Roman tongue. Around them, scattered voices took up the words. Young John's piping voice started a counterpoint—the paternoster in Protestant English. Rhiannon closed her eyes and tightened her grip on Beltran's.

A rising tide of joy buoyed her flagging spirits, nearly lifting her feet from the soil. The old words of power welled up within her like a bubbling spring. Thankfully, she opened herself to the tingling rush of magick—that dizzying force she'd feared never to feel again, summoned by the marriage of Excalibur's magick and the Christians' prayers, the powerful grace of their God.

Raising her face toward Heaven, she cried out the spell.

NINETEEN

THE DISTANT CHIME of bells woke her, a joyous din that echoed and sang through her blood. She stretched and opened her eyes, marveled at the sense of peace and wellbeing flooding through her. Had she somehow returned to Faerie?

But nay. The wainscoted walls of a mortal dwelling coalesced around her, sunlight streaming through diamond-shaped panes across the honey-colored wooden floor. Pewter gleamed on the white-draped table. A fire crackled in the hearth. The good English smells of brown beer and sharp cheese wafted to her nostrils.

Rhiannon pushed back the blankets and sat. Cool air teased her bare skin beneath the clean shift that was her only garment.

"Dear Goddess," she said to Beltran. "Where are we?"

He turned from the window and strode to her side. "Village of Wythe, the innkeeper says. Just within the Scottish border. The Queen of Scots' domain, and thus free of Tudor influence. Your magick proved oddly precise, love."

"My magick...?" Slowly the details spilled through her drowsy brain—the dungeon, the pyre, Uriel raging through the tempest like the Angel of Vengeance he was. The smell of autumn as they linked hands in the spinney, Excalibur shining like a star before them.

She knuckled the sleep from her eyes. "Rather I

think it was *our* magick, thine and mine. Somehow we linked Faerie and Christian magick in a way I've never seen before."

The old Beltran would have denied such a blasphemous notion. Now he merely studied her, a thoughtful frown creasing his brow.

Opting not to hurry him through this radical evolution in his thinking, she smiled and shrugged. "Or perhaps someone was watching out for us. The Lady of the Lake, thy God—perhaps even my father, who can say? Where are the others?"

"In the common room, some of them, keeping the feast day. When those bells started their clamor, Young John ran down to the church for tidings."

"Feast day?" Rhiannon's brow furrowed, the beginnings of alarm prickling through her. "Why, how long have I slept?"

"A full night and day, and we all agreed you've earned it. It's the Feast of All Saints."

"'Tis the Day of the Dead, in Faerie…" The day after Samhain. Anxious, she flung back the blankets and leaped to the floor. Heedless of her undress, fresh-washed hair swirling around her shoulders, she padded barefoot past Beltran and hurried to the window.

Their second-story chamber overlooked the courtyard, the bustling stables and kitchens, the clean-swept cobbles of a village street beyond. Above the thatched roofs of the whitewashed cottages, the rugged sere and bracken of the Scottish moors rolled toward the horizon, under a fleet of briskly scudding clouds.

Astonished, she turned to Beltran. "But this is peace and order! The Convergence should have fallen, the Veil dropped, the way opened between the worlds."

Tenderly he smoothed a loose ringlet from her eyes and folded her hands around a pewter mug. "You were deceived by your sister's witchcraft. Your death would have brought about the event, not averted it. The Lady laid it upon me to tell you."

"Then the Convergence still looms. We've done nothing to avert it."

"It won't happen today," he said firmly. "Drink your beer."

Pensive, she sipped the foaming brown beer. The cool wetness soothed her smoke-raw throat.

Suddenly she was famished, weeks of starvation rations in the dungeon catching up with her. Protective of her welfare as always, Beltran urged her to the table. The polished pewter held simple ware—a crusty loaf of fresh barley bread, sweet crumbling cheese, a steaming tureen of mutton stew swimming with carrots and turnips. Her mouth watering, Rhiannon fell upon the feast.

Between mouthfuls, she demanded, "The others— are they well?"

"Praising God to the heavens for saving them," he said wryly. "I praise God the Blades' hidebound bureaucrats froze my assets when I vanished. I've enough coin to keep them for a bit, until they get their feet beneath them, either here or abroad in some place friendly to Protestants. They're debating where to go—the Netherlands, maybe."

"They ought to be praising *thee*, Uriel." Over the rim of her bowl, she studied him. "Or is it still Beltran? Either way, I'm thankful for both. But how can thou walk the mortal realm?"

Hitching a booted leg on the rung of his chair, he

shrugged. "I inhabit a mortal body, Rhiannon. There's no place for me now in Heaven."

"But after? What happens when thy body dies?"

He frowned, eyes lowered to the remnants of their feast. "I'm still sorting out how it all works. I don't have all the answers. What I do know is that yesterday, I used the killing rage for mercy. For the first time I was able to summon that power, to control it, even to recall it afterward. It doesn't take a flaming hand tracing letters on the wall to spell out for me what that means."

His mouth curved wryly. "He's pleased with my progress, I suppose. Willing to let me keep on with it, and see what other lessons I might learn."

Rhiannon was still grappling with the implications. For so long, she'd believed him dead to her. Too many questions clamored for answers.

"On Avalon, when thou regained thy divinity," she said slowly, "I thought thee returned to Heaven."

"I inhabit a mortal body, Rhiannon, and will until I die—whenever that may be. No man can look upon His face and live. Those are the terms of my exile, set forth by God. When the time comes, I trust He'll find me worthy for whatever comes after."

He leaned forward, his gaze probing hers. "Now I want to speak of *you.*"

The familiar flutter of excitement woke in her belly. Her body reacted to him no differently, it seemed, even after all that had happened.

Vainly she strove to quell the foolish sense of hope bubbling through her. Even if he'd embraced a mortal life, and learned the power of love through mercy as she'd always hoped he would, he was still bound to his order, wasn't he? Surely he'd never choose to abandon his vows altogether. Why give up his calling if he'd found nothing to replace it?

Therefore, their reunion must be a short one.

Still, she would savor it as long as it lasted.

Beneath his piercing gaze, she lowered her spoon and rose restlessly to pace. "What of me? My fate is clear. I gave up my old life willingly to save thine, and I deemed it a good trade. I don't mourn the fact that I'm no longer welcome at the Faerie Queene's chilly court."

She spared him a wan smile. "Indeed, I feel a bit like a condemned prisoner granted a reprieve. Princess I may no longer be, but I'll always be a healer, and my needs are few. There must be a place for me somewhere among these folk."

"You wish to remain here then?" he asked casually. "In Scotland?"

She shook her head. "My plans have not changed, Beltran. My sister Morrigan is not defeated. The Convergence is still coming. My place is at Elizabeth's side—the best hope for peace in both our realms."

"You'll return to England with a death sentence hanging over your head?" He strode toward her, boot heels ringing. "Rhiannon, that's madness! I won't allow it."

Swiftly her chin lifted. Despite all that lay between them, how could he still strike the mutinous spark of her anger so effortlessly? Standing before the fire, she glared at him and resisted the old urge to stamp her foot.

"Thou hast nothing to say about it, my lord! Don't mistake me—I'll always be grateful for thine actions on my behalf. But that doesn't make thee my master."

"Doesn't it?" Dangerous purpose flared in his gaze.

Jaw knotted, he circled the table and advanced upon her. "Why do you suppose I undertook those actions?"

Pulse fluttering, she glanced about for an escape route. But pride made her stand her ground. She'd never shrunk in fear from his anger, and she didn't intend to start now.

"Thou saved me for common decency and from a sense of obligation, just as I saved thee," she fired back at him. "Thou would not have let them burn me!"

"Damnation, girl! Don't be so bloody stubborn." He gripped her arms and held her close, glowering down at her defiant face. "You willful, headstrong, imperious creature, don't you understand me yet? *I love you.*"

The earth shifted beneath her feet. Her breath suspended in her lungs. Robbed of speech, she gaped at him. "I—I beg thy pardon?"

Could it be possible? Nay, surely his Christian God would not work one of his famous miracles for her benefit. Perhaps the mingling of their magick had confused Beltran, just as it astonished her...

"You bloody well heard me." He glared. "What's more, you're in love with me."

"Oh, am I?" Her brows lifted. Of course it was true, every word of it. She'd loved him as long as she'd known him, loved him since the night he walked out of storm and legend into battle and death to save her. Divine yet mortal, invincible yet strangely vulnerable, body and soul driven by harrowing torments only she could heal.

"You must be in love with me." Step by step, he eased her rigid body up against his heat. "There's no other explanation for your actions, the sacrifices you've made for me. The fact that you gave yourself to me.

Good God. Tell me you did these things and felt nothing, and I'll call you an outright liar."

His voice softened. "And I know Arthur of Camelot's
daughter was never that."

Still she hesitated, uncertain whether she dared
grasp the shining miracle of love that shimmered like
a mirage before them. She hadn't forgotten the Archbishop's claim; she was far from the only woman in
life who'd tempted Beltran from his vow of chastity
Yet somehow, his past no longer mattered. Had he truly
said he loved her? Or was it merely something she'd
dreamed up during those days of despair, when she lay
shivering in her cell and thought of him?

The heat of his body was melting her resistance
dissolving her fear. Cautiously, her hands stole to his
shoulders. For the first time since she'd known him, he
was wearing white—cream-colored doublet belted over
his muscled frame, open around the powerful column
of his throat. In her mind, she saw the celestial warrior
glittering with mail, dazzling white and gold, his stern
beauty as he wielded the flaming sword.

Uriel, Angel of Vengeance.

Beltran, Blade of God.

He was both, and neither. He was like nothing she'd
ever known. Yet she never doubted the truth of her
heart.

"If thou art certain of thine own heart, then I shall
reveal the dearest secret of mine," she murmured. "I
love thee. And much good it will do us when—"

His warm mouth closed over hers, swallowing her
objections. His strong arms wrapped around her, hauling her hard against his sinewed frame.

Breathless, she twined her arms around his neck

winding her fingers in the close-cropped golden hair she'd always loved. The blade of his arousal nudged her belly, and heat kindled in her womb.

When he lifted her and carried her across the floor to the bed, she bestirred herself to mount a dutiful protest. "Beltran, there's much to be done. This is no time for dalliance—"

"Never better," he growled, arms tightening around her. "With you, I've learned to seize my moment. And may there be plenty more like it."

Excitement sparked through her as he lowered them to the bed, shift riding up around her thighs, his hard body trapping hers against the rustling straw-filled mattress. Clean muslin sheets, still warmed by her own body and smelling faintly of violets, caressed her bare limbs.

She gazed up at him, arms still twined around his neck. The chiseled, sun-bronzed planes of his face filled her vision—a hard man and determined, eyes gleaming with intent and hooded with passion. Already the hard jut of his codpiece nudged between her thighs, making her womb melt for him. Helpless against the urgency that kindled within, she writhed slowly, sensuously against his heat. With a groan, he found the soft swell of her breast, nipple jutting against the thin shift, fingers teasing the sensitive peak until she cried out softly.

"Lord and Lady, Beltran, this is torment!" she gasped, her hand closing over his to still the delicious friction.

"Good," he rumbled. "I want you tormented. I want you breathless and panting with heat, mad for the way

I feel inside you. I want you begging me to taste your sweet honey, as I did that day on Avalon, remember?"

"Goddess," she whispered, excruciatingly aware of her slick channel spread and waiting for his attentions, barely concealed by her shift. "How could I possibly forget?"

As if he smelled the musk of her arousal on the air, deftly he hooked her shift in his strong hands and tore the fragile fabric down the front. Now she lay wanton and naked beneath him, the extent of her desire exposed—nipples taut and ready for his attention, her woman's mound pink and blushing under his hungry gaze.

Oh, yes, this was what she wanted.

Boldly she reached to unlace his codpiece, though the unfamiliar points and laces might have daunted a less motivated woman. While her fingers worked with unseemly haste at this task, he shrugged out of his cream doublet and the silk shirt beneath. She murmured approval at the hard planes of his chest, the rippling line of his abdomen, the powerful bulge of shoulders and biceps flexing as he unbuckled his belt

At last, the bothersome codpiece fell away. She gazed with mingled longing and bemusement at his jutting length, breath snaring audibly in her throat. She'd never had the leisure to look before, amid the haste of their prior couplings. Now she filled her eye with the proud, potent sight of him. *Hers now, he wa hers, just as she was his...*

Until he tossed aside his breeches and caught he hand in his, wrapping her fingers around his tensil heat. By instinct her hand tightened, exploratory fin

gers sliding down his length and kneading until he
arched into her touch.

"How's this?" she whispered wickedly, knowing
full well he liked it.

"Christ, Rhiannon," he groaned, head flung back
with pleasure, sinew standing out in his throat. "You're
a natural at this."

She could have done this forever, intoxicated by the
novel sensation of having him in her power, being able
to heighten his pleasure with the merest touch. But her
own urgency was building, the coil of passion tightening in her belly, the slow pulse between her thighs
quickening. Even as she stroked him, reveling in his
ragged moans and the slow pearls of moisture that wept
from his cock, her free hand stole to her own aching
cleft. The brush of her own finger against the hard nub-
bin nestled there brought a moan to her lips.

A little abashed, she stole a peek at his face to find
him watching her, gaze riveted to the hand playing between her thighs.

"Aye, that's it, love," he encouraged, voice husky
with his own pleasure. "Make yourself ready for me."

The knowledge that he watched her pleasure herself,
growing still harder at the sight, was nearly too much.
Shameless, she spread herself like a banquet for his de-
lectation, knees falling open, eyes drifting shut. A few
more moments of this, and she'd go over the edge—

The calloused warmth of his hands closed over
hers, delaying her just before she reached her goal.
She nearly mewled in protest. But he lost no time in
fitting his searing length against her channel, the dew
of her passion mingling with his.

A raw shock of arousal arced through her. Crying

out, she twined her legs around his hips and pulled him into her.

He was lightning between her thighs, fierce and tender and crackling with coiled intensity. And the feel of him thrusting into her was pure magick.

Lady of Light, they were both so ready, driven nearly to madness by the prelude to their joining. Beyond reason or restraint, the climax seized her and tossed her high. Helpless in its grip, she dug her bare heels against his flexing buttocks and sank sharp little teeth into the corded muscle of his shoulder.

Spurred by this minor violence, he pinned her fists beside her head and rode her, prolonging her pleasure until she feared she'd die of it.

"Easy, princess," he pushed out, teeth gritted with effort. "You'll finish me."

Forcing her eyes open, she stared fiercely into the burning blue of his gaze.

"Beltran, I can't bear this," she panted. "Merciful Goddess, do it now…"

And she gloried in the primal, feminine satisfaction of her lover's powerful body clenching between her thighs. She shared his low groan of fulfillment as the scalding heat of release flooded through her.

TWENTY

AN HOUR LATER, an excited burst of voices roused Rhiannon from her satiated slumber and brought her struggling upright in the tangled bed. As Beltran grumbled in lazy protest, she slipped from the solid warmth of his arms. Below, Young John was piping in protest, his voice interspersed with a man's impatient rumble and a woman's gentle murmur. Rapid footfalls sounded on the stairs, building swiftly as the entire cavalcade thundered toward them.

Nerves prickling, Rhiannon rolled swiftly out of bed and flung over her head the first garments she could find—an unfamiliar bodice and skirts of sky-blue wool, over a chemise that smelled faintly of lavender soap. Coming fully alert, Beltran sprang out of bed and dragged discarded hose and breeches over his hips.

By the time the door rattled, he was braced before her, Excalibur's cool steel gleaming in his fist.

"Who goes?" he demanded.

"Goddess curse thee, open this door!" a familiar voice shouted back. "Rhiannon?"

"Bright Lady!" Her heart leapt like a stallion clearing a hedge, from solid earth to soaring in a breath. Springing past Beltran's bristling form, she unbolted the door and flung it wide.

Her foster-father burst in, crimson cloak unfurling around his lithe frame, salt-and-pepper curls tumbled, gray eyes sweeping the chamber for danger. When he glimpsed Beltran standing *en garde*, he reached for his saber.

"Sweet mercy, Ansgar! Put up yer blade, man." Lady Linnet Norwood hurried to his side, her fashionable black riding habit dusty with travel, chestnut-streaked ringlets tumbling in disarray beneath her plumed hood. Her sherry-gold eyes warmed when she saw Rhiannon. "Lord Beltran is a friend, aye?"

Then Rhiannon was running forward to fling herself in her foster-father's arms. Too late she recalled his injury—but nay, that was two years and more in the past. Lord Ansgar's arms were strong and steady as ever as they cradled her to his mailed chest.

"Bless all the Gods alike for this moment," Ansgar said brokenly in the Roman tongue. "Child, are you well?"

"Never better." Gladly she embraced him, savoring the life and strength and purpose that burned in him once again. "Dear heart, how did you come here?"

Gently Linnet touched her shoulder. "Glencross Castle lies nearby—my castle, for I'm Countess of Glencross now—"

"Thou art a countess, no less?" Rhiannon was astonished. "Thou've risen high since thy return from Faerie, child."

For an instant, shadows haunted the mortal girl's eyes, but she hurried past the moment. "Aye, and Glencross's only a day's journey from Wythe. We set forth yesterday, as soon as my lord received word."

"It was a vision," Ansgar explained, as Rhiannon enveloped Linnet in a warm embrace. "I saw you i the basin when I was shaving. Sent by the Lady of the Lake, I think. She showed me you were here."

"She has always been kind to me." Rhiannon smiled. "Ansgar, here is someone you should properly meet."

She reached for Beltran's hand and drew him forward. He advanced reluctantly, but at least he'd lowered the sword—a starting point. "This is Lord Beltran Nemesto, Blade of God—"

"No longer," Beltran reminded her.

"—and my promised husband," she finished, both triumphant and defiant.

The two men she loved had met, if one could call it that, when Beltran took them captive in the forest. Ansgar had escaped, greatly to Beltran's annoyance, so she couldn't say relations between the two had ever been cordial.

But her foster-father had taken his sweet time finding her. If he thought now to raise a fuss, that she chose to love a mortal of her own free will, she'd say a few choice words about his tardy arrival!

But the older man's lined face creased in a reluctant smile. "The Lady of the Lake spoke also of thee." Shifting to his antiquated English, he clasped hands with Beltran. "It seems I owe thee a debt of honor, for thy good care of Rhiannon. If anything had befallen my foster-daughter, her father would be greatly wroth with me. I swore him an oath to protect her—a charge I suspect I may now share with thee."

While they spoke, Linnet was quietly bustling, taking Ansgar's cloak, sending a wide-eyed John to tend their horses and fetch water for washing. Rhiannon recalled her duty as hostess and poured barley beer for her guests, which they drank thirstily.

She eyed their travel-stained appearance. "But what befell thee, these two years and more past? How do thou come to be so far north, when…"

"When you left your charge far to the south, near London," Beltran said grimly. He'd sheathed Excalibur in its crimson scabbard. The sword stood propped against the wall within easy grasp, the covert object of all attention. "You're late-come, man, to ensure Rhiannon's welfare."

Ansgar shot a look toward Linnet, who colored deeply and busied herself about the table. "That tale's long in the telling. Suffice it to say I sought Rhiannon high and low, in this realm and the other. Another lady required my aid."

"We rode like blazes for Wythe as soon as we learned ye'd come," Linnet said gently, smoothing the way for all. "Leaving safely at home a certain white cat ye might recall from court, as well as yer gray mare."

"Astolat! And the kitten too. Oh, I can't wait to see them." Smiling, Rhiannon set bowls of stew before her guests. "The Lady sent thee to collect the sword, didn't she, Ansgar?"

Ansgar had the grace to look chagrined. "Even in his dreaming state, Arthur yearns for Excalibur. He's going to want it back, Rhiannon."

"And he shall have it." Beltran's eyes flashed. "I'm no thief, and I can find another easily enough—though none such as this, I'll warrant. Arthur's sword has served its purpose."

While the others spoke, Young John lingered on the threshold, squirming and hopping from foot to foot, his gamin face screwed into a tortured expression. Catching sight of him, Rhiannon smiled gently.

"What ails thee, dear heart?"

Thus freed, he sprang forward. "It's the bells, mi-lady! Ye sent me to hear the news, didn't ye?"

"Mercy, I'd almost forgotten."

"They brung it, them two." The boy gestured toward the newcomers. "I found 'em at the church."

"We had the news from a rider on the road." Lowering her eyes, Linnet crossed herself. Ansgar shuddered and looked away from the holy gesture. "Queen Mary Tudor has laid down her sorrows, poor lady, and passed from this life."

Beltran cursed softly and signed himself. Rhiannon could only stare, numb with shock.

She'd known the Tudor queen was ailing, and had been for months. Indeed, she had Mary's grave condition to thank for Bloody Bonner's absence from Smithfield, and Reginald Pole's preoccupation when she'd seen him. But she hadn't realized Mary was so grievous ill as that.

A dazed sense of reprieve crept through her, made unexpectedly poignant by the sharp stab of grief. Now that the danger was past—to her and all of England—she chose not to recall the bitter, hateful old woman who'd spewed such malice toward heretics, even her own flesh and blood. She remembered instead the grief-stricken wife, abandoned and barren, who'd bravely soldiered through heartbreak and humiliation with her poor, pain-wracked body.

Gradually, the implications came crowding in on her. With Mary Tudor dead, what became of her mirror beyond the Veil, Queene Maeve of the Faeries? Now while their two lands lay so close, with Maeve herself hovering near death, the Faerie Queene could survive only so long as the Tudor queenship thrived. Was snow flying even now in the Summer Lands, white drifts covering the golden orchards of Avalon? Grief twisted her heart at the prospect.

Beltran's suntanned hand gripped her shoulder and squeezed. Blindly she turned toward the refuge he offered.

"What does this mean for England?" she whispered.

Linnet lifted her tear-drowned eyes, and Rhiannon recalled that the Norwoods were an old Catholic family. The girl herself was convent-raised and devout. Mary Tudor's passing could bring only ill fortune for them.

"It means," Linnet said softly, "that our bonnie Elizabeth is now Queen, aye? A Protestant Queen set against the English Catholics and Spanish Philip. Aye, and let's not forget the wee Catholic lass who sits the throne of Scotland."

"God assoil her soul, the Queen is dead," Beltran said gruffly. "God save Queen Elizabeth and guide her hand to rule wisely."

Images of Elizabeth Tudor filled Rhiannon's head—her blazing courage, the wit and cunning bright as her flame-red hair. A Tudor Queen with Faerie blood. What might *that* mean for the two realms?

Whatever it meant, she found fresh hope in it.

Rhiannon shook off her confusion and stepped away from Beltran's sheltering arms. All around her, attentive faces turned toward her for direction.

"We must return to the Queen's court, as soon as we might," she announced. "Or at least, Beltran and I must return there. We've nothing to fear from the Catholics with Elizabeth on the throne."

"And me with ye, milady!" Young John declared, his eyes shining.

"I'd best come as well," Linnet murmured. "A great deal has befallen my family while I idled about in Faerie…and where I went after. My place now is at the Tudor court, if the Protestant Queen will accept a Papist lass among her ladies."

Ansgar stirred restlessly, his eyes narrowed on the sacred sword that stood gleaming against the wall. "If Lord Beltran will escort and guard thee both—"

"With my life, never doubt it," Beltran told him.

"Then my road leads to Avalon, with Excalibur. Arthur has always rested easier with that blade within reach."

When her foster-father had gone with Linnet to make arrangements for their horses and lodging, Young John scampering out to attend them, Rhiannon returned to Beltran's arms with a smile.

"For curiosity's sake, Lord Beltran," she asked lightly, shooting him a mischievous look, "were thou planning to marry me when we reach London? I'm told that's a mortal custom."

"I'll marry you before that, if it suits you." A smile twitched his lips as he stole a teasing kiss.

"It seems a dreadful rush, to be wedded huggernugger," she teased back. When he growled and deepened the kiss, she laughed breathlessly. "But how can I resist such ardent wooing?"

He laughed too. But his eyes were thoughtful as he studied the door where the others had vanished.

"Your foster-father, Lord Ansgar," he mused. "You told me once his name means, what, divine spear?"

"I did." She rubbed her face into his warm raspy throat, his familiar scent filling her senses.

"He speaks as though he knew your father firsthand. Who is he, really?"

"He is who he is." She nuzzled his throat and smiled. "But if thou wish to learn what he's called among mortals, he's known by another name—Lancelot."

"Why am I not surprised?" Shaking his head, Beltran bent to scoop her into his arms.

Feet dangling, she squealed and wrapped trusting arms around his neck. "Thou ought not to handle a princess so familiar, sir! Thou art making a shocking habit of it."

"Get used to it," he said gruffly. A grin quirked his lips as he strode to the door with Rhiannon snuggled happily against his chest. One handed, he levered the bolt into place.

"Where art thou taking me, brigand?" With feigned indignation, she offered a token struggle.

"Be good," he growled softly, blue flames kindling in his gaze as he surveyed her upturned face. "I'm taking you where you belong, princess—to my bed. Together we'll find our own Heaven, on this day and forever."

* * * * *

AFTERWORD

I HOPE YOU'VE enjoyed this fanciful retelling of three legends that have influenced and moved me profoundly as both writer and reader: the time-blurred mystery of Arthurian legend, the colorful and often violent history of the Tudors, and the dark, alluring glitter of fallen angel lore.

I'd like to acknowledge my debt of gratitude to the author who inspired this work most directly: the late Marion Zimmer Bradley. Her epic novel *The Mists of Avalon* is an imaginative retelling of the Arthurian legend, grounded firmly in the history of the Dark Ages, as told by the women in Arthur's life. This magical and moving tale has fascinated and inspired me for more than twenty years.

Magick by Moonrise was a long time coming. I hope you've found it worth the wait.

ABOUT THE AUTHOR

IN HER OTHER LIFE, Laura Navarre is a diplomat who's lived in Russia and works on weapons of mass destruction issues. In the line of duty, she's been trapped in an elevator in a nuclear power plant and has stalked the corridors of facilities churning out nerve agent and other apocalyptic weapons. In this capacity, she meets many of the world's most dangerous men.

Inspired by the sinister realities of her real life, Laura writes dark medieval and Renaissance romance spiked with political intrigue. A member of Romance Writers of America and a former Golden Heart Award finalist, she's won the Emily Award for Excellence, the Georgia Romance Writers Maggie Award, Hearts Through History's Romance Through the Ages, and many others. Although Laura is a multipublished historical author, *Magick by Moonrise* is her first historical paranormal romance. *Magick* won the Pacific Northwest Writers Association award for romance in 2012.

Laura holds an MFA in Writing Popular Fiction from the University of Southern Maine, an MA in National Security Policy from The George Washington University and a BA in International Relations from Michigan State. Living in Seattle with her screenwrite

usband and two Siberian cats, she divides her time
between her writing career and other adventures for
U.S. government clients.